W9-DFQ-728

HIGH PRAISE FOR EDWARD LEE!

"The living legend of literary mayhem. Read him if you dare!"
—Richard Laymon, author of *The Cellar*

"Edward Lee's writing is fast and mean as a chain saw revved to full-tilt boogie."
—Jack Ketchum, author of *Off Season*

"Lee pulls no punches."
—*Fangoria*

"The hardest of the hardcore horror writers."
—*Cemetery Dance*

"Lee excels with his creativity and almost trademark depictions of violence and gruesomeness."
—*Horror World*

THE SLITHERING THING

"I found the hose!" Howie bellowed, running back around the corner. He held the long length in one hand. "Turn it o—" But then he stopped.

"Howie," Leona said with the sickest feeling in her life churning in her belly. "That isn't the hose...."

It hung limp until the moment she'd said that, almost as if it had sensed the trigger of Howie's fear. His eyes snapped down...

Then the "hose" began to move...

Vaguely pink, glistening skin. About an inch thick. It extended from his hand, behind him, its other end still on the other side of the shack. Howie tried to drop the grotesque thing but it was already too late for that. In the space of that synaptic second, the creature energized and wrapped around Howie's upper torso—

Then Howie was dressed in the thing, wearing it like a corselet. His scream was severed when more of its length coiled about his neck. Howie fell over.

His eyes still registered images as his vision clouded, and then the thing's head made itself plain: slightly tapered, less like a snake and more like a worm.

A pink hole dilated—a mouth opening?—then a thinner pink tube of something fleshy slipped out and—

"Howie!" Leona screamed.

—slithered down Howie's throat.

SLITHER

EDWARD LEE

LEISURE BOOKS NEW YORK CITY

For Don D'Auria—
without whom I'd be washing dishes.

A LEISURE BOOK®

November 2006

Published by

Dorchester Publishing Co., Inc.
200 Madison Avenue
New York, NY 10016

ISBN 0-8439-5414-0

Visit us on the web at www.dorchesterpub.com.

ACKNOWLEDGMENTS

Special thanks to: Mike Anthony and Michael Kennedy for my wonderful *Header* movie, Bob Strauss for indefatigable proofing; Cedric Perez for tech stuff; Shay Prentiss and Christine Torres; Noel and Lance at X Ray Productions; Jen and Monica from *Rue Morgue*; Kelli and Kelly from Horror Web; Sascha Mamczak and Francis Hoch; Juan Carlos Poujade; Barry Anderson, Thomas Deja, Aaron Williams, Christine Morgan, Nick Yak. Also Kathy, Mindi, Pam, Tess, and Wendy.

PROLOGUE

When Carol noticed the two ticks attached to her nipples, she very understandably screamed.

She screamed right into Howie's face.

Parrots screeched, lifting off from palm trees; other animals tore away through the brambles. Were he not so shocked himself, it might even have occurred to Howie that Carol's scream barely sounded human. It sounded, instead, machinelike: a bad bearing in a high-rpm motor.

"Ticks!" Carol shrieked after the scream.

Howie stared at the breasts he'd been dying to see all month, and then his mouth fell open. He thought: *Holy Jesus God Almighty! What are those THINGS?*

And the things—barely the size of jelly beans—seemed to be *quivering. . . . .*

Are they . . . are they really ticks?

"Get them off, get them off, get them *off*, Howie!" She shuddered against the tree, her smart and very expensive Victoria's Secret "tankini" top on the ground.

All that remained in the way of·apparel were stylish hot-pink Converse tennis shoes and the tiny floral bikini bottom. Howie had spent the entirety of his junior year yearning to see her like this . . .

But not while she's screaming bloody murder with two—two—two THINGS on her nipples!

She slid down to the ground, probably close to clinical shock now. "Relax, relax!" He tried to calm her. "Don't pass out! I don't think they're ticks and I don't think they're leeches. . . ."

What, then?

Slugs?

Carol's face was paling. Her body began to convulse like slow electrocution.

Oh, shit! Howie hunkered down, gingerly cupped one tangerine-firm breast, and tweezed one of the *things* off her left nipple.

It didn't let go at first, and he couldn't help but imagine the tiniest mandibular hooks sunk into the tender nipple-tip, drawing out blood. When it finally came off, a few minute specks of blood welled up. The bug, tick, slug, or whatever it was felt akin to a cooked pea, only this "pea" was shiny, as if wet, and a strange yellowish white, while its outer sheath possessed scarlet dots. Howie turned the thing over, pinched between his fingertips, and squeezed . . .

Oh, Jesus, that's gross!

There were no mandibles—*no hooks*—but he thought he did detect the tiniest follicles retreat back into the thing's body. *Some kind of parasitic slug or something,* he guessed. When he tweezed it harder between his fingers, blood did indeed effuse, along with threads of some milky liquid.

He pulled the other one off Carol's right nipple and flicked it away.

"Carol?"

She'd already passed out, a shock of brandy-colored hair falling over her eyes.

Some weekend island shindig, he thought. What a bust. *Got to get her back to the shack, got to tell Alan and Leona.* And then, ever the gallant college student, Howie picked her up and carried her back down the trail.

For about twenty feet.

Oh, man!

She wasn't fat at all, but the opposite: trim, svelte, a pixie. Carrying away damsels in distress, however, was only easy in the movies. *I'll never be able to get her back to the shack like this. . . .*

So he left her.

And he ran.

It had been Alan's idea to bring the girls out to Pritchard's Key. "It's the perfect party place," he assured Howie. "Nobody goes there. The island's surrounded by big-ass rocks, and there's no beachfront. No place to dock a boat."

"Then how are *we* going to dock there?" Howie asked.

"I know where the inlets are," Alan answered, "and there're only a few, but if we get there at high tide, we motor the Whaler right in neat as a pin, and no one can run us off—not even cops."

It sounded great to Howie, and what Alan told him next sounded even greater: "Carol finally dumped that jock she was dating, and now she's hot for you, man. She even said you were cute!"

Howie nearly choked on his Corona Light. "How do you know?"

"Leona told me the other night when I was done giving her the best sex of her life," Alan proudly revealed, "and Leona and Carol are best friends. Buddy-bro, we'll get those girls out to Pritchard's Key, get 'em all pissy drunk on Jaeger Bombs, and ball their brains out. They'll probably even do that little lezbo thing they do—and let us watch."

That was all Howie needed to hear.

There was a cabin in the middle of the island that Alan already knew about. "Party Central, man." It looked more like some kind of old maintenance shed when Howie finally saw it. "What the hell is this building doing on an island that's inaccessible?" he asked.

"It used to be some kind of army post," Alan informed him, "but I mean, like, a long time ago, in the fifties or something. They finally closed it down. Anyway, this building was some kind of storage shed."

Howie couldn't have cared less.

Alan and Leona had been setting up the Coleman stove when Carol winked Howie over. "Let's go for a walk," she whispered.

It had been a *long* walk.

Howie knew he was good-looking, and had a certain style that women liked, but Carol was a dish-and-a-half. All long lines and curves, sleek tan legs, broad-hipped and flat-bellied. *She's the best-looking hunk of stuff I've ever been out with,* he realized with some incredulity. *And she's ALL OVER me!* Once they'd had a nice, long hand-holding walk across the island . . .

. . . that was it.

One second they'd been traipsing along, and the next second they were lip-locked.

"I don't usually lust after guys," she confessed through a pant, "but I've been lusting after you for a year. . . ."

And that's when she'd taken her top off—

—and started screaming at the two ticklike things stuck to her nipples.

As he ran, Howie found that the island was bigger

than he'd thought. *Where's the damn trail?* He got lost very quickly, tramping through the lush, tropical woodland. If only he'd brought his cell phone. He wended his way farther and suddenly found himself standing in a bloom of sunlight, looking at water. *The inlet,* he realized, where they'd moored off Alan's Boston Whaler. But—

Wait a minute . . .

There was a boat tied off to some mangrove roots right there in front of him. . . .

That's not our boat. . . .

It was just a skiff with a little outboard in back. *This must be one of the other inlets Alan was talking about,* Howie realized. The small boat rocked gently in the water. So . . .

There was someone else on the island.

Howie stepped aboard the skiff, hoping dismally to find a radio, a cell phone, even a flare gun, but there was nothing. He picked up a small card on the floor.

CENTRAL FLORIDA WEST COAST TIDE TABLE, it read.

Makes sense, Howie thought. *Someone else came out to the island to party, just like we did.* Naturally they'd have a tide table because you couldn't get a boat in here during anything but high tide.

Howie frowned at the card. It was last month's table.

He picked up a slip of paper in the console. *Credit card receipt. Herbster's Marine Exxon.* The captain of the skiff had obviously filled his tank there. *Same place Alan filled up this morning,* Howie remembered. But this receipt was dated three weeks ago. The card holder's name was Robb White.

The gears of Howie's brain turned. *Robb . . . White . . .* Recognition. *That guy on the football team, a senior,* he recalled with a rising dread.

Dread because Robb White and some of his friends had been reported missing . . .

Three weeks ago.

Not cool, Howie thought. But this was just more to process; Carol was the priority. Howie scanned the skiff one last time for a radio or cell phone, came up with nothing, then turned to step off the craft.

Awwwwww, SHIT!

The corpse of a young woman floated languidly just beyond the bow. The way her sable-hued hair fanned out over the water was almost pretty.

The rest of her wasn't so pretty.

She was probably naked, but that couldn't be totally discerned for what was wrapped around her like a pink garden hose: something that had to have been a snake. It coiled about her upper thighs, waist, and bosom, then her neck, and it glistened intricately. Sickening enough as it was, what sickened Howie more was the creature's color: pink, like the inside of someone's cheek. The woman's eyes no longer existed within their sockets but instead floated free, suspended by tendrils of optic nerves. The thing's tail roved listlessly between her wax-white legs, while its head . . .

Howie gaped.

The thing's head burrowed into the woman's mouth, and its elongated body seemed to *pulse* . . . as if pumping something down through her esophagus.

Howie had had enough. *Gotta—get—OUT OF HERE!* But as he leaped off the skiff, something snagged his vision on the other side of the quiet inlet.

His eyes flicked up—

A man was standing between some trees. He wore some sort of black jumpsuit with integrated mittens.

And a gas mask and hood.

Military, Howie thought.

When he blinked, the man was gone.

Howie ran back into the woods as if he were being chased by demons.

CHAPTER ONE

"Would somebody explain to me just exactly why this Pritchard's Key place is so special as far as scarlet bristleworms go?" the bikini'd blonde at the end asked. Her name was Annabelle Omart—noon-blue eyes, and a body like a game show hostess's. She hailed from New York, the *National Geographic* editorial offices. Her body suggested a dedicated regimen of exercise—most likely in upscale fitness salons. The only thing missing was a preeminent suntan. The woman sat demurely, seat-belted in to the helicopter's muster bench.

"It's because of something called a counterstropic rivulet," Nora answered with absolutely no interest. When she didn't elaborate further, Loren Fredrick, her associate, continued, "Which is actually just an uncharacteristic surge of runoff water from the mainland. Gravity and the terrain siphons this water to a single point and a gradient underwater current in the gulf pushes it outward. Pritchard's Key just happens to exist at the same point where the surge begins to disperse."

The army guide wasn't listening, and neither was the cabin master, a gruff warrant officer. They were both looking at the blonde. Every so often, even the pilots glanced back from the cockpit to ogle her.

Professor Nora Craig simply sat there and frowned.

She lapsed back against the cabin wall as Loren attempted to dazzle the others with information about the remarkable scarlet bristleworm. Nora herself let the helicopter's rotor noise lull her away from the creeping trickle of low self-esteem. *Why am I letting that blond calendar girl posing as a photographer make me feel insecure?* Perhaps it was just a case of raging hormones.

She let her eyes move across the cabin, trying to consider everyone in objective terms. Lieutenant Trent looked more like one of those guys who work in a department store appliance section. Pushing forty, smirking, not much going on behind the eyes except a lack of enthusiasm. Evidently he was assigned to the army's public relations unit, the "PR mouthpiece between the military and the civilian contingent," he'd explained. "Whenever civvies need to be shown around army property, I'm the guy they send." Trent's fatigues were crumpled, which might indicate how often this desk driver wore them. If it weren't for the distraction of the blond photographer's cleavage, he would probably be asleep.

Loren Fredrick was Nora's teaching assistant at the university. Totally unsocialized like many professional academics, he sat as gawkily as a textbook nerd. Tall beanpole physique, knobby knees, and a long neck that showcased what had to be one of the biggest Adam's apples in human evidence. Buckteeth, too, and a mop of wiry dark hair. He sat at the edge of his cabin seat, animatedly explaining the evolution of bristleworms in general and their unique "parapodic" means of locomotion more specifically. *He's boring them silly,* Nora thought, *and he doesn't even realize it.*

The army warrant officer was a typical Neanderthal with his green helmet and ham-hock-sized jaw, and the two pilots up front were little different. *Somebody peed in the pool,* Nora mused over their brute, cave-man features. *The gene pool, that is.* They clearly bore no interest in this excursion, and if they were even lis-tening to Loren's grueling dissertation, it was to look at the blonde sitting next to him. *They're just here for the ride and the eye candy,* Nora realized.

"Right, Nora?" Loren asked.

Nora blinked, reined her attention back in. "Oh . . . what?"

"I was telling Annabelle about the reproductive habits of some bristleworms, such as the *Eunice didacta.*"

Annabelle, Nora thought through the bored daze. *Oh, right. The blonde. He's calling her by her first name, like they're best buds.* "The female didacta will actually ingest the entire posterium of the male."

"Posterium?" Annabelle pronounced.

"The rearmost tip of the worm's body," Nora defined.

"Which, in the case of this species, also contains the spermatic reservoir—its penis, if you will," Loren fin-ished, grinning. "That's how the Eunice didacta has sex."

Annabelle's eyes grew wide. "How fascinating!"

The huge-jawed warrant officer elbowed Trent. "Ain't that somethin', Luey? The chick worm eats the dude worm's works. That's how it gets knocked up!"

"Charming."

The warrant laughed along with the two pilots, while Trent simply frowned at the image.

"It sounds like such a specialized subject," Anna-belle said. She perkily pointed to Loren's T-shirt, which read POLYCHAETOLOGISTS DO IT BETTER! "That word you keep using. Polych—"

"Polychaetes," Loren was happy to reply. "That's the class of worm that your employers have sent you all this way to photograph."

Nora felt negligent by not contributing to the conversation. "The scarlet bristleworm, for example. *Scarlata* is the genus, or type, *Polychaete* is the class, and it comes from the phylum known as annelida—which covers all segmented worms."

"Oh," the blonde said, then returned her attention to Loren. "So that word on your shirt—"

"Polychaetologist," Loren explained, "is a scientist, such as myself and Professor Craig, who specifically studies this type of worm. That's our job."

"*Great* job," Trent said, dimly astonished.

The WO called to the pilot, chuckling, "Hey, Flappy, you hear that? These two here are *worm* scientists!"

"And the overall study of worms," Loren continued, "is called helminthology."

"Wow," Annabelle said.

Nora couldn't believe it. *He just told her that he's a worm specialist . . . and she's impressed.*

"I'm just a photographer," Annabelle chatted on. "But listening to a real scientist—it makes me feel so dumb!"

You are, Nora agreed. *She's got the high-paying job, and she's got the looks, but . . . at least I've got a better tan.*

"What I'm looking forward to most of all," Annabelle prattled on, thrusting her bosom forward against the straps, "is getting a tan. I work out so hard in the gym to keep my body fit . . . I guess while I'm in Florida, I should take advantage of the sun, too. Look my absolute best."

Unbelievable ego, Nora thought. She winced out the window. *Even if I DID look like her, I KNOW I wouldn't be an asshole about it.*

As for the trip itself, the university had sent Nora and Loren on the excursion, since they were local and their credentials were unmatched. The whole affair had been chartered by *National Geographic,* no less. It sounded exotic.

It's a shitty little island with no beach and it's uninhabited, Nora's cynicism kicked in. *And we might have to stay there for a week or more. I'll miss* Desperate Housewives *just so this bimbo can snap some pix of a* Polychaete scarlata. Annabelle was one of the lauded magazine's professional underwater photographers. *NG* needed a new picture of the scarlata, one of the world's rarest marine worms. *And it's a hell of a lot cheaper to go to Pritchard's Key than a three-thousand-foot-deep trench in the Mediterranean.* It was Nora's and Loren's job to locate the exceptional worm for Annabelle, for a pictorial on segmented marine bottom dwellers, and since Pritchard's Key technically remained a military reservation, however nonoperational, Trent was sent as the team's official escort.

Hence, the circumstances that had planted Nora's derriere on the hard troop bench of an old helicopter.

What a festival of joy my life has become . . .

"Crabs, fish, sharks, even killer whales," Annabelle distinguished. "I've photographed them all, at some pretty deep depths." She hitched in her seat, to shed an imaginary discomfort, but Nora knew it was a pose. *She's sticking her tits out so the grunts will get all riled up.* Nora felt certain of it. *She's the tribal queen and she's marking her turf, showing the skinny girl that she's got no chance.*

"But I've never shot marine worms," the blonde went on. "What's so special about this one?"

It infuriated Nora the way Annabelle focused her

questions toward Loren and not Nora herself, who was the more qualified expert.

"It's the rarest Polychaete," Loren answered. "And it's probably also the most stunning to look at. Brilliant red stripes run between its parapodia—the rings around its body."

Now a hint of concern came into Annabelle's tone. "How big is it? The idea of, like, *really big* worms? Yuck. That would gross me out. Spiders, roaches, and big worms. That's it for me."

"Then have no fear, because the *Polychaete scarlata* never grows more than a couple of inches long."

"That we know of," Nora pointed out.

Did Annabelle actually glare at the comment?

Loren laughed it off. "Oh, Professor Craig is only kidding, Annabelle. It's impossible for a warm water worm such as this to get any longer than an inch or two."

"Oh, thank God!" the blonde laughed, but when she brushed a tress of hair off her brow, she did it with her middle finger.

A display for Nora's benefit?

Nora put her cheek in her hand. *This is going to be a peachy trip.*

The aircraft noisily touched down on a long-since overgrown helipad carved into one edge of the island. "Oh no! The little lizards!" Annabelle fretted at the window. Nora smiled when she peeked out, saw the helicopter's air-blast blowing countless dozens of little anole lizards out of the palm trees.

"They're so cute!" Annabelle continued to object. "We're killing them!"

Shut up, you airhead, Nora thought. *If those things were bigger, they'd eat you alive.*

"Debark! Heads down, single file!" barked the warrant officer.

Nora was first off, and so slight in frame that the rotor wind almost knocked her down. They all jogged away from the riotous noise.

"So this is Pritchard's Key," Annabelle remarked.

"It's a lot bigger than it looks," Trent added. "Ten square miles, and dense. I'll bet there are parts of it that no one's ever set foot on."

"But I still don't understand what the island has to do with the military."

"Some kind of radar station, I think," Nora said. She had to shield her eyes from the bar of sunlight flashing like a guillotine blade. Palm trees clotted with the greenest underbrush seemed to explode everywhere she looked.

"No, a missile station," Loren corrected. "The locals over in Clearwater used to call it Nike Island."

Annabelle's brow creased. "What do sneakers have to do with missiles?"

Nora laughed out loud.

"The Nike Missile Program wrapped up in the mid-eighties," Trent explained. "It was an army tactical air-defense missile that was first deployed in NATO countries in the late fifties, designed to shoot down enemy aircraft. As the missile became obsolete we started pulling them out of Europe and planting them in the continental United States. Our biggest fear back then was Leonid Brezhnev and his new Backfire Bomber. The Nike was no longer the fastest antifighter missile, but it still had great range against potential bomber threats. The army put fifteen Nikes right here on this island, to protect MacDill Air Force Base and the army's munition depot in Jacksonville. Fortunately, the dreaded Backfire turned out to be the biggest claptrap hunk of junk the Soviet Union ever put in the air, and now there's not even a Soviet Union anymore so we don't need them anyway."

Annabelle seemed alarmed. "You mean there are nuclear missiles on this island?"

"No, no, the Nikes here were never armed with nuclear payloads. The army took them all out of here by 'eighty-five."

The blonde sighed in relief. "Oh, wow, for a minute I thought you were going to tell us that there were radioactive things on the island."

Nora couldn't have been less interested, but by accident she noticed a strange pause in Trent's monologue, as if he were taken aback. "Nope. The Nike was strictly defensive, and we don't need them now. Now we've got the Patriots that take care of the whole ball of wax."

"Not much of a beach," Loren commented of the island's shoreline. Black boulders the size of compact cars seemed to ring the key. "Just a bunch of rocks."

"Yeah, big rocks," Annabelle said.

Almost as big as the ones in your head, Nora thought.

Annabelle hitched at her aqua-blue bikini top. "I was hoping to get a tan in between shoots, but how can I? There's no beach!"

Nora shook her head. *Oh no! Dollface can't get a tan! Poor, poor struggling Dollface!*

"There's a strip of beach on the other side," Trent told them. "It's blocked up by more rocks but there's enough room to lie out. But before we do that—a word to the wise." He passed everyone an OD-green aerosol can as well as a neon-green rubberized repellent bracelet. "This island is Bug City. Let's spray ourselves with repellent every chance we get. And put on your bracelet. They don't smell that great but they work."

"Oh, great. Mosquitoes, you mean?" Annabelle looked like she had a mouthful of lemon juice as she sprayed her arms and legs and put the bracelet on her wrist.

"The mosquitoes aren't that bad," Trent went on, "but there are ticks and chiggers."

"Even worse. I want to get a tan, not Lyme disease."

You're so pompous and annoying, Nora thought, *the ticks won't come near you.* When she was done spraying herself off and donning her own bracelet, she asked, "We're only a couple of miles off the coast. Why go to the expense of the helicopter trip when we could've taken a quick boat ride?"

Trent pointed to the boulders. "Those rocks encircle the island, it's very hard to get a boat ashore, and the current's so quick if you anchor out there and swim in, you might lose your boat. Sure, every now and then some kids get on, use the place to camp out and party. The only reason I know anything about Pritchard's Key at all is 'cause I have to fly out here and check it once a month. Make sure no one's gotten on and done damage."

Nora and Loren traded a glance. *What the hell does the army care about a missile site that doesn't have missiles anymore?* Nora had to wonder. *The only authority interested in vandalism would be Florida Natural Resources.*

The WO and pilots frowned as they carried boxes of supplies off the helicopter.

"Where will we be sleeping, Lieutenant?" Loren inquired.

"Bivouac tents, of course," Trent told them. "And we'll be eating C rats."

"Rats!" Annabelle almost shrieked. "What are you talking about!"

"Rats as in rations. You'll be surprised how good they are. And we do have a field shower, so no one will be getting too stinky."

"There's a domestic water line running out to the island?" Nora questioned.

"No, no, the old missile station has a good old army water purifier and desalinator," Trent explained. "And a generator too, so we'll have some lights."

So we won't be living out here like total aborigines, Nora realized. "Loren and I would like to set up a field lab somewhere so we can catalogue worm samples for the college. We have to use a tent for that?"

"There are fifteen empty head shacks," Trent said. "You can use one of those. It's got lights, electricity for your laptops, whatever you need."

Loren inquired, "Head shacks?"

"That's army lingo for the old launchpads. A head shack is a missile bunker. The missile on its launch rail is called the missile 'head,' so that's where head *shack* comes from. You'll see them in a few minutes. You might have to sweep one out, though. All I do is stick my head in them once a month to make sure there's no squatters."

And ten to one this head shack is chock-full of spiders and God knows what else, Nora considered.

"Could you show us around the island now?" Annabelle asked Trent, a camera slung around her neck. "I'm dying to see it. It looks so exotic."

Trent led them toward a trail. "If you're a tropical nature buff, you'll find this place pretty interesting."

Nora frowned, lugging two suitcase-sized field kits, while Loren carried the laptop and a bigger bag of collection and indexing gear. Annabelle bopped along with her big Nikon bouncing off her bosom. "It's so beautiful," she said wistfully.

You think it might be nice of you to carry one of these for me? came Nora's sarcasm again. She sputtered. *Fat chance.*

Various types of palm trees formed a maze before them. Nora didn't walk ten feet before she noticed three different kinds of geckos, two kinds of parrots, and a squawking gull-billed tern. Just as they entered the trail, a sedate marsh extended, mangrove roots jutting upward like weird plumbing. Clumps of water locus seemed to shiver as they passed; owls looked down at them from high nests in cabbage palms. A minute ago they'd been baking in the sun, but now the woods seemed to draw them into a labyrinthine coolness. Nora oddly felt as though she were traversing worlds.

KEEP OUT! a red-lettered sign warned. THIS IS A U.S. ARMY RESERVATION AND IS UNDER SURVEILLANCE—TRESPASSERS WILL BE PROSECUTED ACCORDING TO THE CIVILIAN STATUES OF THE UNIFORMED CODE OF MILITARY JUSTICE AND ALSO FLORIDA STATE LAW.

"That's what I call a welcome," Loren joked.

"You've got surveillance cameras out here?" Nora asked.

"Not anymore," Trent said, bored as he strode forward. "The sign's all bark and no bite, but it usually does the job."

"A heyday of regional flora and fauna," Loren commented next. A marsh rabbit shot away through brush at their approach. Swamp lilies and wild purple petunias bobbed their heads, and Spanish moss hung like mop heads off low branches.

"There are also leatherback turtles, peregrine falcons, and big-eared bats."

"I'll have to get pictures of *those,*" Annabelle assured them.

"Hate to tell you," Trent went on, "but most of the wildlife out here is so unused to human contact, you'll never see them."

"What about alligators?" Annabelle asked next.

"There aren't any here. But even if there were . . ." Trent indicated the pistol on his hip. "I'm a qualified army pistol expert."

Dirty Harry in green, Nora thought.

Ahead she noted a long wall of sunlight beyond more trees. It seemed uncharacteristic until they broke through. "Wow," someone said. Now Nora saw what had been done: A clearing the size of a football field had been cut into the woods and in it had been erected Trent's drab cinder block "head shacks." They didn't look like shacks at all, more like blockhouses. Fifteen such structures in even rows, forty feet long, twenty high, and twenty wide. Gray-painted metal roofs sat atop each.

"Those are about the ugliest things I've ever seen on an island," Loren remarked.

"In the army," Trent said, "the ugliest is the most efficient. It doesn't matter what it is. A truck, a garbage can, a tie, or a head shack—the army will go out of its way to make it as ugly as possible. Even the Nike missiles themselves were ugly."

"But you said there's no missiles here now?" Annabelle asked.

"Not a one. Like I told you earlier, they were dismantled at the end of Reagan's second term and I think we gave them to Israel."

"Lucky them," Nora said.

Keys jangled. "Say hello to your new field lab," and then Trent opened a black—and very ugly—metal door. Hinges grated. He stepped in and felt around the wall. "At least we *should* have electricity."

"Should?" Nora asked.

"A maintenance crew was supposed to come out here yesterday to fuel the generator and purifiers. The generator runs on diesel fuel."

Suddenly light bloomed, and then everybody jumped an inch off the ground at a series of loud twangy *pops*!

"What was that!" Annabelle exclaimed.

They all moved inside, Trent looking up. "Not as bad as I thought. We only blew about a third of the bulbs."

Nora saw rows of large hooded lightbulbs mounted along the structure's metal roof. "It's good enough," she said. And she didn't see any spiderwebs or wasp nests. "A little moldy but it'll do."

Annabelle gazed down the length of the building. "So, twenty years ago there was a missile in this building?"

"Yep," Trent said. "And if the crew had ever had to fire one, a motor would crank the roof open, the missile rail would rise, then off it goes."

"They'd fire it from in here?" Nora questioned. "Wouldn't there be back-blast, exhaust gases?"

"The crew would actually launch from the missile *station,* not from any of these head shacks."

"Where's the station?"

"On the other side of the island. I can show it to you if you want, but . . ."

"Who needs to see another *ugly* army building?" Loren supposed.

"Exactly."

Nora set down her field case and looked around, trying to come to grips with the environment. *This is going to be a pain in the ass, but I'll at least try to have a decent time.* "Well, everything appears to be in order, Lieutenant. I guess we might as well get started setting up our gear."

"I hate to leave my cameras and dive gear in *here,*" Annabelle fretted.

"I can guarantee that your valuables and important equipment will be perfectly safe," Trent said. "It'd be really tough for thieves to get on the island."

Nora wasn't sure but she thought she heard Annabelle whisper to Trent something like, *I trust you and Loren but . . .* She glanced briefly at Nora, frowned, and turned away.

You DICK! Nora thought.

"Before you get the rest of your gear come along with me to the other clearing," Trent suggested, marching them forward. "It's a perfect campsite."

Nora groaned and left the bulky field cases. The team filed down another trail, through more woods. Nora frowned at Annabelle's bouncy steps as more jealousy percolated. *All women are NOT created equal,* she cursed the Fates. She followed last in line, forced to face Annabelle's hourglass physique anytime she looked up: the tight rump churning in the skimpy bikini bottoms, athletic legs flexing. *I hope she breaks all her nails . . .*

Down the trail a ways, Annabelle pointed, enthused. "Look how yellow they are!"

A dozen large, bright yellow butterflies clung to the brambles, their brilliant wings barely moving.

"A southern dogface butterfly," Loren said. "*Colias cesonia,* at least I think it is."

"But I'm sure Professor Craig knows for sure." Annabelle glanced over her shoulder to Nora. "She is the professor, right?"

Nora ground her teeth at the blonde. "It looks like, well, let me see, like a fucking yellow butterfly, Annabelle. And beyond that I wouldn't know because I'm a specialist in segmented marine worms, not fucking butterflies."

Annabelle grinned at her jab, then complimented Loren, "You're really a smart guy, Loren."

I do not believe this bitch, Nora thought.

"Well, I could be wrong," Loren deflected. "There are thousands of different species of butterflies from six different families."

"How many different kinds of worms are there?"

"Oh, tens of thousands—"

"And fifty-four hundred Polychaetes alone," Nora struggled to contribute, "but it's estimated that there may still be hundreds more that haven't been discovered yet."

Annabelle wasn't listening anymore, lapsing instead into less specific chatter with Loren.

"I did my OCS bivouac training out here," Trent commented. "Had to live on this island for two weeks. Here's where we camped." He'd taken them to another clearing that caught a welcome breeze. "There's plenty of room in the center if we feel like having a campfire."

"Sounds like fun," Annabelle said. "I should've brought marshmallows."

Nora groaned.

Trent pointed up to a tree. "And there's something else we can roast, for any of you who feel adventurous."

Annabelle squealed and began snapping pictures. Lounging on a branch was a long, scaly iguana.

"That's pretty much all I lived on during my survival training."

"Tastes like chicken?" Loren asked.

"Nope. Tastes like . . . crap."

Loren stepped closer to the trees. "Well now, what have we here?" A tall spiky plant was growing out of a patch of sawgrass. "A nettle plant from the Cannabaceae order, more specifically *Cannabis sativa,* I do believe."

"What?" Nora said.

Annabelle squinted. "You mean—"

"A great big pot plant," Loren said of the blooming, six-foot-tall specimen.

"What's a great big pot plant doing on a tropical island?" Nora asked.

Trent walked up to it. "If that's not the damnedest thing . . ."

"I don't know much about marijuana," Nora offered, "but I'm pretty sure it's not indigenous to tropical environments."

"It's not," Loren said. He looked to Trent. "But, Lieutenant, didn't you tell us earlier that kids sneak out to the island a lot to party?"

"Not a lot. More like once in a blue moon, when they're lucky enough to have the tides just right. But, yeah, they do get out here every so often."

"Mystery solved. Some kid was rolling a doobie and a seed fell out. By the looks of this plant, it's been growing for some time." Loren grinned, eyeing the others. "Hey, I won't tell if you all won't."

"Sorry, Easy Rider, but no one's touching the plant," Trent said. "I'll have to report this. Christ, that would look great in the papers, wouldn't it? Marijuana farm on army property. The damn air force would have a field day."

"Shucks," Loren laughed.

"I've never smoked pot in my life," Annabelle said. She giggled. "I'm too afraid of the munchies. That would ruin my body."

Nora wanted to gag.

Trent shook his head at the tall plant. "Well, it'll give me something to do while you guys are worm-hunting. I'll have to look around to see if any more of these things are growing here."

They headed back. *What's wrong with me?* Nora wondered. She knew she was letting herself become aggravated by Annabelle; she also knew it was a juvenile and unsophisticated emotion. *Then I guess I'm juvenile and unsophisticated!* she finally unloaded on herself, still forced to walk behind the photographer and be reminded that she was purely and simply more attractive than Nora.

Floozy. Thinks she's hot shit with her big boobs and

designer bikini. The more Nora tried to let it go, the more she realized she couldn't. Back at the landing pad, the crew had off-loaded all the supplies. The peninsular-jawed warrant officer announced to Trent, "I guess we're done, Luey. Just give my top a call on the radio when you want us to pick you back up."

"You got it. Thanks for the lift. I guess we'll be here a week," Trent figured. He looked to Nora. "How long will it take you to find this worm for Annabelle to photograph?"

Nora sat down exhausted on another field case. "It'll take as long as it takes. The scarlata lives at depths of up to sixty feet but prefers clear, shallow intertidal zones. If we're lucky we'll be able to make do with just snorkeling. Loren and I are experienced divers."

"Oh, don't worry, Professor," Annabelle bulled in. "You won't have to show *me* the ropes. I'm certified to three hundred feet and even have an instructor's license." She flipped her hair in the sun. "Do you have an instructor's license, Professor?"

Nora sighed and looked up at her. "No, Annabelle, I don't, but—"

The blonde grinned at Loren and Trent. "So who knows? Maybe I'll be the one showing *you* where the worms are."

And maybe when you do, Nora thought, too tired now to even be mad, *I'll be the one to shove the worms up your ass.*

"The worms are all yours," Trent said. "I'm not going in the water, and I'm not looking for worms. Not in my job description. I'm just here to show you all around."

"It's gonna be fun," Loren promised. "An adventure!"

"Whatever," Nora said.

Loren grabbed armfuls of rolled tents. "I'll take these to the campground. Then we can start setting up our lab."

"Okay by me." Nora looked around, depressed at the remainder of their gear: diving equipment and several more field cases, weighty stuff for a 110-pound woman. *I can't carry all this junk.* She looked to the warrant officer and the two pilots. *Maybe if I ask nice . . .*

Annabelle rushed ahead, her body blaring in the string bikini. "Oh, sir? Do you think you and your men could help me carry my dive gear and equipment?" She stood erect, hands on hips, giving the helicopter crew an eyeful. "I'd really appreciate it."

"Aw, sure," the warrant officer said. "Come on, boys. Let's give the lady a hand."

A minute later, Annabelle was leading a caravan back toward the head shack.

Nora sat alone now on the shore, mortified. "Well, fuck you all very much!" she said. Eventually, she grabbed a pair of cases and began to drag them toward the access trail.

CHAPTER TWO

(I)

"Zero-one, this is zero-zero. Repeat."

"Zero-zero, I repeat. Four more have entered the perimeter. Two male, two female."

A calculative pause came over the transmission. "A third party?"

"Affirmative, zero-zero."

"So that's a total of eight on the island now still alive?"

"Correct, zero-zero. Eight that we've observed. The first party three weeks ago I'm pretty sure are all dead."

"These latest four—they're all civilian sector?"

"Negative, zero-zero. One of the males is military."

Another, longer, pause. "Other observations?"

"I've found one of the dead females from three weeks ago. There appears to be positive stage two gravidity. Transfection success appears to be positive."

"Roger, zero-one." The major sounded pleased now.

"Terminate all transmissions and return to base. Bring one sample."

"Roger, zero-zero. Out."

Radio silence now. *This should be interesting,* the sergeant thought. At least until they found out about this new military presence on the island . . .

Shards of sunlight stabbed down through the over-brush. The sergeant looked down.

The woman's nipples seemed to float atop the bags of liquefied rot that were now her breasts. *Of course,* the sergeant thought. In this environment? It would be considered tropical. It made dead things rot faster.

The sergeant was not repulsed. He'd seen many, many dead things during his duties. He was fascinated by them.

Ah, heat, he thought to himself. He much preferred the warmer monitoring posts. His last assignment had been the equivalent of ten below at the hottest marks. *That mission seemed to last forever,* he remembered, but at least the project had proved a success. The heat here—the blazing heat day after day—made him feel alive even in the protective mask.

His eyes flicked back down to the corpse.

The kids sure liked to party here. Three boatloads so far. They came to the island in spite of the warning signs and the rock-strewn beachless shore, to imbibe in every chemical and carnal indulgence. This one had been the prettiest of the first bunch, until the things had gotten her.

A few vestiges of her sexuality remained printed on the gray, putrefactive skin. The brown circles of nipples on once-sumptuous breasts, the groove of her sex, even the ghosts of tan lines. She was a skeleton dressed in flesh-tone rags that were falling off the bones.

Yet even looking at it this close left the sergeant unfazed.

It's just my job, he realized.

The island habitat shivered around him. Parrots cackled, lizards scampered up the trunks of palm trees. *It's all so beautiful,* he thought, and then he looked back down at the corpse and smiled.

There would be more corpses very soon.

(II)

"I've never done it in the woods before," Leona informed him.

Bullshit, Alan thought. *You've done it everywhere, with damn near everybody, and I couldn't care less.* He supposed he loved her, though, almost as much as he loved her body and the things she did with it. "It's not really the woods. It's a tropical terrain . . ."

"Whatever."

She was sitting on him, looking down. Beads of sweat glittered on her skin, like jewels. At one point she arched her back to gaze upward at the trees, and her head disappeared in the cusp of her considerable cleavage. "That's a neat trick," Alan said.

"What?"

"Nothin', babe."

Their lovemaking had put him to the test, but he couldn't let her know that. *Jesus. A steamroller.* Her tanlines raved: the Cool Whip–white pubis—hair-free—sitting in the middle of all that peanut butter brown. Alan marveled. *She didn't keep shaved for all the other guys,* he knew. Guys always talked. *I guess I'm special!* The tan lines of her breasts were even more pronounced when she looked back down at him and grinned. "That was great, Alan."

"Oh yeah?"

She jumped off him and scampered away, nude as a

wood sprite. Her carbon-black hair danced around her head. "Come on!"

Shit, I'm too tired to get up! "I'll be in. Gonna lie here for a few, grab some TM."

"Whatever." The chirpy giggle faded.

Man . . .

The island was great. Alan had partied out here about a year ago. Waiting for the high tide had been a bitch, but once they'd found the inlet, the rest was a breeze. At first he'd feared that all Leona saw him as was a rich kid with a nice boat. *Called that one wrong,* he thought to himself. *Guess I'm more of a package than I thought.* It was a gratifying revelation.

Eventually he dragged himself up. He hobbled barefoot over twigs and dead palm branches, and made his way back to the shed. "What are you doing?" he yelled in the doorway.

Leona paused midcut. Still naked, she stood with a pair of scissors at her jeans. "I'm turning these into cutoffs. Didn't know it would be this hot."

Alan was outraged. "I got you those for your birthday! That's a hundred-and-fifty-dollar pair of Sevens jeans!"

Her bare shoulders shrugged as she snipped off the last leg. "Now they're a hundred-and-fifty-dollar pair of Seven-brand cutoffs." She squeezed into them, fastened the button below the slitlike navel, then stood up on her tiptoes and raised her arms. "There. Now you can see more of my legs. What, you don't approve?"

Alan gulped. A topless Leona in cutoffs not much bigger than a pair of panties? "I approve."

"Thought you would."

Alan stepped into his trunks and looked around. This old shack was ramshackle but it would do. They'd brought summer-weight sleeping bags, plus the Coleman to cook on. *And a big cooler of booze,* he reminded himself.

"Look what I found," she said, handing him something.

An embroidered patch. A gold-rimmed shield with three arrows and a lightning bolt. Letters read: U.S. ARMY MISSILE COMMAND. "Where'd you find this?"

"The shelf."

"This place was a missile base a long time ago," Alan recalled, "but the missiles are long gone. The old station is on the other side of the island."

Her eyes widened with a question. "There are army people on the island?"

"No, no. It's all closed down. I'm sure this shack is where they stored stuff. It was ages ago, back when guys like Ford and Carter were in office."

"Who?"

When nature passed out the brains, it gave her tits instead, Alan mused. Now she was puttering with things in her bag, breasts roving. The pose, bent over like that, gave him butterflies.

"So you're sure there's no one else on the island?"

"I'm sure. No one comes here," he said. "Why would they?"

"To party! Like us!"

Alan shook his head. "It's too hard to dock. The only reason I did it is 'cause I'm experienced."

She wriggled her butt in the cutoffs. "You're experienced, all right. I hate to think how much."

"Let's not even go there," he suggested. He'd heard plenty about her, and Carol, too, and plenty about Leona and Carol together, and much else. *Christ, she's only nineteen . . .*

"Fine. I mean, it's normal to be curious," she said, still busying herself and looking spectacular while doing so. "I'd tell you my number if you told me yours."

At first he thought she meant phone numbers, but he already had hers. She meant sexual partners. "Leona," he said, "I'm not that insecure that I have to know how many men you've been with."

"Okay. I'm cool with that." She stood back up, erect nipples pointing. She looked out the frameless window. "I wonder where Carol and Howie are . . ."

"Out in the woods doing what we were doing for the last hour."

"I hope it works out with them. They'll make a great couple, don't you think?"

"Uh, sure." But he could scarcely concentrate on the question. *Holy SHIT, she's good-looking* . . . Her nipples stuck out like dark pink rivets set into the untanned and flawlessly white breasts. Teepees of more white skin pointed to her collarbones: the marks left by her bikini top. She was every college boy's dream, and Alan was very much a college boy. *Thank you, God,* he thought dumbly.

"Come on, let's go look for them."

Alan frowned. "Let's leave them be. They didn't interrupt us, did they?"

"But they've been gone a long time, Alan." She kept rising on the balls of her feet to peer out the window. The gesture tightened her calves and rump in a way that made Alan grind his teeth. "I'm starting to get a little worried," she said.

Chicks. "There's nothing to get worried about. Let me fire up the Coleman. I guarantee you the minute we get some brats and burgers on the grill, they'll be back."

She spun, grinning the way a woman always grins when she wants something. "That's a great idea, but I've got an even greater one. *I'll* fire up the Coleman while *you* go look for Carol and Howie!" And then she shuffled right up and gave him a kiss. Alan grew dizzy from the scent of her hair and the sensation of her tongue finicking in his mouth. Her breasts flattened against his chest, radiating heat, and when her hand momentarily cupped his crotch, he almost fell over.

"Isn't that a better idea?" she breathed into his mouth.

"Um-hmm," he breathed back.

"And when you come back, I'll get some food in you 'cause you're definitely going to need your energy for tonight." And with a parting caress, she scampered outside.

Alan got his breath back and left the shack. Leona was already hunched over the Coleman.

"You're gonna cook burgers topless?"

"Can you think of a reason why I shouldn't?"

His eyes remained stuck on her breasts. "Uh . . . no."

"Good. So how come you're still standing there? Go find Carol and Howie!"

Alan moseyed off, hands in the pockets of his swim trunks. *I wonder,* he thought. *Just how many guys HAS she gotten it on with?* Insecurity. He told himself it didn't matter, because: *The only guy she's getting it on with now is me.* The placation worked, for a while.

"Where the hell are they?" he muttered aloud. "Howie! Carol! Soup's on!" His voice trumpeted, but the woods swallowed the sound. He corkscrewed around the campsite but found no evidence of them. *Maybe they went back to the boat.* Carol was a fussbudget. *A little too prim and proper to fuck in the woods.* She'd be too worried about bugs crawling on her, a real crisis.

The trail narrowed; the woods grew more dense. *Jesus. I practically need a machete . . .* He stopped to rest a minute, leaned against a tree.

What the . . .

Something had poked into his back. *Feels like a nail.*

He examined the palm tree's trunk and, sure enough, sticking out of a seam in the bark was something that looked like a nail or a wood screw. Fatter, though, the width of a cigarette, and maybe a half inch sticking out. But when he squinted closer he thought he saw—

Glass?

A bead of something clear in the center of the nail head. He ran his fingertip over it. Indeed, it felt smooth, like glass.

Glass as might be found in a tiny lens . . .

That's not a camera lens, is it? It couldn't be.

Why? What purpose?

Then it dawned on him: *It's a hidden surveillance camera from the old missile site,* he reasoned. And obviously not operational anymore. The missile site was emptied out, abandoned.

Strange, though.

The most paranoid part of him had to wonder. *Maybe it still is operational.* He looked directly at the small studlike protrusion. *Maybe some army security guy is looking at me right now . . .*

"Naw," he muttered and laughed. *Impossible.* The lens hadn't been hooked up to anything for twenty years.

Snap!

Alan twirled.

Fear surged for a second, but he knew he'd simply been spooked by the camera. Either an animal had snapped a twig, or it had been Howie and Carol . . .

"Hey, you guys! Where are ya?"

The woods sucked up the call. He wended farther out, toward the sound. Then—

What the fuck?

At his feet lay a bikini top. A chartreuse bikini top. *Can't be Leona's.* Hers was back at the shack, and it wasn't this color, and it couldn't be Carol's either because she'd been wearing a bright floral-patterned bikini. Had it fallen out of their bags? *Impossible,* he was sure. When they'd walked to the shack, they came from the other direction. Alan picked up the top. The tag read 32 B. *Definitely* not Carol or Leona's. The top felt damp, and was flecked with bits of dirt and leaves. *Been here a while . . .*

But so what?

Some chick was probably partying out here months ago, and left her top. That had to be it.

Alan grew frustrated. He called out some more, received no response. Overhead, the palm branches were so dense they melded into one another, darkening the forest.

Snap!

"Hey! Come on, you guys! This is a pain in the ass! Where are you?"

This was pissing him off. He stalked forward, peering deeper. Then, for a split second, he saw a girl disappear between some trees about thirty yards away.

A naked girl.

Carol, he knew. The shape of the body looked right, and it was her same long, shiny auburn hair. A second flash of her confirmed it: she was naked save for the hot-pink tennis shoes. Alan dashed clumsily ahead, crunching branches and dried palm fronds. "What the *fuck* are you two up to?"

When he got to where he'd seen her: silence.

Then a jolt shot through him and he almost screamed.

"No peeking," Carol whispered. She stood behind him and covered his eyes with her hands.

"Carol! Jesus Chr—"

"Shhhhhhhhh!"

He stood stock-still, could feel her bare breasts and belly pressing his back. "Keep your eyes closed," came her next whisper. Her voice sounded parched, in need. Her hands slipped down to his crotch.

Well, now, this is very interesting, Alan thought.

"You know what they say," she cooed in his ear. "If you keep your eyes closed, it's not cheating . . ." Her hand worked into his trunks; her hips squirmed against him.

"And *who* was it that said that?" he asked.

"My uncle."

Alan pondered the whispered response, then thought, *Gross.*

"No talking. And keep your eyes closed," she insisted.

Alan couldn't find much of a reason to disobey. He remained standing, and let her continue with her hands . . .

"I . . . I don't even know what they are," she said next. Her voice seemed to *flow,* like some hot, dark liquid. "But it's so wonderful. I feel like I'm coming . . . all . . . the time . . ."

Alan didn't know what she was talking about, and scarcely cared. He felt her move around him now and lower herself to her knees. Her fingers dragged his trunks down.

I am having one HELL of a good day, Alan thought.

"If you open your eyes, I won't do it."

Alan wouldn't think of it.

Her mouth felt so hot on him. The slick friction of what she was doing wound Alan up like a steel spring. What had she just said? *I don't even know what they are . . . I feel like I'm coming all the time.* What did that mean? The only thing Alan figured was that she must be on drugs, X or Oxycontin or something. Her mouth tended him so precisely that he was climaxing himself a minute later . . .

Holy shit . . .

He almost fell over. But now that the fun was done, his fears swooped down. *Christ! Leona might come out here! She might see!*

Alan wouldn't have guessed that this was the least of his fears, when she said, "My turn now," and next thing he knew, they'd traded positions, Alan kneeling before her, his face in her groin, and then he opened his eyes and saw her fingers splaying over the hairless pubis to bare the tip of her sex—and the strange, pus-colored ticks stuck to her clitoris.

Pulsing.

Alan was too revolted to shriek. He tried to pull his face away but couldn't, for her hand clamped to the back of his head, pushing. When she dragged him down and straddled his face, all he could do was squirm beneath her. Her thighs vised his face. Alan could barely breathe.

"Get with it, lover," she cooed.

More horror flowed over him when he managed to glimpse upward. *My God, her skin! Her skin!*

Carol's skin seemed to be patched with rashes, her suntan ruined by large splotches of the same sickly yellowish white hue of the ticks he'd seen. Worse, somehow, were the red spots speckling the patches. *A skin disease or something* . . . He could see her breasts now, and noticed with heightened disgust that two more of the ticks had fixed themselves to the ends of her nipples.

She twisted his hair till his scalp barked in pain. "Put your tongue in, motherfucker," she insisted, then vised her crotch down tighter, threatening to smother him if he didn't obey.

Alan tremored beneath her, and did as instructed.

He passed out from the sheer revulsion when his tongue slid over still more of the ticks that lined the inside of her vagina . . .

CHAPTER THREE

(I)

Big Jaw Swamp, the Everglades

The woman's name didn't matter. Midfifties but holding up well. Blond hair, great tan, and a fitness club bod. A nip and tuck here, a little liposuction there, and a lift or two to buff out some of the wrinkles, she looked like exactly what she was: a rich, Florida divorcée, who, like so many, refused to let go of the vestiges of younger, wilder days.

But the liver wasn't what it used to be, and after a couple of Bloody Marys she was certifiably inebriated. That's when she stumbled and fell off the footbridge, into the swamp.

Don't panic! she panicked. She was a decent swimmer. She splashed around, chin-deep, and finally buoyed herself in a dog paddle. The warm, soupy water did nothing to brace her against the alcohol; if anything, it worsened the effect. She foundered in the water, seeking some bearings.

God, how could I have gotten so drunk? She'd been walking back to the Flamingo Campgrounds when she'd happened upon the rickety bridge. Drinking all day and now it was getting dark. *It's not that deep,* she assured herself, tasting brackish water. *Just swim back to shore . . .*

She found quickly that she was too drunk to call upon her experience as a "decent" swimmer. Dog paddle would have to do. When she looked for the shore, the sign looked back at her.

POSTED: NO SWIMMING! WATCH FOR GATORS.

Oh, shit! Now the adrenaline fluxed with the alcohol, disorienting her. She'd been here all weekend and she hadn't seen a single gator. *Don't overreact!* she screamed at herself. *Just GET TO THE SHORE!*

A *splash!*

Her eyes tore to the other side of the swamp, where in crisp moonlight she knew she saw an alligator tail disappearing into the water.

Madness now.

Only instinct was left to propel her but, lo, she was just too drunk. Sheer horror and about a .08 blood alcohol content dragged her down, into sultry wet *blackness*.

It was true what they said: Her life did indeed flash before her eyes, and she saw now what a shallow life it had been. Cocktails and yacht clubs and fancy jewelry and a supersharp divorce lawyer. That was pretty much it for the woman about to drown in Big Jaw Swamp.

After the life-flash: more blackness. Her brain was misfiring. Did she hear someone shout? Did she hear a loud *clack?* Like her name, none of this mattered. Bubbles exploded from her mouth and then she bucked like a fish on a pier as her lungs filled with water and the frenzied thuds of her heart . . . stopped.

Now the blackness—hell, perhaps—was all-pervading.

Impressions, then. A splash in reverse. Something tugging at her. Hands? Who knew? She was dead.

She vomited water. Thrashing, and a coughing fit that threatened to tear her chest out.

"Got her." A voice seemed proud. "Got her back."

"Ya don't say?"

The woman's eyes shot open in the brightest moonlight. She shivered, heaving, on the floor of a flatboat. A longhaired man with a kind face knelt aside, tending to her.

"You all right, lady?"

Her brain refit the scattered jigsaw puzzle that was her consciousness. Drenched, she hacked up more water, and sucked in hard breaths. Eventually, she figured what happened. "My God . . . you saved my life . . ."

"Sure enough did, ma'am. Pretty fancy piece of work if I may say so."

More sentience gathered. Providence had given her a second chance! She leaned up and looked around. The longhaired man held her hand. At the other end of the boat, a stockier, bearded man was hauling a limp alligator aboard with a grappling hook. The moonlight crisped the image; she saw a hole in the animal's head—the same animal that would've eaten her. *A bullet hole* . . .

What a stroke of luck. God had thrown down a lightning bolt to save her. As she was drowning—and was about to be chopped apart by gator jaws—this pair of poachers had happened by.

"How can I ever repay you?" she sobbed, hugging the longhaired man.

"I'd say you're damn lucky."

"Oh yes, I know! And I'll repay you, I promise."

The bearded one had stacked the dead gator atop of several more. "Lady, you must not know about Big Jaw Swamp. They call it that for a reason."

She nodded absurdly, still partially disbelieving that she was still alive. "Thank you, men. Thank you, thank you . . ."

"You're a long way off from the campground, a damn sight. And this swampland, Big Jaw? It's been closed to campers for years—too dangerous."

The longhaired one: "That's why we're here."

To poach, of course. "Oh, I understand. And I wouldn't dream of telling anyone what you men were doing out here."

Silence.

The woman looked at both men, who remained stone-faced.

"I'd say you're damn lucky," the longhair repeated, "if it was anyone else that pulled you out, I mean."

"Whuh . . . *what?*" she pleaded.

"Nice jewels." Her diamonds were pulled from her fingers. A hand rummaged through the big pocket of her shorts, extracting her soaked cash, ID, and cards. "Um-hmm. ATM card."

Before she could reckon more, her top was torn open. She shrieked, spitting water. Rough hands twisted the six-thousand-dollar pair of implants. "Yeah, she's a looker, all right, for an old one."

"Old one's more seasoned!"

Aghast, she was flipped over on her belly and her shorts were hauled off.

"Please, please!" she tried to reason. "It doesn't have to be like this! I'll do anything you want, and give you money!"

"Um-hmm."

A hand was laid so hard across her buttocks the sound could've been a bullwhip. She shrieked, then shrieked again when that same pinkened buttocks was bitten hard.

"What you gotta understand, lady," the longhaired one said, "is we ain't got time to fuck around. Just some quick fun and we're gone."

"That's fine, believe me," she pleaded more as her spirit turned dark as the water, "that's fine. We can—we can—I'll do anything you want."

The other one sat toward the rear of the boat, near the hulk of fresh-killed gators. "Ain't no fun to poke 'em cold anyways."

They took turns, chortling as they splayed her middle-aged body into shapes she'd never imagined. Gentle lovemaking this was not. The longhair's hand continued to crack her skin like a whip. She yelped as soft flesh was bitten for effect: the buttocks, her nipples, her face.

So this was what providence had saved her for, to bring her back from the dead, for this.

"Yes sir!" the bearded one reveled. "She's a party, all right!"

"Been out in this hot swamp three days. I'll tell ya, this is *just* what the doctor ordered!"

More revel. The woman was raped again, for posterity, perhaps.

Drained by terror and exhausted, she lay pasty, naked, eyes wide in the next inevitable contemplation.

A Buck knife was put to her throat, her ATM card flashing before her stare. "PIN, lady."

She told him without hesitation.

The bearded one appeared to be urinating over the side. Then he dragged up his overalls. "Three more out there. Guess they smell the old bitch's fear."

"They do that, I heard."

She could hear more gators splashing into the water, homing in on the commotion.

Of course, they'd let her go! *They know I have friends at the campgrounds! They won't kill me because they know they can't get away with it!*

"I'll punch her ticket, and then we can leave," the longhair said, hoisting a crowbar over her head.

"No," the beard said.

Thank God! she thought. See, they weren't that stupid.

"Throw her in alive. More fun that way."

No! No! No!

Recompense for a life of deceit and shallow sin? Or just some pretty damn bad luck?

Like the woman's name, it didn't matter.

She didn't even have time to scream when she was tossed nude and thrashing into the water. The gators converged.

"We got a full load anyhow," the beard said. "Let's head back."

"Good idea. After all that, I could use a cold beer . . ."

They watched for a few moments as the woman was hacked apart chunk by suntanned chunk. Then the boat's motor was started and off they went.

"Good goddamn! Life is sure good to us, ain't it?"

"You got that right . . ."

The longhaired's name was Jonas. The bearded one's was Slydes.

(II)

"It just seems kind of bizarre is all I'm saying," Nora cited, setting out a row of specimen jars along the makeshift table they'd set up in the head shack. They'd already put up their tents at the campsite, and Annabelle had decided the light wasn't ideal for much photography today. *Fine with me,* Nora thought.

Loren plugged in the small field microscope, clicked the switch several times to make sure it worked. "You're not yourself today, you know?"

Nora winced. "Oh, bullshit, yes, I am!"

"All right, all right, forget I said that. So what is it? What's so bizarre?"

"Well, for one, the army guy. Trent. He's acting weird, isn't he?"

"No."

"Oh, bullshit!" she snapped.

"Hey, you asked." Loren's facial expression seemed a meld of amusement and confusion. "How can he be acting weird, Nora? You don't know him. So how do you know the difference between him acting weird and him acting normal?"

Nora slammed down an empty case. "Oh, blow me! You'd have to be a moron to not see it!"

"Well, I think my 159 IQ might contravene your assessment. What's your IQ, by the way?"

"Oh, blow me!" She huffed over to the next case of equipment. Nora's was 158, and Loren knew that. "Don't forget, buddy, I am your boss. You're my T.A. That stands for teaching *assistant*. You're still *working* on your doctoral degree and—oh, how do you like that? I already have mine, which is why I'm the *professor* and you're my *assistant*."

Loren laughed. "You do realize I was just joking."

"Yes!"

"So tell me, then. Why, exactly, is it your analysis that Lieutenant Trent is acting weird?"

Nora sighed. *He's right. I'm not myself today, and I'm fully aware of that.* "I don't know. The scenario, I guess."

"The scenario isn't exactly atypical, Nora," Loren pointed out. "We're zoological experts sent by the college to escort a field excursion, in this case a photographic one. *National Geographic* no less. That's pretty cool. They didn't ask anybody else in the state to do it. They asked *us* to do it. Any other time, you'd be so into this you'd be spinning like a top. But no. You're pissed off instead. You claim that Trent's acting weird. Well, I don't think he's acting weird at all. I don't know *where* you're coming from."

Nora paused a moment, rubbing her eyes. *Stop going nuts,* she ordered herself. "I think it's weird, Loren. This place. It's army property that the army has abandoned. It's a missile base with no missiles anymore, right?"

"Right," Loren agreed, still trying to contain his smile.

"Yet they got this guy Trent—some sort of *liaison* officer—who comes out here every month to check the island for damage. What's to damage?" She pointed to the wall. "These ugly-ass brick buildings that are empty?"

"All right, I guess that seemed a little strange at first—"

"There! See? You agree!"

"Not really. Trent's an army gofer, an errand boy. And it just happens to be part of his job to keep tabs on army land that's no longer in use. You heard him. He said they get squatters out here sometimes, and college kids partying. It doesn't matter that the army's not using the land for anything right now. These empty buildings belong to the friggin' army, and so do the water purifiers and the generator and whatever else is out here. Trent spot-checks the place to make sure nobody's screwed with his employer's property. Simple. It's a busywork job, and the military is full of stuff like that."

"I think Trent's hiding something," she finally said.

Loren shook his head. "He's not hiding anything, Nora, and that's not really what's bothering you anyway, is it? Either somebody pissed in your granola this morning—and I happen to know you don't eat granola— or you're having some *giant* PMS, and that can't be the case either because you had that two weeks ago."

Listen to what he's saying, she told herself. *Be honest.* "All right. You're right."

"So what is it?" and before she could answer, he raised a finger. "Ah, but let me guess. The photographer."

Nora's face felt clamped in a cheese press she was frowning so hard. "Yeah, I guess that's it—that priss photographer, and, yes, I know it sounds juvenile and insecure but she really pisses me off."

"That's no secret, the way you were glaring at her for the entire trip over."

She sat down on a collapsible field stool. "How else am I supposed to feel? You saw the way the pilots were gawking at her. And Trent, too. Nobody ever gawks at *me*."

"I do." Loren winked, and made a lewd pelvic gesture. "Hubba-hubba. Any time you want to make the smartest babies on earth, let me know."

Nora sighed. "I'm serious, Loren. It's depressing. What do I need to get some notice? A boob job? A platinum-blond wig?"

"I don't know what you're talking about. You're a good-looking woman. In fact, you're the best-looking female polychaetologist in Florida."

Nora didn't hesitate to give him the finger. "Loren, you know damn well I'm the *only* female polychaetologist in Florida."

"Well . . ."

She plopped her chin in her hands. "I'm a nerd, Loren."

"Don't feel bad. I'm a nerd, too. I can't get laid in a whorehouse with a fistful of fifties. And you know what? I don't care. Sure, Nora, we're nerds, we're geeks, but you know what else we are?"

"What's that?" she droned.

"We're smarter than everyone else, which makes us—" He cut a toothy grin and pointed at her like a gun. "Superior."

Superior, Nora thought. That was the last thing she felt. *I'm thirty years old now and my nickname is still Pipe Cleaner. I'm still a virgin, and in Florida? That makes me more rare than a fucking Gutenberg Bible.*

"Another thing to consider," Loren rambled. He rambled a lot. "Of course, we're smart. Our IQs, in addition to the fund of our general knowledge, probably puts us in the top two percentile of the population, and I mean the *advanced-educated* population."

Nora winced. "Loren! We're a couple of egghead misfits! We're the sore thumbs of the modern American societal mainstream! We're *dorks!* If we walk into a singles bar, we don't even know how to pull up a stool and order a drink!"

Loren ignored the judgment, continuing, "*Aaaaa-aaand,* I might add, with specificity, you and I in all likelihood probably know more about polychaetes than anyone else in North America."

Nora felt like slapping him. "That and six bucks will get you a cup of coffee at Starbucks . . . maybe."

"You are the queen and I am the king of our field. We're marine zoologists of the first water. It may even be—and I mean no arrogance when I say this—that we may be the best polychaetologists in the world. So. *That's* something to be happy about, isn't it?"

Now Nora had to laugh. "I appreciate your positivity, Loren."

"Good. Revel in your life! Celebrate your essence of

superiority in the void of the soul-dead hoi polloi."

"Whatever," she muttered, and forced herself to her feet. "Let's go find G.I. Joe and the Barbie doll, try to keep this day from turning to total shit."

"Well said!"

They left their cinder block lab, headed back toward the campsite. Nora knew she had to snap out of this mood. There was no reason for it. *Midlife crisis and I'm not even middle-aged,* she thought. *What a ripoff.* But was that it, or something else?

The woods pressed in on them as the trail narrowed. "And another thing," she remembered. "That big pot plant."

"What about it?" Loren said, following her up.

"That's pretty weird, isn't it? Something like that, growing *here?*"

"You heard Trent. He told us right off the bat, sometimes kids sneak on the island to make whoopie. Some kid dropped a seed and—presto—it grew."

"Um-hmm, and how convenient an explanation." She glanced over her shoulder at him. "Or maybe I'm right. Maybe Trent really is hiding something."

Loren's chuckling floated forward. "You really have a problem with Trent."

"Think about it." Subconsciously, her eyes roved through the forest's plush vegetation. Searching for spiky plants? "Secluded location, abandoned government land. And the only authority is our buddy Lieutenant Trent. He could have a veritable *farm* of pot growing out here, and who would know?"

"And it must be pretty good weed, too, because you've obviously had a few bowls already today."

"Oh, kiss my ass, Loren!" she snapped back.

"Drop 'em and I will."

"You wish."

"No, *you* wish."

"No! *You*—" But then Nora dropped it. *Listen to us!*

"I know," Loren said after the contemplative pause. "We sound like a couple of kids in junior high."

"Yep. And you know why, don't you? Because that's about as far as we've evolved socially."

"How wonderfully pathetic!" Loren cheered. "But you're not really serious about Trent, are you? Please. Tell me you're not."

Nora didn't say anything, trudging on down the trail.

They stopped at a marshy pond that stretched off to their right. A reddish brown bird with a white head pecked at the water.

"Fresh, not brackish," Nora noted.

"Looks like a brown noddy, too. Haven't seen one of *those* for a while."

Their presence seemed to agitate the bird, which then flew off, yacking. Nora pointed to a scurry of tadpoles in the water. "Southern cricket tadpoles?" Nora questioned. "What's that? *Gryllus dorsalis?*"

Loren stooped to one knee. "Maybe, but look at the flake of the eyes. Probably a *Hyla cinera*."

Nora squinted. "Yeah, you're right. The *Gryllus* doesn't get the gold till the tail falls."

Loren stood back up. The oddest stasis seemed to take hold of them.

Finally Nora said, "This is depressing, Loren. We're looking at a pond and identifying the tadpoles by the Latin classification. That's pretty fucked up, isn't it? I mean, really, that's *not* normal."

Loren scratched his head, cruxed. "Are we really *that* nerdy?"

Simultaneously, they looked back down, eyed their reflections in the water. Like a carnival mirror, the water made Loren's buckteeth look like horse teeth, and his Adam's apple as big as a popover. Nora stood five four, but in this mirror of water she looked seven feet tall and bent, a big frizz-mopped ball for a head jutting from a stick: a geek scarecrow. The knees on her broomstick legs looked grotesque: *Elephant Woman,* she thought.

Are we really that nerdy? Nora repeated the grim question in her mind. "Let's get out of here before I friggin' throw up," she said. They crunched away down the trail, silent.

Neither of them noticed the bloated corpse just a few yards past the edge of the pond. Its mouth squirmed vigorously with shining pink worms.

"God, it's hot!" Annabelle remarked, stepping into the campsite. She unslung the expensive Nikon from around her neck, set it down on a rickety picnic table. Humidity had dampened her blond hair, showing roots. She stretched and took a deep breath, flexing her arms over her head. The pose maximized her toned physique, breasts thrusting outward in the blue bikini top. Her flat stomach stretched, rivulets of sweat trickling down. Her coltish legs shone.

Nora frowned. *That prissy New York phony is doing that on purpose.* Loren's eyes were hijacked.

"I thought you weren't going to take pictures today," Nora recalled.

"Nothing underwater." At the height of her stretch, the edge of one nipple showed. Nora was certain she pretended not to notice, for Loren's benefit. *An absolutely unmitigated TEASE!*

"The best light would be gone by the time I got set up," Annabelle went on. Eventually she fixed her top. "But I did want to get some front shots of the island interior and the shoreline. Tomorrow morning we'll start the water excursions. You and Loren can make some test dives, scout some areas first."

It sounded like an order to Nora. *I'd like to kick her real hard, right in the ass . . .*

"And the hunt for the scarlet bristleworm will begin," Loren said. "We probably won't even need our tanks. Snorkeling will do the job."

"That sounds great, Loren," Annabelle beamed. Then she started stretching side to side, hands on hips.

Yeah, Nora thought. *Real hard . . .*

"Looks like the army's new drug czar," Loren said next. Trent came out of the trail, sweating mightily in his fatigues. He was dragging the marijuana plant, which he'd obviously cut down. "Didn't see anymore, but tomorrow I'll have to check more of the island. I already called this one in."

"Bullshit," Nora said under her breath.

"What are you going to do with it, Lieutenant?" Loren asked.

"Burn it, of course." Then Trent dragged the plant to the other end of the site, began to hack it apart with his knife. It was a substantial plant; once cut up, its pieces formed a pile. Trent began to douse it with lighter fluid.

Loren smiled to Nora. "There goes your theory."

"Don't be an idiot."

"Nora, he's burning the plant with us watching him. What more proof do you need? If he was secretly growing the stuff out here, would he be burning it right in front of us?"

Nora couldn't believe his naivete. "He's doing it for our benefit—like we're stupid enough to fall for *that*."

"You're a laugh a minute, Nora. You really believe he's growing pot out here in secret?"

"Could be." But Nora felt certain. *This little burning session's just for show.* "He's probably got hundreds of plants out here, on the most secluded parts of the island. Who would ever find out?"

Loren just shook his head, chuckling.

Flame leaped from the pile, crackling. "Don't stand too close, Lieutenant," Loren called out. "You don't want to get high in the line of duty."

What they smelled more than anything were fumes from the lighter fluid. Trent backed up, watched it burn down.

Nora felt bored silly already. She looked to Loren but caught him staring more at Annabelle as she continued her "twisting" exercises. Trent, too, stole some glances back at her. *Queen of the May . . . in a Calvin Klein bikini.* Nora smirked through the thought. *I think I know how she got that fancy job at* National Geographic.

The plant burned up in minutes; Trent upended a pail of water on the cinders, then sat down at the table, wiping off his hands.

"I've done a lot of strange things in the army, but that's the first time I've ever burned up a pot plant," he said.

"I'm sure you were right," Loren added. "Some kid dropped a seed a long time ago and it sprouted. It's been growing there for years, and it's probably the only one out here." Then he elbowed Nora.

"Yeah," Trent said. "Never knew what the big deal was with pot anyway. I tried it a couple times when I was a teenager. All it did was make me hungry and stupid."

When Trent turned around toward Annabelle, Nora elbowed Loren back, and silently mouthed the word *Bullshit*.

"Isn't it legal for cancer patients, though?" Annabelle said.

Loren replied, citing the latest from the *New England Journal of Medicine*. "It has been proven to drastically reduce intralobular pressure in the eye as well as negate nausea symptoms in various antitumor therapies . . ."

Nora let the rest of the conversation drown out.

What is wrong with me? she asked herself. She knew she was a smart, perceptive person—an academician and a credible scientist. Here, though, all of a sudden, she felt as though she didn't fit in. *Doesn't matter how smart I am. That's not what the big picture's all about.* She bit a nail. *I'm not PART of the big picture . . .*

The environment enthralled her: This was her element, a tropical island rung with marine life. *It's the blonde,* she knew.

Annabelle was just as professional as she, but also vivacious, beautiful, socially magnetizing . . .

Nora simmered in more envy, eyeing the photographer's pose near the table. Showing off her body, sure, but also part of the crowd, engaging . . .

Fitting in.

The curvy, limber body radiated vitality, not just sexual, but something deeper. She was a picture of health, charisma, and moreover, acceptance.

And I'm not, Nora realized. *I can spout my sour grapes at her all I want but it doesn't change the truth. I'm a virgin curmudgeon, a gawky nerd who's so socially disconnected it's a wonder anyone wants to be around me at all, even Loren.* She felt frumpish in the baggy khaki shorts over the drab black one-piece swim suit. *I'll probably make a terrific old maid. Now all I have to do is wait about thirty fucking more years—*

"—not that I'm in favor of legalization, mind you," Loren was saying, still plugged in and animated in the discussion, "but from the cold scientific standpoint, it's hard to argue with a clinical physical addiction rate of zero, even as opposed to the roughly fifteen percent for alcohol."

"Yeah, but every long-term pot smoker I know," Annabelle offered, "is kind of . . . a moron."

"Plenty of statistics on that side of the fence too," Loren stated. "Pot smoking goes hand in hand with an incontrovertible reduction in long- and short-term memory, thematic apperception. Plus, it remains the leading cause of amotivational syndrome."

"What's that mean?" Trent said.

Nora finally snapped out of it and offered, "It makes you a moron."

"See?" Loren laughed. "The professor speaks! I told you she didn't slip into a coma when we weren't looking."

Jeez, Nora thought. *I really am the life of the party, huh?*

"What about you, Professor? Have you ever smoked it?"

Nora blinked. The question had come from Annabelle. "I . . . uh . . ." Then she smirked. "No."

"I think it's a bunch of silly crap," Trent said. "Call me a redneck, but I'll take a can of Bud any day."

"Still big money in it, though," Loren posed. "I'll bet that plant you burned was worth hundreds of dollars on the street."

Nora couldn't resist. She wanted to watch Trent's reaction. "Secluded island like this? Inaccessible?" She feigned a laugh. "Shit, Lieutenant. You could start your own little enterprise out here, and make ten times more than Uncle Sam pays you."

"No, with my luck, it'd be ten times less," Trent replied, "spending the next ten years in an army prison," and then he laughed himself.

Nora had to admit, her comment didn't seem to jilt him one bit. *I guess I'm wrong about everything,* she thought.

Then Annabelle shrieked.

Every face jerked toward her. Annabelle shuddered, tensed up, her fists at her bosom.

"What's wrong!" Loren exclaimed.

Annabelle pointed to Trent. "There's—there's—"

"What *is* that?" Loren said.

Trent snapped, "What the hell's wrong?"

"There's—there's—there's—" Annabelle stammered some more—

"Something on your back," Nora said.

Trent's eyes bugged. "What? A fuckin' tarantula? What?"

Nora saw it easily. *Hmm,* she wondered, but she didn't want to take any chances. She grabbed one of her scuba flippers, and—

Splap!

She smacked the flipper against Trent's back, but Trent was already jumping up, tearing off the green fatigue shirt. "Jesus! Would somebody tell me what was crawling on my back?"

"Not sure," Nora said, and took the shirt. She spread it out on the tabletop.

"It was a spider!" Annabelle. "Maybe poisonous . . ."

Trent looked outraged. "No way!"

"Loren, did that look arachnoidal to you?" Nora asked.

Loren was checking Trent's back. "No. I didn't see any appendages and the body definitely wasn't bisectional." He slapped Trent on the shoulder. "And, Lieutenant, I'm happy to say you don't have any bite marks."

"Jesus!"

"It didn't look like a beetle, and it was too big to be a tick," Loren added.

Nora was examining the shirt. "But it was definitely motile."

Trent was clearly upset. "What's that mean? Speak English!"

"It means it was moving," Nora defined. "And if it didn't have ambulatory appendages, it must be monotaxic."

Trent appeared as though his entire world had become upheaved. Though not overweight, he was in desperate need of some sun, black chest hair matting on white skin. "What are you *talking* about!"

"Lieutenant, relax, you weren't bitten by anything," Nora reminded him while she and Loren pored over the shirt. "Slugs, limpets, snails, and leeches move by means of what's called a monotaxia 'foot'—"

"The slime pad," Loren simplified.

"—and that's probably what was propelling your little friend here."

"I'll bet it was a *leech!*" Annabelle continued to overreact.

Trent looked on the verge of vomiting. "Shut up!"

"No, not a leech," Nora informed. "Leeches are just another type of segmented worm—an annelid—and I got a good enough look at this to see that it wasn't segmented."

"And this thing's body wasn't ovated," Loren added. "It was circinated."

Trent and Annabelle stood aside, mystified, as Nora finally found the splatter on the shirt. "There, see?" she said. "It's not insectoid, no exoskeleton."

"Well, I guess that means it wasn't a tick." Trent seemed relieved. "I don't need any of that Rocky Mountain oyster fever."

Nora shook her head, bemused.

"Maybe it was a pebble snail," Loren said. "That's about the only monotaxic animal I can think of that has a circular body."

This was definitely circular, Nora remembered. "It almost looked nodulous or ovumular."

"Actually it did," Loren agreed, "but we both know that's impossible."

Trent sneered. "I think it would be really nice if you would drop the college professor talk, and—"

"Ovumular," Nora specified, "or like an ovum—an egg cell. Some marine worms, for example, as well as many marine creatures, have ova that move about by their own means of locomotion once they leave the female's body. These species are mostly parasites; therefore, once the fertilized ovum has been dispersed, it seeks some other form of animal life in which to nurture itself and grow. And nodulous—like a node. Some of these motile ovum are actually carried around in a self-contained node— that protects it and helps it get to a host."

The prospect of "parasites" and "nodes" didn't over-joy Trent. "How do you know that thing wasn't one of those?"

"Because they're microscopic," Loren said.

Trent and Annabelle leaned over now, to get a closer look.

Whatever had been on the lieutenant's back was now just a viscid splotch. What Nora had seen had been about the size of a large-shelled peanut, but circular, like a hazelnut. And yellow, like butter.

"Here's the skin of whatever it was." She pointed, moving the flattened thing with the tip of her pen.

"And, look." Loren squinted, leaning closer. "It's yellow but has tiny red spots."

"Some kind of epidermal pigmentation," Nora said.

"Another vote for a slug, but . . ." His thoughts trailed off.

Nora chewed her lip. "I know. I'm not familiar with any species of land slug that's *yellow*."

"Oh, *yuck!*" was Annabelle's next contribution. "That big splat is its insides?"

"Yep." Nora was secretly pleased by the photographer's revulsion. "I'm not seeing anything that looks like the remnants of an organ system."

"Jesus," Trent said. "It looks like someone hocked a loogie on my shirt, that's what it looks like."

Then Loren brought a hand to his brow. "Oh, shit, I know what it is! It's a spumarius, Nora. Right after molting."

"A what?" Annabelle looked to him.

"An insect called a froghopper," Nora said. She was a little agitated with herself for not thinking of that first. "The larval form of something in the cicada order."

"They're the same size and the same color," Loren said.

Nora handed Trent back his soiled shirt. "Good job, Loren. The mystery is solved. An immature froghopper."

"Are they poisonous?" Trent asked warily.

"They're absolutely harmless."

"Not if you're a shirt," Loren said of the mess.

"Christ, this shirt's blown," Trent said.

"I'm sure Uncle Sam will spring for a new one."

"Are you kidding? We have *uniform* rations in the army. Can you beat that for cheap?" And then Trent walked off, presumably for a clean shirt.

Nora rolled her eyes when she noticed Annabelle's hand on Loren's shoulder as she talked. "Wow, you really know your stuff, Loren. Of all the things it could've been, you identified it in a minute."

"Aw, it was nothing," he chuckled.

Make me puke, Nora thought. *Look at her cozying up to him . . .*

Eventually, Annabelle walked off again with her camera. "See you guys later, for dinner," she said.

Which I hope you choke on, Nora thought.

"Well, so much for the big excitement of the day,"

Loren said. "A friggin' froghopper. Shit, I almost wish it was something interesting, like a rhino beetle or a black widow."

But Nora had already turned toward the woods. "Do you . . . smell that?"

"Smell what?"

"Something in the air . . ."

"You mean the pot that Trent just burned?"

"No, no." She felt sure. "The breeze is blowing south, and this is coming from the north." It seemed vague but very familiar. "I can swear I smell something cooking. Like hot dogs or hamburgers."

Loren sniffed the air, then shrugged. "Beats me. I don't smell anything."

Must be my imagination, Nora concluded.

CHAPTER FOUR

(I)

Leona flipped the burgers on the grill; at least, she guessed she was doing it right. She pulled another Zima from the cooler, then looked into the woods.

Where are those assholes?

The burgers sizzled, their aroma eddying into the trees. Leona wasn't much of a cook. *How long per side?* she wondered. This weekend party had sounded like a great idea . . .

Damn them!

Leona did a good job hiding her insecurities, but the truth was she couldn't stand to be alone. At once she felt foolish, dressed only in flip-flops and her cutoffs. *I'm cooking burgers topless and I'm by myself! What happened to the party?* Her thoughts trailed back to Alan. Sure, he was cute, popular, and seemed very connected to her, but she'd always had the tiniest suspicion that his true interest was Carol.

My best friend, Leona reminded herself.

All was fair in love and war, she knew, but she also knew Carol, especially after a couple of drinks . . .

Alan's probably boffing her right now. Hell, Howie's probably in on it too. She's got them in a three-way, the ho! And here I am, cooking hamburgers in the woods with my tits out!

She shrieked as something scratched up her bare shoulder. She imagined the most disgusting bugs, but when she flung it off, she saw that it was only one of those little green lizards.

"Oops. Sorry," she said.

The lizard landed on one of the burgers. When it tried to run off the grill, it got about two inches before the heat claimed it.

Gross . . . A few moments later, the smoking remains fell into the grill. She looked at the burger it had landed on, then decided, *That's Alan's.*

"Come and *get* it!" she yelled at the top of her lungs. Some birds cackled back at her, as if inconvenienced by her shout. "Where *are* you!"

Sexual excitement wasn't the only thing that hardened Leona's nipples. Anger did too, and said nipples stuck out firm as coat pegs when her gaze fumed back into the woods. *They're out there laughing at me, the fuckers! And Carol, that sleaze! Some best friend. I know she's doing both of those guys—*

She screamed hard when two clammy hands landed on her bare back and shoved at her. Instinct made her grab the spatula for a weapon but just as she would take a swipe—

"Howie?"

Howie collapsed against a tree.

My God! When her own shock wore off, she was seized again merely by the *look* of him. Hair pasted to his brow by sweat, and more sweat drenching his shirt. There was something else on the shirt, too . . .

Did he . . . puke on himself?

He stared up openmouthed for a moment, silent, shaking.

"Howie! What happened to you? And where's Carol and Alan?"

"Carol, Carol," he stuttered, "out in the woods, I had to leave her. She had these—these—these *things* on her, and—"

"What things?"

"Ticks or something, I don't know—"

Leona didn't process the information very well. "You left her in the woods!"

"I—I—I—I had to, 'cause—'cause she passed out, and these ticks, er, well, I don't know *what* they were, but they were this really disgusting yellow color with red spots on them and I think they were poisonous or something—"

Leona fell to her knees and shook him by the collar. "And you *left* her? You *asshole!*"

He yammered on, eyes wide open and bloodshot. "Had to come to get Alan, I couldn't carry her by myself but then—then—then I found a dead body—"

"What!" Leona bellowed.

"I got lost trying to find you and Alan, and there was another inlet with a boat, not Alan's boat, but just a little boat, and that's where I saw the body floating in the water. It was some chick just floating there, her eyes out of her head, and—and—and there was a really long snake wrapped around her, and oh Jesus God, I think it was one of those girls who disappeared a few weeks ago!" And then Howie's torment-twisted face fell into his hands, and he sobbed aloud.

Dead bodies. Ticks. Missing persons.

This . . . was too much for a girl like Leona.

"Howie! You're on drugs! Look, I know lots of people at school are doing the Ecstasy and crystal and this Oxycontin stuff—"

"No, no, no," he blubbered. He hadn't even seemed to notice that Leona was *topless* as she leaned over to talk to him, the orbs of her breasts practically bumping his face. "Do you remember?" he stated more declaratively. "A couple, three weeks ago. It was in the local papers and the paper at school—"

"What?"

"Robb White." He cleared his throat, rested his head back against the tree. "Do you remember that name?"

Do I remember him? Shit, she thought, embarrassed. *I fucked him.* Robb White was one of the classier jocks at school, nice guy for a jock, and, yes, Leona had hooked up with him at the Easton dorm mixer several months ago, after Alan had petered out after too much tequila.

"The papers said . . . he was officially missing," she recounted. "He and a bunch of other kids from school disappeared."

Howie shoved a piece of paper in her face.

What? It was a credit card receipt, for gas at the marina.

"I found that in the boat," Howie declared.

"In *our* boat?"

"No, no, no, in *his* boat. A little skiff anchored at one of the other inlets on this island. It's here now, Leona. And that receipt is from three weeks ago, when he and his pals disappeared. I think that corpse I saw with the snake around it was one of the girls he was fooling around with."

Leona's mind ticked further . . . rather slowly, but at least it was functioning. *Corpse,* she thought stonily. *Snake.*

"And—and . . . *what* about Carol?" she asked. What had he said? Ticks?

"She had ticks on her tits. Yellow ticks . . ."

The idea, the very *image,* made Leona swoon in disgust.

"But that's not all. After I found that body, I saw . . . this guy—"

Leona's anger rose. She was too confused. "What guy? Robb White, you mean?"

"No. A guy in a gas mask and hood. Military."

Yes, this was much too much . . .

"I don't know *what* the hell's going on . . ." Howie's shock was finally wearing off; he was getting his reason back, and this was a good thing for Leona. "We have to start somewhere."

"We have to get off this island!" she blurted back.

"I know. But first we have to find Alan and we have to find Carol, and we need to do that now."

Just as Leona helped him up—

What's that smell? she thought.

"Something's burning!" Howie yelled.

He was up and running toward the Coleman grill.

Holy shit!

Boy, had Leona fucked up! The leaves and sparse brush around the grill had somehow caught fire.

And the fire was crackling toward the shack.

"Jesus Christ, this whole island'll be on fire!" Howie snapped. "The smoke'll kill us before we can get to the shore!"

Leona stood paralyzed, ludicrous now since she was topless.

Howie pointed to the end of the shack. "Turn on that faucet! I'll get the hose!"

Another second, and the seriousness kicked in. This island, this time of year? It was dry as tinders. A fire could engulf everything . . . including them.

Leona sprinted forward, slid to the shack on her knees, and cranked the faucet handle. She grabbed the hose lying there and clumsily aimed the water stream toward the fire. She wagged the hose back and forth, drawing lines of smoking sizzle. The fire had spread out quickly, but just as quickly, Leona had managed to put it all out.

Jesus . . . Relief!

But . . .

She looked around. Where was Howie?

"I found the hose!" he bellowed, running back around the corner. He held the long length in one hand. "Turn it o—" But then he stopped, scanned his eyes at the smoking ashes.

"Howie," Leona croaked. "That thing in your hand *isn't* the hose . . ."

It hung limp until the moment she'd said that, almost as if it had sensed the trigger of Howie's fear. His eyes snapped down. Then the "hose" began to move . . .

Vaguely pink, glistening skin. About an inch thick. How long was it? It extended from his hand, behind him, its other end still on the other side of the shack. Howie tried to drop the grotesque thing, but it was already too late. In the space of that synaptic second, the creature energized and wrapped around Howie's upper torso so fast it was but a silent, pinkish blur in the air.

Then Howie was dressed in the thing, wearing it like a corselet. His scream was severed when more of its length coiled about his neck. Howie fell over.

His eyes still registered images as his vision clouded, and then the thing's head made itself plain: slightly tapered, less like a snake and more like a worm.

A pink hole dilated—a mouth opening?—then a thinner pink tube of something fleshy slipped out and—

"Howie!" Leona screamed.

—slithered down Howie's throat.

Leona stood, uncomprehending, glaze-eyed, as this twenty-foot-long living thing that appeared to be a snake relaxed the pressure of its coils . . . and began to pulse.

Leona wasn't quite sure what she was seeing in those last few moments before her paralysis snapped, but before her feet mindlessly began to take her away into the woods, Howie's body seemed to be *filling up* with something.

Something that the snake was pumping into him, through the fleshy, ringed tube that was its mouth.

(II)

Ruth Bridge's lips looked like she'd been punched in the mouth—hard—if one were cynical enough to look closely; her face, in fact, would easily have been pretty were it not for the permanent, uneven swelling. She'd asked the doctor for "Lips like Pam Anderson!" but received something significantly less. She wasn't even aware of it, though, so what did it matter? A positive self-concept was sometimes more important than the truth.

Her body, on the other hand, looked damn good for a gal worn out by thirty-nine years of dope, booze, and on-the-run living. And her breasts? It had been a Miami plastic surgeon who'd done the work—for free, because Ruth had been his sideline plaything for most of her latter twenties. The doctor's name was Levin, and the manner with which he'd inflated Ruth's meager 32-As to prominent 36-Cs was worthy of a certificate of achievement. Dr. Levin had tired of her, though, after so many hotel rendevous, after which she'd ventured to Beverly Hills for a change of scenery and the pesky warrant for check kiting. Here she'd hooked up with another plastic surgeon, one Dr. Winston Prouty, who, in return for Ruth's pleasures, offered a free lip job. Well, Dr. Prouty—jaundiced by a hidden Demerol addiction—

turned out to demonstrate some howlingly inferior skills. The dirty collagen needle had caused an infection whose scars had never properly healed. Hence, Ruth's overlarge and permanently puffy lips.

In the end, though, it was all relative. These days, most men likely to share company with a woman like Ruth cared less about facial prettiness and more about the auxiliary benefits of unnaturally swollen lips.

The first three dealers in Naples had offered Ruth roughly twenty-five thousand for the watch, but . . . *shit!* They'd also insisted on identification. *Fuckers know the score,* she thought. One had even had the balls to add, "For instance, miss, if I sold this watch and it turned out to be"—he winked at her—"stolen, then I could be charged with a felony." *Fuck you,* Ruth thought. But Slydes and Jonas had really scored a big one this time. The watch they'd ripped off some broad down South turned out to be a French-made lady's Cartier Baignoire Mini, eighteen-karat gold and studded with diamonds and rubies. List price: fifty-three thousand. Ruth had about had an accident in her overly tight jeans when they'd told her that.

The fourth dealer had been a bit more compliant. "I can take one look at you and *know* this watch is hot."

Ruth glared. "What's that supposed to mean? What? I look like some lowlife? Some tramp thief trying to peddle stolen goods?"

"Actually, yes. That's exactly what you look like, and I see people like you every day."

"Aw, fuck you!" she dismissed and was about to storm out.

"And if you want some advice," the proprietor added, "put your wig on right when you're trying to disguise yourself."

She sneered. "Huh?" Then, *Oh, shit!* she thought.

She'd forgotten to take off the cut-price sweeping red-haired wig. When she'd first picked it up, she tried it on for Jonas and Slydes, striking a sexy pose. "Do I look like Julianne Moore?"

"No," Slydes said, beer in hand. "You look like a hose bag wearing a shitty red wig." The bastard! But it was a good idea; she wore it whenever she jacked money from an ATM. They all had cameras now.

And as for this chump jewelry salesman?

She dragged the wig off, revealing the unkempt blond shag. *Fuck him anyway*. What could he do?

She gave him the finger and started to leave when he said, "Wait! Don't be hasty!"

When she looked back, he was holding a stack of bills. "There's no way in hell you'll do better than five thousand. And that would be in cash, by the way."

Ooo . . . Ruth pretended not to be waylaid. *He's right. And . . . that's a lot of money!*

"Plus," he added, "ten minutes of your time. In the back. *If* you know what I mean, and I'm pretty sure you do."

"Buddy!" she celebrated. "You got a deal!"

Ruth was the kind of woman who could relate to those terms. He hadn't even lasted five minutes, which was even better, and now all that money formed a big clot in her purse. She'd already tapped five hundred dollars out of the ATM (you could only take out five hundred dollars per twenty-four-hour period); hence, the wig. It was her job to hit a different machine each day until everything was gone . . . or until somebody found the woman's body and the bank froze the account. The lady had bucks—thirty grand in her checking account!

All in a day's work . . . Back down the main drag in the dented white van the boys had jacked from someone in Georgia. She lived with Slydes and Jonas in their dead daddy's house back at the far corner of Collier County, near the Everglades Highway. When she'd been dating Slydes, she'd cheated on him with Jonas, and when she'd been dating Jonas, she'd cheated on him with Slydes. So they decided to keep it simple; they were both her boyfriends now.

Slydes poached gator; he was the brawn. Jonas grew pot; he was the brains. (While Slydes had dropped out of school in seventh grade, Jonas had actually made it to college, if only for one semester, taking horticulture and botany classes). Beefy, tall, and bearded, Slydes didn't look anything like his short and slightly younger brother. In fact, they had a slew of brothers, none of whom looked anything like each other. Even in areas south of the belt, Jonas and Slydes couldn't have been more different—to put it one way, Jonas got all the brains of the bloodline, while Slydes got . . . something else. The entire observation certainly suggested a moral deficit on the part of their biological mother.

Most of the time, Ruth felt more like their sister than a mutual lover, and given the oddity that Ruth's mother had been good friends with the boys' father—well, that suggested something to them, too (which they never discussed.) Fuck it, was Ruth's overall view. She helped the brothers work their scams and gigs, and they all partied together: a great big happy dysfunctional family. *It works, so why worry about it?*

The ramshackle house sat at the end of an unpaved road that twisted deep into the woods. *Deliverance,* Ruth always thought. She made a face the second she got out of the van. *Fuck! Slydes has the tanning drum going. . . .* Between the hides and the meat, Slydes could make about three hundred dollars per gator—actually, more now that gator ribs were big in all the

Florida restaurants. (Alligators had a *lot* of ribs.) They had a slaughterhouse out back, and plenty of freezers for storage in between runs. He'd sell the meat under the table to the restaurants, and then dealers would buy the untrimmed hides for the European market. Ruth liked gator meat, she supposed, but what made her sick was the smell that often permeated the house: the stench of Slydes's tanning chemicals.

"Hey, baby," Slydes greeted when she pushed open the rickety door. "Give your man a great big kiss."

Ruth did, getting beer fumes along with the passion.

Jonas rose from a beaten chair. "Ruthie, I thought you were givin' your man a great big kiss."

Ruthie smirked. In truth she was starting to get tired of this threesome, but . . . *The three of us work so great together.* She feigned more passion, then tasted more beer breath tinged with pot.

"So what'choo get for the old bitch's watch?" Jonas called over. "It looked damn nice."

"Did ya get five hundred?"

"I got Jack Fuck," Ruth complained. "Twenty-five bucks," and then she handed Slydes a twenty and a five. "Can you believe it? It was a knockoff."

"Huh?"

"It was a fake Cartier. They make 'em in China, and pilots and flight attendants bring 'em back in their luggage to sell here. They're all over the place. Fake Rolex, fake Cartier, fake whatever."

"Well, I'll be damned," Slydes said, scratching his heavy beard.

"Ain't that a kick in the ass?" Jonas said. "The bitch was a phony. Bet her jewelry's all that fake Chinese shit too."

"But I tapped another five hundred from her checking," Ruth said, and handed it over. "So nobody's reported her missing to the bank yet."

"I think we'll be milkin' that one for a while," Slydes projected. "We'll have the account drained 'fore they get wise."

Jonas winked. "And it ain't like they'll ever find the body."

"We'll be going to Clearwater tomorrow, so you can try to pawn the jewelry at some of the shops there."

"Clearwater?" Ruth asked. Finally, a break to the boredom. "We're going to the island?"

Jonas nodded. "Yeah, got no choice. That last pound went faster than shit; my hydro's so good the word spreads, you know? Couple months ago I had ten dealers wanting a pound a month. Now I got twenty—"

"I?" Slydes raised a brow at his smaller brother. "How's about *we?*"

"Aw, shit, Slydes. I'm the grower, you're the poacher. We stick with what we know."

"Right, but we're a *team,* bro. And you keep talkin' like you're the mastermind or some shit. Remember, it's *my* boat that gets us on the island."

Jonas pursed his lips as if he'd just swigged straight lemon juice. "I know that, but I'm just sayin' . . ."

"Yeah, well, you *say* too much."

Ruth shook her head. *What a pair of rednecks.* They split everything down the middle anyway, so she didn't know what they were always arguing about. *Couple of macho morons . . .*

Jonas danced his finger to the words. "We stick with that we know. I know growing grade-A hydroponic pot and you know guttin' gators—"

"And I know bustin' grade-A *pussy,* and you know bitin' the pillow in the cell block and takin' it up the tail."

"Aw, shit on you, Slydes!" Jonas yelled.

Slydes cracked laughter.

Idiots, Ruth thought. Whenever Slydes was at the

back end of an argument, he always tossed up that little "joke," which wasn't totally a joke at all because
Jonas had done five years in Collier County Detent, and
being the skinny white longhaired fella that he was,
well . . .

Jonas finally got back to his explanation to Ruth,
who was now brushing out her blond shag that had
been mussed from the wig.

"Gotta get some more right away or I might lose
some of my bagmen to the competition."

"Well, that's just fine with me," Ruth said. She liked
going out to the island. She pulled up her FLORIDA IS
FOR DRUNK LOVERS T-shirt, showing her perfectly flat
belly. "I need to work on my tan."

"Not this time, baby," Slydes informed. He stuck out
a leg and farted.

Gross, Ruth thought. *Chili.*

"We're in and out real fast; no time for layin' out in
the sun this trip."

"Oh, wait a minute," she remembered. "I thought
you said we couldn't go to the island for at least another week, some nature photographers out there or
something."

Slydes nodded his big block head. "Which is why we
slip in and slip out, at night. High tide's at eleven p.m.
tomorrow, and that's when I'll be pullin' up."

Fuck, Ruth thought. She liked to keep tan—it was
good for tricks when Jonas and Slydes were too busy to
realize what she might be doing on the side. And the island was perfect. But all this running around lately—
mainly running *their* errands—she'd lost most of that
Hot Tramp Florida tan.

"Have some chicken nuggets, hon." Slydes offered a
plate. "Jonas just got back from Chik-fil-A."

Ruth was famished. "Thanks!" she said, crunching a

few down. "These are great!" When silence filled the room, she noticed Jonas and Slydes staring at her.

Then they both burst out in laughter.

"Those ain't chicken nuggets, hose bag!" Slydes roared. "It's fried gator dick!"

"You *fuck*!" Ruth yelled.

Slydes was cackling. Then he hugged her and smacked her another kiss on her big overly swollen lips. "Aw, it was just a joke, baby, and, mmmm—" One big callused hand slipped under her shirt and up her back, the other hand slipped down her jeans from behind. Ruth's nipples shot right up. She was . . . a reactive woman.

He sniggled her neck, the big hands still roving her skin. "Aw, baby, I really missed you."

"You did?"

"Aw, shit yeah. I just got a serious *need* to have my hands all over your beautiful body."

"Slydes! How sweet!"

"Tell her why, Slydes," Jonas bid.

" 'Cause, ya see, baby, I'm all out of towels and I sure as shit need *something* to wipe all this gator slime off on."

Ruth couldn't have been more offended. "Fuck you!"

Slydes and Jonas heehawed like a couple of donkeys.

"Now be a good girl and drag them jugs back to the shed."

"And on your way back," Jonas added, "bring us a couple more beers. If you're lucky"—a cocky grin—"I'll lay some on ya later," and then he spread his legs in the chair and squeezed his crotch.

Yeah, she thought. *If I'M lucky. That skinny slob!* At least the blockheads bought her jive about the watch being fake. That was five big ones in her little pocket, and—damn it—she deserved it. For all the shit work she did for those two?

Ruth's back creaked when she picked up the jugs. She weighed a hundred pounds on a "fat" day, and each of those three-gallon jugs must've weighed twenty-five pounds apiece. PROWASH: REPTILE HIDE DEGREASER, one read. The other: TRU-TAN SKIN PREP. It was the stuff Slydes used on the gator skin, and it *stank*. To herself, she admitted, Slydes was a great lover—the big, rough type, which she went for most of the time. But everything, his hair, his skin, his clothes—*Even his jism!* she thought with a knot in her gut—stank of these chemicals, all mixed, of course, with the fishy malodor of alligator.

The brothers swigged beer as they watched her lug the jugs—true gentlemen. "Oh, Ruth?" Slydes called out. "One other thing."

"Huh?" she replied, aggravated.

Slydes lifted his leg, twitched a hip, and farted.

The brothers laughed uproariously.

What a pair of perfect assholes, she thought, humping the jugs out the back door. *Too bad I'm in love with the both of them . . .*

CHAPTER FIVE

(I)

The major looked up at the sergeant. "This is impressive, Sergeant."

The microscopic scans flashed on the viewing screen, displaying the rate of success before their eyes. *A live birth through a test host,* the sergeant realized. The sergeant wasn't a technician—he'd been trained in surveillance and covert security procedures—but he knew this was what the brass wanted. Previous births using people and higher mammals hadn't worked out; after the ova had matured, the juvenile had been dead.

As the sergeant understood it, the human element had been an accident. *There weren't supposed to be any people on the island,* he knew. Until now they'd been testing on birds, for their migratory assets. This made perfect sense, of course: The transfections could be used more effectively against a potential enemy.

Yeah, the brass'll be shitting their pants over this. There's a big difference between the lab and the field.

"This is better than we could have ever hoped for." The major typed some notes into his operating report. "Try to find some other bodies," he said. "If the nodic dispersals are as successful as these, we've hit some serious paydirt. We'll all get promoted, even the field contingent such as yourself and the corporal."

"That's good to know, sir." But all the while the sergeant was thinking, *I won't count on that. The brass will hog it all, like they always do.*

It didn't matter, though. The sergeant liked being in the field. It was the only thing that made him feel real.

"So you were saying." The major kept typing, never looking up. "Four more people have come onto the island?"

"Yes, sir."

"And one of them is military?"

"Yes, sir. I think it's just some sort of escort assignment. He's showing some civilians around."

"A field trip." The major almost laughed. Almost. "That's amusing. And the other two groups of four?"

"Four are dead and have already been infected—the first group from several weeks ago. The second group's half gone."

"But this third group . . . you're not worried about them?"

"Not at this point, sir. Nobody knows anything yet. I'm sure we'll have a positive infection rate in all of them soon. And by the time anyone from the mainland knows—" The sergeant shrugged. "We'll be gone."

"Good. Keep me posted. And I want you and the corporal to plant more cameras. Keep a close eye on this latest group."

"Yes, sir."

The major turned off the sampling screen. "Meanwhile, I'm going to go tell the news to the colonel. Good work, Sergeant." And then he left the lab.

The sergeant frowned. He was glad he'd never wanted to be an officer.

Bam, bam, bam! He slammed the metal locker in one of the rear utility rooms that they were using for their barracks.

"Come on, Sarge!" the corporal complained, leaning up in his bunk. "I thought I was going to get to sleep today."

"You thought wrong, so roust it. Four more people came onto the island today, three civilians . . . and one officer."

"Damn it . . ."

"You're telling me. And the major says you and me have to mount more cameras out in the woods, so get up and get the night-vision gear ready."

The corporal rubbed his eyes, muttering. "Why can't you get the gear?"

"Because I'm the sergeant."

The corporal dragged himself up.

"We'll wait till it's dark. Then we go out." The sergeant left and went down the hall, to the old office he'd set up as an ops room. His surveillance screens glowed.

"That's one." The sergeant indicated the screen. *The colonel wants me to keep a close eye on this latest group.* He switched around the various camera zones.

This latest group looked like it might be very interesting.

On the screen, the blonde was taking off her clothes.

(II)

Annabelle wasn't terribly inhibited about taking her clothes off in the woods. (She'd done that any number of times in high school.) Nor was she terribly concerned about the prospect of someone catching a glimpse. It would be a visionary thrill for Trent and the college boy—and by the looks of them, they could both use it—and she admitted to herself that she'd actually *love* for that envious bitch Nora Craig to see her body. Why?

To show her who's got it and who doesn't.

Annabelle had had a few sexual experiences with women in the past, and though it wasn't anything she'd ever really sought out, she didn't object when the prospect came up. But, no, she had no physical attraction for Nora at all—a short, reedy, and barely bosomed bookworm—however, Annabelle had no problem flaunting her body to keep other women in their place. *It's not ego,* she reminded herself as she took off the bikini top. *It's honest self-awareness. It's confidence. I can't worry about other girls being jealous just because I'm more beautiful than them . . .*

She frowned at the off-the-wall shower: an olive-drab curtain hanging from an elevated steel ring. Stenciled letters read FAIR-WEATHER FIELD HYGIENE UNIT.

She thumbed off her bottoms and stepped through the ugly green curtain. Inside, she glanced down at her body and smiled. *Sorry, girls. I can't help it that I am All That.* Her only displeasure was the absence of a suntan, but she'd be working on that here. She gritted her teeth reaching for the steel knob—*I'll bet the water's going to be ice-cold!*—then squealed when she found out she was right. It was hot today, yes, and humid too, but even with that, the spray made her shiver, made her lustrous white skin go tense. This was a bit more than refreshing. When she turned her breasts into the spray, she squealed again as her nipples shot up.

A moment later, though, the water turned warm, then hot enough that she had to adjust the knobs. *I'm impressed,* she thought. Why go to all that trouble to provide hot water? But then she thought about it . . .

Of course they did. They're pulling out all the stops because they know I'm a nationally known nature photographer with a famous magazine . . .

Or at least she liked to think so.

Suddenly her nerves felt charged as she sudsed herself. *Of all the places to get horny—an army field shower!* Annabelle believed in honest acknowledgment with regard to sexual desire. There was sex, and there was love, and there was sex with love, and then sex without love. *Sport fucking,* she remembered her roommate in college calling it. Annabelle was very open sexually; if she was attracted to a man, she'd let him know and never felt slutty about it. *I'm just being honest. What's wrong with that? When a guy sleeps around, that's okay, but when a woman does, she's promiscuous.*

Annabelle didn't care. She knew that most women envied her looks, so naturally they'd throw any available stone.

But the pickings here were slim. Loren was a cross between *Revenge of the Nerds* and that Alfred guy on *Mad Magazine.* He'd be good for some signals—she always needed someone to carry her bags—but that's as far as *that* would go. Lieutenant Trent was no prize, either. *Over the hill,* she thought. But she supposed he'd do in a pinch. He seemed very serious, so maybe he'd be that way in bed . . .

Annabelle adjusted the knobs to make the water cool. *Perfect* . . . Shampoo turned her hair to a pile of fragrant foam. *I should've recolored my hair before coming,* she worried. *I hope my roots aren't showing.* Parrots cawed over the hiss. When she tipped her head, the shampoo's foam sluiced between her breasts to her pubis, which she lathered lingeringly. Without thinking, she slid her hands up over her belly; her skin seemed hypersensitive. Next, her fingertips were playing over the already firm nipples, and then the most lusty sensations roved through her body. No, there was nothing sexy about this assignment—bristleworms!—and nothing sexy about the people with her. But—

The only thing Annabelle needed . . . was herself . . .

Her feet parted. Her fingers slipped overtly between her legs, through bubbly hair to the folds of her sex. She found she didn't need men, nor images—she was enough, her robust body, nerves squirming like electric current as the cool spray stimulated her skin. She murmured a chuckle to herself—*God, what if someone IS peeking?* She could almost envision Trent, the army stick-in-the-mud, or Loren the Nerd, huffing with an eye to the curtain gap. Just to satisfy her curiosity then, she opened her eyes to check the gap . . .

Of course, there was no one there.

Common sense returned. *I didn't come here to play with myself in a portable shower!* And then she rinsed all the soap off, reached to turn off the water—

Her shriek whistled through the air. She tore out of the shower, dripping and never more naked. Her bare feet crunched over dried brush and palm leaves, and when she remembered exactly what she'd seen in the shower, she shrieked again.

Annabelle manically patted her hands over every square inch of her body that she could reach, feeling for the things. She had only enough time to wrap a towel around herself before Trent, Loren, and Nora bolted into the cove.

"What's wrong!" Trent exclaimed.

Annabelle stood huddled, shivering but not from cold. "Those things! They were in the shower!"

"What things, Annabelle?" Loren asked.

"Like that thing on Lieutenant Trent's back earlier! That yellow thing with the red spots! But there's a bunch of them!"

Nora flung open the green shower curtain. The others shouldered in behind her.

"More spumarius," Nora observed. "Froghopper larvae."

On the inside of the shower curtain, a drove of the bizarre off-yellow buds seemed adhered. A few more dotted the water pipe that led to the showerhead.

"Wow," Loren said.

"Get some collection vials," Nora told Loren. Then she leaned to peer more closely at the things. They crawled along on the plastic sheet, perhaps moving an inch every two or three seconds. "I can't believe the rate of locomotion," she said. "Didn't think they moved that fast."

"You're damn right they move fast," Annabelle blurted, her fist clutching the towel to her wet bosom. "They were almost at my *feet!*" She pointed down.

More of the yellow things bumbled around in the sopped ground. One was almost at the tip of Nora's sneaker. When she stepped away to the right, the viscid buds shifted right. Nora frowned, then stepped to the left.

The things on the ground shifted to the left.

"That's really strange for froghopper larvae," Nora informed them. "They're not predatory at all, and they don't have the necessary sensory organs to detect other living things in proximity."

"They're sensing something now," Trent said, still irked by his own experience. "When you move, they move."

Nora stepped out, confused. "Right, and another strange thing is the size. Froghopper larvae are about the size of BBs, but this genus is significantly larger."

Annabelle fingered wet hair off her brow. "Who gives a shit? Would somebody please kill those things?"

Nora pursed her lips. "Annabelle, we already told you, they're harmless."

"How do you know?" Annabelle challenged with a scowl. She turned in a huff and stalked back toward the camp.

Nora was leaning farther; several of the things weren't but a few inches from her face as she inspected them. "Maybe I . . ."

"Maybe what?" Trent said. He seemed aggravated.

"Maybe I was wrong about this—"

Before Trent could respond, Loren reappeared with some collection tubes and forceps. "A spumaria *this* size? You know what I'm thinking, right?"

"That it's—"

"That we've discovered a new species."

Nora shook her head. "Loren, what *I'm* thinking is that maybe these things aren't froghopper larvae at all."

Loren stalled with the poised forceps. "All right. Why do you say that?"

"The dorsal region. Look how they're moving. I'm not seeing any parapodic structure. It almost looks like cilia."

Loren maintained his stalled poise. Then he winked at her. "Can't be. It's too big." Now he redirected his attention to the slowly moving things on the curtain. "Come to Papa, you ugly little buggers." And then he plucked several up with the forceps.

Nora didn't know what she was thinking. "Come on, let's get them under the scope for a good look."

"Wait a minute," Trent said as they were about to go back to the row of head shacks. "I was going to take a shower."

"Go ahead," Nora told him.

"Just get a broom," Loren added, "and sweep the things out. They won't bite."

Loren and Nora walked away with their specimens.

Trent looked back at the shower curtain and grimaced. "Maybe I'll skip the shower for now," he muttered.

CHAPTER SIX

(I)

Banks of gray-black murk chased the sun behind the horizon. Slydes nodded his approval as the weather-worn cabin cruiser churned ahead. *The darker, the better,* he thought at the wheel. Clear nights were so much riskier.

Ruth sat hunched at the bow, her feet dangling off the side as she watched for other boats. Not much traffic this far off Clearwater, but they always had to sweat the local police marine patrols and the Natural Resources boats.

Everything looked nice and clear.

Jonas could be heard clattering belowdecks, making room for what they'd be bringing back: several pounds of high-grade hydroponic marijuana.

They'd only started growing it at the island a few years ago, and since then, Slydes was secretly jealous. His brother's product dwarfed his gator poaching profits. *But we're family,* he reminded himself. *Share and share alike.* Jonas took care of the brainy horticulture stuff, while Slydes took care of details, like getting them on and off the island quickly, gauging the tides and the weather. Ruth was just squeeze, but she helped in her ways too—*Mainly in bed,* he thought, but she had lots of street contacts and helped out immeasurably in their sideline jobs, like pawning stolen goods, jacking ATMs with cards they ripped off, and helping the brothers bury the occasional body.

It was a system that worked.

"Is it high tide yet?" Ruth called back from the railed prow.

Slydes swigged more beer, burped, then nodded. "And there's the island."

A mile ahead, the island's bulk began to form in the murk.

It was a great gig. Before they'd found out about it, Jonas truly was a pissant pot grower. They rented rooms in some of the bum motels, and that's where Jonas set up his hydroponic gear, but these days the narcs were wise to everything, eyeballing erratic and nontypical electricity bills. *Fuckers think of everything,* Slydes bemoaned. He didn't smoke weed himself (beer and women were all he needed), but the market couldn't be better. And the stuff Jonas was growing was so topdrawer he was getting a rep as the man with the best. All the punks and college kids in these beach towns? They couldn't buy enough of the stuff. Hydro was the New Deal, and Jonas was cornering the market.

Because of the island.

The way it worked was like this: The bigger the plants grew, the more potent the THC, but you needed a place big enough to grow them past ten feet. Solution: the island. And you needed square footage, too. The average dupe could grow a plant or two in his apartment without anyone getting wise, which didn't amount to anything but small-time dealing. But what if you had a place where you could grow *hundreds* of plants? And keep twenty-four hours of light on them without having to worry about the narcs getting wind of your sky-high power bill?

Again, the solution was the island.

All the space we need, free electricity, free running water, and twenty-foot ceilings, Slydes thought. A pot grower's dream.

"Got my stows all ready," Jonas said when he came up from the cabin. They'd rigged some panels to pop out just behind the head. "But look what I found." Jonas giggled.

He held up a severed foot.

Slydes stared with alarm, then remembered. "Oh yeah, that ritzy business-looking chick we carjacked last week." They'd pinched a chunk of change off her, all right. Fancy laptop, big-ass wedding ring, not to mention her Mercedes, which they'd sold to the chop shop. They'd brought her back to the boat for a little party, but as they'd been dragging her clothes off, she'd kicked Slydes a swift one in the nuts. *Hadn't planned to kill the bitch,* he thought, *but, shit, she asked for it.* He figured the best way to teach her a lesson was to cut off the foot that had kicked him. They'd had a good go-round with her and then rolled her off the deck. In these waters? The sharks took care of them quick.

"We gotta be more careful, brother. Can't be leaving shit like that sittin' around in the boat."

Jonas laughed. "Hey, you're the one who cut off her foot." He threw it over the side with a paltry splash.

"What was that?" Ruth asked, jerking around.

"Beer can. Shut up and watch for boats."

Jonas leaned over to whisper, "How long we keeping her around?"

"I thought you liked her."

"Sure, for a hose bag, and she does the mouth thang mighty fine, but you know, after a while they all get an attitude. Start to think they have power 'cause they know your whole operation."

Slydes knew this but . . . *She sucks a mean one . . .* "Shit, let's keep her a bit longer. She's a good gofer, and she don't mind jacking the ATMs and that shit." Slydes chuckled under his breath. "Besides, she's crazy in love with both of us, so let's ride that awhile. When some better trim comes along, we'll put her in the drink like we always do."

"Cool." Jonas peered out into the night. "There's the island."

"Yep. Be there in a few. Just remember, no fuckin' around. We're in and out."

Jonas pushed long strings of greasy hair out of his face, which the gulf wind immediately replaced. "Photographers, you say."

"Underwater photographers or some shit, takin' pictures of fish or something for a big magazine. Won't be here long. Just grab a couple pounds. We'll get more when they're gone."

Jonas nodded. It would have to do. "Just so I can get me something. Sure as shit don't want to depend on what you make selling gator. I have college, brother. I'm too smart for that rinky-dink stuff."

"Here's your gator," Slydes said, pointing to his groin. He hated it when Jonas implied he was smarter, even though he knew it was true.

Jonas laughed and slapped his brother on the back. "Think I'll grab some quick tail off our hose bag. Have fun steerin' the boat, Captain Tug."

"Oh, I *got* something for you to tug. Tell me the truth. When you're laying peter on Ruth, you think about all them big rednecks who corn-holed you in county detent, huh? Go on, you can tell your brother."

"Fuck you, Slydes!" Jonas yelled and stepped out of the cockpit. He stalked off down the manway and shouted to Ruth. "Hey, Ruth! Downstairs!"

When Jonas and Ruth disappeared belowdecks, Slydes thought, *Jesus. It was just a joke.* Made him wonder a little, though.

Slydes checked the tide table again, then his watch. *Right on the mark.* Out in the murk, the island's obscure shape grew larger.

Of course, he had no way of knowing that things weren't going to go quite as smoothly as he thought.

(II)

Nora and Loren sat up late in the head shack, bleary-eyed and hot in the harsh overhead light. Night had come to the island like a fog bank. The head shack's metal door stood open, letting in humid air. This late the woods outside sounded like a jungle.

"You were right earlier," Nora said. "There's no sign of a developing organ system." By now her eyes felt welded to the microscope, whose lighting element reminded her of an optical exam. It was giving her a headache.

Loren sat next to her at the table, wielding tiny forceps and wire-thin dissection probes. For several hours now, they'd been examining several of the things they'd found in the shower. "It's not even a complete animal." He looked up a moment from the legged magnification frame under which the specimen lay. "I've never dissected anything like this in my career. It's almost like this thing is just a tumor or a multicelled cyst."

"A multicelled cyst that *moves,*" Nora added.

"About the only thing we *do* know is it's not a damn froghopper."

A motile cyst? she thought. *A nodular cell cluster*

that has a system of locomotion? "I wasn't imagining it when I saw these things *moving,* was I?"

"No, they were moving pretty damn fast," Loren assured her. "And they had direction volition. When you moved your foot on the shower floor, these things shifted their direction. I'm positive. We all saw it."

Nora sat back in the fold-down army chair. She rubbed fatigue out of her eyes, or was it confusion? *It's impossible. It's fucking impossible.*

Loren yawned, a fist to his mouth. "Maybe we really have stumbled on something. Maybe this is a previously unknown infantile mite or something."

"Come on, Loren," she objected. "This big? You and I both know that it's impossible for something like that to get this big. It's contrary to insectoid life."

Loren nodded dumbly.

It was the feeling in her gut that bothered her most. She felt tacky in the gritty humidity. Patches of sweat darkened her T-shirt like blotches. "It's able to move at will," she almost droned, "which means it's functionally motile. But—"

"No parapods, no legs, nothing even close to a monotaxic foot," Loren finished for her. He looked back a moment at the mag frame, then shook his head at the evidence bright before his eyes.

"It looks like it moves on bristles or cilia."

Loren pointed errantly to the specimen. "Come on, Nora. They *are* cilia, and we both know that. We're looking right at it."

Nora let out a long sigh. "Which means we're looking at something that's impossible." *I can't say it,* she fretted. *Loren would think I was ridiculous.* When she looked back at him, he was staring right back at her.

But it was Loren who broke the ice that she was afraid to, afraid because her peers would think she was being absurd. "We were right earlier, weren't we?"

"The thing on Trent's shirt and the things in the shower are the same, and they're not some *undiscovered species* of mite or sebaceous parasite. We both know exactly what these things are, but neither of us is saying it. It's a motile worm ovum."

Loren nodded, confusion lengthening his expression. "A motile worm ovum the size of a coffee bean. Which doesn't exist."

Indeed, they'd both seen the same thing before, but under *electron* microscopes, not little 100× field scopes.

Now Nora rubbed her face in the most bewildered frustration. "There's no such thing as a motile ovum this size. They're all microscopic, they're just simple cell clusters with a cilia-based system of locomotion."

"Um-hmm." Loren held another plastic collection vial up to the light, and shook the bean-sized thing inside around. "Well, this ain't microscopic, Nora. So what do we do?"

Good question. "Collect more samples, look for the annelid that these things come from, and report to the college. That sounds like the best bet."

Loren stared grimly. "Sure, but that's ignoring the consequences of something, isn't it?"

"I know. The annelid that these things come from must be . . ."

"Really big," Loren said.

She gestured her microscope. "On one side of this one, there are some apertures behind the cilia roots. And I'm pretty sure I saw a stylet ring there."

"So did I, and now that we've decided what this really is, why should that be a surprise? Most other forms of motile ova have them, it's the delivery system to the host, and right now we're both wondering if one of these things could infect a human."

Nora nodded wearily.

"The infection constituents would be incompatible in humans, wouldn't they? And of course the ova themselves would be too. A human immune system would destroy it immediately." Loren blinked. "Right?"

"I think so," she said very softly.

Loren seemed suddenly enlivened. "So let's not freak out. This is actually exciting; it's a polychaetologist's dream. It might be a new species."

"Yeah, that would be great, Loren." But she didn't sound convinced. "But we're still ignoring the size."

Loren looked back down onto the radiant magnifying frame. "It's big, all right." He seemed to be chewing the inside of his cheek. "And I mean *really* big."

CHAPTER SEVEN

(I)

They moored the beaten cabin cruiser at the usual stop just when high tide hit; Jonas, hip-deep in the lagoon, caught the rope Slydes tossed and tied it off to a sweet-gum tree.

"It's creepy tonight," Ruth commented as she lowered herself off the back ledge.

"What are you talkin' about?" Slydes asked.

She looked up and around, wading clumsily. "It's just . . . different. Feels weird. It's my female intuition. We have that, you know. I saw it on that *Oprah* show."

Slydes climbed off, frowning. *Bitch is drunk again, or fucked up on something.* The water lay like black glass. No moon roved overhead; more cloud banks were rolling in. Ahead, the island's wall of trees looked like an obscure, dark bulk. Slydes didn't feel quite right himself, but he didn't admit it.

Once ashore, the three of them stood dripping.

Ruth's T-shirt clung to her breasts. When she raised a flashlight, Slydes snatched it away.

"I told ya, no lights. There's people on the island tonight."

Jonas seemed aggravated that he was wet. "Any idea if they're camping near the headshacks?"

"No, so that's why we gotta be extra careful." Slydes shirt read ST. PETE BEACH—A QUIET LITTLE DRINKING TOWN WITH A FISHING PROBLEM. "So remember what I tell ya. We get in and out fast as we can. I'll keep watch and Jonas, you get in, grab some product, and leave. Then we come back to the boat. We need to get out of here in a half hour before the tide goes back down too far."

"What do I do?" Ruth asked for instructions.

"You can tweak your titties for all I care. Just don't make any noise. It's past midnight now, and these photographer people are probably asleep. But you never know."

"Any of 'em chicks?" Jonas asked.

"What do you care!" Ruth objected and gave him a hard slap to the arm. Jonas had always had something of a voyeurism problem, and Ruth knew it. He actually had a lot more problems than that, but that was another story.

"Two of 'em, I think," Slydes said.

"And that goes for you, too!" Ruth added, and slapped Slydes.

Slydes latched a big, dirty hand to her face and squeezed her cheeks between her teeth. "Keep your voice down, ya pain in the ass."

Jonas swatted at a mosquito. "Now that I think of it, how about if Ruth stays here?"

"The fuck I am!"

"She's high as a kite and'll be yappin' the whole way." Even in the darkness they could see her face redden.

"I'm *not* stayin' here by myself! There's gators and snakes and stuff!"

"And leeches and ticks," Jonas added. "Oh yeah, and them big spiders that paralyze ya when they bite."

"Fuck that shit!" Ruth conveyed as eloquently as she could. Right after she'd said it, a bat squeaked by. "Fuck!"

Slydes pointed a smudged finger. "All right. No more noise or we leave ya here."

"Fuck," she whispered.

"So let's quit fuckin' around and get moving."

They moved slowly down the trail. Visibility was poor even when their eyes acclimated to the darker woods. Unseen animals could be heard scampering through brush. Slydes felt as though he were walking through fog.

A hundred yards in, he whispered, "Not a sound. Look."

They peered past trees. A light flickered. Tents had been set up in a small cove, and a campfire crackled. A blonde in a bikini sat before the fire, writing in a notebook.

Oh, man. There's a party, Slydes thought.

"Damn," Jonas whispered. "Would you look at the—"

Ruth glared. "I'll pop your nuts off if you even *think* about looking at her!" came a hot whisper in response.

Slydes chuckled. He had to admit, it might be fun to have a roll with this one and then maybe tune her up Slydes and Jonas–style afterward. After all, Slydes had his skinning knife on him, and he had a pair of pliers on the boat that he sometimes used to pull out gator teeth. *Yeah, we'd get her screaming something fierce.* But . . .

Not tonight.

We just get in and out, he reinforced to himself.

"Shit," Jonas whispered next. "How come these folks aren't sleeping?"

Someone else emerged from the woods and approached the blonde, who looked up and started chatting. In the firelight, Slydes could tell the guy was a big-time geek: skinny, lanky, stoop-shouldered. *Who the hell's this turkey-neck? One of the photographers?* "Let's move on," he whispered.

They crept away, swallowed by the woods again. The trail veered.

"What if there's people at the head shacks, too?" Jonas asked.

"There won't be. Ain't no reason," Slydes felt sure, then, *Good god-DAMN!*

The outside light glowed bright at the first head shack, and the door stood open.

"Aw, shit, Slydes!" Jonas whispered.

"I can't fuckin' believe this shit. There's no reason for any of these people to be here, for shit's sake!"

At least none that they could think of. It was the farthest head shack Jonas used for his hydroponic operation, at the other end. He knew if he took a chance now and blew it, they'd lose the whole works and a hell of a lot of money.

"I say we go in and get the dope anyway," Jonas said.

"No way," Slydes insisted. "We'd be morons to do that."

Ruth smiled in the dark.

Jonas wasn't happy. "Shit, Slydes, I don't even think there's anyone in that first shack anyhow."

"Then why's the door open, dick-for-brains? Why're the lights on?"

"Maybe—"

With no warning, Ruth squealed like a referee whistle.

Slyde's heart surged. He slapped his hand over her mouth to seal off the shriek, and felt her tremoring in his grasp. *What the shit!*

What was wrong with her?

"Quiet, quiet!" Jonas shot another whisper. He held up Ruth's quivering arm, which displayed a small thin snake. "It ain't nothin'," he said and plucked the snake off with his fingers and tossed it away. *Shit, a little snake's all it was,* Slydes thought. He kept his huge hand clamped over Ruth's face, and took a few silent moments for him and his brother to see if anyone inside the head shack had heard Ruth's outburst.

A shadow appeared in the bright, open doorway, and a figure stepped out.

Another chick, Slydes thought. *What the fuck's going on here?* And it didn't matter, because if she'd heard them, and called authorities, they'd have to beat feet off the island and leave everything.

All that pot.

The woman in the doorway looked wan, slim. She walked out and glanced around as if indeed looking for trespassers.

Then she shrugged and went back inside.

"We lucked out," Slydes said under his breath. "She didn't hear." He gestured with a jerk of his head to move off.

When they got to another clearing, Slydes realized he still hadn't let go of Ruth. She collapsed out of his arms when he released his grip.

"Shit, man!" Jonas exclaimed. He seemed almost amused. "Is she dead?"

Moonlight broke through some clouds. Ruth lay crumpled and still at their feet. *I didn't smother the bitch, did I?*

He began to worry just when her chest heaved and she snapped back to consciousness.

"Damn," Jonas remarked. "We could only hope."

Her eyes batted; she leaned up on her elbows. Then awareness returned. "Holy fuck! That snake!"

Slydes looked down, hands on hips. "You're as dumb as they come, girl. You almost blew it for all of us."

She seemed outraged by the comment. "There was a snake on me!"

Slydes dragged her up by the T-shirt collar and slammed her against a tree. "It was just a baby pine snake, you empty-headed fuck brain."

"It was gonna bite me!"

Her eyes bugged when Slydes, again, slapped his big hand over her mouth. "If you don't keep your fuckin' voice down, baby, the next time I go trolling for gators, it's *your* ass I put on the hook."

Jonas smiled, popped a brow at the threat.

"Pine snakes ain't poisonous," Slydes went on, "and that one was too small to bite anyway. You are about the dumbest set of tits on two legs." He dragged his hand away and pointed at her. "We hear one more peep out of you, and you're gonna be a *dead* set of tits, you hear me?"

"All right, Jesus," she complained.

"What do we do now, Slydes?" Jonas asked. "We don't grab the weed soon and get out, we'll miss the high tide."

Slydes grumbled, rubbed his beard. "I know. We only got two choices. Leave now and come back when it's safer—"

"Let's do that," Ruth dared in the lowest voice.

"—or wait till that chick at the head shack goes to sleep. Then we grab some weed and go camp out ourselves in the middle of the island somewhere. And wait twenty-four hours for the next night tide."

"I can't put this off, Slydes," Jonas insisted, shaking his head. "If I don't put more product on the street, I'll lose all my bagmen to the competition. Don't matter *how* good my hydro is, I'll lose my rep if I can't put the shit on the street."

"Then it's settled. We wait till later and grab the stuff tonight."

Ruth's expression showed what she thought of that. "So we gotta sit in the woods for twenty-four hours? With all these snakes?"

Jonas smiled. "Yeah, baby. Maybe we'll tie ya to a tree and let 'em bite your titties. Or stuff a handful of 'em down those little shorts of yours."

"Oh, fuck *you.*"

"Let's go back to the boat and wait a bit," Slydes said. "I need a beer." His thoughts strayed during the walk back. *Tonight'll be a hassle but it's worth it,* he knew. His brother's hydroponic pot demanded top dollar on the street for its quality, and it was a hell of a lot easier than dealing with that illegal gator meat. *All in a day's work,* he dismissed. Up ahead, he watched Ruth turn at a crook in the trail, caught a fine side glance of her body. *Yeah, she's a big-time pain in the ass, but . . .* The body was the thing, and her knowing what to do with it; hence, the chief reason he and Jonas kept her around. She'd tied off the T-shirt in a big knot, revealing a belly good enough for one of those ab-cruncher commercials. The night's humidity moistened the cotton fabric, which only divulged more of the large, heavily nippled breasts. As she walked, the bottom of her butt cheeks edged out under the shorts.

Yeah, he knew. *She probably will be gator bait some-day . . . but . . .* In fact, a little romp back at the boat might help tone down some of the night's aggravations. *I need to tap my love vein,* he thought. He knew that Jonas was already sick of her, but as for himself? *She's too good-lookin' to kill just yet.*

When they got back, the clouds were breaking well. At least they'd have a little light now. Ruth sat back up on the prow, the breeze parting her hair, while Jonas snoozed in the back fishing chair. The boat rocked languidly in the water. The night seemed serene now: the moonlight fluorescing the woods, the crickets and peepers thrumming their drone. Slydes could appreciate none of this, however, not the transcendental type. He clattered belowdecks, snapped on the cabin light, and reached for a beer.

"The fuck . . ."

He'd nearly slipped on the ice, which was melting on the floor. The beer cooler had been tipped over. The cover to the map box hung open, and he was sure it had been closed earlier. And when he looked at the toolbox, the tools seemed . . . disarranged.

"Get down here!" he barked.

Jonas and Ruth rushed down.

"What?"

"Which one of you tipped my cooler?" Slydes demanded. "Were ya born in a barn? You knock something over, you pick it back up."

"I don't drink that shit," Ruth said. "I could use a line of coke, though. Or some crystal."

"You were the last one to get a beer, Slydes," Jonas reminded him. "The fuckin' thing probably tipped over during the trip."

Slydes gave it some contemplation. *He's probably right, but*—"The map compartment's hangin' open, too," he added. "I didn't even use a map tonight. And see the toolbox? It's messed up. The rachet's always on top 'cause I use it all the time. I even used it today before we left. Now it's on the bottom."

"Like someone was looking through it," Ruth presumed.

"The door to the head's open too," Slydes added. "And I'm positive I closed it and put on the latch."

"Oh, fuck," Ruth groaned. "You guys are scaring me!"

Jonas' eyes were narrowed as he thought back. "I

may have pissed after you, Slydes, and I don't remember if I latched the door, and come to think of it, I may have fished around the toolbox for the stub-head screwdriver 'cause I remember wishin' I had one when I was taking the screws out of the insulation panel I hide the weed behind."

"The map compartment could've just fallen open," Ruth said.

"What about the cooler?" Slydes asked.

Jonas laughed. "You're worrying about bullshit, man. A swell probably came through when we were on the island, tipped the fucker over."

Slydes mulled it over. "Yeah, I guess you're right," he finally conceded. He picked some beers off the floor and followed his brother and Ruth topside.

In truth, however, Slydes was right. Someone *had* rooted through the cabin when they'd been out.

But he was wrong about something else . . .

The thing that had landed on Ruth's arm earlier wasn't a baby pine snake.

(II)

"I repeat, zero-zero. Three more are on the island. Two males, one female."

The radio line seemed to stall over the information. "I don't understand this. The island's supposed to be uninhabited."

"It's not now."

"Is the latest group military?"

"Negative, zero-zero. All three are civilians. They're acting discreet, though." *Transients,* the sergeant guessed. *They're up to something. Why would they have come to the island at night?*

"Be extra cautious." A hesitation. "We can't take chances at this point. If any of them see you, kill them."

"Roger, zero-zero."

"Out."

The sergeant stood in the brambles, thinking. He didn't know if this was good or bad. The more people who came out here, the more test subjects for the specimens, and so far that phase of the operation was working. Each day they were getting a more accurate picture of gestation periods, ovatic dispersal and function, mobility efficiency, etc. This was a lot of effort and expense for a biological feasibility study . . . but it was working. It was proof that genetically transfected hybrids could be used as weaponry.

So long as we don't get caught out here.

The sergeant didn't particularly like to kill civilians.

The corporal was finishing up with the cameras; they needed to monitor more of the island's outer perimeters.

"All done," the corporal announced.

"Good work."

"What did the major say about the new ones?"

"He didn't like it, and neither do I. All of a sudden this deserted island is getting crowded. And if any of them see us, we're supposed to kill them."

"No problem," the corporal remarked, looking around.

They already knew that the transfected species was perfectly compatible with the environment. He suspected that Research Command had a lot to do with it now. *They want to know what it's doing to the civilians we've infected . . .*

They moved back to the head shack area; the door was still open at the first unit, the lights on.

What is she doing in there? the sergeant thought.

"How come you went on the boat that docked earlier?" the corporal asked.

"Just a quick check for weapons, and I disabled their emergency radio."

Then the lights went off at the first head shack.

The corporal pressed up against a tree. "Look. There she is again . . ."

They could just see her in the moonlight. The woman with the frizzy short dark hair came back out and closed the door.

"She's finally going back to the campsite. Now we can get a look in there and see what she was doing all this time."

The corporal's face shield turned. "Hey, Sarge, she doesn't look too bad, you know?"

What is WRONG with him? "None of that."

"Why? The major just said we can kill them."

"With discretion, and only if we're seen. You'd fuck an animal if you had to. You know what happens if you get written up."

"You'd write me up for *that?*"

The sergeant just looked at him.

No sense of duty, he thought.

When the woman disappeared down the trail, he was about to proceed toward the head shack, but the corporal grabbed his arm.

"Wait, Sarge. Look. They're back again."

They pulled back behind the trees. It was the three that had arrived tonight. They'd staked this area out earlier but then left. *What are they up to?*

They were loitering at the farthest head shack, then . . .

They opened the door and light bloomed.

The lights were already on in there. The sergeant mulled the fact over, and couldn't imagine why.

Then the three civilians went inside and closed the door behind them.

"This is getting pretty interesting," the sergeant commented.

"I really like the girl—"

"Shut up."

I'd really like to know what they're doing in there, the sergeant wondered. He had a feeling this was going to be a long night.

(III)

"There's my babies," Jonas said. There was pride in his voice. They all looked up at the twenty-foot-tall marijuana plants growing out of their urns.

All three of them squinted in the long room's strange, silverish glow. Sheets of aluminum foil lined all four walls. Stranger was the incessant drone, like a bubbling hum, from the airstones and their small aerator pumps connected to each.

"I love these rooms," Ruth said, stepping forward toward the erect, green-spiky rows. "The sound, and the silver light. It's like mellow acid."

Slydes rolled his eyes. "Our little hippie."

"Look at 'em." Jonas grinned upward. "They're busting twenty feet, I'll bet. They don't even get that big in nature, under the best circumstances."

Forty such plants filled the former missile silo, and they had forty more in the next head shack, too. "I'm getting nine, ten ounces of the highest THC content pot per plant, every three months. Average asshole only pulls two to four."

"Look at the flowers!" Ruth celebrated. "They're beautiful!"

"Yeah, baby, they sure are. And they're *big*. The bigger, the better. There's more THC in my pot than *anyone's*."

"Quit bragging and let's get on with it," Slydes complained. He was tired, and they'd missed high tide going out. *Which means we gotta stay on this island till tomorrow night . . .* The skinny bitch in the first head shack had stayed there for another fucking *hour*. They hadn't counted on that. *Shit, it's past one o'clock now . . .*

Hydroponic homegrowers had several methods to choose from. Jonas used the "wick system," with ebb and flow urns; this was the best system because it grew the biggest plants, but the least popular because it consumed the most water and electricity. Water and electricity weren't a problem here, of course, because Jonas simply tapped into the army's unmonitored supply; hence the brightest lights round the clock, and unlimited fresh water. His only expenses were airstones and aerator pumps, Perlite, Pro-Mix, coconut planting fiber, and a *lot* of aluminum foil, which doubled the photosynthesis effect by bouncing back the light. That's why Jonas's plants were bigger and more concentrated. The average grower was limited to closets and basements, but with ceilings this high—and all this free light—Jonas was giving the plants more than even nature could provide. Charging a little more for superior pot was only good business. His customers just wanted more.

They checked the next head shack where, if anything, the plants grew even hardier. Then they moved to the third head shack.

"A damn good thing you have some ready to go," Slydes grumbled.

This was where they did the cutting, drying, and weighing. Jonas had tables and chairs set up for the various tasks, plus *cartons* of plastic baggies.

"That's because I always think ahead," Jonas bragged. "You always have your next delivery ready in advance. You know, Slydes, if you ran your poaching business like I run my pot business? You might actually make some money."

"Bend over real hard and blow yourself, brother."

Ruth giggled. "That I'd like to see." But then her

eyes opened wide when she looked at the cement floor, and she shrieked, "Fuck!"

The men walked over.

"What the hell's that?" Jonas queried.

On the floor a small, bright pink worm squiggled across the cement. It was about three inches long.

"Ain't no earthworm, that's for sure," Slydes noted. "Not movin' that fast."

The worm made more tracks, leaving tinseled slime. It had traversed half the width of the head shack in the time they were looking at it.

"Well, ain't that just the shit?" Jonas said. "There better not be any of these things on my plants."

"It just looks . . . disgusting," Ruth said and glared. "Somebody kill it."

Jonas seemed very concerned. "What the fuck is that? A corn worm?"

Slydes stepped on it. "Nope. It's a dead worm. Now let's quit fuckin' around with worms and get the fuck out of here."

When Slydes lifted his shoe, all that remained of the worm was pink slime.

Jonas grabbed a plastic bag full of a pound of trimmed marijuana, then snapped off the lights.

Before they left, none of them happened to notice that the squashed remains of the worm were sizzling.

CHAPTER EIGHT

(I)

Why did she feel so unsettled? *Weird night,* Nora dismissed. She'd expected the sounds emanating from the woods to help lull her to sleep; instead, they'd annoyed her. She supposed they'd all need to be up early tomorrow, for Annabelle's shoot, but now, going on two o'clock, it would be impossible to get in a decent night's sleep.

The little polyester tent pressed in like a coffin. She'd tossed and turned in the summer-weight sleeping bag. Each time she tried to clear her head of the day's aggravations, her temples began to rage in a headache. She'd drifted off once but was then bolted awake by, of all things, a sexual dream.

You've got to be kidding me . . .

She never had sexual dreams . . . an *odd* fact for a virgin. The little bit of dating she'd done in college and grad school had always wound up getting torpedoed by a term paper, a study session, or a test. The academician in her always wound up walking on her womanhood, asserting the priority. Whenever a potential relationship would fail, or she'd miss out on a perfectly normal fling, she'd always be satisfied to tell herself: *You're not in school to make whoopie. You're in school to get your doctorate.* Objectively this was all true, but by now it left little to console her womanhood. Her sexuality felt like something moldering. Her desires were fruit whose seeds would never touch the earth to give root.

The dream:

The man's face reminded her of the door knocker at her grandmother's house. It had been mounted on the ornate door's center stile, an oval of tarnished bronze depicting a morose half-formed face. Just two eyes, no mouth, no other features. The peculiar knocker was one of Nora's earliest childhood memories, for whatever reason. Her parents took her to Grandma's house every Thanksgiving; she remembered the knocker but not the rest. Why would that be?

One sleepless night, at age four or five, she'd gotten out of bed to go to the bathroom. The darkness of the musty hall had confused her; she'd opened the wrong door. *This isn't the bathroom,* she realized. *It's the room Mommy and Daddy are sleeping in.* But—

Her big eyes stared out. Mommy and Daddy weren't sleeping. She didn't know *what* they were doing—just that they had their clothes off and Daddy was doing something weird on top of Mommy. Nora shuffled away, bewildered.

The day after Thanksgiving, they'd driven away, and Nora could see that scary door knocker shrinking in the distance. Grandma died the next day.

And now her dream. The man's face was just like the knocker: half formed, just two blank eyes. He didn't need any more facial features than that, for he was just a body to suit her needs. His arms felt hot beneath her; he was carrying her through teeming woods—these woods?—deliberate footsteps crackling over twigs. He laid her down naked on the forest bed, and stood between her spread legs, looking down. The moon glowed behind him, blocking out the unnecessary details of his face. A face would give him a persona, a humanity, but her desires had taken her so completely, she didn't care *who* he was, or even how he might feel about the real *her*. He was only a symbol—of deliverance—just as her body, in this hot, compressed dreamscape, was a symbol—of her own unbridled lust.

When he turned a moment, the moon cut him into a silhouette of raven black, the outlines sharp as newly cut glass—including a stout, erect penis. Nora whined, cringing atop fallen leaves. Her belly sucked in and out as she stared up at him almost teary-eyed. The sweat on her skin felt slippery as glycerin when she smoothed her hands up her stomach to her breasts and plied her nipples as if twisting screws out of a wall. The pain drilled the most delicious sensations through her belly to her groin, where they all settled like an overcharged battery waiting to be tapped.

The silhouette seemed content to watch for now. Was the faceless figure touching himself, so incited by her body? Nora hoped so because, next, those electric sensations summoned her hand back down the slick abdomen. She gruelingly held herself back, her fingers never quite being allowed to hit the final triggers that would flatten her right there in the leaves. More and more of those sensations mounted, and soon she was moaning to let them out, but . . .

Not . . . yet . . .

She wanted him to see it all, to bear witness, and

then to spend himself on her from where he stood. The live-wire sensations mounted; the moon bathed her glistening skin. Then her guest began to lower himself.

Yes . . .

Callused hands began to massage her. The compounded sensations were driving her mad; the stars blurred in her eyes. As the rough hands kneaded her breasts, her nipples burned hot as embers embedded in her flesh. But just as she thought he'd lie atop her, he pulled back . . .

The hands pushed her knees back to her face, and his mouth found her sex. His tongue did things she didn't think possible—she'd never known that the web of her sexual nerves was capable of feeling such things. She closed her eyes and let the frenzy take over. First, one finger entered her, then two, then three; she was biting marks into her knees. The ministrations went on and on. Was her tongue hanging out? Was she shrieking her pent-up bliss?

Now! her mind screamed. *Now!*

The coal-black shadow moved upward, arms like struts that kept her knees pinned back. She could feel his hot, muscled flesh slide against the backs of her legs, and then he positioned himself. The penis nudged the entry of her sex, teased her as it threatened to enter—

Now . . .

—but that's when Nora woke up.

Her first sexy dream in ages, and look what happened. *I don't believe it,* she thought in the deepest frustration. *I can't even get laid in a dream!* The hot night was compressing her within the cocoon of the sleeping bag. She'd been sweating so profusely, it felt as though someone had dumped a bucket of hot water on her.

She'd been sleeping in her swimsuit. The cooler air caressed her when she finally got out of the bag. This was maddening; it was the middle of the night and she couldn't sleep. Worse was the dream's aftereffects, which left her skin prickly, her nipples aching as if plucked. *Gotta get out of here, go for a walk or something . . .*

She grabbed a lantern and unzipped the tent, crawled out as if fleeing a hornets' nest. Once outside, she stood in moon-tinted darkness, caught her breath, and let the frustration beat down.

She kept the lantern dim. Loren's tent remained zipped up; she could hear him snoring. *Sounds like a busted chain saw—jeez!* But the other two tents . . .

The strangest curiosity seized her. She wanted to look into the other tents—she didn't, of course, but she wanted to. They both stood unzipped.

Are they . . . in there?

Trent and Annabelle would be foolish to sleep with their tents unzipped. Their exhalations would summon droves of mosquitoes. But where would they be at this hour?

Who cares?

Nora walked down a trail, not even really aware of any direction. Her flip-flops crunching over twigs could scarcely be heard over the night sounds that pulsed all around her. Lizards scattered wherever she pointed the lantern light. An array of multicolored winged creatures buzzed around her.

The head shacks stood dark now, a row of lonely bunkers. She got her mind off the frenzied dream—and the utter letdown of its conclusion—and thought back on the details of the day.

Those things in the shower . . .

There was little room for error after so close an examination. She and Loren were indeed the experts, and they both knew now what the things had to be.

Motile ova. From some species of tropical annelid.

A worm.

She sat down on a stump and pondered. Some worms were sexed, some were asexual, while others were hermaphroditic. The phenomenon of ova motility among species of worms was well documented. The ovum, via its own means of locomotion, would seek out its own place to hatch, and certain parasitic varieties would seek out a living host for that purpose. But these were all marine species, and—

They're all tiny, she knew.

A mature worm ovum the size of a coffee bean? How big would the ovum be when it was *im*mature?

Then the most obvious question struck her:

How big would the gestating worm be?

The question totally confounded her, and she knew it was doing the same to Loren. *I can't wait to get those samples back to the college,* she thought. If she told any of her peers she'd found a motile ova that big, they'd laugh at her.

But now they'd be able to see for themselves.

Let it rest there, she decided. For now she knew she needed to concentrate on the task at hand: finding a scarlet bristleworm for this smart-ass blond photographer.

Nora blanked her mind on the subject of Annabelle. It was like at school. Sometimes you had to work with someone you didn't like, and that's just the way things were. Nora had never had a problem with clashing personalities.

So why now?

Something felt ticking inside her. She turned the lantern all the way down, to draw fewer bugs, and to think about anything *but* Annabelle . . .

That's when she realized her eyes were focused on something . . .

With the lantern off, darkness reclaimed the cove.

So . . . what the hell is that light?

It wasn't coming from the first head shack that she

and Loren were using as a lab. *One of those down there . . .*

She kept the light off, and walked quickly down the row of old missile units. She kept her eye trained, thinking it would go away as she approached, that it was just an odd reflection of moonlight, or some fox-fire. But no . . .

A thin beam of light seemed to be leaking out of the roof of the head shack at the very end of the row.

She walked right up to the long brick building and stared upward. *Yeah. That's definitely light. Electric light.* The building's roof of corrugated metal was arch shaped, and there was very clearly a hole in it. The beam of light shot up into the trees.

Why would the inside lights be on? None of these head shacks had been used in years.

Then the obvious answer came to her. *Trent checks these places every month for signs of squatters and vandalism. He probably forgot to turn the lights off last time he checked.*

No big mystery.

But when she turned to leave, something else caught her eye.

More light.

At the very edge of the next building's roof, where the metal met the brick, she saw the faintest line of light leaking out.

Hmm.

She checked the rest of the head shacks and found no further evidence of lights on inside. Then she checked the doors and found them all locked.

I'll have to remember to tell him tomorrow. . . .

She looked around and realized she was suddenly ill at ease. She supposed this was a creepy place to be alone in. Earlier, when she'd been studying the ova, she thought she'd heard voices outside, even a shriek, but she knew it was either her imagination or a night bird somewhere.

She strode hastily back to the campsite, or so she thought when she realized she'd taken the wrong trail.

She was about to turn the lantern back on when—

A voice fluttered.

"God, that's good . . ."

A woman's voice.

In another small cove, she saw pale shapes moving. She kept the lantern off, squinting as the moonlight brought out details. At first she wasn't sure, then—

I don't believe what I'm seeing . . .

It was Trent and Annabelle, both naked.

How tacky, Nora thought. *They're doing it standing up.*

Evidently Trent was stronger than he looked. Annabelle's arms and legs were wrapped around him as Trent's pelvis stroked her in an almost machinelike rhythm. Her breasts squashed against his chest, her ankles locked; she was hanging on to him—a monkey on a tree, only Trent was the tree. Judging the noises that came from Annabelle, it was apparent she was enjoying it, but—

Nora was aghast. This was making love? This was a physical gesture of passion? Nora's mind broke it down to bare parts: *They're just standing there, screwing. They don't really even know each other!* It was true, they'd only met this morning, and here they were, two animals in the woods.

Is that what it's all about? Nora wondered dismally. *I guess that's just the way some people are . . .*

Eventually, Trent lowered the blonde to the ground, to continue, and then she broke into a new round of gasps and moans, Trent's hips pounding onward, a mindless derrick. Nora continued to watch from behind a tree without even knowing why. She didn't have a voyeuristic streak at all, and there was certainly nothing enticing about the scene. Annabelle's back arched, her long, bare legs shooting up into the air in a wide V. Nora had never seen anything so perfunctory in her life.

Just leave, she told herself. *This is depressing.*

She should've obeyed herself, but she chose to watch a few moments longer, and in those moments, Annabelle's face turned toward her . . .

Nora's heart jolted.

In the moonlight, Annabelle's eyes met hers. *Oh my God! She sees me!*

Annabelle never said a word. She simply smiled.

Nora pulled herself back, turned, and ran away.

A crush of emotions buried her. She fled haphazardly back toward the campsite, images swimming in her head. By most people's standards, what she'd witnessed was of little consequence. *So what?* she tried to convince herself. *There must've been some spontaneous attraction between the two of them, so then one thing led to another.* Nora was a scientist; she should be able to understand that with no problem. But she knew what a psychologist might say: that the real reason the scene upset her was that Trent had selected Annabelle instead of her. It didn't matter that Nora felt no attraction to the army officer at all, it was merely the process of natural selection.

Being seen was the worst part. *My God,* she fretted. *That bitch will never let me live it down.* Nora knew she shouldn't care but she did anyway. The scientist in her was losing out very quickly to the human.

Just go back to the camp and go to sleep. Forget about it.

She stopped a moment to rest, that jolt to her heart finally wearing off. She placed her hand against a tree—

—then flinched.

What *was* that?

Her hand touched something.

A stud of some sort.

She turned the lantern up to look . . .

In the bright halo of gaslight, she couldn't have appeared more puzzled. A screw of some kind had been embedded in the tree trunk, but there wasn't a screw head at the end of it, as she expected.

Instead it was a clear glassine bulge. Like a lens.

(II)

Slydes lounged back in the fishing chair at his boat's aft. He raised his leg and farted, and found an inexplicable satisfaction in the act. He felt content now that they'd gotten in and out of the head shack without being seen, and more content in knowing that Jonas would turn that bag of pot into at least a thousand dollars in cash very quickly. It did secretly bother him, though—that Jonas made more money with his gig than Slydes did with his. Jonas believed that was proof of some intellectual superiority, but—

I'm smart too, damn it, Slydes reassured himself. He knew how to catch gator and effectively butcher it, didn't he? And he even knew how to prep and tan the hides, and that wasn't easy. Once he and his poaching buddies had thrown a gator-skinning contest (Jonas had had the audacity to *not* bet on his brother), but Slydes had won lickety-split. *I put 'em all to shame,* he remembered.

He didn't have anything to prove to anyone.

He lobbed the next beer bottle over the side. *Goin' through 'em tonight* . . . And why shouldn't he? It was hot and he'd worked hard all day. But now all those beers were leading to the inevitable result. The deck creaked when he lumbered to the stanchion cable and opened his pants. More inexplicable satisfaction arrived when he leaned back and pulled a hard piss over the side. *Ahhhhhhhhh . . .*

After a couple of minutes, Slydes was still urinating. *Damn! Come on, peter. I ain't got all night.* He half expected to see the lagoon rise an inch or two. *Bet it pisses the fish off,* he allowed himself the scholarly hypothesis. But when he was shaking off, he . . .

He squinted at the sensation. Not an itch, but—

Something tingled very slightly.

On his scrotum.

Not a modest man, Slydes pulled his "bag" up and looked at it in the bright moonlight.

Fuck!

A beetle or something was clinging to one of his testicles. Bean-sized . . . and very disconcerting. At first he thought it might be some sort of sore—he'd had those in the past—but then the "sore" was moving. And the color?

That was the grossest part. The thing's shell was the color of pus.

He plucked it off with haste, then turned on one of the deck lights. *Damn!* he thought, outraged. *The fuckin' thing was on my 'nads!* He squinted at it.

Some piss-yellow bug, but it wasn't hard as he'd expect a beetle to be. It felt hot, wet.

"Fucker," he grunted. "You're fish food," and he flicked it over the side.

Thank God it hadn't bitten him—whatever it was. He surely would've felt a sting of pain on so sensitive an area. If anything, the area he'd plucked it off felt . . .

Kind'a cool and tingly, he noted. It wasn't unpleasant in any way.

How'd the fucker get in my pants? he wondered next. No biggie, it was gone now, but he figured it must've crawled up his leg when they were cutting through the woods to get Jonas's dope.

Suddenly Slydes twitched in place, stood up straight and wide-eyed. Now he felt *another* sensation.

"You gotta be shittin' me!" he muttered and stuck his hand down his pants in the back. He fished around and, sure enough, pulled another one of the things out.

It had crawled right down into the cleft of his buttocks. *Another one in my ass crack!*

In truth, though, Slydes had to feel sorry for the bug.

Dumbfounded, he checked his entire body and found no more of the things.

Some squirmy kind of leech or slug, he reasoned. He'd picked it up in the woods, so that meant Jonas and Ruth probably had too.

He thunked down the steps to the cabin.

"Jonas! Ruth! The two of you's better check yourselfs for bugs. I just picked two off me."

But when he looked around, no one was there.

Belowdecks reeked of pot smoke. He'd seen them down here earlier, toking up some of the stash they'd brought off the island.

Slydes climbed back up and popped the cap off another beer. He looked out toward the island's massive tropical forest. *I wonder where the hell they went . . .*

(III)

The warm bare wood beneath Ruth's nakedness felt weirdly luscious; in fact, her entire body felt that way—cocooned in the wonderful, lulling buzz. Jonas took them to this old shed when they'd left the boat; he'd seen it on previous trips, just an old storage shed of some kind. *A lot better than doing it in the woods,* she thought, *with God knows what kind of bugs crawling around.* Not to mention that snake that had jumped on her earlier . . .

Jonas was already up and had his clothes back on.

"Want another toke, baby?" He hoisted his favorite carved-wood pipe.

She grinned and shook her head, hair disarranged and skin teeming with sweat.

Jonas took a few more hits, then popped a brow. "I swear my stuff gets better and better. No wonder my bagmen are screamin' at me to grow more."

Ruth slowly sorted her thoughts. "A year from now, you'll be rich, Jonas. When we start more plants in the other head shacks."

"Damn straight." Something seemed to catch his eye in the corner. "What's this?"

Ruth felt too lazy now to even lean up and look.

They hadn't noticed it before, but Jonas picked up a drawstring bag. He curiously inventoried the contents: "Swimmin' trunks, towels, suntan lotion . . ." Then he looked at her. "Shit, Ruth, someone left their shit here."

"The photographers?"

"Naw, they're keeping their stuff at the campsite."

"Slydes said that college kids come out here sometimes," Ruth recalled. She had her flashlight set on end, shining at the ceiling. It brought down a murky umbrella of ringed light that Ruth found fascinating. "They must've left it."

"Hmm. Yeah. Guess so." He seemed satisfied with the conclusion. Another conclusion might've occurred to him had he been observant enough to notice the portable grill outside, and the beer cooler full of melting ice.

"Let's get going, I'm tired."

Disappointment overwhelmed Ruth, something she was used to with this pair. "I thought we were going to sleep here. Let's cuddle!"

Jonas frowned. "Come on, put your clothes on and let's go back to the boat."

She leaned up on her hands. Why couldn't he or Slydes ever do anything *she* wanted? It would be romantic to sleep here.

"I'm sleeping here!" she insisted.

"Cool." Jonas stuffed his bag of pot in his shorts pocket. "Thanks for the piece of ass. I'll see ya back at the boat in the morning."

Jonas left the shed.

A piece of ass. *Prick!* So much for romance. It didn't matter, though. She felt so good right now, she wasn't going to let his selfishness spoil the mood.

She lay back down, sated and high. That pot was strong as hash; the warm buzz pulsed from her heart to her toes.

She snapped the light off and let the grainy darkness come down like the softest blanket. At least the sex had been decent this time—it wasn't always that way with Jonas. The beer he'd been drinking all day gave him some much-needed endurance. *Five minutes is better than two,* she reminded herself. With two lovers, the situation could've been worse. What Jonas failed to provide in the way of her womanly needs, Slydes usually took care of, and vice versa.

Jonas had left the door open, which permitted a trace breeze. The moon came in like an accidental guest, and the sounds of the forest began to pulse along with her buzz. She lolled in the dark, decided not to even put any clothes back on, and in her sleepy mind she saw her dreams with Slydes and Jonas come true. One great big happy family. More and more money coming in each month. A new washer and dryer, and one of those big fancy flat-screen TVs where she could sit between her two lovers every night and watch wrestling . . .

Warm semen trickled between her bare legs, but she

felt too tranquilized to even move, much less wipe her-self. Her eyes closed, and her unusually large lips turned up into a contented smile. Sleep carried her away oh so deeply . . .

She never even felt the thin, foot-long pink worm that slithered into her body through her vaginal canal.

CHAPTER NINE

(I)

The sergeant and the corporal watched the longhaired man leave the shed. *He's leaving the woman,* he realized, which seemed odd. But that was better for the field analysis. The woman would be much more vulnerable sleeping alone in the shed.

"How long till you think one of them gets her?" the corporal's voice issued through the earphone.

"Could be hours, could be minutes. No way to tell. The worms' sensory organs are supersensitive, and the ovum too. They'll seek out the largest heat signature as well as the most profound pheromonic emanations."

"Pheromonic?"

The sergeant couldn't believe the deficient level of tech training the younger NCOs were getting these days. "Airborne glandular emissions of bombykol molecule groups that come out of the skin, particularly the skin of genitalic regions. They're picked up by olfactory VMO receptors and stimulate pleasure centers in the brain. Chemical triggers, you know, from the tech classes you *passed* to get this duty assignment. They trigger innate reproductive responses."

The corporal clearly remembered nothing of these classes. "Fine, but since you just said it might take hours for one of the specimens to get her, I think we should go in there right now and have some fun. We'll get her pheromones going, all right."

The sergeant glared at him through the visor of his protective mask. "Any more comments like that, I'll write you up."

"You're not serious, Sarge."

"Try me." The sergeant would *not* have that sort of thing going on while he was ranking NCO in the field. It didn't matter that all the subjects would eventually die, it was protocol. That sort of thing could get out of hand. "She's probably got all kinds of diseases. I don't want to have to be quarantined when we get back to the post."

The corporal grumbled.

I really don't trust these new kids at all, the sergeant thought. "We're done for now," he said. "Let's get back."

"What about the two men on the boat that came in tonight?"

"They'll be infected by morning, if they're not already."

They slipped away from the shed, then turned on their low-light lenses to refind the trail back to the field HQ. They passed one corpse along the way, one of the women infected by the ovum. She hadn't released the brood yet, but the dead belly quivered from all the immature larva that bloated it.

"She hasn't been dead long," the corporal said after lancing a dead arm with the portable chromatograph. It had been calibrated to read serum levels of putrefactive gases. "A few hours maybe."

"A 'few' hours isn't good enough." The sergeant passed his troop the lance thermometer. "Check the drop-fall time against the mean-to-zero brain temperature."

The corporal looked lost. "I've never done that."

Damn. The sergeant snapped the gauge away and uncapped the lance. "I can't believe they're graduating you kids through this occupational specialty. This is supposed to be one of the first things you learn." He turned the unit on, input the readout of the air temperature, then—

Crunch.

—jammed the lance into the corpse's nostril. The breasts seemed to quiver a moment, but that was just reflexive. When the thermometer beeped, the sergeant slid the lance back out. "Hour and eleven minutes," he read.

"How's it work?"

"By comparing the brain's temp against the air temp and calculating the drop time."

"Oh."

Yeah. Oh. The sergeant snapped some digital pictures for the file. "The mutation element is incredible. Look at her skin."

"Yeah. Neat," the corporal remarked.

The woman's skin had fully turned now, to the same translucent yellow, peppered by bright red spots. But the sergeant couldn't help but notice how his underling's eyes were fixed on the cadaver's swollen breasts. "You're an animal. You're gaping at a dead woman's breasts. If I weren't here, you'd probably be having sex with it."

The corporal shrugged.

What can you do? The sergeant guessed he was just getting old. It wasn't the victim's former beauty that captivated him, it was the level of mutagen-transmission.

The Transfection Unit that made these specimens really knew what it was doing.

"Take a tissue sample so we can get out of here," he ordered. "I think the colonel's going to be really pleased about this."

(II)

"I slept great last night," Loren enthused, picking out his Sigma flippers and snorkel. "The clean, fresh air of the great outdoors, I guess."

"Me too." Annabelle appeared just as lively, blond hair shining in the morning sun. Today she wore a bright parrot-green bikini that seemed to cover even less of her body than yesterday's apparel. "I got to sleep pretty late," she said, inadvertently looking around for Trent, "but slept very well. I'm surprised how quiet the forest is at night."

"Quiet?"

"Oh, sure. You should hear the racket the woods make in Brazil and Southeast Asia. Ten times louder than this."

"Wow, you've been all over the place."

"Indeed I have. My job's sent me on shoots all over the world, from the Sahara to the Arctic Circle."

"What about the Arctic Circle?" Trent asked. He looked exhausted when he came out to the narrow strip of beach, his uniform crumpled and circles under his eyes.

Loren found his diving mask. "Annabelle's a world traveler, from her job."

"A world traveler, huh? I believe it."

Annabelle gave him a sultry smile. "This little island's more like a vacation to me."

Trent rubbed his eyes. "Yeah, me too."

The blonde untopped a tube of waterproof suntan lotion. "Would one of you mind putting some of this on my back?"

When Trent stepped forward to take the tube, she gave it to Loren. Trent frowned.

"You'll definitely need this," Loren said, hands already shaking as he smoothed the lotion over her skin. "Shallow water magnifies UV rays. You'll have to reapply this all day; waterproof means it won't wash off for ten or fifteen minutes."

"Where's Professor Craig?" Trent asked.

"She's already out in the water."

Trent gazed out into the Gulf of Mexico, arms crossed. "So today's the big hunt for the scarlet bristleworm, huh?"

"Yuh—yep," Loren confirmed. His hands gingerly spread the lotion around the strap of Annabelle's bikini top, then shakily slid lower.

"Loren, since you're down there, would you mind doing the backs of my legs?"

"Shuh—sure," Loren said. Now he knelt to find himself face-level with Annabelle's derriere.

Trent frowned again.

Annabelle glanced over her shoulder. "That's enough, Loren. Thanks."

His hands continued to shake when he gave her back the tube. Annabelle fitted on her diving mask, then propped it up on her forehead. "I'm ready when you are, Loren."

"Damn, I forgot my collection bag. It's back at the head shack—I'll be right back." He jogged off into the trail.

Trent laughed when Loren was gone. "You really made that kid's day. See how he was shaking?"

"Well, I wasn't *trying* to intimidate him."

"It's probably the first time he's ever had his hands on a woman."

Annabelle grinned but didn't look at him. "Your hands were doing all right last night."

The comment caused Trent to stall. "That's good to know."

"I hate to tell you this but what's-her-name saw us."

"Who? Professor Craig?"

"Um-hmm."

The lieutenant mulled it over, then shrugged. "Doesn't bother me *what* she saw. I couldn't care less about her. You're the one I'm interested in."

Annabelle coyly tapped his nose. "Oh, don't get all mushy on me. Last night was just one of those spontaneous things, you know."

"Yeah, well, we need a lot more of those *spontaneous things*."

"We'll see," she said, still not looking at him. Now she checked the underwater housing for her camera. "And I'll bet seeing us last night made *her* day."

"She and the kid are a real pair."

Annabelle chuckled. "Geek Patrol."

"You really have to wonder about people who devote their lives to studying *worms*."

"She and Loren are peas in a pod, I'm afraid."

Trent nodded smugly. "Right, and now that you've changed the subject, I want to see you again tonight. And I want your number."

"Oh, the assertive type, I like that. But you don't need my number. It's not practical for us to continue seeing each other. I live in New York."

"They have these things called planes."

"We'll see," she said.

"One way or another, before this worm thing is over, I'll get your number."

"Shhh! He's coming back."

Loren reappeared with a net bag full of plastic specimen tubes. "Got 'em."

Now Annabelle was checking her snorkel. "I really can't wait to see one of these worms. I'll be credited with having the most recent photographs of it. Loren, how long till you think it'll take to find one?"

The young man had regained his composure after having had his hands on her preeminent body. "Well, keep in mind that Pritchard's Key is the only known place in North America to have them. It's very rare, because of the shifting water temperature, like I was saying yesterday. It might take all day to find a scarlet bristleworm. It might even take all week. You don't just turn over the first rock you see and, bam, there it is."

Nora trudged up to them in her flippers, dripping water. She pushed up her mask and handed Annabelle a specimen tube. "Here's your scarlet bristleworm."

"You gotta be kidding me," Loren said, amazed. "How did you—"

"I turned over a rock and there it was," Nora told them, unimpressed.

Trent was laughing. "Outstanding. The rarest worm in North America and Professor Craig finds one in five minutes."

Annabelle held the clear tube toward the sun, peering at its brilliant bristly contents. "It's really disgusting-looking but it's also . . . incredible. The color—it's so bright, like a glowing ember."

"I just swam out to about a ten-foot depth," Nora explained, shaking off more water, "found a cool-flow, and started turning over rocks. There're lots of them out there. You'll see a narrow trench cutting down near that cool-flow. At the tip of the trench, there's a big chunk of reef about the size of a bus—that's where the nest is."

"This I gotta see!" Loren exclaimed, visibly excited. He dorkily plopped down the beach in his flippers and waded into the water.

Trent was still chuckling. "The kid acts like he just won the lottery."

"He's never seen a live one before," Nora said. "To a polychaetologist, that's like a coin collector finding a two-headed Buffalo nickel. Oh, and we'll be having spiny lobster and stone crab for dinner. I've never seen so many in one area before."

"Outstanding," Trent said again. "Professor Craig—you are one squared-away polychhhh—polywhatever. I'll let you two finish the big worm hunt while I go look for more pot plants to burn. Have fun."

Nora stopped him. "Oh, Lieutenant? I wanted to ask you something. Didn't you tell us yesterday that the army took all the surveillance cameras off the island when they closed down the missile site in the eighties?"

Trent seemed piqued by the question. "Yeah, sure. This used to be a high-security military reservation. Why do you ask?"

"I think I found a camera, last night." Nora pointed back toward the edge of the forest. "It was on this side, somewhere between the campsite and the head shacks."

"I guess they could've missed one," Trent supposed.

"And it was the strangest thing—I mean, I think it was a camera of some sort; it definitely had a lens. But it was really small."

"A surveillance camera *would be* small," Annabelle said.

Nora restrained most of a smirk. "Small as in *tiny*. It was like a half inch long, sticking out of a tree, and about as thin as a pencil. Just a stub."

"Might have been an old proximity sensor or motion detector," Trent reckoned. "But it's long been disconnected. Were there wires coming out of it?"

"No."

"Any indicator lights?"

"Nothing like that, either."

Trent didn't seem concerned. "Show it to me later, okay? It's probably just one of those old-generation electric eyes that would trip an alarm if someone crossed it."

"I'm sure you're right," Nora said. "It just gave me this really uncomfortable feeling. Like when I looked in it, someone was seeing me."

Trent smiled at her paranoia. "I guarantee you, whatever it is, it hasn't been hooked up in over twenty years."

Trent walked off toward the trail.

"Spy cameras in the woods, huh?" Annabelle leaned over to adjust her flippers. "But *you* were the spy last night."

"Pardon me?" Nora couldn't believe what the woman had said.

"Oh, you know what I'm talking about, Nora. But don't worry, I'm not mad." She smiled to herself. "I'm not the inhibited type, being watched never bothers me. But, honestly, I never figured you for a voyeur."

It was too early in the morning for this. "Hey, I was just going for a walk in the woods. I had no idea you'd be out there *fucking*."

"Don't get so upset," Annabelle chided. "Nature has a way of taking its course, especially in an environment like this." She stood back up, her posture accentuating her bikini'd bosom and table-flat stomach. "I told you, I wasn't mad."

Nora glared, a headache pecking at her. "I don't give a flying *shit* if you are."

"I was just going to say"—the blonde maintained a quiet, controlled tone—"that Lieutenant Trent's pretty good, and I'm not a territorial person. So you can go for it, too, if you want. I don't mind."

"You're outrageous!" Nora almost shrieked at her. "I can't wait for you to go back to New Fucking York!"

Now Annabelle tinkered again with the big encased camera.

"Professor Craig—profanity doesn't become you. And you don't have to worry about being embarrassed around Lieutenant Trent."

Nora winced so hard that creases seemed permanently etched into her face. "Why would I be embarrassed?"

"I didn't tell him that you were spying on us last night."

"I wasn't spying!" Nora flat-out yelled.

"Shh! Calm down. Loren's coming back. You don't want him to hear, do you?"

Before Nora could yell further, Loren trudged back up to them, seawater running off his body in rivulets. He seemed frustrated. "Nora, I couldn't find that cool-flow you were talking about."

Nora's teeth were grinding back and forth. "I'll be out in a minute."

Annabelle lowered her dive mask over her face. "Loren and I will find it, Professor. But you did a great job finding that first worm. I'm really looking forward to that lobster dinner you mentioned. Maybe later, you can show Loren and me where they are." She absently put a hand on Loren's arm. "We'll have a cookout to-night, it'll be fun!"

Then she and Loren walked back toward the water.

Nora fumed after them.

She didn't know *what* kind of game the photographer was playing. She looked around, wide-eyed in rage. *Have I EVER been this mad?* She sat down in the sand for a few minutes, trying to rein back in some composure. *They can find the fucking worms,* she decided. *I'm done for today. And . . . the NERVE of that phony bitch!*

As a breeze began to dry her skin, she tried to reflect on herself. *Is it me? There are lots of assholes in the world. I can't get this bent out of shape every time one crosses my path.* Maybe this was why she'd chosen an academic-based career instead of something more socially connected.

And she knew she had to consider something else, too.

Deep down, in her most hidden subconscious fibers, was she actually jealous of the more attractive woman?

Hell no, she decided. *And what was she talking about with Trent? Like now that she's "had" him first, it's okay for me . . .*

The notion just infuriated her more. Trent was a dullard.

She took a few more minutes to shake it off. She was sitting right in front of a vinyl beach bag . . .

That's Annabelle's bag, she realized. It contained towels, flip-flops, sunglasses, and the like. And right next to it lay a tube of sunblock.

What was Nora thinking?

She looked to the water. Annabelle and Loren had already gone under. So she picked up the tube of sunblock and without even much forethought, scooped a hole in the sand, emptied the lotion into the hole, and covered it. The tube read SPF 45.

Nora refilled it with her own SPF 2.

She looked up to the blazing sun and nearly giggled. *Now the bitch can go back to New York barbecued!*

She felt like a juvenile delinquent pulling such a prank, but she figured she deserved it. It had been the comment regarding Trent that bothered her most, *Like he's her property that she's giving me PERMISSION to use! Yeah, she thinks she's the queen of the hive, all right. Like she's on some horse's ass reality show. Annabelle Island. And Trent's one of her puppy dog grunts.*

Nora was discovering her very own Peyton Place.

She pulled off her flippers and mask, then lay back

on her towel. The sand beat heat into her back. In spite of the sour mood, she admitted, the water was perfect—clear as gin and just a degree above cool—and she did enjoy snorkeling. She was trying to motivate herself to do something—go back on the worm hunt, catch some lobsters, anything. Or she could return to their makeshift examination lab and make some more notes on the strange yellow ovum they'd found in the shower stall. But a sudden fatigue hauled her down. *Not enough sleep last night,* she realized, eyelids drooping in the sun. She began to nod in and out, the mildest surf-sounds rocking back and forth in her ears . . .

When she roused herself, it seemed like she'd been sleeping about fifteen minutes. Then she looked at her watch.

"Oh, for God's sake!"

The sun had moved halfway across the sky. It was past noon. Annabelle, lying belly-down on a towel, turned her head to look at Nora. Loren knelt at her side, slowly applying more suntan lotion on the photographer's back.

"Look who's awake," Annabelle said.

"Hey, Nora. You slept the morning away." Loren looked over at her quite sheepishly, while his hands tended Annabelle's back.

"Hope you don't mind me borrowing your associate, Professor Craig. Loren, if you ever decide you don't want to study worms anymore, you'll make a great masseur."

Nora frowned, watching Loren spread more lotion on Annabelle. *Look at him. He's getting his jollies being her personal cabana boy.* At least there was a tiny satisfaction, though. *She thinks he's using heavy sunscreen but it's really only SPF 2. She'll look like a fire truck by the end of the day. The bitch.*

Annabelle and Loren suddenly seemed to be squinting over.

"Nora, did you forget to put on sunblock?" Loren asked.

Then Annabelle: "You're looking pretty pink, come to think of it."

An alarm shrieked in Nora's brain. She'd been too busy sabotaging Annabelle, she'd forgotten about herself. She looked with dread to her arms, then her legs, and found herself pink as deli ham. *Oh my God! How could I have let this happen?*

"I did," she finally admitted. "I forgot to use my block." Then she held up the empty tube, disgusted with her secret.

"You know better than that," Loren told her. "We're marine zoologists, Nora. We're out in the sun ten times more than other people. You've been lying out here for three hours with no block? Of course you'll get burned."

When Nora rubbed her face, even her cheeks hurt. *Now I'M the fire truck . . .*

She had a feeling this wasn't going to be one of her better days.

"Loren found a really big nest of the scarlet bristleworms, right in front of an underwater trench and the most fascinating coral configurations," Annabelle informed her next. She spoke with her eyes closed as Loren continued to massage her back. "I got great pictures!"

"Actually it was Nora who found the nest," he at least had the presence of mind to say. "She told us where it was. Thanks, Nora. You were right. We hit the jackpot."

Who gives a shit? Nora glanced, embarrassed, at her pink arms. "That's wonderful. So we can go now?"

"Oh no," Annabelle piped up. "We'll be here a few more days at least. I need pictures of every aspect of the worm's life and its environment. The sun hits the water perfectly at midafternoon. Loren and I need to dive again tomorrow."

It didn't even anger Nora anymore: the way Annabelle excluded her from everything.

"I'm even going to have Loren in a few of the underwater pictures, so his name can go in the article, too."

The only reason I don't bury you, Nora replied in thought, *is because I'm too tired to dig the hole.*

"And I got plenty more samples for us to catalog for the college," Loren added, "plus some pretty interesting echinoderm fossils that look like they go back to the Cambrian Period."

"The what period?" Annabelle asked.

"Cambrian," Nora answered with no interest. "About sixty million years ago, when invertebrate life was just beginning to soar."

Annabelle was careful not to acknowledge Nora at all. "You also found some other weird things, didn't you, Loren?"

"Couple of translucent megalodae, some multicolored Clitellatas, oh, and a sea potato."

"A sea *potato?*" the blonde asked, amused. "It's not like a potato we eat, is it?"

Nora smiled. "Yeah, Annabelle. Loren will cook you up some fries in a jiffy."

Loren intervened. "No, it's just *called* a sea potato. It's actually a sediment-dwelling sea squirt."

Annabelle looked right at Nora and silently mouthed, *Kiss my ass.* Then she winked.

What gall! For each hour that passed, it occurred to Nora that a conflict would erupt eventually. *I guess I shouldn't be getting in any catfights,* she realized. *The bitch would probably beat me up.*

Annabelle rose to her feet and did a long stretch, giving Loren an eyeful. "Thanks for the back rub,

Loren. You're a master. But after all that swimming, I think I'll go take a nap." She glanced down to Nora again. "You might want to put some sunblock on Professor Craig, though. She's turning as red as a fire truck."

You would say fire truck. She even steals my analogies.

"Oh, and, Professor? What time will you be cooking that lobster dinner you promised?"

About five minutes after I put my foot up your ass, Nora thought. Instead she just said, "About seven, if that doesn't cramp your sophisticated itinerary."

"Oh, don't worry, it doesn't. See you later!"

A lot later, I hope.

Annabelle traipsed off to the woods.

"What's with all this friction between you and Annabelle?" Loren asked.

"She's just a bossy, arrogant, territorial bitch, that's all. No friction. Women mark their turf, Loren, especially women with *implants*."

"Oh no, she's natural, she told me."

Nora smiled to herself.

"And there's no reason for the two of you to not get along," he added, fishing in his bag for more sunblock. "We're all in this together, you know."

"Not if you ask her. She treats me like I'm not here."

"You're imagining it. She's actually very nice. Emotionally unfolded, professionally dedicated, and intellectually diversified."

Nora leaned up, squinting outrage. "Loren! She's a ditz with big tits! She's phonier than Al Capone's secret vault. She's a mover, Loren; she uses her body and her sparkling eyes to manipulate men for her personal benefit."

Loren almost got mad—something she'd never seen. "That's harsh and judgmental, Nora. I'm surprised that an academician such as yourself would make such a shallow invective. It almost sounds defensive, even insecure."

Nora laughed. "She's got bigger boobs than me—big deal. I'm not insecure about it. She's more attractive than me, lots of women are, but you know what? I don't care! I could shit care less and whistle Dixie at the same time. But since you're not just my assistant—you're a good friend—I only feel it proper to warn you."

He seemed defiant now, lower lip trembling at the challenge. "Warn me?"

"She's a textbook floozie who's *wheeling* for you. Don't let her pull the wool over your eyes. Girls like that eat guys up and spit them out like gum when they're done with them. And she'll do it to you if you let her."

Loren glared; now his lower lip was *really* trembling. "That hurts my feelings, Miss Perfect. I'm glad you have such confidence in my acumen with the opposite sex." His head bowed, almost as if he were about to sob.

Oh, jeez . . . "Loren, I'm sorry, I only meant—"

His head jerked up in a grin and a loud clap of his hands. "Had you going, moron! Jesus Christ, I know she's a bogus, manipulating, saline-stuffed bitch. I'm just playing Poor Little Infatuated Nerd-Boy so maybe she'll feel sorry for me and give me a sympathy fuck. Believe me, I ain't looking to hold hands in the fucking park with that Paris Hilton wannabe."

Nora signed, relieved. "You're such a tool, Loren."

"Damn right, and a big, *big* tool at that—like a friggin' roll of cookie dough if you want to know the truth. I'll hump her so hard she'll sound like someone stomping on a squeak-doll."

"Loren!"

"Now shut up and flip over so I can put sunblock on your back. Otherwise you'll get redder than a—"

"Don't say fire truck!" she insisted.

"I was *going* to say scarlet bristleworm." He grabbed a tube of his own sunblock.

Sputtering, Nora flipped over on her belly. "I guess you're getting to be an expert at this."

"I'm an expert in everything," Loren claimed.

"I feel like chopped liver here."

"Why?"

"You were too busy rubbing all over Barbie, you didn't even stop to *think* that maybe your *boss* might need a back rub."

"And what's wrong with chopped liver?" he said, squirting lotion on her back.

She tensed a moment as his hands slid over some sunburned fringes, but then relief began to work in.

Loren chuckled. "I overheard Annabelle talking to a friend on her cell phone, and she referred to me as The Geek."

"Are you sure she wasn't talking about me?"

"Naw, you were Professor Dork."

"How flattering."

"And here's the best part—she's yacking away to her friend and eventually tells her that she's certain you and I are both virgins. How's that for a laugher?"

Nora smoldered and kept silent.

"What? I say something wrong?"

"No, just—"

"I'm no virgin, that's for sure. I've had sex a bunch of times, and my first one was with this foreign exchange student who stayed at my house while my brother went to Sweden. This girl was *hot*! She even—"

"Loren, I don't want to hear about your sex life!"

"Wow, you're really testy today," he said. "Guess Annabelle was right."

"What?"

"She also told her friend on the phone that you had permanent PMS."

Nora almost yelled, "That insufferable bitch! I'd like to mop my floor with her bleached-blond head!"

"Calm down," he urged, his finger daintily spreading the cool sunblock around her top straps. "Can I ask you a personal question?"

"No!"

"*Are* you a virgin?"

"No. Of . . . course not! And even if I were, it's none of your business. Just put the damn stuff on my back, mouth shut."

"Sorry." His fingers paused. "Wait, take this off before I goo it up."

My cross, she realized. Her grandmother had given it to her eons ago at her confirmation. She rarely ever took the tiny golden cross and chain off. "You take it off, I can't reach, and I'm too lazy right now to sit up."

He carefully worked the tiny catch and slid it off. "I've been working for you over a year and never knew you were a Christian."

Nora thought about it. "In truth I guess I'm a pretty *shitty* Christian. My grandmother gave it to me and she was cool. I always wear it under my top."

Loren grinned behind her. "I like the dichotomy. The symbol of the man who died for our sins, and you keep it between your breasts, which are the symbols of female sexuality."

She rolled her eyes under closed lids. "Loren, my boobs aren't exactly pillows of carnality."

"Oh, that's right, I forgot. You *did* admit that you're a virgin."

Nora knew he was just pecking at her for fun, which normally she went along with. But now, here, the conversation filled her with dread. Throughout her adulthood, she hadn't even been "saving" herself for the right man. *I couldn't GIVE it away . . .* She didn't suppose she was downright *ugly,* and she was at least complex enough to realize that not *all* men went solely for Annabelle-types. *Jesus, I can count my heavy makeout sessions on ONE hand.* Then a worse possibility assaulted her:

Maybe Annabelle's right. Maybe I really am a great big case of permanent PMS. For one thing, what guy wants a woman whose career field revolves around worms? And for another, what guy wants a woman who's bitchy, unhappy, and cynical all the time?

But was that really her?

When she felt the cross slip out from between her breasts, she couldn't even remember if any man in her life had actually had his hands on them . . .

Now Loren was doing the backs of her thighs, multitasking the application of the lotion into a pretty good massage. Nora blanked her mind of all negativity . . . and felt better.

Her thoughts drifted to last night's dream: the crude sex-fantasy. It had been a gratifying dream, of course, until the end, when she'd wakened unfulfilled.

Just sex, she thought. She focused on the dream's details—the faceless night suitor with no identity. The rough, intent hands on her flesh, the urgent tongue that incited her nipples and her sex. *That's what I need,* she joked to herself, *a man who's just a body.*

A body for *her.*

She could almost fall back to sleep now. *The Bimbo's right; Loren gives a killer massage . . .* Now he was working her feet, firing nerves she didn't know she had.

"The feet are an erogenous zone, you know," he said.

"Your point being?"

"Clinical reflexology. As scientists, we should be intrigued by human reproductive response systems, and all their intricacies."

"Loren, please." Slippery fingers glided back and forth across her arches and insteps. "Just be quiet and keep doing it."

The sensations overwhelmed her; she felt woozy in some carnal way. Her buttocks clenched when his hands slid back up the calves, then thighs. She knew this was absurd: she was letting an innocent back rub become much more, she was stealing something from it. She tried to imagine Loren as the lover from her dream, but then some distant moral twinge disallowed it. More sensations flowed from her thighs to her groin, somehow squeezing her sex with a lewd, hot pressure, and in another mental recess, she imagined herself turning around in the sun and masturbating, or worse, brazenly inviting him into her.

The mental alarm bell clanged louder, and the fantasy dissolved with her realization of the truth. *My teaching assistant is putting sunblock on me and I'm getting horny. Nora, congratulate yourself on a new low.*

"That's enough, thanks," she blurted. She flipped back over quickly, assailed by an inexplicable guilt. At least if she were blushing, her sunburn would hide it. "I can do the front," she said.

"Damn, I was just starting to have fun."

Nora frowned. *I'll bet. Probably musing over the Bimbo.* She rubbed more lotion on her front shoulders and arms. The tingling between her legs mocked her; she struggled for a harmless subject. "So what's on the rest of today's agenda? Are you and Miss Priss going out for more worms?"

"You heard her," he said, lying back on his own

towel. "She wants more underwater shots when the light is optimum, she said. And she wants to try to get some mating shots. Probably tomorrow afternoon."

Figures. "Did you sex the samples you brought up?"

"Of course. All today's samples are back at our field lab. I've got them in some field aquariums." He chuckled. "And don't worry, I won't let Annabelle dupe me. Today she kept brushing against me—what a tease. I'll let her go on thinking I'm a virgin. Then she'll really want me, right? I mean it's true, all women want to crack a male virgin?"

She shook her head to herself. "How about if we stick to more professional subjects?"

"Come on, it's true, right?" he insisted. "Everybody wants to be somebody else's first. It's completely biogenic, it's got to be. In a sense, we're all still back in Neanderthal days. Part of our brains believe this."

"Remnant Darwinism in sexual function," she murmured, closing her eyes again and lying back. "Let's stick to scarlet bristleworms, huh?"

"I'd rather talk about sex," he thwarted. "It's fun. I'm going to play Annabelle's game, let her think what she wants, and execute my right to your remnant Darwinism in sexual function." He nearly giggled. "I'll wind up giving her the best balling of her shallow, insipid life!"

Nora looked over, shielding her eyes. "What's gotten into you? You never talked so—"

"Libidinously?"

"That's not quite the word I was looking for. 'Trashy's' more like it."

"Same thing. Why mince words? I don't know, it must be the environment, the air, the sun, just the four of us here in the cusp of nature's beauty. It all reaffirms my vitality as a sexual entity."

"You sound like a horny redneck, Loren."

"I *am* a horny redneck, baby," he said, his giant Adam's apple bobbing. "And when I get back to the mainland, I'm gonna tear it up! Watch out, girls!"

Jesus, I've created a monster-nerd . . .

"And speaking of abandonment of modern morality," he said, "here's your cross back."

She'd forgotten about it—a symbol, perhaps, of her forgotten religion. She reconnected the chain and slipped the cross beneath the top of her one-piece. The tiny tidbit of metal felt cold between her breasts. "What about you?" she asked. "Are you spiritual at all? Do you have any religious beliefs?

"Sure," he answered at once. "I believe in scientific conclusionary phenomenalism."

Nora almost hacked. "What the hell is *that*?"

"Reverence to the acknowledgment of the contradiction that space and time are forms of intuition. Man's spiritual absolution can never be made manifest in our finite minds but in the genetics beyond the *whole*. Follow me?"

"No."

"What I mean is, salvation is a consistence of a judgment pursuant to other judgments, fitting in ultimately to a single absolute system."

Nora rubbed her eyes wearily. *Never ask a genius what his religion is,* she told herself.

"It's just a neo-Judeo-Christian attitude, that's all," he dismissed. "Quasi-existential dynamics—and if there really is a hell, you can bet that Sartre and Nietzsche are there. We'll only find out who's right when we die; until then, there's only faith."

Interesting gobbledygook, but Nora thought about that. *If God exists, where will I stand in the end?* she wondered with a chill. *I'm not a bad person, but am I really a good person?*

And if there isn't a God . . . does that really mean

nothing matters? The ideas frustrated her, even as she unconsciously felt her cross beneath the swimsuit's fabric. She looked for any escape. "You're covering a lot of bases today," she pointed out. "Now you're talking heavy theology and five minutes ago, you were telling me about how you're going to connive Annabelle into thinking you're a virgin just to get laid."

"But lust is innate," he responded. "God forgives all."

Nora smirked. "I've had enough sex-talk and God-talk." She got up and brushed sand off her skin. "Now I'm going to do something that *really* matters."

"What's that?"

"Catch lobsters."

CHAPTER TEN

(I)

Ruth hadn't felt this awful . . . ever. She awoke in the woods, and after a minute of thinking through a catastrophic headache, she remembered: *I fell asleep in the shed last night, didn't I?*

Yes. She and Jonas had gotten high on some of his potent weed, and had made love in that little shed. He'd gone back to the boat but . . .

I stayed, she knew. *I slept on the floor—I'm positive.*

And if she'd slept on the floor . . .

How did she wind up in the woods?

When she leaned up, more shock hit her: she was still naked. She almost shrieked when she brushed some bugs off her thighs and stomach, then thought *Fuck!* and flicked a slimy tree frog out of her belly button. Dismay shot her head around; then she saw that she lay less than fifty feet from the shed. Sunlight struggled down through high branches. The door to the shed remained open.

My clothes must still be in there, she realized. She wiped sweat off her brow and smacked her lips. *Yuck!* Her mouth tasted dry and stale, and her stomach squirmed to remind her how hungry she was. *Jonas's ass-kicking pot always leaves some ass-kicking munchies.* She was probably dehydrated, too. In this heat? Even last night it didn't feel as though the temperature had dropped below eighty. *And I slept in it. In the fuckin' woods?*

She must've been so stoned, she'd tried to walk back to the boat, but then passed out. It was the only explanation. When she looked down more closely at herself, it almost seemed as if she'd been laid out deliberately: legs spread wide, arms out, flat on her back and nude. But when she tried to get up—

"Oww! Fuck!"

Her hands flew to her bare heels, which suddenly barked in pain when she'd dragged them across the ground.

Her heels were scuffed bloody, and her buttocks and bottoms of her thighs sparkled in pain, too.

What the fuck happened to me?

She helped herself up, blinking her confusion through the headache. Now her eyes scanned back toward the shed and she saw two lines coming from the doorway and ending—

Exactly where her heels had been.

"This is fucked up! I didn't pass out in the fuckin' woods! Somebody dragged me here! They dragged me out of the shed and left me!"

But who? And why?

Jonas? Slydes? Why would they do that? *Or maybe one of those nature photographers,* she thought, but that didn't make sense either.

Then she thought again of her position. Like she'd been deliberately laid out spread legged—in wait of something.

Like bait, came the next, odder thought. *Somebody left me here on purpose . . .*

The rustling chopped off her remaining thoughts. Just a few feet away, she noticed leaves moving on the ground. *I don't need this fuckin' shit!*

She ran back to the shed and slammed the rickety door.

"Fuck!" she exclaimed yet again.

Ruth's less than complex mind crapped out on further contemplations. Dread and terror left her winded. *We just need to get the fuck off this fuck-hole shit-bird island,* was about the most sophisticated assessment she could make of her situation.

And whatever had been outside rustling beneath the leaves . . .

Ruth didn't think about it.

The heat inside the shed wrung more sweat from her pores, which plipped like rain on the dry wood floor, leaving dots. *Fuck! You could cook pizzas in here!* Her marijuana hangover hindered her as she pulled her shorts and top back on. It was so hot she paused a moment and leaned against the wall.

And noticed that the spots her sweat had made on the floor—

Ruth stared.

—were moving.

She steadied herself, squinting.

Her vision shifted further: dehydration, fatigue, mental trauma, and now the oppressive heat all conglomerating. Was she seeing double?

More . . . spots seemed to be converging on the spots that her sweat had left. The more she stared, the more clear it became.

The spots were moving.

Fuckin' Jonas! He must've laced that pot with PCP or opium!

Ruth needed to know that; she needed an explanation that her mind could fathom. So she walked shakily to the middle of the floor, put her hands on her knees, and leaned over. She opened her eyes as wide as she could, and *focused*.

Some of the spots weren't drops of sweat. They were beetles or something—snot yellow with tiny red dots.

They encroached on the sweat drops, as if to drink. Then some of them began to inch toward Ruth's feet.

"Fuck this shit, man!" she declared and stumbled out of the shed.

The outside air revived her. Then, on her first stride toward the exit trail—

Flump!

Ruth fell flat on her face.

No profanity now could allay her frustration, no variations of her favorite transitive verb that began with the letter F. Instead, she sobbed loudly, pounding her small fists into the dirt. Dust from the ground stuck to her perspiry skin, smudged her cheeks, arms, and legs, while bits of leaves and other detritus hung in her blond hair. She looked like the Wild Woman of the Forest . . . save for the notion that the Wild Woman of the Forest probably wouldn't have breast implants or a cotton-candy-pink T-shirt that read YUCK FOO!

Ruth, in essence, was having perhaps the worst day of her life just now. For all she knew Jonas and Slydes had raped her in the woods last night and left the island without her. She felt nauseated, hungover, and—come to think of it—her . . . private regions hurt. She was hallucinating yellow bugs, and to top it all off, she'd just tripped and fallen flat on her face.

Finally, she cut loose and bellowed, "Fuck-fuck-fuck-fuck-fuck-fuck-*Fuck*!" at the top of her lungs.

The forest fell silent; the emotional release putting her a little more at ease. But an added confusion slapped her in the face when she looked to see what she'd tripped over . . .

A portable camping grill.

The grill lay tipped over, and several overcooked hamburgers lay in the dirt, being feasted on by ants.

A portable grill?

And at the corner of the shed sat a cooler quite different from the one Slydes kept on the boat. Ruth kneed her way over, opened it, and discovered several bottles of beer and wine coolers.

This stuff hasn't been here that long . . .

The last thing Ruth needed was another mystery, but the identity of whoever owned the cooler became immaterial in the next second, when something that could only have been a hand slammed down on the back of her head and grabbed her hair.

She shrieked like a smoke alarm. The unseen figure shoved her face in the dirt and sat on her back, pinning her, and whoever he was seemed agitated by the noise she was making because each time she shrieked, he smacked her head into the ground.

Ruth only screamed a few times.

Dizzy now, and her vision dim, she felt herself being dragged yet again away from the shed. She was perhaps half conscious, her brain screaming to rebel, but any genuine attempts to fight back were enfeebled by her daze.

She was dragged into the leaves and flipped over. The shots to the head kept her from focusing. Her shorts were ripped open and yanked off, and then her top was hauled up, her breasts pawed by a hot, humid hand that seemed intent on milking out all the saline.

Something remotely similar to a human voice splattered down into her face, uttering, "Shut up and lie still. It won't hurt much," or something like that.

When more of Ruth's vision cleared, she noticed that he'd dragged her back to where she'd been last night, her legs spread wide open to the deeper woods.

"Look," the voice gargled over her like someone with a rotten larynx. "There's more."

Before she could think, *More what?* Ruth looked down between her legs and saw—

The leaves . . . moving . . .

She remembered the rustling earlier, and she remembered seeing something moving beneath the leaves.

And whatever it had been began to come forth.

What Ruth saw vigorously wriggling forward was so revolting she nearly passed out altogether. Shock riveted her so completely that she was past screaming anymore.

Churning out of the leaves were several glistening, bright pink snakes, about the diameter of garden hose. No eyes could be discerned on the things, just that glaring, wet *pinkness*. The head of each one appeared to be tapered, even skull-less, with a small hole where the mouth should be.

They were *shivering* toward her, as if even in their blindness they sensed the presence of her body.

And they just kept coming, their tails never appearing from the underbrush.

Had she been less traumatized, she might have wondered how long they were, because right now they'd shivered out at least fifteen feet . . .

"Don't move," the phlegmatic voice ordered. "It won't take long. Just lie there and keep your legs spread."

This was not the situation where Ruth would be favorable to such a command. But her daze began to fade, and more of her strength returned. She began to flail in the dirt, and shove her heels at the grotesque pink things, but each time she did, her captor tightened the grip on her hair and thumped her head back to the ground.

Don't let the fucker knock you out! she managed to order herself. Because if she were unconscious, she knew damn well where those snakes were going.

Instead of kicking out this time, Ruth lunged up, grabbed her attacker's own hair, and pulled. He was strong, though; he didn't come down, she went up, and—

Her attacker gargled out a splattering scream.

Ruth bit a sizable chunk of upper cheek right out of his face.

The hand released her hair, and Ruth got up and ran, just as the first of the snakes would've entered her vagina.

The roar of objection splattered behind her—a hideous, barely human sound—as Ruth's feet shot her away into the trees. She spat the chunk of cheek out of her mouth like a chunk of hot chewing tobacco.

Get out, get out, get out!

She stopped only for a split second, and looked around to see who the man was who'd tried to feed her to the shivering pink things.

She screamed again—louder than she ever had—for her attacker was barely a man at all but more like an erect cadaver, with eyes like raw oysters and enslimed yellow skin flecked with bright red spots.

Holy fucking shit! she thought, running. *It's a fucking zombie . . .*

(II)

Robb White's former mind was barely functioning by now, taken over by mutagens expelled by the aggressive ovum that were now well insinuated throughout the island. These microscopic pieces of viral proteins—

common among many species of invertebrates—had intricately mutated his instincts and motor responses by infecting his central nervous system. In other words, most of what existed between Robb's ears was now mutated porridge.

He could still talk a little, and still think a little less, but everything else was essentially overridden. He'd lived much longer than the friends he'd brought here, but then he was good strong stock, a jock, a college athlete, a health and physical education major. How could he have ever imagined that all his health-mindedness would only lengthen his life as a human carrier for mutated worm ovum? The few synapses that still fired dragged back the dimmest etchings of memories. Their weekend party on this little island hadn't lasted long before the others began to disappear—

And reappear later, but not in the best of shape.

By the time he knew he had no choice but to get back to his skiff—and abandon his friends—it was too late. He'd already been duly infected by those little yellow beetles or ticks or whatever. He would retain enough sentience, though, to figure that the disgusting little things probably had some direct connection to the ten-foot-long pink worms that had started showing up too. Before his own infection, he watched one coil about the voluptuous body of his latest girlfriend and burrow its head down her throat.

Robb trudged on back toward the shed, not even consciously aware of his mission. Neither was he aware of the fact that his skin had mutated to an ill shade of yellow highlighted by brilliant red specks.

Every now and then, though, some cognizance did flare in his mush-brain and register appropriate thoughts, like: *Ugh! I'm royally fucked up!* and *My fucking father's gonna kill me if I don't get the skiff back in time!* and *Pretty decent set of tits on that trampy blonde*. And as for that trampy blonde, he'd promptly dragged her out of the shed to leave her closer to one of the nests. He hadn't been *consciously* aware of this; he'd simply done it because an instinct told him to.

But when he'd returned, she'd been trying to escape. Hence, his altercation, and, yes, after roughing her up and popping her in the head a few times, those acts of violence did seem to trigger some long-lost sexual reaction. But that was all for nothing now.

Robb's penis had rotted off his body a few days ago.

His yellow hand felt at the gouge she'd bitten out of his cheek. Something like pain registered . . . along with something like defeat.

A woman had beaten him. Robb, an all-star athlete and muscle rack, didn't care to be beaten by a woman at anything.

He stood shakily between two palm trees, staring at the woman's escape route with gray, runny eyes. Then he looked down at the tiny pair of cutoff shorts he'd pulled off her. *Shhhhhhhit!* his infected brain thought.

"Gonna find the bitch and really fuck her up," his phlegmatic voice rattled aloud. "I'll stuff the worms up her snatch myself if I have to."

(III)

The brisk snorkeling session livened her up. *I feel human again! I feel like a real, live polychaetologist in the field!*

Nora had wound up snorkeling for hours, actually, marveling at the scenery beneath the tepid, crystal-clear water. Flippers pumping, she glided through schools of pinfish, blue tang, and damsels. Fire sponge and fernlike sea rods branched up from clumps of orange and yellow coral. The languid water caressed her, cool and warm simultaneously, and the sunlight seemed to float above her like lightning-white lava. Sea horses frolicked among stalks of phallic club coral, and when Nora diverted her direction, a lustrous green and blue parrotfish turned briefly to show her teeth like a hand-ful of nails, then returned to eating algae off a rock. The fish was the size of a bed pillow.

Being right back in the face of nature rejuvenated her, reasserting her love for marine habitats. *Nothing up there is as beautiful as this,* she thought. *I'd proba-bly enjoy life a lot more if I were a friggin' fish . . .*

She let these underwater spectacles enrapture her; she got lost in all the variations of beauty. A sensation nearly erotic titillated her when a funnel of minnows shifted di-rectly into her; it gave her the impression that she'd just swum into a cloud made of glitter. When she checked her watch, she couldn't believe so much time had passed. *I came out here to catch lobsters,* she reminded herself.

Within fifteen minutes, her catch bag was full.

Back on the beach, she realized it would be getting dark soon. She trudged ashore with difficulty, dragging the bag, and hooked the cumbersome flippers to her belt. Out of the water, the lobster bag revealed its true weight: over ten pounds; the creatures flapped and rus-tled. A trail of water dripped behind her as she marched up the beach and entered the woods.

The bag dragged at her arm. She huffed down the trail, but as she neared the campsite, she thought she heard a hissing sound.

She stopped, squinted.

A gaze through some branches showed her the field shower. Nora's squint transformed to a frown. It was Annabelle in there, and the shower's ugly tarplike cur-tain was only halfway closed.

Exhibitionist floozy, Nora thought. *I'll bet a million bucks she left the curtain open on purpose.* Of course: She was hoping Trent or Loren might catch a glimpse of her body in the raw. *Wants to keep them whupped up*. Earlier, Trent had sprayed the shower down with some bug repellent, which would likely deter any more of the bizarre yellow ovum from venturing in.

Though she only glimpsed the other woman for a moment, Nora couldn't deny the pang of jealousy. Annabelle stood angled in the cramped stall, showing the curve of her buttocks and the edge of a breast. She turned slowly, almost as if aware of being watched, then stretched as the shower water pushed suds down her breasts and abdomen.

Nora silenced her thoughts and moved off. However, she hadn't walked far before she heard—

Snap!

She stood still, listening. Then came a quick scuffle: someone obviously dashing off through the woods.

Nora followed the sound, peered through trees. The sound disappeared as quickly as she'd detected it. At first she felt alarmed, but then realized her earlier assumption must be right. *Annabelle WANTED one of the men to see her body*. The escaping footfalls could only have been from Trent or Loren.

Probably Loren. That blonde tease has got him ALL twisted up. She held her gaze on the woods awhile longer, but saw no one running off. *Who cares?* she thought.

The lobsters stirred. *Better quit fooling around and get these in the cooler*. She stepped up her stride, got back on the trail, then winced and fell to a knee.

Damn it! That HURTS!

She'd stepped on something; her bare foot blared pain. *What the hell is that?*

She awkwardly crooked her leg around. Something metal on a string stuck out of the bottom of her foot. "Bastard!" Grimacing, she yanked it out as a small amount of blood dribbled from the tiny wound.

Her first notion was that it reminded her of a key on a pendant, as someone would wear around the neck. A straight, flat piece of metal on a looped cord, three inches long and an eighth of an inch wide. She wiped the blood off it, took a closer look. *Jewelry?* she considered. Some party kid could've dropped it. But why the string cord instead of a chain? When she rubbed her fingers against the tip, she felt ridges of some kind. Then she thought of keys again, something to unlock a security cable on a laptop.

Shit on it, she thought and stood back up. The damn thing had just been lying there in the trail, and she'd stepped on it. It didn't even look like it had been there long . . .

When she'd hobbled back to the campsite—bowed to one side by the lobster bag—she found Annabelle in a new bikini whose fabric was shockingly flesh-toned— sitting at one of the old picnic tables. Her hair was up in a towel now, and she was passively painting her fingernails. Trent sat across from her, scribbling in his army pad.

Nora huffed forward, her pierced foot throbbing. "Hey, Annabelle, could you give me a hand with this bag of lobsters?"

The blonde looked up and sighed. She displayed her shiny red nails. "Sorry, my nails are wet."

"Here," Trent offered. He took the bag and appraised it. "Wow, this is great. There must be two dozen lobsters in there."

"About that, and all still alive and kicking. But we've got to keep them cool before dinner."

Annabelle looked at the impressive bag but said nothing. She sat with her legs demurely crossed, and blew on her nails. "I'll stick them in the cooler I've got hooked up to the generator," Trent said and walked off.

"Ouch, ouch, ouch," Nora muttered when she hobbled the rest of the way to the table and sat down.

"Still aching from your sunburn?" Annabelle asked.

"No." Nora resisted the impulse to yell.

The blonde took a pleased glance at her own arms and legs. "I tanned great today. Not a trace of burn. Good genes, I suppose."

Which I guess means my genes are inferior. Nora couldn't believe the photographer hadn't burned while wearing only SPF 2. *Must be my karma.*

Annabelle beamed to herself. "I'll have the best tan when I get back to the Big Apple!"

Bully for you, you pompous bitch, Nora thought very calmly. She opened the waterproof first aid kit, extracting some antiseptic and a Band-Aid.

"Step on a thorn?"

"No. Some key or pendant or something." Nora put the stringed object on the table. "Somebody dropped it on the trail, and I stepped on it coming back from the beach."

Annabelle felt the ridges on the end. "Oh, this isn't a key and it certainly isn't a pendant. I'm pretty sure it's a jeweler's file. I used to date a jeweler, and he always had something like this around his neck, along with an eyepiece."

"A jeweler's file?" Trent asked, returning. He sat down with a bottle of water.

"Nora stepped on it." Annabelle passed it to him.

"Hmm." Trent turned it around in his fingers. "And you say you *stepped* on it, Professor?"

"Yes." Nora applied the Band-Aid to her foot, knowing it would probably fall off within an hour. "On the trail back from the beach. Do you have any idea what it is? I was thinking it must be some kind of key someone was wearing around their neck. Annabelle says it's a file."

Trent raised a brow. "Looks more like an old calibration tool for army PCR radios. There's a slot on the side you stick this in, to change channels." He gave it back to her. "You should get a tetanus shot when we get back to the mainland."

Nora got one every year, for her job. *A calibration tool,* she thought, looking at it. *Another boring mystery solved.*

"I'll bet some grunt with the missile team dropped that thing here twenty years ago," Trent said.

Twenty years ago? Nora wondered. The tool didn't even look tarnished.

She put it away and forgot about it. In truth, though, the object wasn't a calibration tool, nor was it a jeweler's file. Nora had been right in the first place. The object was—

CHAPTER ELEVEN

(I)

My key! the corporal thought in the worst kind of alarm. When he'd returned to the control center, he reached to his belt where the key's lanyard had been attached but—

It was gone.

I must've tied the damn thing on wrong! he realized.

This was not good. Especially considering the classified nature of this assignment, the key was considered a sensitive access device. The corporal sweated beneath his protective mask. *If one of those civilians gets hold of that key, they could get into the command center!* The corporal's career would be over. He'd be busted, written up, fined, and probably thrown in the stockade. The entire mission could be compromised . . .

He stood a minute to compose himself, and think. *Maybe . . . maybe no one will find out,* he thought. *I won't tell anyone I lost it until the assignment's over.*

The sarge is coming out on rounds in a minute anyway; I won't even need my key . . .

It was the only plan he could think of.

A minute later, the door did indeed open, and the sergeant emerged. "Why didn't you come inside?"

"I was just taking a last look around before shift change."

The sergeant didn't question the lie. "Well, come in here. I want you to see something."

The corporal entered and followed the sergeant to one of the old power rooms that they'd converted for their own use. They used several of the rooms to monitor growth rates on some of the hosts.

The one named Howie, the corporal saw behind the quarantine enclosure's protective screen. The kid's body was so bloated that he'd busted out of his shirt and shorts. He shuddered, pouring sweat.

"He's still alive, isn't he?"

The sergeant nodded, and pointed to the vital signs meter. "Yep. Hope the poor bastard isn't feeling anything, but . . ."

"But he probably is," the corporal said.

"Yeah."

The corporal didn't care.

"Looks like he's about to blow," said the major, coming in behind them.

The sergeant and the corporal both snapped to attention.

"Yes, sir," the sergeant said.

"At ease." The major peered through the glass, intent on the spectacle. "So far the transfections have been close to perfect. And the infection rates from the worms and ova alike are occurring in less than twenty-four hours." The major looked more pointedly at the subject. "Is this a single-ovum infection?"

"No, sir," the sergeant answered. "A multiple gestation. He was infected by several ova and three or four live worms."

"Are the recorders on?"

"Yes, sir."

"Should be any minute—"

As if on cue, Howie's body began to buck, his wet skin slapping on the floor. His arms and legs seemed to vibrate, and it looked like his eyes were going to jettison. Then—

His back arched upward; the convulsions trebled. Soon the bloated body began to deflate as Howie's mouth poured forth a slew of live, inch-long worms. More worms—hundreds of them—began to evacuate the colon . . .

"Beautiful," the major whispered. His eyes glimmered on the scene.

The sergeant and the corporal traded glances. *I'm about to puke,* the corporal thought, *and this guy thinks it's beautiful?*

Moments later, Howie lay dead in a pool of shivering pink worms. The worms were peppered with hundreds more immature yellow ova.

The major grinned. "Gentlemen, that's what I call positive reproductive success of a genetically hybridized species. I can't wait for the colonel to see this replay." He pressed his hand to the glass, musing. "Look at all of them, will you? All of that just from one single human host . . ."

The sergeant winked at the corporal.

"Decon the room," the major finally said. "I want all the worms dead."

"Yes, sir. Should we clean the room for another host?" the sergeant asked.

"Not necessary. With a success rate like this? We'll be leaving very soon."

"What about the one in the next room, sir? The female from the first group."

"Oh yes, the in vitro. Leave her to hang awhile, we'll take readings on her till the very last minute."

"Yes, sir."

"As you were," the major said and left the room.

"He's so happy, you'd think he just got laid," the corporal said when it was safe.

"That's an officer for you." The sergeant took a last look through the glass. Now the worms were massing over the host, to eat.

The sergeant pulled a lever and then the specimen room filled with orange-hued gas, a combination dehydrant-bacticide aerosol. "All in a day's work," he said.

Whatever you say, Sarge, the corporal thought.

(II)

"Christ, I feel like I just got run down by a semi rig," Jonas groaned. He dragged himself to the deck, a hand to his head. He squinted past the bow in disbelief. "You're shitting me! It's almost dark."

"No, shit, Sherlock," Slydes remarked from the captain's chair. "We both slept the whole day away."

Jonas scratched his straggly head. "Ain't that the damnedest thing . . . You sick?"

Slydes made a face. The old cabin cruiser creaked as it pitched slightly in the water. "I feel sicker than a shit-eatin' dog. Don't know what it could be."

"Me neither." Jonas steadied himself on a stanchion cable. His face was pale as cream. "I thought maybe the dope was too strong . . . but you didn't smoke none. And I've never been seasick in my life. Shit, man."

"How's Ruth? Is she sick, too?"

Jonas mouthed Ruth's name, then jerked his gaze around the deck. "Ain't she up here?"

"Hell no. I thought she been belowdecks with you all day."

"We . . . fuck! I can't remember! We smoked some of my weed last night at that old shack and got pretty fucked up. Then . . ." Jonas worked what little brainpower he had. "I came back to the boat but she passed out in the shack."

Slydes grimaced when he leaned up and looked at his watch. "Well, go find her and bring her back 'cause the tide's gonna start coming in soon."

Jonas looked to the darkening island and moaned. "Aw, man, I don't want to go lookin' for her. I feel like shit. Let's just say if she don't show up by high tide, we leave her."

Slydes spat over the side, grimacing at a taste in his mouth like when he was ten and his daddy made him eat some dirty cat litter for talking back to him. "You must've passed those college smarts out your ass the last time you took a shit, Jonas. If we leave her here, she'll get really pissed and turn our whole pot operation over to the cops once she finds her way back to the mainland. We can't leave her, you moron."

Jonas waved a bored hand. "No, but we can *kill* her. Maybe I'm just getting old, brother, but chicks are just too much hassle. She'll come back on her own before long. Then we'll take off, and when we're out to deep water, we'll just toss her over the side."

Slydes felt too lousy to do much calculating. "If we kill her, who's gonna clean the bathroom back at the house?"

Jonas rubbed his face, nodding. "Good point."

"So get off your skinny, pot-smokin' butt and go bring her back."

Jonas wearily climbed off the boat and staggered into the woods.

Slydes knew they would undoubtedly kill Ruth one of these days—probably on a gator troll: no evidence—but not just yet. *Not till I tag her a few more times,* he resolved. As the sky darkened, the island's noises rose. Slydes felt like throwing up again—the boat was rocking more now as the tide began to draw in—but he knew there was nothing left to upchuck. *Don't even feel like drinkin' beer,* he realized, and that meant he was *really* sick.

What'd I come down with?

Then he thought of those things.

Those squishy yellow bugs he'd found on himself last night. Slydes ground his teeth at the image. Had one of them bitten him, and passed him some germs?

Well, shit, goddamn . . .

A mild fever seemed to be seeping into him now; he was just nodding back off in the captain's chair when he heard . . .

Sobbing?

That's what it sounded like—like a woman coughing and crying at the same time. Slydes smirked.

Ruth's back, he knew.

Sure enough, just as the realization kindled, a sobbing and very distraught Ruth pulled herself up the side ladder.

"Where the hell you been, girl?" Slydes asked with feigned authority. "You been out in the woods all last night and all day?"

Her face looked drained, her hair a mess—that is, more of a mess than it usually was. She collapsed to the deck, then drew her knees up like a scared child. "It was awful, it was awful!" she hacked.

Slydes had no concern whatsoever as to what had

traumatized her. "You see Jonas? He just went out a few minutes ago lookin' for your sorry ass."

"I was almost raped, you asshole! And I was almost attacked by these big pink snakes!"

"Big pink elephants is more like it."

"Fuck you!" she belted out, tears streaming. "Didn't you hear me! I was almost raped!"

"Raped?"

"Yeah, fucker! I was almost raped by a yellow zombie!"

The good hard laugh which followed helped Slydes feel better. "Uh-huh. Yellow zombies and pink snakes."

"Twenty-foot-*long* snakes!" she added hysterically. She dragged herself up, her unknotted T-shirt swaying. Slydes eyed the large unbra'd breasts tossing beneath . . .

She seemed desperate, searching the deck. "Holy fuck, is there anything to drink on this tub?"

Slydes pointed a serious finger. "Watch what you call my boat, girl."

"I'm dying of thirst!" she bawled some more. "I was burning up in those fucking woods today."

"Why didn't you just come back to the boat?"

Her tense face glared at him. "I was hiding from the zombie!"

Slydes could only nod through another smile. "There's still a few beers downstairs—"

"I don't want beer, I want water!"

"Well, there ain't no water, unless you wanna drink the Gulf of Mexico."

She thumped belowdecks, then resurfaced, chugging half a beer in one pull. Her face blanched, she looked cross-eyed; then she threw up over the side. "Fuck!"

Slydes was not too sick to object. "Don't you be puking up perfectly good beer! I got a mind to bitch-slap you. What's wrong with you?"

"Shit, I'm sick . . ." Less than ladylike, she spat more

bile off the deck with a retching sound worthy of a longshoreman.

Sick, Slydes thought. He scratched his beard. "Did you find any bugs on you?"

Ruth snapped a glare. "Bugs?"

"Yeah, piss-yellow little things, with red spots. Like ticks or beetles, but soft."

"No!" she barked back. "I told you I got attacked by worms! Same color as that one that landed on my arm last night—only fuckin' *huge!*"

When she bent over the stanchion again, Slydes couldn't help but notice she wore nothing but the fluorescent-pink T-shirt. "Your bare ass is showin', girl. Where's your shorts?"

"That big guy ripped them off!"

"What big guy?"

She bellowed at the top of her lungs, "The zombie! The zombie that almost raped me! And I think he wanted the snakes to rape me too! He laid me out naked in the woods last night when I was passed out—"

Sooner or later the drugs burn your brain, Slydes thought. That's why he stuck to beer. *Jonas must've tricked up some of his reefer,* he deduced. "I'm tired of looking at your brown-eye. Go put some pants on."

She huddled back down. "I don't have any more! The zombie took them!" Then she cradled her stomach and began to rock.

A thought more serious snapped into Slydes's mind. A big guy. A big *zombie.* Slydes didn't believe in such tripe, but he did believe in drug-induced hallucinations.

What if this "zombie" of hers was a real person?

One of them photographers . . .

His tone grated with import. "Hey, girl. When you were out running around in the woods, did anyone see you?"

"The zombie saw me!" she continued to shriek.

"Yeah, yeah—the zombie—I know. But I mean anyone else, like maybe one of those photographers?"

She groaned, shaking her head back and forth. "Holy fuckin' shit—I feel bad . . ."

"Go belowdecks and get some sleep," Slydes told her. "You're all fucked up. Sleep it off. When Jonas gets back, we'll be going home."

"Oh, good, good," she continued to sob. "I just want to go fuckin' home . . ."

Breasts swaying beneath the T-shirt, she dragged herself up again, and thunked downstairs.

Crazier than a shit-house rat, Slydes thought. If she didn't have that dandy mouth with the lips all puffed up from that plastic surgeon she'd been shacked up with, Slydes knew he wouldn't be quite so quick about keeping her around.

He wondered if he was feeling a little better himself, then convinced himself he was. But something else nicked at the back of his mind, now that he thought of it. Just before Ruth had gone downstairs . . .

The chick was in good shape, he'd give her that. Those big implants sticking out like grapefruits and nary a trace of fat on her body.

Slydes scratched his beard again, perplexed as the sound of peepers rose from the woods.

Had it been his imagination, or was Ruth's belly starting to look a little swollen?

CHAPTER TWELVE

(I)

Campfire light shifted on their faces. Nora had dragged the pot off the coals to serve directly, and by now the four of them sat back in the sand, stuffed.

"That's the best lobster I've ever had in my life," Lieutenant Trent proclaimed. Empty shells formed a pile of bright red debris in front of him. "To hell with the C rations."

"Yeah, Nora, they really were good," Loren said, occluding a burp with his fist.

Nora felt stuffed herself. "Freshness is everything."

The only one not to compliment the night's cuisine was Annabelle. Still in her bikini, she sat in a lotus position finnicking with a plump tail. "How come these lobsters don't have claws?" she seemed to complain.

"These are spiny lobsters," Nora answered. "Ah, let's see—*Panulirus . . .*"

"Panulirus argus," Loren finished.

"Warm-watered species don't have claws. In fact, most of the world's commercially harvested lobsters are clawless. The meat's all in the tail."

Loren slipped a tube of white meat from his last lobster. "And *that's* what I call a piece of tail."

"Hilarious," Nora said. She'd also thrown some stone crabs and sunray clams into the pot, all of which were readily devoured.

"You think we could have this again tomorrow night, Professor?" Trent asked.

Annabelle, as might be expected, frowned.

Nora sighed at the weary title. "Sure, and please stop calling me Professor, okay?"

"Why? You earned it. Must've been a lot of hard work."

"Yeah," she admitted, "but it's just the word that bothers me. Professor. Every time I hear it, I think of that guy on *Gilligan's Island.* Just call me Nora."

Trent and Loren laughed.

"There's still one more." Nora indicated the pot. She tonged out the last of the crustaceans. "I'm too full to even look at it."

Annabelle grabbed the lobster. "I don't usually make a pig of myself, but . . ." She smiled, sitting erect in an obvious pose that highlighted her roll-free stomach. "I *live* on Atkins. No carbs, keeps me brimming with energy."

Keeps you brimming with pretentiousness, Nora interpreted. *Why don't you eat my shorts, too? They're low-carb.*

Loren and Trent were doing a bad job concealing their gaze at the blonde's body.

Jesus. Nora was just about to settle back in the sand when Annabelle screamed.

Trent and Loren went bug-eyed, and Nora lurched up as if stung. *What the hell's she screaming about?*

Annabelle had just broken the lobster open at the carapace, then flung it away in disgust. "Oh my God, that's so gross!"

"What?" Loren exclaimed, surging toward the blonde.

"Worms!" Annabelle shrieked.

Worms? Nora moved around the fire as Loren picked up the opened shell. She could see in the firelight—the lobster meat seemed pink and squirming.

Instead of disgust, Loren's face registered excitement. "Aha! Looks like we've got a decapod-targeting parasitic marine annelid."

Annabelle was shaking, she was so repelled. She looked like she was about to be sick in the fire. "It's a bunch of fucking *worms* in my lobster! Oh, Jesus— they look like dog-shit worms!"

There was an image Nora didn't need. Closer examination showed her a pack of the tiny worms churning within the red carapace.

"Most of them are dying," Loren noted.

"The cooking process," Nora said. But something bothered her. "But the worms closer to the center are still kicking. They don't look right for a nonsegmented parasite, do they?"

Loren agreed. "The hydroskeletons are all wrong. And they don't look like Polychaetes, either, or anything gastropoda."

Annabelle's beautifully suntanned face looked sapped of all color. When the silence settled, she looked dismayed at Loren and Nora as they continued to examine the nest of tiny parasites.

"I could've eaten those disgusting things," the blonde complained. "Are they poisonous?"

"No, no," Loren assured her.

"Then why are you looking at them like you just found the Holy Grail?"

Good question, Nora realized. "Because we've never

seen a parasitic marine worm like these, which is disturbing because . . ."

Loren finished the statement for her. "Because we're America's leading authorities on the subject. We've never even seen a marine worm body configuration like this—not a chitin-penetrating species."

"Chitin-penetrating?" Trent queried.

"The ability to penetrate a chitinous exoskeleton—an insect shell, or a lobster shell, in this case." Nora was transfixed. "Chitin penetrators that live in seawater are always segmented, yet these don't appear to be."

Loren continued with the late-night worm lesson. "Certain types of marine worm parasites attack crustaceans by disgorging a corrosive digestive enzyme onto the host's shell. The enzyme burns a hole through which the worm can either consume the innards of the host or inject eggs, or—" He and Nora looked at each other with raised brows.

"Or what?" Trent asked.

"Or inject fertilized ovum," Nora said. *Like the ova we found in the shower . . .*

"How can you even see them?" Annabelle asked next. "They're tiny."

"You're right," Loren said. He stood up with the lobster, and Nora got up right next to him.

"Which is why we're going to go look at these under the microscope." Transfixed now, she and Loren stalked away to their field lab.

The fire crackled. Trent smiled and slipped his arm around Annabelle. "How do you like that? All of a sudden you and I have this cozy campfire to ourselves."

The grotesquery of the parasites she'd nearly eaten vanished. She grabbed Trent's hand and urged him up. "I'm not interested in romance, Lieutenant. While those too nerds are looking at their worms, you and I are going to find a place to fuck."

Trent followed Annabelle—and the rest of his good fortune—down another trail.

The fire crackled some more, painting the trees and surrounding brush with lines of light that squirmed, almost like worms.

(II)

"They're resilient, that's for sure," Loren said, gunning up his microscope. "The cooking process didn't kill them all, and this lobster looks pretty well cooked."

The fact didn't impress Nora much. "There are worms that live in underwater thermal vents that survive at hundreds of degrees. I just want to find out what these damn things are."

Neither of them said anything at first. Nora adjusted the comparator microscope, while Loren sat at the table beside her, changing stages on a smaller scope. Each had placed several of the tiny pink worms under their lenses. "I'm seeing something else immersed in the fluidity between each worm."

"Me too," Nora admitted. "Could it be mesenteric debris from the lobster?"

"Lobsters don't have mesentery. They have semisolid blood-processing organs that are green. This carrier fluid's clear. And there are specks in the fluid. You got those on yours or am I seeing things?"

"You're not seeing things," Nora said. "The specks are off-yellow."

"Just like those ova we saw in the shower stall."

It was difficult for Nora to frame words, but she knew Loren was thinking along the same lines. "The shower ova were the size of jelly beans and these are so small they're practically microscopic. You and I both know the size differentiation means that these specks came from a completely different species."

"A worm ovum this small couldn't grow to the size of a jelly bean. Now, correct me if I'm wrong, but didn't the shower ova have red spots on their sheaths?"

"Yes," Nora grimly replied. "And I'm sure you just did the same thing I did, Loren, and upped your magnification."

"There are red spots on these too."

"Which means that these and the shower ovum *did* come from the same species of worm—"

"A conclusion that's zoologically impossible," Loren finished.

Nora sighed at the table. *One thing at a time. We've got some chitin-penetrating worms that are fluxed with some accessory debris that looks like motile ova.* "Let's focus on the worms," she ordered.

The microscope's light stage showed Nora another world, a circular world of brilliant colors, vibrant details, and stunning light. She had several of the worms on her slide; each one, if extended, might stretch a quarter of the perimeter's border.

The worms shimmered, squirming with vigor. Their fresh pink bodies glistened like squiggles of some bizarre molten metal.

"No segmentation," Loren said.

"And no striations on the skin, either. No plating, so we know it can't be a gastropod or anything from the molluska line. It almost looks like a shipworm—"

"But shipworms are really clams in tubular casings, and this . . . ain't that," Loren added to her observations.

Nora sat back in her chair and rubbed her eyes. "Conclusions? Hypotheses?"

"Either we're not as smart as we thought," Loren said, "or we've stumbled on an undiscovered species of parasite."

"Um-hmm, and if this were a channel in Antarctica, that would be a reasonable deduction. But in the Gulf of Mexico, North America's nucleus of warm-water marine biology?"

"The chances of this particular research community missing *this* is impossible."

Finally they'd both given voice to the gravity of the dilemma. "I wish these worms were a little bigger. Then we could dissect one even with these small scopes," Nora said.

"This will have to do." Loren cast his boss an odd look. "Both of us should be really jazzed about this. How come we're not?"

"Because it's too fucked up," she didn't hesitate to profane. "Us not knowing what this worm is would be like a military history professor not knowing the date of the Battle of Hastings."

"October fourteen, 1066," Loren said. "The English were winning the battle until their king, Harold the First, caught a flaming arrow in the face."

"Oh, Loren. You really are a hopeless nerd."

"I know, but your point is well taken. These worms are big-time super-duper screwed up. They shouldn't even be in an environment like this. They look like land-dwelling worms, but we know they're marine because they attacked a lobster. And that means their motile ova are water-dwelling, too, but we found a much larger version of the same ova in the shower and on Trent's shirt—hundreds of yards away from the closest seawater. Which means they're obviously land dwellers."

Nora sprang up in her seat. "Wait a minute. We took samples of the shower ova, didn't we?"

"Yeah. I vialed a bunch of them up."

"Let's compare them directly to the ova from the lobster."

"Why didn't I think of that?"

"Because I'm the boss."

They both hustled to one of the other tables where they'd placed their specimens. The small plastic saltwater tanks Loren had hooked up for the scarlet bristleworms bubbled away from their air pumps. Loren's hand eagerly reached for the vials he put the ovum in, but—

"What the hell!"

Nora stared.

The small vials were all empty.

Loren held several up to the overhead lights. "They're burned through at the bottoms. It's like the ova melted the plastic and got out."

"There's a few of them there." Nora pointed.

Several of the grotesque yellow nodes were inching up the wall. "The ova must possess the same corrosive enzymes of the worms that bred them."

"Chitin-penetrating *and* plastic-penetrating," Loren remarked. His mouth fell open when he turned his head. "Hey, Nora . . ."

"What?"

"Look at the tanks."

Nora lowered her face to the pair of mini aquariums. "Holy shit!" she yelled. "They've infected the bristleworms!"

In the farthest tank, all of the scarlet bristleworms had at least one yellow ovum attached to their bodies. The worms themselves shuddered. But events had progressed further in the closer tank.

Several ova lay dead on the tank's floor. But the bristleworms they'd attacked seemed to throb, and were bloated from within. The worms were still alive but barely moving. Then one of them—

"Unbelievable!" Loren exclaimed.

The bristleworm began to disgorge a slew of much tinier worms.

Within a few minutes, the other bristleworms in the tank did the same, until the water was tinted pink with so many tiny worms.

Nora was flabbergasted.

"Like the Tessae worms in central Africa," Loren murmured. "And the—"

"And some of the Trichinella family. Our little pink parasite has the ability to attack a different annelid species with free-ranging ovum and force it to bear its young."

But the revelations didn't stop there. Nora and Loren squinted harder as the minuscule newborn worms began to slither en masse up the face of the tank. Eventually they were twitching out over the side.

"I'm starting to get a little freaked," Loren said in a low drone. "They're coming *out* of the friggin' water, Nora."

"Just wait a minute. It won't take them long to die. They have to suffocate . . ."

They waited for another minute, then another.

"Jesus . . ."

Ten minutes later, the newborn worms hadn't died. They were all out of the tank and moving across the table.

"Well, how many impossibilities can we take for one day?"

"A marine worm with air-breathing capabilities," Nora said very slowly. "Every worm in the world that can do this has been exhaustively catalogued." Her face felt hot in aggravation. "There's no way—no *fucking way in the world*—that an annelid like this could remain uncatalogued."

"No fucking way in the world, huh?" Loren directed his displeasure in the obvious direction of the mass of worms. They were moving *toward* them on the table.

And the bean-sized ova that had crawled up the wall, too, had changed direction now, once Loren and Nora had come over to the table.

"They're *detecting* our presence," Loren said.

"Fibrotic sensory pores," Nora guessed. "They're reading the carbon dioxide we exhale—which triggers their instinct ganglia that a potential host is near."

"Uh-huh, and I don't want to find out what happens if one of those little things gets on me."

Nora sloughed that one off. "If one of them got into your bloodstream, your immune system would kill it."

"Yeah? I'm not going to wait for my immune system to do the job." Loren picked up a can of mosquito spray. Nora was about to object—they were *specimens*— but . . .

Not a bad idea, she recanted. The chlordane and diethyl-meta groups in the repellent would kill the worms just as it had killed the ova in the shower stall. The just-hatched worms on the table were so tiny yet so abundant that they looked more like spilled pink lemonade—lemonade that moved of its own instincts.

Loren smirked as he sprayed down the table and wall. He sprayed more directly into the tanks.

In a few moments, the ova on the wall dropped off dead, and the worms shriveled and died.

"So much for them," Loren said.

"Loren the Worm Killer. But we're going to have to preserve some of these and take them to Florida Natural Resources. I guarantee you, they don't know about this. Chitin-penetrating parasites like these? That reproduce this actively and can attack multiple hosts? If these things broke out, they could decimate the gulf's crustacean harvest."

"Well, at least only one lobster was infected," Loren noted, calmed down now. "This could be a fluke infection, you know."

Could be, Nora thought. *Maybe it was a lucky hit on the part of the worm. But if they wiped out these bristleworms that easily, it could wipe out an entire food chain.*

Loren had used the lab's forceps to place one of the dead shower ovum under his microscope. "These are the same, Nora. Just a lot bigger."

Nora had figured as much. The hunch wouldn't let go. She took Loren's slide and placed it under her own dual-lensed scope, to properly compare the dead ova against the smaller ones mixed with the worms from the lobster. When she switched on both fields . . .

"Oh my God."

"What?"

"See for yourself," Nora said.

Loren looked in the comparator scope. He only looked for a second before he lifted his eyes away.

"Oh my God is an understatement," he said.

Nora had seen it first, and wanted clarification.

The tiny worms from the lobster weren't so tiny anymore. They filled the entire space of the slide's viewing perimeter now, and the ova in their proximity could now easily be detailed.

Loren stood erect, dumbfounded. Confusion made his eyes looked glazed. "This can't be."

"Tell me about it," Nora said. "Those things are ten times bigger than they were twenty minutes ago."

Loren nudged her back to the microscope. "Look back in there," he said, a little jittery now. "Keep your eye on them for a full minute, then tell me your observations."

Nora did so.

She knew what he was driving at in significantly less than a minute.

She could actually see the worms and ova growing before her eyes.

CHAPTER THIRTEEN

(I)

"What do you make of it, Sergeant?" the colonel asked, having made a rare appearance from his makeshift field office. The sergeant had logged the observed activity at the old head shack, believing it to be "atypical."

We must be getting ready to leave, the sergeant pondered. *Why's he so interested in a bunch of civilians all of a sudden?*

The corporal was manning the monitor controls, zooming the military's very best lenses, but he seemed more fixed on the slender woman with frizzed hair. *Have to get that kid's mind out of the garbage,* the sergeant thought.

"Look at that," the colonel said. The image on-screen lurched forward from the zoom: a closer shot of the slender woman in the dark one-piece swimsuit. She was leaning over a computer now, typing something.

The colonel added, "I don't like it. It looks like she's recording data. Data on what?"

The sergeant stepped closer. "I'm not sure, sir. As I noted in my log, the civilian activity in that building seemed harmless. But I could be mistaken."

"It looks like they're keeping specimens of some kind in there."

"That wasn't the case earlier, sir."

The colonel faced the sergeant directly. "In your estimation, is there any way the civilians know we're here?"

"In my estimation, sir—no."

"What about you, Corporal?"

"No signs of detection, sir."

"The only civilian who ever saw me was in the second arrival group . . . and he's dead. That's verified and recorded. The fourth group's craft has been disabled. In fact, every civilian to come on the island is now infected, this third group being the only exception. What they're doing seems routine and unalarmed. I think it's some kind of nature excursion—the blond woman appears to be a photographer."

The colonel thought on it, then watched the screen some more. "You're always right, Sergeant, and I'm not disputing your assessment. But I still need to know what they're up to. I need you two men to make another trip outside and guarantee me that what they're doing won't compromise our tests."

"Yes, sir," the sergeant said.

"Good, then do it. Do it tonight."

The colonel's boots snapped as he left the room.

The corporal looked up when the door closed. "I wonder what's up his ass."

"He's bucking for general, and he'll probably get it if this mission yields positive results. That guy's been doing these field jaunts for years—it racks up promotion points. He's not going to let anything screw this up."

The corporal rolled back in the chair, put his feet up on the old desk that was once used by missile-control officers. "The hybrids are duplicating better than we ever expected. We already know that they don't hesitate to attack human hosts. The worms and the ova alike have already proved that they can live in multiple environments. Why can't we just go home now?"

"Because the brass says so, and you can bitch about it all you want, but it won't do any good." The sergeant laughed and slapped the corporal's back. "Just think of all that extra-duty pay you'll get."

Fuck that, the corporal thought. *I want to get laid.* He'd been in the military long enough to know that whenever you thought sure a mission was about to end . . . you could slap on another week or even a month.

"I'm going to go finish my shift log," the sergeant said. "In the meantime, keep an eye on the civilians." He pointed to the screen. "Let me know when they lock that place up for the night. That's when we go back out."

"Sure thing, Sarge."

The corporal switched to another camera once the sergeant left. Now he had the low-light on and was watching the blonde.

That's more like it.

The blonde was already naked, and sprawled out on the beach. When she climbed on top of the guy, her back arched, which couldn't have displayed her breasts more perfectly in the moonlight.

But the corporal knew that looking would suffice for only so long.

One thing I know for sure, he told himself, *before we leave this island, I'm going to bang that blonde . . .*

(II)

That wasn't bad, Annabelle thought in the so-called afterglow. *Out here I have to take what I can get.* She wasn't used to that—not with her looks and her social status back in New York. Young power players were more her speed—and Trent was neither of those—but he did have an aggressive way about him. He was perfunctory and direct, no frills, all business. If she viewed the island photo shoot as an adventure, she'd feel more content.

Cool gulf breezes diced up the night's blanket of heat. They both lay naked and sweating right up at the wood line, their clothes flung this way and that before them. Soft waves fell twenty yards beyond—the tide was coming up—and the beach sand looked bizarre in the subdued moonlight, like cold smoky glitter.

Trent looked haggard in the same light. *I'm wearing him out,* Annabelle thought with an inner giggle. She reached into her beach bag and pulled out a flask.

"Holding out on me, huh?" he said.

"I wouldn't call what we just spent the last hour doing 'holding out.'" She took a long sip—dark rum— and smiled. The sudden swell of heat in her belly made her think of a penis going from soft to hard in the channel of her sex. *I'm a dirty girl tonight,* she joked in thought. *Can't get my mind off anything but sex.* It was the hot night, she knew, and this exotic environ and its circumstances: stuck on an island with no way off, and only two men in her midst, both lusting for her faultless physique. The notion lit primal fuses in her psyche, unleashing the bitchy, antsy, slut-in-heat disposition. She knew she shouldn't be drinking—it only laxed her inhibitions more—but the moment seemed to warrant it. She passed Trent the flask, deliberately brushing his shoulder with a hot breast.

He drank gratefully, and sputtered a satisfaction. "This busywork assignment has turned out to be a great time."

"Yeah, and we're both getting paid."

"But I don't think I'll be writing this part down in the report to my CO. Drinking rum on a moonlit beach at midnight, with a foxy blonde. No, that wouldn't wash."

Just foxy? She took exception. *I'm a hell of a lot more than that and you know it. Don't get cocky.* She stretched out. A couple of hits of rum right after sex was an ideal tranquilizer. Trent lay angled away from her; she could see him gazing out at the surf, his middle-aged desires clearly sated. A younger, more acceptable man would be on top of her again. She had that way with men—to make them want more than they could handle. She reveled in the impression of herself.

"Can't believe you're not married," Trent muttered.

"That's so proverbial," she teased. "You can't do better than that?"

"Yeah," he admitted, "but I'm too tired right now—thanks to you."

"My pleasure."

"No serious boyfriend back in New York?"

"Nope," she lied through her teeth. She'd been stringing along the same fiancé for a year. A successful stockbroker, whose family owned one of Wall Street's biggest brokerages. He was great for jewelry and the Porsche, of course, and she supposed she really would marry him someday. It would be worth her while. And he was so busy with his job, he didn't have time to monitor her. She cheated on him with impunity, any time the magazine sent her on a shoot. As long as she kept her infidelity out of the city, she could have the best of both worlds.

She caressed her breasts when she knew he wasn't looking.

"Yeah, well, I think I'll be visiting you in the Big Apple sometime soon," he asserted.

In your dreams! Now he was annoying her, the way he wielded his personality the same way he had sex: with assertiveness. *I'm the one doing YOU a favor,* she wished she could say aloud, *and it's only because Loren is LESS my type than you.* "We'll see," she said instead. She wanted to keep his fire fanned. Then she added, "If you're a good boy."

"Oh yeah?"

She stretched her toes out as far as she could, flexed her long legs. She let her mind wander.

She imagined herself being taken right here on the beach, not by Trent nor her fiancé but by a coterie of men from her past. Her nerve-charged body, her spread-open legs and narrowed eyes summoned them, and then they were lying atop her, thrusting into her fast and rough, one after another. The fantasy titillated her as the sea breeze slipped up and over her bare skin. . . .

"Be right back, gotta take a leak," Trent said and got up.

Charming, she thought, but now that he'd left, she could focus on the greedy invention of her mind. Hot, muscled bodies squashed her, callused hands mauled her breasts. Raving sensations pinpointed at her nipples, which were either torqued by fingertips or sucked out by fervid mouths. Stout penises delved into her most private places, spending themselves in a fever-pitch only to be replaced by more. Back in reality her own hands succored herself . . .

Mmmm . . .

"Hey, Annabelle! You got a flashlight?"

Trent's voice shattered her pleasures. *That asshole,* she thought, disgusted. *Can't even have a minute of fun with myself.* She leaned up with a frown. A flashlight? *What's he want that for? He needs to SEE where he's pissing?* "I think so!" she griped back.

"Bring it here, will you? I need to see what this is."

Probably means his cock . . . She pulled the light out of the bag and got up, followed the annoying voice to the edge of the woods.

There he was.

The moonlight painted his naked body. He was leaning over, looking at a tree. Annabelle's smirk couldn't have been more severe, her senses still buzzing from her self-stimulation. "Here," she said testily.

He pointed the beam on a tree trunk, lighting it up. "There. See?" His finger indicated a nub of some kind. "Definitely not part of the tree. I scratched my damn leg on it."

Poor you . . . Annabelle looked closer. "It's a nail. So what?"

"I don't think it's a nail . . ." It looked more like a black stud. "It's coming loose," he said, yanking on it with his fingers. "It's working free."

Annabelle shook her head, hands on bare hips. "Is there a reason I'm supposed to care about this?"

"It's got—" He squinted harder, the image ridiculous now: a hairy-backed man fiddling with a tree in the middle of the night, buck-naked. "Remember what Nora was saying earlier?"

"That skinny wuss?"

"She said she found something that reminded her of a camera lens attached to a tree." Finally he prized it loose. "It's almost like it was *nailed* into the tree."

"A camera that small?" Annabelle objected. "That's ridiculous."

He held it right up to the flashlight, the splayed beam throwing wedges of dark and light against Annabelle's bosom, belly . . . and frown. "She was right. It's got a tiny piece of polished glass inserted in the top, like a lens."

"Read my lips. Who cares?"

He seemed amazed by the find. "I guess I was right. It's an electric eye sensor from the old missile site probably. They left these things in the perimeter because it was easier than removing them all. They're probably all over the place."

"Read my lips. I'm *bored.*"

"Oh, sorry." He caught himself. "It's just kind of interesting, isn't it?"

"How about . . . *no?*"

"I'll have to show it to Nora, see if it's the same thing she was talking about."

The comment made her fume. As far as Trent went, she could take him or leave him. The man was just a sideline distraction because there was nothing better around. But he was still part of her sexual turf and there was no way she'd allow him to be in proximity to that bitch.

"We can show it to her tomorrow," she said, emphasizing the pronoun "we."

They moved through moonlight back to the beach; Trent placed the object in his bag. "Well, you're bored, so I guess that means you want to get back to the camp," he presumed, and reached for his pants.

"Not *that* bored."

"Oh, okay. Let's lie out here while longer," he said. He got back down on his towel.

What a moron. "I'm not done yet," she said bluntly.

"Not done with what?"

She stepped over him, looking down. "With you," she said, and sat on his face.

CHAPTER FOURTEEN

(I)

When Slydes awoke, he felt akin to a reanimated corpse rising from a lime pit. *Mooooooooother-FUCKER!* he thought. Had someone hit him in the head last night? Had he fallen down? But when he awoke, he remained in the captain's chair behind the wheel, where he usually took his downtime on the boat.

Ruth's tousled head emerged from belowdecks. She looked cross-eyed and dehydrated—about the same way Slydes felt just now. "When are we leaving?" her shrill voice inquired. "Isn't it high tide yet?"

Bonehead, Slydes thought. "We missed it by ten hours," he gruffed. His watch told him it was seven in the morning. *We fucked up again . . .* "What the fuck is wrong with us!"

"I don't feel good, Slydes!"

Them bugs, he remembered. *They MUST have bit me.* "We all must have got some jungle fever or something. We keep passin' out." He tried to roust himself. "I'm gonna try to get us out of here in low tide. Shag Jonas's ass and get him up here."

"Jonas ain't down there!" she railed. "You said he went looking for me last night!"

Ruth's whining voice was killing him. "He never came back? That goddamn pain in the ass!"

"Where do you think he went?"

"You know damn well where he went! Probably went back for more dope, the shithead! We never should have come out here in the first place. This is his fault." The solution was simple; they needed to bring him back so they could leave. But he was still out in the woods, and the woods were where they'd picked up those gross-ass yellow bugs.

Slydes eyed up Ruth. "Go to the head shack and bring him back."

Ruth's face screwed up at the suggestion. "Fuuuuuuuuck you, motherfucker! I ain't going back in those woods by myself! I told you! There's a zombie out there that pulled my pants off and tried to rape me! And he tried to feed me to those giant pink snakes!"

Here she goes with the zombie again. There's nothing like a drug burnout to make a fucked-up situation MORE fucked up. He took the keys out of the boat's ignition. Did he trust Ruth?

Hell no.

"I'll go find him, you stay here," he ordered.

"I don't want to stay on this creepy boat by myself!"

"Quit whining! You sound like a fuckin' dog toy. Nighttime's one thing, but this is broad daylight. You and I both can't be thrashing around in the woods, not with them photographers up and about."

Ruth crossed her arms. "If you go, I go."

"Yeah?"

"Yeah."

Slydes punched her right in the forehead. She fell to the bottom of the short steps, out cold. *Best way to win an argument with a gal,* he thought.

Slydes stepped off the deck ladder into the water, and waded toward the island.

(II)

Nora thought back to her old lit classes as she meandered through the woods at just past dawn, Henry David Thoreau and all that. Being alone amid this plush wilderness—just as the new day began to arrive—put one in a sedate frame of mind. The beauty shimmered around her; it seemed to invite her to venture deeper, that and her curious solitude.

It feels damn good to be away from everyone else for a little while, she admitted, and she knew it was more than just escaping the envious angst that Annabelle incited. It let her free her mind, and now, for these cherished moments, she delighted in the luxury of thinking about nothing at all.

She roved deeper, down trails she hadn't been aware of. The pink light of the sunrise shot bolts down through dense branches. All that spiced the silence were chirping birds.

She wasn't sure why she'd risen early. She'd woken to obscure dreams and a headache. The other tents remained zipped up, so she sprayed herself down with some repellent and quietly wandered off, if only to take a look at more of the island.

I better be careful I don't get lost, she considered. The tropical forest grew more dense as the next trail continued. She supposed she was looking for more signs of the worms and ova she and Loren had stumbled on last night. Soon the dilemma ruptured her mood.

I'm getting paranoid, she realized. Everything she

knew about worms that produced motile ova insisted that they were harmless to humans—so what was she afraid of? But—

A bienvironmental species? A worm as well as its ova that can function on land? And the worm itself did resemble certain worms from the Trichina and Trichinella families, and some of those could *definitely* infect humans . . .

Be realistic! she finally commanded herself. *I'm an expert, and my professional inclinations are that these things are no more dangerous to humans than ladybugs.*

The determination made sense, yet the back of her mind wouldn't let go of the creepiness.

Her next step was snagged—something on the ground. *Vine,* she thought at first. She looked down to see what had caught the front of her flip-flop.

Not a vine, a cable.

She detached her foot and knelt. A black cable—an inch thick—stretched across the overgrown trail. *What's this doing in the middle of the woods?* she thought. *It's a power cable.*

Nora followed the cable back toward the camp and head shack areas, and didn't go more than a hundred or so yards before it terminated and split. One end branched to a conical voltage regulator that provided the lights and electricity to the head shacks. The other end veered directly into a tin shed that contained two bulky machines. Stenciled spray-paint letters identified one: FIELD PURIFICATION UNIT, WATER, PROPERTY OF U.S. ARMY. A series of hoses ringed through the second machine, and most of the joints and connections on the hoses were streaked with white crust. *Salt,* she knew at once. *This must be the desalinator Trent was talking about.*

Then she turned around and followed the black power cable back, where it would undoubtedly terminate at the portable generator that Trent had also mentioned on the day they'd arrived.

She followed several hundred yards farther, expecting at any moment to hear the chugging sound of the generator.

She walked on and on . . . and didn't hear a sound.

Finally the cable ended at a fat metal connection ring set into a square of concrete. *The generator's underground?* she thought. But she knew better. *That can't be . . .*

Something white could be seen behind some leafy branches. She pushed back a bough and found a metal sign on a post. The sign was white with red borders, and it read KEEP AWAY! RADIOACTIVE MATERIAL IN USE!

Nora ran back to the campsite. She didn't hesitate to open Trent's tent and stick her head in. "Hey! Lieutenant!"

Trent's head rose groggily in the lightweight sleeping bag. "Huh?"

"Is there a hot radioactive source on this island?"

The question slapped him out of sleep. "What the—" Then his face drooped. "You found the . . ."

"Yeah! Is it live?"

"Wait for me while I get dressed."

He knows all about it, Nora felt sure. *And he lied. He specifically told us that the generator ran on diesel fuel.* A minute later, Trent came out, dressed in crumpled fatigues.

"There's no *diesel* generator on this island, is there?" Nora demanded.

"Well, uh, no."

"Then how come you told us there was? You've got an RTG in the ground out there, don't you?"

"Keep your voice down," he said, glancing at the other tents. "Over here."

He took her out of the campsite and down the trail

to the field shower area. "Now I can talk," he said. "I'm not supposed to let any civilians know about it. You know what an RTG is?"

"Yeah," Nora said testily. "Radioisotope thermal generator. I have a lot of friends who've seen them on Arctic specimen expeditions, and the government puts them up in the mountains, too, to provide power to remote observation posts. It's a nuclear battery."

"Exactly, and you're right, the government uses them all the time, in places where there's no practical way to deliver fuel to run gas and diesel generators. A small radioactive pellet produces heat that's changed into electricity through a thermocoupler. Same sort of thing NASA puts on satellites, Mars probes, things like that. It's a battery that lasts a hundred years." Trent sat down on one of the old picnic tables, rubbed sleep out of his face. He looked worn out. "Since I had to escort civilians to the island, my orders were to lie about the power source. No one knows about the RTG and there was no reason to think it might be discovered—it's all the way on the other side of the island." He looked right at her. "What the hell were you doing that far into the woods?"

"I was going for a nature walk," Nora said, and she didn't feel the need to apologize.

"Great. Now you'll have to be debriefed when we leave—big pain in the ass."

"Debriefed?"

"The location of the RTG is classified. You'll have to be interviewed in Jacksonville by the Army Security Agency and sign a National Secrets Act nondisclosure form."

Nora felt outraged. "That's ridiculous!"

"Hey, you're the one who had to go on a nature walk."

My God, she thought, frowning. "So that thing was installed for the missile site?"

"Right. It provided all the needed electricity for the control station and the launch circuitry."

"How come it wasn't removed when the missiles were dismantled?"

Trent smiled and shook his head. "The RTG itself is only the size of a lunch box . . . but it's seated in a thousand-pound shielding box, and then they embedded the box in fifteen tons of steel-reinforced concrete."

"Too big to move."

"Yeah, but if no one knows it's there, it's not a security risk." He rubbed his eyes again, aggravated. "Now someone *does* know where it is. You."

"Well, I'm certainly not going to tell anyone about it."

"Good, because if you do, you can get five years in jail and a quarter-million-dollar fine. In this day and age, can you imagine the uproar if the public found out there was an RTG on an island two miles off the coast of Florida? Every nut job and wannabe terrorist would come out here trying to dig it up. You know, the psychological element. Theoretically, if you took the uranium out of that RTG core—someone could make a dirty nuke. So mum's the word here. If Annabelle mentions in her bristleworm article that there's a friggin' nuclear battery on Pritchard's Key, I turn into a buck private real fast. My whole career will be in the toilet."

Now Nora got the gist. RTGs were safe alternate power sources whose fuel was inaccessible, but in today's climate of terrorism, dirty bombs, and overall radiological paranoia, public knowledge of their whereabouts provided a huge security breech.

"All right, now I get it," she said. "And of course I won't tell anyone. So we can skip the debriefing part, okay?"

"*Not* okay. I'd lose my job."

Nora grimaced. "You really are by the book, aren't you?"

"Pretty much. That's the way it's got to be. Next time you go on a nature walk—*don't* go. Most of this island's unexcavated. There's quicksand, sinkholes, all kinds of trouble. Please. Stick to the safe areas. And I couldn't repeat it enough: *Don't* tell Annabelle or Loren about the RTG. And once you're back on the mainland, don't tell anyone else. Ever. The military's really paranoid about this stuff. You'll have your phones tapped, your mail swiped, all your data sucked out of your computers, oh, and the IRS. And all because you know about a little piece of radioactive material that's smaller than a BB."

Nora looked bug-eyed at him. "Lieutenant, trust me, I'll sew my mouth shut."

"Good, 'cause this is no joke."

Damn. The riot act, Nora thought. *Can I help it I decided to go for a friggin' walk?* There were better ways to start a day.

"Oh, I forgot to tell you," Trent said next, the sour topic finally closed. "Remember when you mentioned you found something like a tiny camera in the woods?"

"Yeah, it was stuck into a tree, almost like a nail."

"I found one too, last night. I'll show it to you later. It's in my tent somewhere."

"You said it might be an electric eye, right?"

"Yeah, and I still think that's what the things are."

Old electric eyes from an old missile installation, she thought. *What could be duller? But the RTG?* That and last night's surprise discovery: the tiny pink worms and ova that seemed to grow at an extraordinary rate. She'd love to get a look at one of the worms under a lab-grade microscope. *The ones we found in the lobster were too small for these little field scopes.*

At least it would give her something to do while Annabelle and Loren continued to search for more scarlet bristleworms.

She was just then reminded of something that had slipped her mind. "Damn, I forgot. You left the lights on in the last two head shacks."

He looked at her funny. "You mean the one you and Loren are using?"

"No, the buildings on the other end. I saw light leaking out from the roofs the other night." She chuckled to herself when she realized how little it mattered now. "On the other hand, I guess the army's not worried about wasting electricity. The power from the RTG is unlimited and free."

"That's true, but there still shouldn't be any lights on. In fact, no one *could* have turned them on. I only have the key for the head shack you're using. The other head shacks are locked up and I couldn't get in them if I wanted to. The rest of the keys are back at my post's property room. I better check it out anyway. I can't see the army sending anyone else out here, not without me knowing. I'm the only one who ever checks this island."

"The only one that you know of," Nora posed.

"Well, yeah, but it wouldn't make sense. As far as the army's concerned, this is dead property."

Not quite, Nora elected not to say. *Not with a nuclear battery buried in the ground.*

In an instant, Trent's eyes lit up as he looked past Nora. "There she is," he announced. "You're up early."

"So are you," Annabelle replied. Wrapped only in a towel, she frowned at Nora. "What are you two doing sitting there?"

Discussing the mini nuclear reactor that's hidden in the woods, Nora thought. *Why don't you go sit on it for a few days?*

"Nora was just telling me about scarlet bristleworms," Trent lied. "They're remarkable creatures."

"Um-hmm. Remarkable." Annabelle strode for the field shower. "If you're that interested, you could snorkel with Loren and me later, when I go out to do the rest of the shoot."

"I just might do that," Trent said.

Annabelle was clearly perturbed by Nora's presence with Trent. Nora loved it. *What a drama queen.* "I'll be on my way," she said and rose from the table.

Annabelle pulled back the shower curtain, brazenly hung up her towel so that both could see, then stepped in.

Another deliberate move. *That self-absorbed bitch just can't stop showing everyone that her body's better than mine.* By now, Nora couldn't care in the least.

"Oh, shit!" Annabelle bellowed. "Not again!" And then she leaped back out of the shower and flung the towel back on. "What is wrong with this freak-show gross-out island? I'm sick of it!"

What's she shrieking about now? Nora followed Trent over and looked in the shower.

"Looks like a piece of pink yarn," Trent said.

"Last night I had those disgusting worms in my lobster," Annabelle railed, "and now there's a *snake* in the shower."

That's no snake, Nora knew at once. The thing was a foot and a half long, glistening, and pink as bubblegum. *I can't be this lucky,* she thought. She dropped to one knee. The ground that served as the shower's basin was wet from the water that had accumulated; there was a half inch of muddy water topped by floating bits of leaves.

Nora leaned closer.

"Don't touch it!" Annabelle exclaimed. "It'll bite."

"It's just kind of floating there," Trent said. "Looks dead to me."

"It is dead," Nora affirmed. She looked up at Trent. "The insecticide you sprayed in here the other day saturated the ground." Then she looked at Annabelle, explaining, "And this isn't a snake. It's the same species of worm that infected the lobster, just older and more mature."

"Great, a worm. That's even *more* disgusting."

But Nora wasn't disgusted at all; she was intrigued. The bands of the coelum matched those they'd examined last night with the microscopes.

Again, her observations were verified: This was not a species of annelid that she recognized.

Nora got her wish: a bigger specimen to examine.

"What's that stuff coming out of its mouth?" Trent asked. From the tip of the worm's eyeless head floated a plume of something nearly granulated and yellow.

"Ova," Nora said. "Motile ova. They're underdeveloped versions of those yellow things that were in here two days ago."

"You mean the worm's eggs?" Annabelle asked.

"Carriers of the worm's eggs," Nora corrected. "Once mature, they can move about independently. Some invertebrates don't *lay* eggs that hatch from a stationary nest, they *disperse* the eggs. Moving hairs called cilia or rings of muscle called parapods enable the ova to find its own hatching place. In the case of a parasitic ovum, the hatching place is another living thing, like a lobster, for example."

"Or a human?" Trent asked.

"With this type of worm, I don't think so," Nora felt confident in saying. "Not mammals of any kind. Once a worm or an ovum like this entered the bloodstream of a mammal, the macrophages in our immune system would kill it immediately. I don't think we have to worry about infections ourselves. The main thing I'm worrying about is getting in a thorough examination of this before it decomposes."

Nora looped the dead worm over her pen and lifted it up. *Now I have something to do today!*

CHAPTER FIFTEEN

(I)

Slydes barely slipped back into the woods in time; he'd just finished checking the head shacks where Jonas grew his pot, when—*Goddamn! Not her again!*—the skinny woman in the black one-piece turned the corner. Slydes ducked behind the trees. If he'd been a second slower, the woman would have seen him.

What the fuck is she doing in there?

She seemed intent on something, a half smile on her face as she bopped up to the first door. *She's spending an awful lot of time in there . . .*

Slydes noticed that she was holding something. It looked like a piece of pink string draped over her pen.

"Come on, worm," she absently remarked. "Let's see what you're all about." And then she went into the building.

Worm? Slydes thought. *Is that what she said?* So the pink string was a worm, obviously a dead one. But now that Slydes thought about it, the worm was the same color of the thing that had landed on Ruth two nights ago, and the same color of the worm they'd stepped on in Jonas's dope shack, but a lot longer.

And . . .

Ruth said something about snakes, too, didn't she? Giant snakes that were . . . pink . . .

Giant pink snakes? Or maybe giant pink worms . . .

He caught himself. *Don't be an ass.* There'd be all kinds of worms on an island like this. Not to mention that Ruth was fried crispy from drugs. The dumb-ass girl had hallucinations all the time.

He couldn't ignore the coincidence, though. Ruth harped about pink snakes, and now here was this skinny chick with the frizzed-out hair walking into the head shack with a pink worm . . .

Longest fucking worm I've ever seen . . .

He felt too lousy to dwell on it, though. He had a doozy of a fever now; his nose was running and stuffed up, and the headache throbbed constantly. He was out here trying to find Jonas so they could get out of here, but there'd been no sign of him yet. *Fuckin' low-life pothead brother, fuckin' everything up. We wouldn't be out here now if it weren't for him and his damn souped-up dope.* He slipped away from the old missile buildings. *If we'd never come to this damn island, I wouldn't be sick . . .*

But he knew he couldn't go anywhere until he'd found his brother.

Slydes searched for another hour, branches swiping at his face, vines threatening to trip him. Toward noon, the humidity was soup-thick; Slydes *poured* sweat. Just when he thought he'd keel over from the heat, he found a narrow freshwater stream. He thunked to his knees, then cupped cool water into his mouth and over his face. *That's the ticket!*

Then he looked down into the water and saw some inch-long worms crawling about.

The worms were pink.

If he'd had anything in his stomach, he would've vomited. Instead, he trudged away, revolted.

This island's a pile of shit . . .

Slydes's heart almost burst when a hand grabbed his wrist.

"Aw, brother, we are seriously fucked," the low, guttural voice told him. Slydes jerked away from the clammy hand.

It was Jonas.

Jesus . . .

Jonas stood leaning against a tree, his skin yellow like a bruised banana, but dotted with brilliant red spots.

"What—" Slydes gulped back some nausea. "What happened to you?"

"Them things, you know? Them little yellow buggers. Some of them, when they bite you, they change your insides. And some of 'em are just . . . eggs."

"Eggs? What the hell are you talking about, Jonas? You're talking crazy." Slyde's power of cognition was on a rough track. "Where you been? You left the boat a night and a half ago, and we haven't seen you since."

Jonas kept on the subject. "They're eggs for the worms."

Worms, Slydes thought in the back of his head. *Worms . . .*

"You've seen 'em."

Slydes's eyes widened in thought. *The skinny chick, with the pink worm . . .*

"One fell on Ruth the other night, and then we saw that smaller one near my plants." Jonas's watery eyes looked like wads of phlegm. "They're using us, Slydes. We're the subjects for their experiment."

"You're not talkin' sense!" Slydes yelled hard. "Experiments? Subjects? Man, we gotta get off this island! It's all fucked up, brother!"

"There were two parties of college kids who got here before us." Jonas scratched at the red dots on his arms. "They're all toast now—except for the big one. Usually a host'll kick the bucket after a couple of days, a week, maybe. But that big one's still walkin' around here. So just remember that, Slydes. The big one."

"The fuck you talkin' about? Big one?"

"Big, big guy. Like a football player. I guess he adapted better than most. Shit, maybe he changed over completely, ain't gonna die at all. He's a big guy. Watch out for him. He's trompin' around here like a fuckin' zombie."

The words dragged Slydes's memory back like something on a hook. *Big guy. Like a zombie.* Ruth had said the same exact thing. And she'd also said a bunch of shit about—

"Tell me about the worms . . ."

"They're the whole experiment, Slydes. And like I said—we're the subjects. Any poor fucker who's dumb enough to come to this island . . . becomes part of the experiment them guys are doing."

Slydes's voice ground like gravel. "What guys?"

"You ain't see 'em? They sneak out every now and then to check on things. Military guys. Army, navy, I ain't sure. They're wearin' these camouflage rubber suits, and gas masks."

Slydes just stared at the information his brother had given him. "Shit, man—" Jonas's knees shook, and sweat made his yellowed face shine like baby oil. With difficulty, he sat down at the base of the tree. "Ahh, yeah, that's better. You gotta get your ass out of here now, Slydes. Get out of here before I turn over."

"What do you mean, turn over?"

"I been infected by those yellow things. They look like fat ticks, and they got red spots on 'em."

Slydes suddenly felt like he had a belly full of spoiled meat. He knew what his brother was talking about. Dread nearly closed his throat off. "Jonas, I picked a couple of the selfsame things off my body the other night. Am—am—am . . . I infected too?"

"You ain't turning yellow so probably not. Maybe you got 'em off before they could bite. When they bite they inject this shit in your blood . . . that changes you. Changes you yellow. Changes your insides . . . so the worms can grow in you better."

Slydes looked at his arms, saw no signs of the insane infection that had stricken his brother.

"But it also changes your brain, too, after enough time's passed. I ain't there yet, but I will be. It's almost like you start to take on the instincts of the worms."

"You mean like that little one in the pot house? And I just saw some more in that creek, little tiny things."

"Them's the worms I mean."

"But—but . . . but Ruth said she saw some worms ten feet long. That ain't true, is it? Tell me it ain't true."

Jonas grinned through gray teeth. "It's true. Them little tiny things in the creek? They grow fast, and they grow *big*."

"Not ten feet!" Slydes protested.

"Oh, shit, man—they get bigger than that."

The information wasn't what Slydes needed to hear.

"The big ones are the worst, 'cause they need to eat more. They dissolve your insides, brother, and then suck it out. That's what they eat. They choose smaller people to lay their eggs in, and bigger people to eat." Jonas's brow popped up. "And you're a pretty big guy, Slydes. So what I'm sayin' is you gotta get your ass off

YES! ☐

Sign me up for the Leisure Horror Book Club and send my TWO FREE BOOKS! If I choose to stay in the club, I will pay only $8.50* each month, a savings of $5.48!

YES! ☐

Sign me up for the Leisure Thriller Book Club and send my TWO FREE BOOKS! If I choose to stay in the club, I will pay only $8.50* each month, a savings of $5.48!

NAME: _____

ADDRESS: _____

_____

TELEPHONE: _____

E-MAIL: _____

☐ **I WANT TO PAY BY CREDIT CARD.**

☐ VISA   ☐ MasterCard   ☐ DISCOVER

ACCOUNT #: _____

EXPIRATION DATE: _____

SIGNATURE: _____

Send this card along with $2.00 shipping & handling for each club you wish to join, to:

Horror/Thriller Book Clubs
20 Academy Street
Norwalk, CT 06850-4032

Or fax (must include credit card information!) to: 610.995.9274.
You can also sign up online at www.dorchesterpub.com.

*Plus $2.00 for shipping. Offer open to residents of the U.S. and Canada only. Canadian residents please call 1.800.481.9191 for pricing information.

If under 18, a parent or guardian must sign. Terms, prices and conditions subject to change. Subscription subject to acceptance. Dorchester Publishing reserves the right to reject any order or cancel any subscription.

JOIN NOW!

this island right now. Get Ruth off too. And leave. Now. While you still got a chance."

"I'm taking you with me, get you to a doctor back on the mainland."

Jonas shook his head. His yellow finger trembled when he slipped a reefer from his pocket and shakily lit it up. "It's too late for me. Get out before I change more, 'cause you know what happens then?"

"What?" Slydes croaked.

"I'll come for ya. I'll try to infect you. Watch." Jonas coughed wetly into his hand, then showed it to his brother. Amid the wad of appalling phlegm, several of the yellow things twitched. Jonas picked one out and popped it between his fingers. "This one here, it ain't got a worm in it 'cause it's one of the ones that changes you. That white stuff inside."

Slydes saw white strings in the slime.

"It changes your cells or something, to make you a better host." He popped another one. "Ah, here's one. Here's a fertile one. See, Slydes, some of these things have the white stuff, and some of 'em have worms. This one's got a worm. Look."

Slydes could barely do so . . . but he looked anyway. In the dab of muck hanging off his brother's fingers, he saw the tiniest bright pink worm wriggling away.

"How do you know all this stuff?" Slydes asked.

Jonas's head tilted at the question. "I think because I'm changing. The more I change, the more of the worm's instinct I get in my brain, I guess." Jonas scraped the crap off his hand and got back to his reefer. "Get out of here now, brother . . . before I try to infect you with the same shit."

Crazy, Slydes thought. *It's crazy.*

But he knew now that it had to be true.

"Shh!" Jonas bid. "Listen. . . ."

Slydes stood still.

He could hear something rustle, and when he looked through some trees, the brush was stirring.

It was stirring a lot.

"Go!" Jonas whispered. "One of 'em's coming."

When Slydes saw the pink shine roving beneath the brush, he ran like a madman.

(II)

"Report?"

The major had called them into the security room. He appeared perturbed, but then, he generally did.

"Early this morning we investigated the first structure, where members of the third party have set up a field lab of some kind," the sergeant replied.

"I know, Sergeant. We all saw that on the monitor last night. They look like they're examining something in there. Didn't the colonel order you to find out what they're examining?"

"I did that, sir." *He's already in a bad mood. Now it's going to get worse.* "They're examining the subject."

"*Our* subject?"

"Yes, sir."

"Our worm, you're saying? They've found samples of *our* worm?"

"Yes, sir. And the examples of the motile ova. They were newborn hatchlings."

"Were the members of the party infected during the process?"

"I can't say for sure, sir, but they didn't appear to be."

The major leaned over the table. "Corporal, punch up the camera we have installed there."

"Yes, sir." The corporal put it on the main monitor. "She's in there again, sir." On the screen, the same slender woman was back inside, at the worktable.

"She's in there a lot," the major noted. "You're sure you found progeny of the subject in there? Are you sure it wasn't something else?"

"It was our worm, sir," the sergeant offered. "They're replicating well, all over the island, and not just in humans. There seem to be many examples of the indigenous animal life that are adaptable. And that's actually good news."

"Yes, it is. But not if we're disclosed." The major wagged his finger at the corporal. "Play back from the moment she reentered the building."

The corporal hit some buttons, and next they were watching the slender woman in the one-piece swimsuit unlocking the door and walking in.

Draped across an ink pen was a worm.

"I guess I can't argue with that," the major remarked. "That's definitely one of ours."

"Yes, sir, it is. And they had samples of the ova as well. The ones last night probably weren't big enough to examine closely—not with the field equipment they have on hand, but—"

"The sample she just took in there is fairly mature."

"Yes, sir."

Silence stood with them in the room. Then the major said, "If they know about the worm, then they may know about us."

"I don't think so, sir," the sergeant said. "I think they're just zoological scientists on a field excursion. They discovered our subject by accident, and at this point they have no reason to believe it's part of a genetic experiment. If they knew about us, they would have notified some authority."

"You're right." The major was thinking. "And that's our good luck. Turn on the jammers so they can't call out. We can't take any chances—the experiment's gone too well so far. We're going to be leaving soon."

The sergeant nodded. "I'm confident that everyone on the island will be infected by the time we leave."

"I agree, but we only have a few more maturation tests to do in the meantime. Keep an eye on them, and confirm infection." He looked the sergeant dead in the eye. "If you can't confirm one hundred percent infection within twenty-four hours, I want you to go out there and kill whoever's left."

The sergeant and the corporal looked at each other.

The major turned at the door. "I realize that may sound like an unorthodox measure, but it's all in the interests of the mission's ultimate success. Will that be a problem, Sergeant?"

"No, sir. No problem at all."

(III)

"I thought you were going for another swim with Annabelle," Nora posed when Loren ducked into the head shack.

"Yeah, but not till later in the afternoon." He walked in, then looked enthused. "Wow, where'd you get that?"

"Your pretentious blond friend almost stepped on it in the shower earlier."

"Hey, just because I worship her body doesn't mean she's my friend."

"You a betting man?"

"Sure."

"Okay, I'll bet you that before this shoot is over, she's putting overt moves on you."

"You're high," Loren said. "And I'll tell you something. I'm pretty sure she and Lieutenant Trent have something going on."

Nora laughed at the worktable. "You're *so* perceptive, Loren. What a bright light you are."

"Why do I detect unremitting sarcasm?"

"She and Trent have been doing the naked pretzel since the first night."

The surety of her words stunned him. "Really?"

"Yeah, and she wants to make Trent jealous—she loves games. She has no identity unless she's the center of male attention. That's why she'll be coming on heavy to you soon. Accept it. And don't be a dope. Don't feed her atrocious ego and utter lack of character by responding like a horny mutt."

Loren's head rose in an arrogant pose. "Hey, just because I'm a few years younger than you doesn't mean that you know more about human romantic behavior."

"No, but the fact that I'm a woman *does*. I'm betting that she puts hard moves on you and you fall like a house of cards. You'll be absolutely convinced that she's crazy about you. Too chicken to bet?"

"You're on," he said, grinning. "Loser buys dinner at the winner's choice of restaurants."

Nora shook on it. "Now let's stop yacking about that ultraboobed peabrain and take a look at this."

Loren sat down at the worktable, eyeing the foot-and-a-half-long worm. "You killed it?"

"No, it was already dead from the seepage at the bottom of the shower stall. Trent sprays it down with bug spray every day since we found those first motile ova." She slid the microscope over to Loren. "And I'm pretty sure we were right last night. This worm here is the same species as the tiny ones from the lobster. Which means we weren't seeing things last night. It's a species that grows at an exponential rate."

Loren's eye lowered to the scope. He went silent for several minutes. "There's no doubt. The pore scheme in the coelum is identical, and so are the mucoid ducts in the parapodal bands." He shook his head in studied amazement. "There's nothing else I've ever seen that's even remotely like this. *This* size? Good God."

"This is a species that the helminthology community is unaware of," Nora pointed out.

"We've discovered a new annelid." He took his eye away long enough to grin at her. "We get to name it ourselves."

"Yeah, but it's still a rip-off when you think about it."

"What do you mean a rip-off? It's every zoologist's dream to get credit for discovering a new species of animal life."

"Sure, Loren. But look at the fact of the matter. If a paleontologist discovers a new fossil, he makes a fortune. Somebody discovers a new enzyme, a new bacterium, a new friggin' fish—you name it—they make a fortune and they become famous in their field." Nora snorted. "We discover a new worm, and nobody will care."

"Yeah, and we won't make jack shit. But so what? We'll be the stars of the next issue of *The American Journal of Worms* . . . for about a month."

All of a sudden the new find seemed almost more trouble than it was worth. But Nora could still retain some level of excitement in their next step. "This one's big enough to dissect. You want the honors?"

"Damn straight."

"Start cutting, Doctor."

Loren got up for the case of exam and dissection implements, as something occurred to Nora. "One thing," she said. "We can't tell the others anything about this."

"You're right. They'd overreact in a big way."

"We'll just tell them the worm is typical and nothing to worry about. Any other way would be—"

Loren laughed. "Can you imagine Annabelle's reaction if she thought there was an undiscovered parasitic worm out here—that doubled in size in twenty minutes? And that they were in her *lobster*! She'd have a cow!"

"I'd love for her to have a cow, and every other conceivable farm animal," Nora remarked. "But I'd be more worried about Trent. He'd have an army quarantine crew out here."

Loren sat back down and unzipped the dissection kit. With forceps he readjusted the body of the worm across the stage, then applied stage clips. The case contained cutting instruments called microscalpels, which looked nothing like typical scalpels. Honed needles composed the blades, some made of steel, some made of hard resins. The kit also contained intricate pipettes, probes, and section lifters. "Yeah, this one's plenty big enough," Loren muttered. "Let's see what's going on in here . . ."

Nora waited.

"Same mucoid ducts that we saw on the parapods of the ovum," Loren observed.

"Mucoid ducts in the coelum mean it's a skin-breather—like an earthworm," Nora said, cruxed.

Loren daintily cut some more. "Plus gill sacs connected to the secondary dorsomentral channels. So we were right again. It can breathe air and also process oxygen when it's in seawater. Like lungworms and snakeheads. And it's definitely not a Polychaeta." He pushed the microscope over to Nora, frustrated. "I can't even guess what the family is on this thing."

Nora changed the numerical aperture and upped the light field. With microshears and a teasing needle, she peeled back the layers of the worm's coelum—its outer musculature that served as skin as well as the main sensory organ carrier. "This looks like a roundworm but demonstrates features of other nematodes and annelids. No evidence of triphasic rhythm fibers. Part land rover, part free-range seaworm, but the outer physicality smacks of what we thought last night. Roundworms. Pink from oxygen saturation—"

"The Trichinella family."

"Um-hmm, and that's impossible because no Trichinella, nor Trichina, exists without triphasic rhythm."

Loren laughed, if a bit nervously. "When we discover a new species of worm, we sure do pick doozies."

Nora wasn't laughing. "Plus motile ova, plus chitin-penetrating digestive enzymes." She didn't say anything more, but jacked the microscope to its full 400× magnification. "Damn, what I wouldn't give for an SEM, or even just a scope that cranked to a thousand or fifteen hundred."

"Tell me about it."

Nora went silent again, then slid the scope back to Loren. "Tell me what you see."

Loren looked. "Muscular symmetry that looks both radial and spiral," he declared.

They both sat a minute, saying nothing. Only experts of their kind knew the ramifications. "This can only mean its motile ova are bifunctional. A mutator. Like—"

"Like a fair share of Trichinosis species. And if we're right, then these things can *easily* infect humans . . . I'm going to check the midlevel striations now." He cut some more, then said, "My hands are full. Get something to gently raise the stage clip, will you?"

The kit lay on the other side of Loren, so Nora looked around for a pen or something small to lift the clip. *Damn* . . . There was nothing near her. She slipped her finger in the key pocket of her swimsuit, but the only thing in it was that small, corded metal strip she'd found the other day. *This'll have to do,* she thought, and used it to raise the stage clip.

"What's that thing?" Loren asked, obviously seeing it under magnification.

"Something I stepped on in the woods. Not sure what it is. Trent said he thinks it's a calibration tool for an old army radio."

"It's got some funny markings on it," Loren told her.

"Okay, thanks. Lower the clip now."

Funny markings? She took the metal strip away and decided to look at it under the other microscope. "You're right," she said, focusing. "What *are* those markings?"

"They're raised, like Braille almost," Loren said back while still concentrating on the next incision. "Reminded me more of a bar code or something. Trent said it was a radio tool?"

"Yeah. But he wasn't certain."

"Looks more like a key to me."

"That's what I thought too," she murmured, and looked more closely at the object beneath the magnifier.

The markings looked like this:

-:.:-:.

"Forget about that thing," Loren said next. "I just found the stomach process and the enzymatic sac."

"Did you puncture it?"

"Yeah, and guess what? The fluid is sizzling. It's even smoking a little."

"The chitin penetrator," Nora said.

Then Loren said, "Holy shit. It's not burning the glass slide, but the stuff melted the tip of my probe."

"Is the probe tip made of resin?"

"No. Stainless steel."

"Strong stuff," Nora commented. But this wasn't terribly surprising. There were a number of invertebrates that possessed highly corrosive stomach enzymes: to burn through the shells of animals they were attacking, and to even burn burrows into coral. "Remember that article we read about the Norwegian lugworm? It released its enzymes all at once and burned a hole through the aquarium's slate floor."

"Yeah, slate, but not steel. This is really tough stuff, Nora."

She could see threads of smoke rising up from Loren's microscope slide. "Can you drip some onto the floor?"

With larger forceps, he kept the dead worm crimped to the slide, then lifted it all off the stage. Careful not to dribble any on his fingers, he tipped the slide. Several drops of the brownish fluid plipped onto the concrete floor.

Threads of smoke began to rise.

"Jesus," Nora said. She grabbed another probe and ran it across the smoking drops. "This stuff is *really* tough. It's burned some small indentations into the cement."

"We'll have to be very careful getting some more of these things to take back to the college," Loren said.

"I wonder what the preferred habitat is. Water or land?"

"Probably water. Something that gets this big isn't going to settle for beetles and bugs to eat. It'll go after larger crustaceans, the bigger meal ticket."

Like the lobster, she recalled. "When you're out looking for more bristleworms with Annabelle, keep an eye out for more of these. It'd be great to get some live ones to take back."

"I'll find some." Loren felt sure. "And speaking of that, I better start getting ready. Annabelle will probably want to start the next shoot soon."

"See Spot run," Nora said. "And don't forget our bet."

"Oh, I won't. You'll drop big money when you lose that one," Loren said. Then he winked and left.

Poor fool, Nora thought. *The ignorance of youth.*

She continued dissecting the worm . . . and continued to find physical features that seemed to borrow from several different species: epidermal pores to draw in oxygen from the air—like an earthworm—but also gill filters for water breathing—around intercoelic channels that stored seawater—like free-ranging Polychaetes. Ovaries that produced independent motile ova were possessed of many roundworm species—like the Trichinella classes—while the worm's physical appearance, too, looked like some of the nonmarine orders of Trichinella and Trichina.

On its own, though, Nora knew that the specimen could not be any of those.

Almost like a genetic hybrid, her mind whispered.

When she'd dissected all she could, she jarred the worm in preservatives and spent the next hour inputting notes into her laptop. That's when Trent walked in.

"Going for a swim?" Nora asked, for the lieutenant was wearing trunks and an olive-drab army T-shirt.

"Yeah, I might as well," he replied. "I've been stationed in Florida for the last ten years, but I don't think I've even been to the beach more than a few times. I thought I'd tag along with Annabelle and Loren, while they're looking for their scarlet bristleworms."

"Have fun."

"But I wanted to show you this first." He approached the table and handed her something. "Is that like the thing you mentioned?"

Nora placed it in her palm and knew at once. "The little camera lens, yeah. The one I saw was stuck in a tree, almost like it had been nailed into the bark."

"Same thing here, but I pried this one out. Originally I thought it must've been an electric-eye sensor, or maybe an infrared perimeter alarm, but I don't see any terminals on it."

"I didn't see any on the one I saw either. No connection posts or anything to hook wires to. When the army was using these things, how did they establish a circuit?"

"Beats me. But there does seem to be glass in the head, like a lens."

"I know," she said next. "Let me take a closer look . . ."

She placed the cigarette-butt-sized object on the microscope stage, then focused down.

"Yes, it's definitely rounded, polished glass. A bulb, maybe, an indicator light?"

"Can't imagine that. In the woods? And what would the power source be? See any terminals on it, or anything like a hole for wires to go in?"

Nora studied the odd cylinder more closely. "Nothing on the sides or on the butt end."

"See if there's any markings on it. I'll bet there's a defense contractor's name on it somewhere, or an army property line," Trent said.

Nora slowly revolved the object on the stage with forceps. "Wait a minute." She paused. "There is something."

"What's it say?"

Nora rubbed her eyes and got up. She bid Trent to sit. "Tell me if you've ever seen *that* before."

Trent sat down and put his eye to the scope.

What Nora had seen was oddly familiar. Etched along the object's side were markings like this:

..-::-

CHAPTER SIXTEEN

(I)

Annabelle stretched her bare legs to the sun. The tan was deepening, made more prominent by a blazing white thong bikini. She glanced down at herself and immediately thought, *Lookin' good, Annabelle—as always.*

She wanted to catch a few more rays before she and Loren went back in the water for the last of the bristleworm photos. *He'll be here soon,* she figured, so she took off her top, to let herself be "caught." The sudden sun seemed to lick her nipples, raising them in the heat. She wanted to keep Loren stoked: Sexual anxiety among the men in her range always kept things interesting. *Poor little Loren. He'll have blue balls for years. . . .*

Her bare breasts looked like fresh white fruit atop the nougat tan of her belly. She lounged back on her towel. The narrow beach extended off, gentle waves flapping over each other as seagulls glided silently overhead.

Her snorkeling and photo gear lay beside her. The

sun was heating her up. *Might as well make some calls while I'm just lying around.* She couldn't wait to tell her friends about this little expedition. When she opened her cell phone she noticed that her fiancé had left several messages. *Better to let him wait,* she decided. She liked to let him stew; it kept him wondering. *He needs to appreciate me more . . .*

She called her best girlfriend in New York and got to chatting. "The funniest thing of all is how dumb these people are," she was saying. "None of them know I'm a newbie; I've got them believing I'm the magazine's premier nature photographer—they don't know this is only my third assignment. The idiots think I've been all over the world!"

More chatter.

"Well, of course! There's this army guy here, nothing to write home about but he's good for some diversion. I wouldn't pay him the time of day back home, but on this island? Why not? And, no, I don't consider it cheating at all—strictly recreational. What I do is my business. Shit, my fiancé's the lucky one. What he doesn't know won't hurt him." Then she giggled. "But I better *never* catch him cheating on *me*! What I'd do to him would make Lorena Bobbit look like Shirley Fucking Temple."

Still more chick-thing chatter.

"Oh, and you wouldn't believe the damn professor—she's a *worm* professor, can you believe it?—this skinny frizz-head cunt with permanent PMS. Looks like Olive Oil on Popeye. I'm playing so many head games with her, it's actually fun, and I'll bet she's never been laid in her life! She's so jealous of my bod that you can see steam coming out her ears. Oh, and she's got this dork assistant named Loren—nerd and a half. I'm always giving him an eyeful to keep him riled. That poor kid probably plays with himself ten times a day! When I'm bored, I tease the shit out of him. It's so much fun!"

Suddenly the line fell silent, and after a moment, all she could hear was fuzz.

I knew I shouldn't have changed my service. She leaned up, frowning, and redialed.

Nothing but fuzz over the line.

Then she dialed her fiancé.

Fuzz.

"Goddamn cell phones," she muttered and put it away.

(II)

"Are those numbers that have just worn away from age?" Nora suggested.

"No, I don't think so," Trent said. He still had his eye pressed to the microscope, focusing down on the tiny lens or element or whatever it was. They were trying to figure out the ..-::- markings. "They don't look like they're worn or eroded at all. It must be some kind of a microbar code. The military uses nomenclature codes to mark security equipment. Same thing as a model number, only coded."

"Security equipment," Nora said, "which makes sense on a camera lens that small. So that other thing I found on the cord—it must be a security *key.*"

Trent looked back at her. "Thing on the cord?"

"The thing you said was a radio calibrator," Nora reminded him.

"It had the same markings?"

"See for yourself." She placed the object on the stage.

"The configuration is different but it's the same style," Trent observed now.

"And you said you've seen them before?"

"I've seen the same sort of *thing,* but nothing exactly like these. Usually they're numbers or letters."

"A newer system?"

"It's got to be. For certain kinds of specialized equipment, the army needs to mark it in a way that can't be deciphered by an enemy in the field. I'm sure if you ran a scanner across these markings it would tell you exactly what this thing is, when it was made, model number, lot number, stuff like that. It would also tell you what it's a key *for.*" Trent paused, puzzled. "I'm going to call the S-3 officer at my post, see if he knows anything about this island still being used for anything."

"But you're the guy who checks the island every month," Nora pointed out. "Wouldn't you be the first to know?"

"Not necessarily," he said. "This thing's got me thinking." He held it up. "A key, then a security lens, and what you told me this morning."

"Huh?"

"About the lights being on in some of the head shacks."

Oh yeah, Nora thought. *And he said he didn't have access to them.* "You didn't turn the lights on." She saw the simple deduction. "So it must've been someone else."

"Someone I don't know about. So maybe the army is using the island for something . . . and I don't know about that, either."

Trent snapped open his cell phone, hit a dial key, then waited.

"Damn," he said.

"Busy?"

"No, just static. I'd say we were in a bad cell out here, but my cell phone worked fine yesterday and the day before." He dialed another number and got the same effect.

Nora called the college, just to see if she'd get through. "I'm getting static, too. Sort of a throbbing buzz."

"Have you made any other calls?"

"A couple times since we got here. The reception

was fine. Maybe a tower went down, or a solar flare broke up some satellite waves."

Trent kept his phone to his ear, listening. Then he shook his head and closed the phone. "The way the static rises and falls . . ."

"Yeah?"

"It almost sounds like a military signal jammer."

Nora frowned. "That doesn't make sense."

Trent thought about it and shrugged. Then he agreed, "You're right, that's ridiculous. I'm sure it's just a good old case of technical difficulties. Why would anybody jam *us?*"

(III)

"Loren? Do you mind if I snorkel without my top on?" Annabelle asked. The large, tan-line-delineated breasts stared back at him as if they themselves awaited the answer.

Loren amused himself by imagining an array of responses. *Of course I mind! What kind of an immoral cad do you think I am?* Or, *I would find that unduly offensive, Annabelle.* Better yet: *That's sexual harassment! Expect to hear from my attorney!*

"I—I—I . . . don't mind at all," he said.

"Oh, that's good." The breasts rose in a perfect pose when she adjusted her diving mask. "It feels so wonderfully natural underwater, you know?"

"Yeah," he droned.

The dark pink nipples—larger than poker chips—infiltrated him like a hypnotist's totems. She was a centerfold come to life, standing before him in utter nonchalance. Nude now, save for the white thong's tiny triangle, she was all glimmering skin and voluptuous lines. *I'll bet the suntan oil on her body weighs more than the thong,* he thought.

When she leaned over to step into her flippers, Loren could've collapsed.

This is going to be a really great day . . .

Mask propped up on his forehead, Trent appeared from the trees. He almost dropped the flippers he was carrying when he noticed Annabelle. He paused to gulp. "This is going to be a really great day . . . the weather, I mean."

"Yeah, not a cloud in the, uh, sky," Loren added.

Annabelle giggled. "That's great. A threesome."

"I figured you might need some army expertise finding these bristleworms," Trent added.

"The more, the merrier." Annabelle leaned over one more time to pick up her camera.

"The beach really is the best place to appreciate natural beauty," Loren remarked.

"I hear ya," Trent said.

"First time in my life I ever seen a woman wearing a Dorito."

"Come on, boys!" Annabelle strode off, attributes bobbing. Loren and Trent followed her like two puppies.

They waded in behind her. Mild surf lapped at their thighs.

"You two know where the bristleworms are?" Trent asked. "Or is it just potluck?"

"Loren knows," Annabelle called back. "We'll follow him."

Damn it! Loren thought. He wanted to be the one following her, considering what he'd be looking at. "You remember, Annabelle," he urged. "We'll just swim out till we feel the cool-flow, then look down for the trench. The end with the yellow coral banks is where the nest is."

"Okay," she agreed. "Then you guys can follow me."

"Smart move," Trent said aside to Loren. There was no need to hide their obvious sexism. "She'll be snapping pictures for a long time once we get to the nest. Which means plenty of eye time for us."

"Precisely."

Once they'd waded to chest-level, they all mouthed their snorkels and dove . . .

Loren thought of floating within a liquid prism. The warm water seemed extra buoyant. He marveled at the sea's schools of silver fish flowing en masse like splinters of metal, clumps of coral, and squirming anemones, large yellow-tailed snappers cruising lazily and bright as neon. Some spine-balls that were urchins rolled below them like tumbleweeds, and when a hefty octopus spotted them, it froze, tentacles extended, then shot away before a wake of black ink.

The three of them saw the trench and then the canary-yellow mass of crenelated coral. That's when they surfaced, treading water.

"You all saw the coral right at the tip of the trench," Loren said. "That's where the bristleworms are. Just start turning over rocks and you'll see them." He finnicked more specimen tubes from the net bag that floated off his belt.

"I'm ready," Annabelle said, hoisting her camera.

Both Trent and Loren were clearly diverted by the vision of Annabelle's floating breasts. "Are we going into the trench?" Trent asked.

"It's not advisable," Loren said.

"Why?" Annabelle asked. "I could get some great shots."

"What's in the trench?" it was Trent's turn to ask.

"Well, seafans, featherduster anemones, light-emitting coral that flashes like Christmas lights," Loren began.

"That sounds pretty cool," Trent said.

"Oh, let's go," Annabelle urged.

"And probably moray eels that are big enough to bite the limbs off humans . . ."

"Oh, let's *not* go," the blonde corrected herself.

"Thank you. So we'll stick to the coral clusters, and we should find some great scarlet bristleworms."

"No time like the present," Trent said.

The outcroppings of coral were about twenty feet below them. A group of shining pinfish followed them down as if part of their group. Loren's eyes scanned past the coral to the end of the trench, which looked narrow and hundreds of feet long—a minor chasm that had likely been formed thousands of years ago during an underwater plate-shift. For a moment he actually considered investigating, but then noticed some baby hammerheads loitering at the trench's rim.

Naw, he thought.

His eyes invariably rose back to Annabelle, who hovered over the coral, looking down. Her legs would slowly open and close to stabilize her position as she fired off some test shots with the big camera. She might as well have been nude in the water, all that immaculate flesh suspended before rising bubbles. The image compelled unshakable fantasies . . .

But it was all primordial, he knew. *Eye candy,* he thought, *inciting my male genetic propensities.* He knew now there was nothing really likable about Annabelle. She was the stuck-up leader of the cheerleading squad, who'd only settle in the end for the quarterback, the idea of social status raised to a personal priority. Shallow. Loren had encountered plenty of shallow people in his life of nerdom, and he'd had enough . . .

The only woman he really liked was Nora, but . . .

She's my friggin' boss.

Such was life.

Trent was staring at Annabelle too, right at the tiny triangle of fabric between her legs. *He's a caveman, all right,* Loren thought, *and wants to drag her back to the cave by the hair.* It was clear they had something going on; Annabelle had already made her selection. *Survival of the dumbest,* Loren tried to rationalize. It was easier than admitting he'd never be the kind of tough guy most beautiful women were attracted to.

He moved in and started flipping over rocks alongside Annabelle. Beige sea dust rose in billows. But then Annabelle upturned a large flat rock, and . . .

Recoiled.

Loren and Trent immediately spotted her reaction, and swam to her.

She jabbed her finger down violently toward a mass of scarlet bristleworms.

They were all bloated up to the size of Ping-Pong balls, some bursting before their eyes to release spews of tiny pink worms and minuscule yellow ova.

And these things have lungs AND gills, he reminded himself. *They could be moving all over the island by now.*

Trent and Annabelle swam back ashore, leaving Loren to tread the water in place.

He debated the idea for several more minutes. Then—

Got nothing better to do . . .

He dove back down, to collect more samples.

CHAPTER SEVENTEEN

(I)

Slydes got back to the boat after noon. Was it his imagination or did he still feel sick?

Imagination, he hoped. He'd felt so lousy the past day or so, but wishful thinking told him that maybe it was just the flu or something. Trekking back to the boat he quickly got lost—the island was a labyrinth of vegetation—but for the entire time he kept glancing at his arms . . . to see if his skin was beginning to yellow.

Like Jonas.

Like a nightmare, he thought.

But he'd seen what had happened to his brother— the most morbid infection—and he'd seen the worms himself. He hadn't stayed around long enough for a detailed look. The simple glimpses of the long, pink, hoselike *things* had been enough.

Ruth wasn't bullshitting . . .

The air was still, the heat beating down when he climbed back aboard. He swatted at mosquitoes, squinting through sweat.

Part of him still couldn't believe what he'd seen . . .

Ruth lay sprawled across the dingy cot downstairs, either sleeping off the oppressive heat or . . .

The thought seized Slydes.

She ain't dead, is she?

He had to jostle her a full minute before she came awake.

"Wake your ass up," he ordered. "It's time to leave."

Her face, arms, and legs looked tacky. Her eyes puffed up . . . almost as bad as her lips. When she managed to reclaim some awareness, she said, "Did you bring Jonas back?"

"No. Jonas is . . . sick. We're leaving without him—"

"What!"

"And we'll bring back a doctor," he told her. How could he tell he the truth? *We're leaving without him 'cause he got infected by the worms, and he turned yellow—with red spots—and he'll try to pass that shit on to us.*

Slydes wasn't prepared to say that.

Ruth didn't argue with the lie—her true face. She didn't care anymore, and neither did Slydes. "I just wanna go home," she half sobbed.

"We're gonna do that, right now." Slydes helped her up the steps. The long pink T-shirt was pasted to her flesh now, her blond hair darkened from so much sweat. When he grabbed her arm, the skin felt slippery, but . . .

It don't look like she's turnin' yellow, he observed, *and me neither.* That's all Slydes could hope for.

Abovedecks, the hot air stood still, and the sun glared off the water so harshly he could barely see. "The tide ain't high enough, but we're going anyway."

"Good, good! Just start the motor and go!"

The shrill exclamation grated his nerves, only to be answered by a sound even more shrill when he turned the ignition key. The engine chugged as metal shimmied.

"What the fuck's wrong now?" Ruth wailed.

Slydes barked back—with more nervousness than authority: "Sounds like there's no oil in the damn crankcase!" and then he hauled open the engine compartment on the back deck.

Smoke rose.

When Slydes hunkered down and looked, his heart fell into his belly like someone dropping a stone off a high bridge.

"Whatever it is—*fix it!*" Ruth screamed.

But there'd be no fixing this.

"Someone fucked us good," he conceded to the sight. "The engine's grenaded."

Ruth crawled forward on bare, scraped knees, the dark circles under her eyes like charcoal smudges. "What? What?"

"Someone drilled holes right through the valve covers into the cams . . ."

Ruth didn't want to believe it. "Who would do that? Why would someone do that?"

A relevant question, but the answer wouldn't do them any good.

The V-8's valve covers did indeed exhibit several holes, but the closer Slydes looked the more it occurred to him that they weren't drill marks. The tiny holes varied in diameter, their edges . . . irregular.

Slydes put his face right up to a cover. "Looks more like something burned through the metal . . ."

"Fuck!" Ruth blurted. She began to sob again. "What—what's that down there?" A dirty finger pointed to the bottom of the engine compartment.

Slydes saw it at once.

Curled up in the oily bilge were several dead worms.

(II)

Annabelle threw her snorkeling gear down in the sand. "That was really gross. Did you see that?"

"Sure did," Trent said. He sat down to rest, trying very hard not to overtly stare at Annabelle's almost totally naked body. "Looks like those little pink parasites made mincemeat out of your bristleworm nest. Chalk one up for the good old order of nature."

Wet now, Annabelle's bare skin shone in the high sunlight. "Those little worms looked just like the ones in my lobster, and you know what? I think they're just baby versions of that really big worm I found in the shower. I think they're the same type of worm."

Trent's eyes followed the line of her legs. "Could be, I don't know from worms."

"It's just *gross*," Annabelle emphasized. "That shower worm was over a foot long. They're probably all over the island but we just don't know it . . . along with those yellow ticks—or whatever she said they were."

"Nora said they were worm eggs, I think. Ova. I don't know what you're all bent out of shape over. They're just *worms,* Annabelle. You see a worm, you step on it."

Annabelle made a sour face at the recollection.

Now Trent was staring at her fat-free abdomen as she bent over to get something from her bag. The way her breasts hung down in that pose . . .

Trent was grinding his teeth. *Those things should hang in the National Gallery of Art. . . .*

Annabelle pulled out her flask and took a long hit.

Trent swatted at a few mosquitoes, then withdrew some repellent from his own bag. "What are we going to do now?"

Annabelle frowned toward the gulf. "I don't know about you, but I think I'll get drunk."

Now you're talking, Trent thought. She was a prize, all right, and more so when she had a few in her. He rubbed the repellent on his arms and neck. "That sounds like a plan, but I need to do a radio check with my post first. I've been doing it with my cell phone, but there hasn't been any reception all day."

"Mine crapped out earlier, too."

"So did Nora's. You can't trust technology these days, but one thing you *can* trust is an army radio. I've got a portable in my tent."

They meandered back to the campsite, trading hits on the flask. Annabelle's anxiety over seeing all those worms seemed to recede as the rum worked into her. *Aw, Christ,* Trent thought. *I am one lucky son of a bitch . . .* She had her arm around him as they made their way down the trail, her damp body bumping against his. *She sure as shit makes it easy getting into her pants,* he thought. *She never wears any . . .* When they got back to the camp, though, she pulled on a tube top.

Damn.

Trent quickly came back from his tent, bearing the weighty handheld radio. He switched on the service frequency.

Annabelle sat idly on the picnic table, wagging her legs.

"Jay One, this is Area November calling for radio check," he said into the unit. "Do you copy?"

When he released the transmission key, all that came back was throbbing static.

"I'm going to go take a nap," Annabelle decided and got up.

Trent was pissed. "I thought we were going to get drunk."

"I changed my mind." Moments later, she was getting into her tent.

Moody bitch, Trent thought. *Always jerking guys around.* Frustrated, he rekeyed the radio. "Jay One, this is Area November. Do you copy?"

Just more throbbing static.

This is really fucked up, he thought. Cell phones were one thing, but this was a secure military radio band.

He frowned, and still couldn't shake the inexplicable notion: *I'll be damned if that doesn't sound just like a jammer . . .*

(III)

Loren snorkeled concentric circles around the largest body of coral. Any evidence of bristleworms was just as disconcerting as before. They were all either bloated . . . or emptied out and dead. His flippers languished, then stopped when he happened upon a thorny starfish. The creature didn't move when he picked it up. *Is it dead?* he wondered.

When he flipped it around, he saw a stream of tiny pink worms exiting the aperture that was the starfish's mouth. With his finger then, he flipped over a common urchin, and found its underside pocked with tiny yellow ovum.

Jesus! The parasites are all over the place!

He came up for air a few more times, finding more and more evidence of infection. *The worms attack any invertebrate in their path . . .*

He floated around more incrustations of coral, and found himself looking straight down the slope of the trench.

In the water, it looked like a long black gouge in the sea floor. *Can't hurt to go in just a little,* he told himself. He knew his earlier warnings of moray eels and sharks were exaggeration; both creatures rarely attacked humans. Loren wanted to see if their odd pink parasite had ventured into the trench, too.

He entered slowly and turned on his flashlight.

A one-second glance was all it took.

Bubbles erupted from his lips. He shot to the surface and immediately began to swim to shore.

What he'd seen lying in the mouth of the trench was a human corpse with slabs of dough-white flesh hanging off its bones.

CHAPTER EIGHTEEN

(I)

Nora tried to make calls on her cell phone for the rest of the day—to no avail. *I've never heard interference like that before . . .* The odd, throbbing static over the line. When she went out toward the very end of the beach, hoping for a clearer track to the mainland . . .

The same throbbing buzz.

Trent said it sounded like a jammer, she recalled, but she knew he wasn't serious. Jammers were used by the military, and this site was of no importance to the army anymore. The lieutenant's later suspicions were something else altogether, but the more she thought about it, the more she realized how ludicrous the idea was.

"No phone calls today," she muttered to herself and snapped her phone off. She headed back. *Where is everyone?* She hadn't seen any of the others for hours. *If they're still out in the water looking for bristleworms, that's one long swim.* Actually she was more interested in their newest discovery as far as worms went . . .

Nora couldn't deny her first impressions. Both the newborn hatchlings from the tanks as well as their foot-and-a-half long specimen looked like trichinosis worms.

And there's no trichinosis worm like that . . . unless Loren's right about us discovering an entirely new species . . .

More exciting things had happened in her field, just not to her. She posed questions to herself as she walked back to the camp, a number of what-ifs.

What if this worm really could infect higher mammals?

The most famous of the Trichinella species did exactly that: the *Trichinella spiralis,* notorious by its ability to infect all carnivores and omnivores. *But that's an inborn worm,* she reminded herself, *almost microscopic. And it's NOT a marine parasite.*

That's when Nora spotted the nest of possums at the foot of an old pine tree.

Possums were common in Florida, a clumsy rodent-like marsupial mostly known for waddling into the middle of highly trafficked roadways, but they actually flourished in tropical woodlands. Nora leaned over to look at the nest of animals.

They're all dead . . .

It was a mother, with a half dozen young. The adult lay askew, mouth and eyes opened, little legs stiff. It appeared to have died recently—no sign of flies, maggots, or other parasites. Nora got down on one knee to look closer . . .

The infant possums weren't moving either, but they seemed . . .

Bloated, she saw.

So young they remained hairless, the newborns all possessed bellies that looked distended.

Nora quickly retrieved a box from the head shack, returned, and transferred the adult possum and one baby back to her lab.

It didn't take her long to get one of the infants under the microscope. *Oh no,* she thought the instant she sectioned the hairless abdominal wall.

Somehow, she wasn't surprised.

In the bright, magnified circle, it was almost stunning the way the hundreds of tiny ova poured forth. The cilia on each yellow egg roved vigorously. To a person in her field, this spectacle was fascinating.

And potentially horrifying.

Now . . . don't take your eye off, she ordered herself. *Don't even blink . . .*

It wasn't her imagination. Very minutely, the ova were growing.

She barely noticed Trent coming in behind her.

"Ready for something weird?" he asked.

I'm LOOKING at something weird, she thought. "What's that?"

"I still can't get a call out on my cell phone, and now I can't even get out on this."

Nora saw that he was holding up a clunky green radio, antenna extended. "You're kidding me. Are the batteries dead?"

"Nope. Full charge. All I get is that same static that wavers in and out."

"I kept getting the same thing on my cell phone just a few minutes ago. I even went out to the far end of the beach facing the mainland."

"Like I said before," he told her. "It sounds like a military jammer. What do you make of that?"

Trent distracted her. She wanted to continue with her dissection. "Why would the army jam this island?"

"There's no reason that I can imagine, and that's what bothers me. I just have this funny feeling that something's going on here that they didn't tell me."

Nora thought about it. "You know, it could simply be some other kind of interference." She pointed to the door. "Or maybe there's some naval ship out in the gulf, testing its jammers."

"That's an idea," he agreed. "Or it could be the air force base in Tampa, or the National Guard on maneuvers somewhere."

These were logical explanations, so . . .

Why is he paranoid? she wondered.

"What's this?" he asked next, spying the dead possum in the box.

"I found a nest of them, all dead. And—well—I guess I should tell you this now—but they were killed by the same parasite that was in Annabelle's lobster. And it's the same species of worm that she found in the shower yesterday."

The information jolted him. "But that thing was as long as my forearm. The worms from the lobster were *tiny*."

"They grow fast," was all she could say, and when she looked back in the microscope, she saw that the ova had doubled in size. "We could have a bit of a problem here. These worms can infect mammals, and . . ."

"*We're* mammals," Trent said very dryly. He stared off through his next contemplation. "And we don't have any way to get off the island, and to make matters worse—"

"No way to call out to someone," Nora realized. "But we shouldn't overreact. Small mammals are one thing, but humans are much more sophisticated, not to mention we have much more efficient immune systems." It seemed an appropriate thing to say, but there still wasn't much consolation. "But we'll still have to safe-guard ourselves."

"What do you mean?"

Her eye was back at the microscope. "We don't know what this is, but if it's anything like what we *think* it is we shouldn't take chances." The ova continued to grow under the microscope, a shimmering, yellow spectacle.

"What's the worst-case scenario?" Trent asked. "What are the chances of these things actually being able to kill humans?"

A lanky shadow crossed the room. "They may have already done that . . ."

It was Loren who'd come in.

Nora was almost shocked by his appearance: drip-ping wet and trembling.

"You look like you've just seen a ghost," Trent said.

"Not a ghost, a corpse," Loren replied.

"What?"

Loren dropped his gear. "I went back out to the bristleworm nest. The parasite's infected everything—I couldn't believe how fast it tore through the area. Then I found a dead body."

Trent squinted. "Are you sure? The three of us were out there an hour ago. There was no body."

"It was in the trench."

Nora stood up and faced him. "Loren, this is very important. Was the body infected by the parasite we've found?"

He sat down, brushed wet hair out of his eyes. "I couldn't tell, it was too decomposed."

"So it's been there a long time," Trent figured.

"Not necessarily. In water this warm, plus bottom feeders? A body wouldn't last long at all," Nora said.

"And who the hell's body is it?" Trent asked next. "We're the only ones on the island."

Nora looked to Trent. "Go find Annabelle and bring

her in here. We're going to have to have a group discussion. Her little photo shoot isn't important anymore—we don't know what we might be up against, and with no boat and all our phones inoperable, we might be in some serious trouble."

"What about the phones?" Loren asked with some alarm. "My cell phone worked fine yesterday."

"Try it now," Trent suggested. "Nothing's been getting through all day, not even my radio."

"Lieutenant Trent says the interference sounds like a jammer," Nora added.

Loren's brow creased at the comment. "That's ridiculous." And he dug his cell phone out of his bag, dialed some numbers.

"You're right," he muttered a minute later.

The dilemma trebled with each thought. *Can't get off the island—no boat. Can't call for help—the phones and radios aren't working for some unknown reason. There's a parasite on the island that might be able to infect humans . . . oh, and by the way, we've also got a dead body in the water, and nobody knows who it is . . .*

"Wasn't Annabelle with you when you found this dead body you think you saw?" Trent said.

Loren clearly didn't care for the structure of the sentence. "I *saw* a body. I don't *think* I saw one, I *saw* one."

Trent held up his hands. "Fine, but how do you know the body isn't her?"

The question silenced them all.

"Couldn't be," Loren insisted. "You and Annabelle went back to the beach when the three of us were looking for bristleworms. I stayed out. That's when I found the corpse."

Nora tried to rein in some reason. "One thing at a time. Forget about corpses and jammers and parasites right this minute. Lieutenant, I think the best idea is for you to find Annabelle, while Loren and I do some more tests on this worm."

Trent didn't seem overly pleased, but he agreed, "All right," and left the head shack.

"So you were right—it can infect mammals," Loren said when he noticed the dead possum. He looked into the scope. "Jesus. Some of the ova are still growing, while others have already hatched."

"You're kidding . . ." Nora hadn't seen that. *Another fluke.* "It looks like a Trichinella, and it's acting like a number of species from the order, but—"

"Nora, this worm is acting like a whole bunch of *different* worms," he said, "and we both know that."

When Nora took another look herself, she saw that some of the tiny ova had already hatched into worms that were already a half inch long. "This is going to become a mess real fast. They're growing off the slide."

"Isolate one ovum and one worm, then—"

"Kill everything else," she finished his thought. She placed a worm and an unhatched ovum in a petri dish, then scraped everything else into a plastic container and sprayed it with repellent. "I want to see what this ovum's going to do."

"It might be an infertile mutagen carrier," Loren speculated.

"That's what I was thinking." But it was also what she was *fearing.* Once a species got this big, who knew what effect it would have on humans? "And we're going to keep this worm alive—to see just how big it gets." She left the ovum in the dish and forceped the now inch-long worm into a glass beaker. "Why don't you check out the mother possum?"

Loren slid the box over and pulled up the other microscope. "At least it doesn't stink yet. The only thing grosser than a possum is a rotten possum."

"It had already given birth to the babies," Nora told him. "It's obvious it hasn't been dead more than a few hours."

"And just more proof of a parasite that can live on land and in water."

"Um-hmm."

Loren wasted no time in making a transabdominal incision on the adult possum. When he parted the rive with dissection probes, he simply stared. "I don't even have to put any tissue samples under the scope to see that this possum is seriously fucked up."

"Huh?" Nora leaned over and looked.

"There's nothing inside. All internal organs are absent."

"That's impossible. It hasn't been dead long enough to suffer that level of putrefaction."

"I'm not even smelling putrefaction, Nora, not a trace. Somehow the entirety of its organ systems was removed before any cellular deterioration could take place."

"Eviscerated by a predator?"

"The body was intact," he objected. "No cuts on it, no bite marks. If a skunk or another possum ate this thing's innards, there'd be bite marks on the abdomen."

Now Nora could see what he meant. "And it couldn't be a bacterial infection or a corruptive stomach virus because there'd still be signs of decomposition."

"And there isn't any," Loren finished, frustrated. He pushed away from the table, arms crossed in thought. "So you know what I'm thinking now?"

Nora nodded. "This is the same way that chitin-penetrating nematodes *eat*."

"Yeah, but they don't eat five-pound mammals, they eat quarter-ounce crustaceans and mollusks." He looked over at Nora's microscope. "What's your ovum doing now?"

Nora eyed the scope. "Shit, it's about half the size of a marble now. A half hour ago it was smaller than a pencil point."

Trent came back in, looking just as flustered as Nora and Loren. "What's wrong with you two? You looked pissed."

"Not pissed," Loren offered. "More like aggravatedly confounded."

Trent frowned. "I can't find Annabelle anywhere."

"That's not good," Loren said. "Especially if we've got the kind of trouble we think we might have."

"What are you talking about?" Trent demanded, losing some patience.

"Well, Lieutenant," Nora began, "we seem to have a tiny parasitic worm that lives on land and sea and may be able to grow to unheard-of proportions. Big enough, at least, to attack, and kill, that." And she pointed to the possum on the table.

"Before you started cutting on it, it didn't look *attacked*," Trent said.

"Something sucked this thing's guts out for food," Loren specified.

Nora tacked on, "And then laid eggs in all its babies. And the eggs were the same yellow things we saw in the shower stall the other day."

"You can't be serious," Trent dismissed.

"Look familiar, Lieutenant?" Nora picked up the microscope slide and showed him what was on it: a yellow ovum with bloodred spots, the size of a pea.

"Holy shit . . ."

"This thing's probably increased in size a hundredfold in less than an hour."

Trent rubbed his brows. "How is that possible?"

"We don't know," Loren said. "High infantile growth rates among worms and other soft-bodied invertebrates aren't uncommon. But motile ova like this are another story. They always stay the same size before they hatch."

Trent eyed the ticklike pod. It was moving about very slightly via its cilia. "So that thing's going to hatch into a worm."

"Maybe, maybe not," Nora said. "Certain types of ova—like certain types of sperm cells—aren't always fertile."

"That one's big enough to dissect now, Nora," Loren reminded her.

"Good idea." She placed the slide back under the scope, then carefully wielded forceps with one hand, and one of the microscalpels with the other.

"Ten to one there's no embryo in it," Loren said.

"I'm not following any of this now," Trent admitted. "I thought an ovum and an egg were the same thing."

"Not quite," Loren offered. "An egg always carries an embryo, while ova sometimes have dual purposes."

"I still don't get it."

"Be patient . . ." Nora held the yellow bud down with the tines of the forceps, then gingerly cut into the rubbery outer hull. The ovum popped more than split, and out issued a dollop of jellylike muck laced with something like white threads.

"You were right," she said. "There's no worm larva inside, just some white strands. Probably a mutagenic protein." Next she plucked up several of the previously killed ova and similarly cut them open. "Looks like half of these have infantile worms in them—"

"And the other half contain the mutagen," Loren already knew. "Just like a lot of the Trichinellas."

Trent shook his head. "Would somebody please explain what you're talking about?"

Nora sat back and began, "Motile ova—in other words, egg carriers that move about independently—

are part of this worm's reproductive system. Typically a parasitic worm will lay its ova in a living host. The non-fertile ova release a mutagen that genetically alters the host's own reproductive systems to make it a more compatible natal environment. Later, the fertile ova hatch. The mutagenesis has occurred in order to force the host to bear the worm's young."

"Yuck," Trent remarked.

"Sure, but a perfect system that increased the odds of positive reproduction. A similar thing happens in many mammals including humans, believe it or not. Not with ova but with sperm cells. Most people don't know that only about half of a man's sperm exist to fertilize a female egg. The remaining sperm have alternate duties: to kill sperm from other males, for instance, to run interference against bacteria that possess spermicidal traits. Some sperm even release protein secretions that fool another male's sperm into believing it to be an egg, wasting its potential. All for the sake of increasing the chances of reproductive success."

"You're right," Trent admitted. "I didn't know that. I thought all sperm was the same."

"Well, it's not, and neither are ova. This worm's ova have multiple purposes, too: to genetically adapt a host—crab, mollusk, shrimp, and in this case even a possum—to become an unwilling reproductive vessel. And that's exactly what alarmed Loren and me about this worm. It looks a lot like an order of roundworm—or nematode—called Trichinella and Trichina."

"That sounds familiar for some reason," Trent said after a pause.

"Sure," Loren said. "Everyone's heard of trichinosis."

More recognition in Trent's eyes. "The stuff you get from eating uncooked pork."

"Right. That worm—the *Trichinella spiralis*—and others like it can mutagenically change a host to make it more habitable to its own young, too. But the difference is—"

Nora took it from there. "Those kinds of worms never grow more than a few millimeters in length—but look how big this one's gotten just in the last hour."

She held up the beaker.

"Christ!" Trent exclaimed.

The worm inside was now eight inches long and squirming vigorously.

"The similarities are interesting," Nora continued, "but so are the differences. The *Trichinella spiralis* is an inborn worm—meaning it doesn't live on land or in water. The species exists entirely in hosts, transferring from one to another through food and excrement."

"Lovely," Trent said, making a nauseated smirk.

"But there are plenty of Trichinella-like nematodes that live on land as free-ranging worms, and plenty more that are marine and freshwater species. None of them, however, can do both."

"But this one can," Loren said.

"The most alarming thing about this worm is that it actually resembles several totally different types of worm all in one."

Loren: "It's almost like this thing is part earthworm, part leech, part clam worm, and part trichinosis worm."

"A mutation?" Trent attempted. "From chemicals in the water or something?"

"No mutation could cross-breed multiple species," Nora informed him. "We've seen evidence that it's a chitin penetrator—like a clam worm."

"From the lobster," Trent remembered.

"Exactly. The worm initially infected the lobster by burning a hole in its shell with its digestive enzymes and then injecting its ova through the hole. These kinds of worms also eat the same way."

"Eat?" Trent questioned.

Loren indicated the dead possum. "By filling a host's abdominal cavity with the same corrosive enzymes. The enzymes dissolve the internal organs, and then the worm sucks it back out. A liquefied meal. Lots of worms eat this way, and lots of insects too. Flies are the best-known example."

Trent was staring at the possum. "Wouldn't it take, like, a *really big* worm to eat all the organs in that possum?"

"It sure would," Nora admitted. "And that's another reason we're worried about this." She held up the beaker again. The worm was now pushing ten inches. "We've seen how big this thing has gotten in less than an hour. How big will it be after a full day?"

"Or a full week?" Loren posed. He gulped at the thought. "A worm that could successfully attack a possum this size and be able to consume probably a full pound of internal organs . . ."

Now it was Trent's turn to gulp. "How . . . big . . . would a worm like that have to be?"

Nora took a guess after a few moments of uncomfortable silence. "Two or three inches in diameter, at least. And at least ten feet long."

Priorities, Nora was thinking now. *We've got a few.*

"All this talk of worms," Trent remarked. He brushed his arm as if there might be bugs on it. "It's making me paranoid."

"I keep looking over my shoulder," Loren added, "thinking there might be worms behind me, or ova."

They were back at the campsite now, sitting solemnly at the old picnic table. There was nothing more they could do in the lab.

Nora grabbed her snorkeling gear. "We have to identify some priorities. If it turns out this worm *can* infect humans, we could be in a heap of trouble, especially since we can't seem to get off the island right now."

"What should we do?" Trent asked. He was the group's official leader, but now he seemed to be showing some insecurities. "We *have* to find Annabelle."

"Right," Nora agreed. "And that's what you and Loren should do."

"You're going back in the water?" Loren asked.

"I have to. You said you saw a dead body out there near the trench. I hate to say it, but are you absolutely sure it wasn't Annabelle?"

"Impossible." Loren felt certain. "It was too decomposed. She'd been with me and Lieutenant Trent less than an hour before."

"And she came back ashore with me," Trent added.

Nora looked at him. "Where did she go then?"

"I . . . don't know."

"The body did appear to be female," Loren admitted. "There was still some blond hair hanging off the scalp."

"Shit!" Trent said.

"But there was almost nothing left," Loren went on. "The flesh was hanging off the bones. The body's probably been out there for days."

"Sharks, eels, and a variety of bottom dwellers can reduce a human body to next to nothing real fast," Nora reminded. "I have to have a look, to make sure it's not her. And I also need to examine it as closely as possible. Whoever's body it is, I need to see if the worms could be responsible."

"We should go with you," Loren said.

"No, we need to maximize our time. You two look for Annabelle. Split up, check everywhere. And keep trying your cell phones—and your radio, Lieutenant."

Trent seemed unsure, even shaky. "What do we do if we can't find Annabelle?"

I don't know, Nora thought truthfully. *I'm more worried about what we DO find. More worms. BIG ones.* "You'll find her. Let's meet back here in two hours exactly. And good luck."

The two men branched off while Nora trudged down the trail toward the beach. Now she knew what Trent and Loren meant about being paranoid. With every step she looked to her sides, half expecting to see some very large pink nematodes squirming in wait. She couldn't pass a tree trunk without inspecting it for signs of the yellow motile ova. *I just cannot BELIEVE what we've stumbled on,* she thought.

On the beach she noticed the tide was coming up, with a rougher chop than usual. She took an uncomfortable glance at the sun. In another few hours there wouldn't be enough light to snorkel at all. . . .

She pulled on her flippers, lowered her mask, and waded in.

Skimming along the bottom, she knew it was her imagination when she began to feel inhibited. The water wasn't *really* murkier, and there weren't *really* fewer fish about—she simply imagined it. Farther out, she snorkeled a deep breath and dove.

Several sea urchins lay upside down—dead. Next, she picked up an upside-down stone crab and looked at its hard-shelled underside. There was a hole in it.

She wended around a large boulder, then stopped. Another dozen crabs lay similarly upside down. *They've all got holes in them!* she saw.

Evidence of a chitin-penetrating parasite.

Another sea urchin quivered in a small crevice. Nora flipped it over and recoiled.

Fixed to the urchin's mouth was a six-inch-long pink worm.

Nora thrust away with her flippers, repulsed. *The worms are killing everything . . .*

The next outcropping of boulders was crawling with yellow ova . . .

I have to be real friggin' careful! she yelled at herself.

When she got to the magnificent coral deposits that flagged the trench, she saw nothing but a carpet of dead scarlet bristleworms. They lay curled up like red litter, tossing slightly in the current.

The entire nest has been routed . . .

The impulse to leave couldn't have been stronger, but there was still one more thing she *had* to do.

The corpse.

Maybe he imagined it, she wished. *Maybe it was a dolphin skeleton or something . . .* She skimmed by more clumps of coral, and there it was: the darkening decline that marked the tip of the trench. *Deeper than I thought,* she realized, flipping downward. And it was darker. She kicked out and glided another dozen feet.

Nora stared through the prism of her mask.

The arrangement of flesh and bones lay before her almost as if it expected her. Scraps of fabric around the hips indicated shorts too skimpy for a man, and another band of fabric about the rib cage was clearly a bikini top. It was orange.

Does Annabelle have an orange bikini? She couldn't recall.

Nora felt haunted as she hovered over the remnants of a living person. Eyeless sockets looked back at her, and something like a grin struggled through the waxen, swollen traces of flesh around the mouth. White teeth glimmered through. A flap of white skin floated off the chest, darkened by the circle of a nipple. Nora found herself fingering her own gold cross as she hovered closer. Bones were all that remained of the feet, and off the femurs and shins, more white flesh wobbled like jelly. White hipbones broke through the skin of the pelvis.

She heard her own teeth grinding when she peered again to the flesh-specked face. Loren was right; clumped tresses of hair floated tentacle-like off the scalp, too light to be brunet, but it seemed longer than Annabelle's hair.

I'm pretty sure this isn't her.

But if it wasn't Annabelle . . . who was it?

The intense grotesquerie of what she was looking at felt as palpable as a gust of current. She wanted to leave now, but . . .

She knew she'd have to look closer for another moment, for any evidence that the worms might have done this.

There were no ova *on* the body, but what about inside?

Aw, shit, I don't want to do this!

The cadaver's bare abdomen was stretched across the hips tight as a drum skin, and as white. The belly button was a concise pock against the bloodless flesh. The idea of pulling the corpse ashore for a makeshift autopsy was out of the question; it would fall apart at the joints from the turbulence.

I'll part the belly a little, take a look inside . . .

She shone down her flashlight, while her other hand unsheathed her utility knife. She thought of grave robbing when she brought the tip of the blade to the corpse's abdomen.

The sharp steel tip hadn't penetrated more than an inch before three long pink ropes flew out of the cadaver's mouth.

Nora's heart felt stabbed. For a moment, she blacked out from the shock of what she'd witnessed, dozens of feet under water, in dead silence.

But there was her evidence.

The worms were a yard long each. They corkscrewed away from her, their grotesque bright pink skin shimmering.

Holy, holy, holy SHIT! she thought.

Then she froze in the water when a fourth, longer worm shot out of the knife hole and wrapped around her waist so quickly it was on her before she even saw it—

CHAPTER NINETEEN

(I)

But when Slydes noticed the dead worms floating in the bilge, he also noted that the bilge line seemed a little high.

This is turning into one FUCK of a shitty day, he thought. *My brother's dead, a bunch of fuckin' worms somehow ate HOLES in my engine block, and now I guess they ate holes in the hull, too!*

Yes, the bilge line was very slowly rising. He leaned back out of the engine compartment, veins thumping at his temples.

"The boat's sinking!" he snapped to Ruth.

"The *fuck* it is!" she bellowed back.

"Come on!"

"Come on *where,* for shit's sake?"

Slydes was beginning to see the limits of his patience. He lowered his voice, his eyes hard on her.

"Ruth. I just got done telling your dumb ass that the boat's *sinking*. That means we need to be *off* the boat."

Too much stress and confusion had taken too great a toll on poor Ruth. Things just weren't working right upstairs. "I don't wanna go back on the island!"

"We ain't got much of a choice, do we?"

"The snakes! The zombie!"

Those worms are so damn big she thinks they're snakes, he reminded himself. And Jonas had mentioned some big guy out there, who was all fucked up from the worms, and something about military people in gas masks. But it gave him an idea . . .

"There's gotta be another boat somewhere on this island," he said.

"The photographer people!"

"Naw, they came by helicopter, but there's some other people here. Jonas told me about 'em. We'll rip off their boat."

"Fuck yeah!"

There wasn't much to salvage. Slydes grabbed the flashlight, a knife, and some tools. "We'll hide out at the head shack till dark, then find us a boat. Let's go."

Ruth, still dressed in nothing but the long pink T-shirt, stood hesitantly on the side ladder, peering down. "Slydes? There might be more worms in the water."

Slydes took a handful of her hair and—

Splash!

—heaved her over the side, then stepped down after her.

The tide was up now, the water up to their chins. When they struggled ashore, Slydes looked back at his former pride and joy.

The boat sank before his eyes.

(II)

"Annabelle!"

Loren was winding himself by the constant calling out. He'd searched the entire north point of the island—Annabelle hadn't been found at the campsite, shower, or head shack area, and there was no sign of her on the beach. Her camera and snorkeling gear were stowed in her tent.

Where the hell is she! he thought in an uncharacteristic flare of anger. *We might have a serious parasitic threat going on here, and she's out lollygagging.* He stomped through more brush, whacking branches out of the way. Every so often he'd see an ovum or two on the trail, which he gladly stepped on. They popped like bubble wrap.

The farther trails were so unpronounced they barely existed. *Pretty clear no one's walked here in years.* There was no reason to, even when the missile site was up and running.

A cigarette butt on the ground looked relatively new. *None of us smoke,* he reminded himself. The knowledge gave him a creepy feeling in his gut. Then he noticed something shiny. *A quarter?* he guessed.

Loren picked it up.

It was a cap from a beer bottle.

This wasn't terribly surprising: *Trent said that college kids sneak on the island sometimes.* But like the cigarette butt, the cap looked brand-new.

Just as he thought the trail would diminish to nonexistence, it fanned outward. Loren followed it another hundred yards and—

How do you like that?

—found himself standing at the edge of a well-enclosed lagoon. Anchored right off the rocky shore was a long—and very new-looking—boat. A Boston Whaler, he knew at once. A nice, pricey little pleasure boat.

So we're not alone here after all.

Loren didn't hesitate climbing aboard. The boat was obviously unoccupied. Storage bins lining the deck were filled with life jackets, towels, and assorted boating gear.

Damn . . .

No radio. But the boat hadn't been here long. *At least we can get off the island now,* he realized. *All we have to do first is find the owner of this thing.*

But then another thought drummed in his head.

That is, if the owner's still alive.

For all Loren knew, the owner of this Boston Whaler and the rot-riddled corpse he'd found in the trench were one in the same.

He needed to think. He sat down on a rolled-up tarp in the aft area, but—

What the SHIT!

The tarp thrashed when he sat down on it.

"Get away, get away, get away!" a muffled voice was suddenly shrieking.

Loren stumbled back at the shock.

There's someone under the tarp!

When the tarp came unraveled, a dark-haired young woman emerged, just as terrified as Loren. She wore bikini bottoms, a sweat-drenched T-shirt, and sneakers. And the nearly insane look in her eyes didn't set Loren at ease when he noticed what was in her shaking hand:

A big revolver.

"Don't shoot," Loren's voice cracked.

"Who are you?" she wailed.

Loren hoped he hadn't had an accident in his trunks. "Loren Fredrick," he answered in a voice as shaky as this woman's gun hand. "I'm an associate professor at the University of Southern Florida. I'm here as part of an escort group for a nature photographer—it's all sponsored by the college." Sweat was dripping into his eyes. "Now, could you please put the gun down? I'm not going to hurt you—I'm just looking for a way off the island."

The pistol jiggled as she stared back at him, weighing his words. Finally, her gun hand lowered.

Thank you Jesus, Mary, and Joseph! "Now that you know who I am, who are you? And whose boat is this?"

She sat at the aft rail, her hair disheveled, stringy from the humidity. "My name's Leona Long," she said. Her terror finally wound down. "I came here with some friends—Carol, Howie, and Alan—this is Alan's boat."

"Came here to party?"

She nodded, and forearmed sweat off her brow.

"We need you and your friends to take us off this island," Loren told her. "Where are they now, and . . . Why were you under that tarp? It must be hot as hell under all that thing."

Her eyes looked dull and lost when she gazed back at him. "My friends are all dead. I was hiding here."

"Hiding from what?"

She spared a sardonic chuckle. "You have no idea what's going on here, do you?"

The remark seized Loren. "Well, I think I do—at little, at least. Were you hiding from the worms?"

"Yes!" she cried. "You know about them? And those little yellow bug things?"

"They're called motile ova," Loren explained. "They're the worm's eggs. The worm itself is a kind of parasite that we've never encountered before. We think that these worms as well as their ova can infect humans."

"You think right," Leona asserted.

"So your friends were killed by—"

"Yes—Jesus—yes. The worms were actually *growing* inside them. And I saw other bodies too; there was a group of students who came out here several weeks ago. I'm pretty sure I'm the only one left alive. The only thing I could think to do was hide here; I was hoping someone would just . . . find me, eventually." She looked around groggily. "I hid under the tarp—I didn't want those other guys to see me."

Loren's brow shot up. "What other guys?"

"There's military people on this island, too. I think they put those worms here to see what they'd do to humans. They've got these little cameras all over the place—they're *monitoring* us, for God's sake. It's like we're part of some scientific test."

Now, here was some news. *Military,* Loren thought. *Cameras . . . one of the things Nora found . . .* "And you've seen these military men yourself?"

"Yes, a couple of times," she murmured. "They never confronted any of us—they just kept back in the woods. We'd catch glimpses of them. I even saw one of them taking pictures of one of the bodies—after it had been infected by the worms. They're in gas masks and black suits with hoods."

"Well, how did they get on the island themselves? Do they have a boat too?"

"I don't know," she said. Her shoulders drooped. "And I don't care." She began to choke back sobs. "I just want to go home."

"Don't worry, we'll get you home . . ." Then Loren looked down at the boat, and blinked at the incongruence of what she'd just said. "How come you're still here? If you knew your friends were all dead, why didn't you just take the boat out of here yourself?"

"No keys. Alan's got them, and he's long gone."

A hope glimmered. "Where's his body? We can still get the keys."

"He's out rotting in the woods somewhere!" she

whined. "I don't know! You want to go digging through a dead man's pockets when he's full of those things?"

She's right about that, he realized. "We don't even need the keys. We can push the boat out of the cove if we have to, let the current take us—one way or another, we're getting out of here. Come on, I'll take you to where my friends are."

Leona stiffened. "I—I don't think I want to do that. I'd rather stay here."

"You'll be perfectly safe," Loren assured her.

"How do you know your friends aren't infected by now?"

"They're not, trust me. I just saw them a little while ago—"

She was shaking her head. "You don't understand. Those little yellow things are all over the place. They'll fall on you from the trees if you're not careful. And some of the worms are really big. I'm not going back into those woods; I'm lucky enough to have made it this far without one getting me." She paused, eyeing him. "Why don't you and I leave right now?"

"That's impossible," Loren told her. "My friends aren't infected. I guarantee it. But I can't just leave without them."

"I think you should," she said, fingering the gun.

Oh no. This is going to be a problem, Loren realized. Should he go for the gun? Loren knew his karma didn't work that way. *I'd get my skull parted . . .* "Okay, look. You stay here and wait for me to get back with the others. Will that work?"

The lost gaze searched his face. "Yeah, I guess. I'll be able to tell if any of them are infected."

Loren assessed her comment. *Interesting.* "How *can* you tell, by the way? You seem to know a lot about this. If a person's infected initially, how do you know?"

"By looking at him," she said. "My boyfriend—Howie—he turned real fast. Had to have been less than an hour before the signs started showing."

"What are the signs?"

"Your skin turns to this mucky yellow—same color as the eggs. After a while you even develop red specks along with the yellow."

More information of interest. *She's talking about the mutagenic element. Contagion would depend on the level of viral admission, and also antibody resistence of each infectee.* And Loren also knew—based on his knowledge of the Trichinella order itself—that a positive infection could bring about much, much more than a change in skin pigmentation. *No need to tell her that part,* he considered. Then he remembered Annabelle. *Hopefully Trent's already found her by now. I'll just go grab Nora, and then we can get the hell off this island.* But as he was about to do so he thought he noticed . . .

Wait a minute . . .

Her dull gaze came alert. "Why are you looking at me like that?"

Loren was looking at the crotch of her bikini bottoms. "What's . . . what's that? Down there?" He pointed.

The girl slowly looked down at herself. An uneven crescent of skin emerged right at her bikini line.

The crescent was yellow, almost like a stain, or a rash.

Then dread seemed to bloom over her head like a halo. "Oh no, no, no!" she groaned.

She yanked up her T-shirt.

"No," she whispered.

Her abdomen had turned yellow, with bloodred specks. Her eyes welled with tears as, next, a dozen motile ova began to inch out of her bikini bottoms.

Loren didn't even have time to lunge for the gun—or even implore her not to do it—when she put the revolver's barrel to her head and—

Bam!

Leona's horror was gone, along with the side of her head. Loren could do little more than stare through the shock. The woods froze around the lagoon, the silence now somehow more deafening than the discharge of the bullet.

Shit, was all he could think.

He quickly pushed her body overboard, then picked up the gun and made a swift exit off the boat . . .

(III)

Darkness was beginning to sift into the woods when Trent heard the shot.

He froze in place, eyes snapped open.

Yes, it sounded like a single, distant gunshot.

No. It couldn't be. He patted his gun belt, felt the butt of his army-issue 9mm strapped snugly into the holster. *There's only one person on this island who's armed,* he reminded himself. *Me.*

The mainland was only a mile or two away; sounds could carry in strange ways, especially over water. *Probably a truck backfiring,* he considered. *Or maybe a sonic boom from a jet flying back to the air force base.*

Yes. Maybe.

He stomped through most of the island's western end, but still no sign of Annabelle. *This shit is getting old,* he thought with a gripe. *I don't care how good-looking she is. I'm tired of bushwhacking through these woods . . .*

And in the back of his mind he remained all too aware of Nora's and Loren's concerns. *Maybe this worm stuff really is serious, too. They seem to think so, and they're experts.*

But during his annoying trek, he hadn't encountered any worms, nor their accommodating ova.

Trent began to feel like an idiot before long. *A wild-goose chase, only the goose is a brick shit-house blonde*. His watch told him it was almost time to be heading back. Nora would have more information about the dead body out in the water—*If there really IS a dead body*. The kid could've been mistaken. Anna-belle was probably back at the campsite by now . . .

Probably drunk, he added the thought, *from that flask full of rum. And I'm running around out here looking for her* . . . More irritation bristled.

Yeah, he thought. *I'll bet she's passed out drunk some-where, so to hell with this. I'm going back to the camp.*

Just as Trent turned to abandon his search—

whap—

Something landed on his head. He flinched away, aghast, swatting about his head. *What the fuck was that! Did one of those worms just land on me?*

He flung something long and stringy off his neck.

"I thought that might get your attention," a sultry voice said from somewhere. Trent's shock faded when he saw what had hit him in the head . . .

Not a worm. A white G-string.

Annabelle grinned coyly at him. She leaned against a tree, stark naked, her tan lines raving at him.

"Where the hell have you been?" he almost yelled.

"Just wandering around. Where have *you* been?"

"Looking for you!"

Her eyes narrowed a little, she pouted at him. "You sound mad."

"I am mad! We've been looking for you for almost two hours! Nora and Loren think these worms might be dangerous to humans. We all need to stick together and think of a way to leave the island."

"Oh, let's not leave yet." Her voice remained sing-songy, flirtatious. Trent noticed her beach bag at her feet, and the uncapped and obviously empty flask. *Just as I thought.* "Come on, you're drunk. Something serious might be going on, and you're out here getting loaded."

"There *is* something serious going on," she said. "Me and you. Right now."

Trent couldn't help it, but at least he was fairly sure that no other red-blooded man could either. His anger dissolved and then he was walking right up to her. *Here we go again* . . . His gaze slid up over her body, lingering over every perfect curve. Suddenly, worms, dead bodies in the water, and inexplicable electronic jamming were the furthest things from his mind.

He just couldn't help it.

The image of her body and its accommodating promise dragged him to her as effectively as a chain around his neck.

"That's better," she whispered when they embraced. Her hot hands seemed impatient when she lifted his T-shirt over his head, and a moment later he was back in his lustful heaven, his bare skin pressed against the warm, plenteous bosom. *Oh God, I am so pussy-whipped!* Trent gave up altogether. Nature was calling again, and he simply didn't have the will to say no.

He could feel the turgid nipples pressing against him, could feel the heat radiating off her body and surrounding him, pulling him. Trent was none too daintily sucking her neck when he felt her fingers teasing around his groin. The sexual energy between the two of them was merging into a cocoon of antsy, hot static.

She was about to unfasten his gun belt and delve into his trunks when she suddenly nudged him back.

"Let's get kinky," she whispered.

"Huh?"

Annabelle picked up the beach bag and slipped out the drawstring. Now her fingers spidered across his chest. "Tie me up."

Trent was thrown off guard. *Tie her up? In the*

woods? I just want to get laid again. Trent had never really been into such things but . . .

"You really are buzzed," he said.

"Um-hmm." Her big, wanton eyes blinked. "Makes me hotter." She put the drawstring in her hand and offered her wrists.

What a nut . . . but I guess I don't really care. He lashed her wrists together, and thought, *What now?* but she pointed just above her.

"Lift me up. Right there."

The crook of a broken bough stuck out of the tree. Annabelle held her arms up, elucidating her breasts, as Trent palmed her hips, raised her enough to get the lash hooked on the bough, then released her. Now she stood before him on her tiptoes, stretched out like something for display. Her breathing grew heavier at once.

She's really into this kooky stuff, he realized, but scarcely cared. He began kissing her breasts and tonguing around her neck. Words weren't necessary now, just primal action. Her stretched body trembled as Trent's mouth embarked on a hot, wet trek from the dimple of her throat, and down . . .

"Lower," was the only word she breathed.

The officer knew what she wanted, and took his time getting to it. His mouth sucked fresh sweat off her skin, between the valley of her breasts, then more tan skin, then her navel. Her body was quivering now. Trent lingered at the navel, knowing that it only maximized her expectations; now *he* was toying with *her,* a notion that seemed ultimately satisfying.

After minutes more of excruciating mouth-play on her abdomen, he finally lowered himself to his knees.

She breathed through hisses, then quickly raised her legs, splaying everything before his face. The bottoms of her thighs rested on his shoulders.

Trent tinkered further with her angst, refusing to arrive at the mark. She was truly hanging now, her arms straight as rods, her bare heels thunking his back, trying to pull his mouth closer. Trent just kissed and sucked ever more along the insides of her thighs.

The way she began to shudder, he would've thought she was climaxing even before his mouth finally found her sex.

Annabelle let out a delicious moan. If Trent had been able to see her face, surely her eyes would've been squeezed shut in the most potent pleasure, and every muscle in her flawless body flexing beneath the tan skin.

Her moans rose to repeated crescendoes, her flesh quaking, then—

Just as he expected her climax to let loose—

"Get me down!" she shrieked. "There's someone behind you!"

Trent heard an unpleasant metallic *clack!* of some sort, and before he realized it might have been the sound of something hitting him on the back of the head, his vision began to blur. It seemed that black ink had been dumped over his consciousness, and—

Trent collapsed flat on his back.

Only one second of awareness ticked by before he'd fully blacked out, and in that second, he saw two things:

Annabelle hanging helpless and naked against the tree.

And a man in a decon suit, gas mask, and hood reaching out for her.

CHAPTER TWENTY

(I)

Nora corkscrewed in the water as the pulsing, pink worm tightened its coil around her waist. Somehow her instinct turned off her panic and turned on her defensive mechanisms; as the worm coiled in one direction, she violently flailed her body in the opposite, hoping to retard the thing's efforts to fully encircle her.

She thrashed, wielding her knife. No thoughts of horror or fear filled her head—only reaction. The worm seemed the width of a garden hose, but it had to have been ten feet long. Eventually it wrapped around her body several times, then began to constrict.

Its strength was dizzying, as though two hefty men were pulling on each end of a rope looped about her waist. Had it gotten around her neck, she knew she'd be strangling now, but this wasn't much better. The worm was trying to squeeze all the air out of her body . . .

Her free hand clamped just under the tapered cone

of flesh that was the worm's head; this was all that kept it from slithering about her throat . . .

Nora was running out of air. Her flippers kicked to the surface, but the worm's posterium—its tail end—raveled around her legs, tightening more.

Meanwhile, unvented carbon dioxide began to swell in her lungs . . .

Through her mask she viewed the worm's eyeless head and the sphincter of muscle that composed its frontal duct. The fleshy ring opened and closed akin to a heart valve, driven to attach itself to her mouth through which it would either empty its digestive enzymes—to feed—or empty its ovarial reservoirs—to plant its eggs.

The mouth had no jaws—just the grotesque, pulsing ring—and no teeth, but instead something worse: a circle of "stylets" that would sink into the meat of her back throat like fishhooks, to keep the worm's body securely attached to the host. The most revolting sensation of Nora's life was the feel of the worm's own throat clamped in her hand, its skin—or hydrostatic sheath—moving back and forth—like the foreskin over an erect penis.

At that moment, she thought: *I'm going to die now* . . .

She felt something tear through her swimsuit—and her skin. Seawater burned into a six-inch-long gash down her abdomen. The worm was now a belt tightened around her waist . . .

Nora's knife had shot down, then, and cut the belt in half.

She'd done it without thinking, cutting herself in order to cut the creature . . .

Half of the worm's length drifted away, dead.

But this left the top half, still alive and squirming.

Nora's blade blurred across her eyes, and severed the worm's head. It floated away, a squirming, pink lump.

The rest of the body unraveled, the clipped end releasing a plume of tea-colored digestive enzymes as well as a slew of underdeveloped ova. In a split second, Nora watched those same corrosive enzymes burn up any ova it came in contact with.

She managed to kick away, as still more of the acids came only inches away from drifting into her face.

Her legs kicked independently from her mind. To escape the corrosive ooze, she'd kicked backward, farther into the trench, and then her back collided with something . . .

A moment of thinking passed.

Then she shot up to the surface, where her head broke the water only a few heartbeats away from the point in which she would've drowned . . .

I'm alive! was her first genuine thought.

She was slowly treading water, to stabilize her metabolism out of shock. Her chest heaved as she sucked in breaths.

I have to get back to the others, she knew. *But . . .*
But . . .

What had that *been?*

Not the worm, but the abutment she'd backed into just after decapitating the worm?

Something not right . . .

Her confusion waylaid her. She was swimming *back* down to the trench, knife in one hand, flashlight in the other.

What the hell was that!

She had to know. A culvert of some sort? An oil pipeline? But what purpose could such things serve twenty feet beneath the Gulf of Mexico near a useless island? She knew there were more worms down there, yet her curiosity seemed fevered. The worms had more than likely swum away, and the enzymes from the one she'd killed would have dispersed in the current. So . . .

I just have to see. She felt driven. *What was that thing I backed up against?*

Her flippers pumped furiously; she swam back down to the trench. Crystalline water glittered, prism-bright. Ys and Ws of coral branched out from the bank, skeletal fingers that seemed to be pointing to secrets.

Nora slowed her descent, then stopped.

The trench stretched onward, probably several hundred feet, and widened to thirty. The sun's angle kept the underwater gouge blotched in cool, teeming darkness. She couldn't see what she'd touched, and only knew that it felt out of place, but . . .

Something's there, she noticed through a squint.

She'd have to surface for more air in another minute, but not till she got a look.

She reached back out into the inkiness and felt it again: a smooth, flat surface, slightly curved. Like metal.

That's when Nora—mildly alarmed—veered the waterproof flashlight around.

She became *severely* alarmed when her eyes registered what she was seeing, and then she shot herself back to the surface, gulping air.

That's—that's—that's . . . CRAZY! she thought.

What she'd seen lying in the trench was an object that could only be a naval submarine . . .

(II)

He was supposed to be here an hour ago, the sergeant thought. He checked all of the rooms in the old control station. *Where the hell is he?*

The sergeant wasn't the overexcitable type. When something went wrong, he simply fixed it, with a calm professionalism. He'd sent the corporal out a while ago, to retrieve the climate sensors and the little bit of field equipment that had been posted outside, but there was no sign of him. *Just what I need. A man away from his post when the mission's winding down . . .*

He was about to check the monitors when he heard footsteps coming down the hall.

The major walked in. "Good news, Sergeant. All of the project's findings have been logged and processed, and every duty protocol has been completed. It's time to leave. The colonel's very pleased with the mission's success."

"That is good news, sir."

"Looking forward to getting back to the post?"

"Yes, sir."

"Get the collection and security gear ready to take out. I'll be securing the specimen data. We'll debark tonight."

"Yes, sir."

The major eyed him. "You seem . . . reserved, Sergeant. Is something wrong?"

The sergeant sighed, his shoulders slumping. "Yes, sir, it appears that there is."

"It *appears* . . ." The ranking officer looked around the room. "Where's the corporal?"

"I sent him out in the field earlier to take the climate sensors off-line. He should have returned by now."

"So he's away from his post without authorization, is what you're saying?"

"Yes, sir, at this point, I'd make that conclusion."

The major muttered something under his breath, then leaned over the security monitors. "He's not in any of the surveillance sectors. I know he was thoroughly screened before this assignment. Do you think he abandoned the mission?"

The sergeant was sweating now. "No, sir. I just can't see that. He knows that we'd find him."

"Does he have any abuse problems?"

"I don't think so, sir. Things like that are usually easy to detect on missions like these. But . . ."

"But what, Sergeant?" the major asked sternly.

"He may have a problem with unauthorized interaction."

The major went silent for several moments. "Don't mince words, Sergeant. You mean you think he's out there *fucking* one of the populace."

"I suppose it's possible, sir. Just based on some comments he's made."

The major shook his head, blank-faced. A blank face, the sergeant knew, was worse than a tirade from any other officer.

"If anything botches this mission, Sergeant, we'll all be ruined. The colonel won't stand for it. He'll be busy for a while so . . . let's suit up. We've got to find the corporal ourselves and get him back here."

"Yes, sir." But the sergeant groaned to himself. This was one of the worst things that could happen.

He grabbed his protective hood and mask, thinking of the corporal. *I should've known. I'll kill him myself, if the major doesn't beat me to it.*

(III)

Part of him felt gypped. These people here were obviously into some bizarre sexual shenanigans. The blonde was *hanging* on the tree, already naked.

All ready for me, the corporal thought.

He knew it was risky . . . but he also knew there was *no way* he'd end this mission before getting a piece of her. At least he wouldn't have to fight with her—she was hanging there for him, like a suit of clothes in a closet. Less time fooling around. *I'll be able to get right to the goods . . .*

But her nakedness did make him feel a little gypped. One thing he'd been looking forward to all this time was the thrill of ripping her clothes off.

Neither of them had seen him watching. The man was on his knees, getting to business. That's when the corporal stepped out and jacked him in the head with his service tool.

The blonde had seen him in that last second. The look in her eyes was delicious: pure horror. *Yeah,* the corporal thought. He liked that. She'd only had a second to scream when—

Clack!

The corporal jacked her out, too. She hung limp from the tree now. Had he killed her?

Who cares?

The corporal had to make this one quick, *real* quick. The sergeant thought he was out pulling in some field equipment, but the corporal had already done that. *If I got caught out here, that would be it for me.*

But this blonde was too much. Some things were worth the gamble . . .

There were other risks, too—the worms and ova, especially. But his field suit and hood would protect him. The thalate and ethylene fibers in the fabric would repel the worms like tear gas, at least that's what they'd been told. The corporal unzipped the front of the suit down to the crotch.

He degloved, too. He *had* to touch her.

Oh, man, this is some prize, he thought, kneading the plump breasts. His hands slid down her sides, reveling at the sensation of warm, damp, tight skin. He could stand only a few moments of this before he lifted her down and dropped her to the ground.

The rape was simple and precise. No frills. *Too bad you won't be conscious for the best fuck of your life,* he thought. He just climbed on and did it. One, two, three.

For some reason, it was always more satisfying when it was against their will.

Now you have something to remember me by.

She hadn't moved a muscle throughout. Again, he thought she might be dead, but then after he made a last grab on her breasts, he felt a heartbeat. The idea of killing her crossed his mind, but the corporal knew he didn't even have time for that. *I better get back to the field station before the sarge gets wise.* He zipped his suit back up and redonned his gloves.

Yes. The corporal really liked these field assignments.

He took a last look at the blonde, who lay crumpled and spread-legged, wrists lashed over her head.

No, he decided. *I won't kill her. I'll leave her for the worms instead.*

He was about to make tracks back to the station, but stopped cold. He thought he'd heard a sound.

A metallic *click.*

Then came the last sound he'd *ever* hear.

Bam!

The corporal collapsed right on top of the blonde, dead from the bullet that had slammed into the middle of his back.

(IV)

Gun smoke stung Loren's eyes. He couldn't believe what he'd just done; he hadn't even given it a thought.

Holy fuck! I just shot a guy in the back!

Only after the pistol pumped out its round did Loren remember he'd never fired a gun in his life. The weapon kicked so hard, it flew out of his hand . . .

He stared through vertigo for several moments, listening to his heart beat. Annabelle's rapist had collapsed right on top of her. When Loren snapped out of it, he rushed over, yanked off the motionless assailant, and tended to Annabelle.

Oh no . . .

Her hands were tied and lay limp over her head. Her legs were disarrayed. Loren felt encased by dread when he put a finger to her throat to check for a pulse. After what seemed a minute, he found one and sighed in relief. He jostled her around, gently slapped her face, but she remained out cold.

"Goddamn, what the hell happened?" Lieutenant Trent had just come to. He sat up, a hand to his head, then stared in disbelief at the scene.

"That guy in the suit raped Annabelle," Loren's voice cracked. "So I . . ."

Trent saw the revolver on the ground. "You shot him?"

"Yeah. Uh, in the back."

Trent instinctively checked his gun belt, found his own pistol intact, then leaned over the man in the suit. "Man, this is really fucked up. Who *is* this guy?"

"I don't know but that gear he's wearing looks military to me," Loren said. "We need to get out of here right now and find Nora. That guy's got colleagues who are going to be looking for him."

"You're right . . ." Trent grabbed the gas-masked man's shoulder, to look at him. "He's military, all right, but I can't tell what branch." The mask's eye portals were mirrored. Trent yanked at the hood but couldn't get it off.

"Help me with her," Loren said. "We need to leave." He picked the revolver up and stuck it in his waistband.

"Where'd you get that?"

"Long story, I'll tell you on the way."

They each shouldered one of Annabelle's arms and stalked off.

"This is crazy," Trent muttered. "Military personnel in decontamination suits?"

"Yeah, and surveillance cameras in the woods and our cell phones and your radio being electronically jammed. Plus a parasitic worm that looks like a genetic hybrid, a damn gene-splicing experiment or something—all on an island nobody knows about."

"I'll bet that guy's with the Army Research Command. We walked right into the middle of one of their black projects by accident."

It sounded too coincidental, but after he thought about it, Loren had no choice but to agree. "I can't think of anything else it could be," he said. "We're in the middle of it, all right, and now we have to get out before we wind up dead. Other people have died on this island—"

"The body you said you saw in the water—"

"Not just that. This pistol I have I took off a dead college girl. She'd committed suicide with it, after telling me that other people have been killed by the worms."

"What?"

Loren sighed. "Just wait till we find Nora. I'll tell you the whole story."

They huffed through more brush. Annabelle didn't weigh much, but under these circumstances, the burden was wearing both men out.

"Stop!" Trent said in a sharp, sudden whisper.

"What?"

The lieutenant stared at Loren. "Did you hear that noise?"

Loren looked desperately about, listening. "I . . . I don't think so . . ."

"Something rustling." Trent seemed sure. He looked up into the trees. "It sounded like it was above us."

Loren looked up, too. "Probably, uh, probably one of those big iguanas, or a tree-nesting bird."

"Yeah," Trent muttered back. "You're . . . probably right."

Before Loren's perceptions could register, something fell from the tree, as if unraveling. He thought of a hose being dropped: *pink* hose, and that's essentially *all* he could think before the two-inch-wide, twenty-foot-long worm unfurled from unseen branches, deftly coiled about Annabelle's chest, and began to lift her upward.

"Holy shit!" Trent yelled.

"Hold on to her!"

Annabelle's unconscious body was being lifted as if on a towline. Trent lashed his arms around a thigh, while Loren grabbed her feet, but then—

"Fuck!" Trent shouted.

They began to rise too; the worm was lifting all three of them. Trent and Loren, out of futility, dropped back to the ground. Trent drew his service weapon and fired several stray shots higher into the branches. "It's like trying to shoot a piece of rope!"

Annabelle's nude body disappeared upward.

Loren shook off his shock and still not really thinking jumped up for some branches. His flip-flops scuffed against bark as he tried to hoist himself up.

Trent grabbed his shoulder. "Forget it, man."

"We can't just leave her!"

"She's gone. There's nothing we can do to help her. What? Climb the tree? You'd never get up there, and even if you could, how are you going to shoot a worm that moves faster than a sidewinder?"

Loren knew he was right, but he still couldn't break his instincts. He tried to pull himself up again: useless. He hung off a short branch like a kid trying to do a pull-up.

"Forget it, man," Trent repeated.

The realities began sinking in all at once. Loren didn't know what to think, but he *did* know that Annabelle was gone.

He dropped back down, and the two men ran off as fast as they could.

Nora, pondering some bizarre realities of her own, stumbled back to the campsite just as Loren and Trent sprinted into the clearing. The three of them nearly collided with one another.

"I found the dead body in the water," Nora announced. "And it was full of worms. At least now we know. These things do attack and infect humans."

Trent sat down at the picnic table, winded. "You can say that again."

"Annabelle's . . . gone," Loren said.

"What do you mean?"

"A worm got her," Trent said.

Nora tried to cogitate. "I saw four of them in the water, and they were all over ten feet long."

"This one was twenty, at least," Trent confirmed.

Loren was getting his breath back. "It could've been longer than that. It was impossible to tell how far it went up the tree."

Here goes, Nora thought. "I also found a submarine."

Loren and Trent stared at her.

She recited the experience in detail.

"I saw that trench," Trent said. "A submarine couldn't fit in it."

"No, no," Nora explained. "Not like a nuclear submarine full of missiles. It was a lot smaller—"

"Like a submersible?" Loren said. "A research submersible? The military uses those all the time. They use them to map transport routes for the navy."

"That's more like what I'm talking about," Nora

said. "And I'm *certain* it wasn't a pipeline or anything like that. It was a submarine. It even had some fins on the side."

"Were there windows?" Trent asked.

"I didn't have time to look over every inch. There were still plenty of worms down there. One of them almost got me . . . till I cut off its head."

And, next, Loren and Trent explained their own encounter.

"A man in a decontamination suit and gas mask?" Nora questioned. "Every new thing we discover looks more and more like a military experiment of some kind."

"And you can bet there are more of those guys on the island somewhere," Trent offered.

"But where?" Loren questioned. "On the submersible?"

"Maybe, but I'd guess they've got their own field station set up out here somewhere," Trent said. "And another thing you can bet on. Whatever this experiment is they're doing, it's definitely a top-secret project. They're not giving a flying fuck about any civilians who get killed. It's almost like they're *hoping* for that—"

"Right," Nora picked up. "That's what the experiment's all about. To see how vulnerable humans are to the worms and ova."

"A potential antipersonnel weapon," Loren posed. "The girl I got this gun from said she came here with several friends, and one by one they'd all been infected by the worms. She said these military guys seemed to be surveying them, which makes sense because of all those tiny cameras out here."

"As far as the military is concerned," Nora said, "we're expendable."

"Yeah," Trent added, "and we're being jammed and there's no way off the island."

Loren sat bolt upright. "Shit! I forgot! There *is* some good news in all of this."

Nora and Trent looked at him.

"We *can* get off the island. Because I know where there's a boat."

"You're pulling our legs?" Trent said. "We could never be that lucky, not after all this shit."

"Well, we *are* that lucky. There's a Boston Whaler anchored in one of the coves. No keys to start the engine, but we can push it out of the cove and drift back to the mainland. It'll be tough if the tides aren't right."

"I'll drag the fucking boat out with my teeth if I have to," Trent said. "If we stay here much longer, we'll be worm food."

"I guess we should leave now . . ." Nora's eyes widened on the others. "But . . . I don't feel right, about—"

"Annabelle," Loren said.

"Should we try to find her?"

Loren and Trent both slowly shook their heads. "There's no way she could've survived," Trent said. He seemed reflective suddenly. "This is a stupid thing to suggest but . . ." He stared off.

"What?" Nora asked.

"I'm really curious about something. I think we should take a chance and stay for at least another hour. The tide'll be higher then anyway, easier to get out." He took out his gun, checked the slide. "I want to have another look at that guy Loren shot."

"What the hell do you want to do that for?" Loren objected. "I thought we wanted to get out of here ASAP."

"We do, but I really want to check that guy's dog tags, see what branch of service he's in."

"That's actually a good idea," Nora offered, "if it's

not too risky. I'd like to know who exactly is behind all this."

Loren maintained his protests. "What difference does it make? Army, navy—who cares? If there's a submersible out there, it's probably the navy. I don't give a shit. Nora, one of those worms lifted Annabelle up into the trees!"

"We'll be careful," Nora said, hoping she wasn't being too naive. "I'm curious about something too. While the lieutenant's checking out that guy in the gas mask, you and I can go check something else."

"What?" Loren asked.

"The other side of the island. Where the original control station is for the old missile site."

CHAPTER TWENTY-ONE

Ruth grabbed Slydes's beefy arm, her eyes wide in trepidation. "We're not going in *there!* Fuck that shit! I'm not going *near* that place!"

Slydes frowned as he sized up the old utility shed. "Keep your voice down," he gruffed. "And what's your damn problem *now?*"

"That's where I fell asleep the other night! Then the zombie dragged me out and dropped me in the woods, for the worms!"

The zombie again. What could Slydes do? It wasn't a zombie, he knew, but it was almost as bad: an infected human. "The zombie ain't here, Ruth. And there might be food in that shed. We ain't eaten anything in a couple of days."

"I ain't fuckin' hungry! Let's go!" she pouted.

"Plus, I'm dyin' of thirst, and don't tell me you ain't either." Slydes pointed through the trees. "There's a cooler right there. Maybe there's something in it we can drink."

"There's nothing in it!" she kept complaining. "And even if there is, it's hot by now. That thing's been there for days." She jerked around, pointing down. "Look, there's a stream. We can drink that water. Then we won't have to go into that fuckin' shed." Animated, she rushed to the narrow brook, got to her knees. She was about to cup some water into her hands, but—

"Fuck," she muttered.

Slydes smiled.

The stream was full of tiny pink worms.

"Yeah, you go ahead and drink that, Ruth. Go ahead."

She rushed back over, grossed out. "Let's just get out of here. You said all we had to do is find one of the other boats."

"We will. In a minute." He grabbed her hair and shoved her toward the shed.

"Fucker!"

"Now come on," he ordered, "and quit being a pain in the ass." *Jesus, this is too much work,* he thought. *Right now her pretty backside ain't nothing but a ball and chain . . .* He followed her as she stumbled forward.

The heat was crushing them; Slydes felt like slow-cooking meat in his jeans and boots, his shirt drenched. Ruth's pink T-shirt looked like wet tissue paper pasted to her bosom and belly. *Pretty soon there won't be any water left in me to sweat out . . .* He didn't know much about medical stuff, but he could imagine that in this heat, with no water, they wouldn't last much longer. In spite of his physical strength, each step reminded him how weak he was getting. Ruth looked like she'd keel over any second.

"Fuck! Look!" she yelled next.

Crawling very slowly down the shed's front wall were half a dozen yellow ova.

Those fuckers! Slydes thought. He remembered them

well. *Some of 'em have baby worms in them, and some of 'em . . .* What had Jonas told him? *Stuff inside that changes you when they bite.* "Just steer clear of them," he told Ruth. He flipped open the cooler sitting out front.

Aw, shit!

It was full of worms and ova. They seemed to be percolating in there, incubating. *They must like heat,* he considered.

He flipped the lid closed. "Nothing in there."

"Oh yeah!" Ruth seemed delighted. She bent over a portable Coleman grill next to the cooler. Dried-up burgers lay on the ground, but next to them lay a barbecue fork. Ruth wielded it like a sword. "Now we can defend ourselves!"

Slydes winced. "All that bong resin's clogged your brain. What are you gonna fight with a barbecue fork?"

"The worms! Next time one sneaks up on us, I'll jab it with this."

"You do that." Slydes dismissed her banter. "Let's just look inside."

Ruth stepped back from the door. "Slydes, I'm fuckin' serious. I don't wanna go in there. The zombie might be there."

"Ruth, if the zombie's in there, I'll shove his head up his ass, okay? Then I'll stick him with your barbecue fork, and that'll be that."

Her puffy lips pressed together. "You don't even believe there *is* a zombie, but I don't give a shit."

"Fine. Now let's go in. I'll even go first." He opened the creaky door, then—

Oh, what the hell?

—grabbed Ruth by the hair and shoved her in first.

"You're a fuck, Slydes! You're a lyin' piece of fuck!"

"Yeah, yeah." He stepped in after her, looked around. At least it was cooler in here, out of the sun; the little windows were open, letting in a bit of a cross breeze.

"See, pea brain? No zombies in here."

Ruth gusted out a relieving sign. "And—shit!" Her dirty bare feet thunked to the corner. "Food!"

Some plastic bags lay on the floor, full of potato chips and cheese curls.

At least that's somethin', Slydes thought. It was the closest he'd come to thanking the Fates. "Any sodas in them bags, any bottled water?"

Ruth bumbled through the bags. "No. But at least we've got something to eat." She ripped open the cheese curls. A moment later, her cheeks looked stuffed as a chipmunk's.

If we don't get some water soon, we're gonna die, Slydes thought point-blank. He didn't dare voice this to Ruth, though. He opened a bag of chips and began munching. *But if I could get that little gas grill lit outside, I could boil some of the creek water.* That would kill any worms or ova. "You got a lighter on you?"

"Fuck no," she said, crunching more curls. Her fingers and puffy lips were orange.

"You gotta be shitting me. You smoke pot like they're cigarettes and you don't have a lighter on you?"

Ruth glared. "Well, I had one, Slydes, but like I told you, before the zombie tried to rape me he tore off my shorts! And the lighter was in my shorts! Does it look like I got any pockets to carry a lighter in?" She faced him arrogantly in the drenched T-shirt, then flapped the damp hem up. "See any lighter, Slydes? Huh?"

"All I see is your dirty camel toe." He pointed to the other corner: some clothes and towels. "There's a pair of shorts there. Put 'em on."

Ruth made a face, as though the suggestion were outlandish. "I'm not putting on some other girl's *shorts*! She might have crotch rot."

"I guarantee you, Ruth, your *own* crotch rot'll kill

anything on them shorts." And then he grabbed her hair and shoved her forward. "Now put 'em on! Every time you bend over, I gotta look at your ass hair."

"I don't have ass hair, you fuck!"

Slydes stared her down. "Your lips are gonna be a lot fatter in about one second—"

Ruth smirked, and pulled on the shorts. She reached into one pocket. "Hey! Money!" She held up a small roll of cash. "And—" From the other pocket she extracted a cigarette lighter.

"All right." Slydes snatched the lighter away from her and headed for the door.

"What are you gonna do?"

"Boil some of that brook water, Einstein. Kill the worms."

"You're a genius!"

He went back outside. He'd hoped that eating something would make him feel better, but instead it made him feel worse. *Yeah, shit, we're probably dyin' of dehydration and don't even know it yet . . .* But maybe some luck had come his way.

He set the grill back upright and opened the small propane cannister to high, then snapped the lighter over the element.

The lighter worked fine, but the grill didn't catch.

Don't tell me . . . He put his ear to the element.

There was no hiss.

God is really kicking our asses today. He chucked the lighter into the woods, disgusted.

Some char marks seemed to sweep up the shed's wall. *Must've been a fire here,* he realized, *but somebody managed to put it out.* A logical deduction.

Yet who was the bigger "pea brain"? Slydes walked right back into the shed and never even noticed the water hose lying at the other end.

"Ain't no fuckin' gas in the tank," he said, back inside.

"Fuck." Ruth sat against the wall, an orange hand to her belly. "I feel like shit, Slydes. I feel like I could croak. Maybe those worms infected us."

Slydes wanted to throw up, in part from how he felt, and in part from remembering exactly what Jonas looked like the last time he saw him. "If we got infected, we'd be turnin' yellow, like Jonas. We ain't infected, we just need water." Darker thoughts entered his head. He kept looking at Ruth . . . and the stark veins standing out in her sweaty neck. He knew this:

When hunters couldn't find water, they could drink the blood of any animals they killed. Blood was mostly water.

In which case, Ruth was a veritable *bucket* of water.

Am I that much of a scumbag? he asked himself. The question almost bothered him.

Almost.

He had his Buck knife right there on his belt. He'd skinned and gutted many a gator with it. And compared to gator skin, cutting Ruth's throat would be like putting his knife through mashed potatoes.

The question appeared to be answered.

But if he was going to kill her for the water in her blood, then—

I just gotta have it one more time, Slydes figured. His lack of reservations, perhaps, represented his human truth, so at least he was being honest. He was going to use her mouth for his own sexual pleasure and then drink her blood. Great guy.

He sat down and put an arm around her.

"What are you doing?"

"Cuddlin'," he said.

Ruth rolled her eyes. "Now?"

"Now, or any time. You're always beautiful."

Ruth was stunned by the compliment, however phony. Slydes held her tighter, caressed a breast. "Come on, baby. I've been missin' you fierce."

Ruth's expression showed sheer befuddlement. Any other time, she'd be happy to oblige, but under *these* circumstances? Jonas dead along with God knew who else? Giant worms, and a zombie in the woods? Plus, she was feeling really lousy. . . .

"Slydes . . ." She tried to push his hand away, but by now he'd already pulled her T-shirt up. "I feel like shit, like I'm gonna throw up."

Slydes's beard tickled her when he kissed her neck. "Please, baby, don't leave me hanging. I'm needing you really bad."

"I'm not in the mood, Slydes!" she outright whined.

He had his jeans opened, and pushed her head down. "It'll only take a minute, sugar. See, Ruth, you're so beautiful, it just makes me hot for you all the time."

Ruth frowned and shrugged. It wasn't the first time she'd performed a sex act simply because there was nothing else to do. Slydes groaned once her expertise was upon him. He obviously wasn't the most considerate of men, and given that he'd been sweating and stinking on this island for the past three days only proved more of Ruth's resilience. *Yeah, she's a trooper, all right,* he thought, the sensations building already. In which case she'd be a *dead* trooper very shortly.

Just as Slydes would have his moment, she stopped and looked up at him. "Oh, fuck, what a couple of morons we are!"

"What!" he shouted, outraged. He pushed her head back down. "Come on, girl! You don't stop right before a guy's going to—"

"I just thought of where we can get water!"

"Huh!" The distraction spun in his head. *Yeah! Your neck!* Again, he tried to force her head back down.

"Would you *wait* a minute!" she managed to blurt. "We can get all the water we want at the head shacks where Jonas grows his pot. The drip lines, from that old army filter or whatever the fuck it is!"

Slydes eyes widened. *Holy shit, she's right!* Unbeknownst to her, Ruth's perceptivity had just that second saved her life. "That's good thinkin', baby!"

"Fuck yeah!"

"But finish the job." And then he shoved her head back down.

Ruth, indeed, finished the job, treating Slydes to a potent climax, the residue of which was displaced into her mouth.

"Aw, yeah, honey, that was great . . ."

But Ruth sat bolt upright, eyes pried open. Her lips puckered in distaste, as though she'd taken in a mouthful of turpentine.

"What's wrong with you?" Slydes asked, refastening his pants.

Ruth spat loudly on the floor, and when she looked at what she'd expectorated, she grimaced. "Oh, fuck! That's fuckin' *gross*!"

"What'choo talking about?" Slydes leaned over and looked.

Oh, fuck. That IS fuckin' gross, his thoughts heartily agreed. There were no other words.

Roiling amid his spat-out semen were hundreds of tiny yellow beads, smaller versions of the ones he'd plucked off his body the other night.

"You're infected with those worm things!" Ruth shrieked at him.

"Bullshit! I ain't infected. They came out of *you!* They came up out of your belly or somewhere!"

Ruth jumped up. "They didn't come out of my stomach, Slydes, and you know it! They came out of your *pecker!*"

Slydes stroked his beard. Had they? He looked at his arms, looked under his shirt. *My skin ain't yellow,* he saw. *Jonas said you turned yellow if you were infected.* But . . .

Ruth wasn't yellow, either.

And the ova came from somewhere. "They were on the floor already, like the ones outside," he tried to convince himself.

Ruth stomped around the shed, spitting incessantly. "I could feel 'em squirming in my mouth, Slydes!" Then glared as though he were a leper.

Slydes didn't much care for that look.

"You're infected! I'm getting out of here!"

The predicament irritated Slydes . . . so he decided to kill her anyway. *I know it ain't me who's infected,* he kept telling himself.

What else could he believe?

As he reached for his knife, though, he cast a glance at the semen again.

Those little yellow worm eggs . . .

Had they doubled in size in the last two minutes?

"I'm fuckin' sorry, Slydes, but I gotta get away from you," Ruth declared. "I don't wanna get infected with those fuckin' things."

I'm carving her up, Slydes resolved. It was a matter of pride. He'd done a lot for her, and now she was abandoning him.

Low-class.

Slydes shucked his knife just as Ruth opened the door to flee the shed.

But she didn't flee.

She screamed and just stood there.

Someone was blocking the door, and when she jerked backward, Slydes saw who it was . . . or, not really even *who* anymore, but *what.*

He would have no way of knowing Robb White by name, he only remembered Ruth's claim of a big yellow zombie lurking around, and then Jonas's dying revelation that the very first person to be infected by the worms continued to live through repeated mutations. *He's a big guy,* Jonas had related. *Watch out for him. He's trompin' around here like a fuckin' zombie.*

This person/thing was a "big guy," all right. He stood huge in the open doorway, hair all gone now, replaced by mottled yellow scalp, old swim trunks essentially rotting on his pelvis. The eyes looked more like wads of spit, but somehow they seemed to recognize Ruth.

Then the ruined, yellow face . . . smiled.

"He's come back for me!" Ruth shrieked. She dodged a swipe from a huge arm, then ducked behind Slydes. "Stick him with your knife, Slydes! He's gonna kill us! He wants to feed us to the worms!"

Moments of consternation such as this were difficult to reckon. Slydes was scared shitless and paralyzed as he stood there, Ruth hiding behind him. His first instinct, indeed, told him to fight. But when he took a closer look at the thing that was thunking into the shed with mutated arms outstretched, he knew there was no point. He wouldn't be fighting a man, he'd be fighting an organic monstrosity.

The face beamed back at him, yellow and runneled. A gray tongue emerged to lick segmented lips. Slydes noticed a chunk missing from the guy's cheek, revealing a sore crater in pus-rife flesh. Muscles and veins flexed beneath the shiny, runny skin, and worse than the inhuman sick-yellow hue were the blazing red spots.

And, yes, the thing was smiling.

It's smilin' at Ruth . . .

"Don't let him get us, Slydes!" she screamed.

"Us?" Slydes questioned.

This would be even better than cutting her throat.

Ruth's screams cartwheeled around the room when Slydes turned, grabbed her by the shoulders, and threw her into the waiting arms of the college jock formerly known as Robb White.

Was the thing giggling? Slydes thought so. It wrapped its arms around Ruth's slender physique, dragged her to the floor, then wrapped its stout legs around her too.

"You coward piece of fuck scumbag motherfucker, Slydes!" Ruth cut loose in her loudest scream yet.

Slydes stepped around them, and slipped out the doorway.

"Oh, fuck, no, no, noooooooooooooooo!"

Slydes took one last peek inside. Ruth's zombie had pulled down its rotten swim trunks, and was now yanking down her shorts. Slydes closed the door and jogged away.

(II)

"I've never been this far across the island," Loren said. He followed Nora through the thickening woods. Time and disuse had narrowed the trails this far in, to mere overgrown scratches; they could barely see them enough to follow them.

"I've explored a little," Nora confirmed, "but not quite this deep. According to Lieutenant Trent, the old control center is this way."

"You really think there's someone there?"

Nora tried to weigh the question in concrete terms. What they'd discovered thus far almost seemed unbelievable, but then she *knew* she believed it all because she'd *seen* it all. "Actually, Loren, I really do."

Loren gulped, and went silent.

"Seriously," she went on. "I can't deny what we've

seen. A parasitic worm that displays features and traits of multiple species? Their hydroskeletons and ova growing exponentially? That sounds like laboratory-induced mutation."

"I know, but—"

"And we *have* found surveillance cameras all over the island. I've seen them, you've seen them. Now, you and Trent just told me that Annabelle got hauled up into a tree by a twenty-foot worm. That's an unbelievable story—but I believe it because I just saw several worms almost as long back in the trench. You and I both know worms like these can't grow this large or this fast without some kind of artificial catalyst inducing it." She paused. "And I *know* I saw a submarine out in that trench. It wasn't oxygen deprivation, Loren, and it wasn't hallucinosis spurred by variances in water pressure."

"I believe you saw a sub or submersible," Loren admitted. "And I believe something really screwed up and unnatural is going on here. But aren't we asking for trouble now? Aren't we getting in too deep?"

"One of our party is already dead," Nora reminded him, "and we know other people have been killed on this island recently. We already *are* in too deep."

"I want to know what's going on, too. But if there really are people at this control center, what are we going to do? Ask them what they're doing? Invite them to lunch?"

"No. We're going to apprehend them, with that gun you have. We're going to get to the bottom of this."

Loren laughed hard—and nervously. "They're military, Nora! They have guns too, and the big difference is they know how to use theirs. I'm just a mild-mannered polychaetologist, not Wyatt Earp."

Nora shoved away some branches and moved on. "Relax, Loren. We're just going to take a look. You're a scientist, too—aren't you curious about what's going on here?"

"Um-hmm, and Magellan was curious about what was going on in the Philippines . . . and he got butchered by a bunch of pissed-off natives."

Nora shook her head. "Just come on."

"What's that there?"

Loren had noticed a small tin shed that seemed to be humming.

"It's the filtration and desalinator for the island's water supply." Then Nora pointed to the black power cable and metal box it branched off from. "And that's the voltage regulator."

Loren stared at it. "And the generator is . . . where?"

"It's over there some place," she said quickly. "Come on."

Loren followed the cable, finding its terminus at the large slab of concrete on the ground, and the accommodating sign: KEEP AWAY! RADIOACTIVE MATERIAL IN USE!

Loren frowned at her. "No wonder I've never heard a generator motor. There isn't one. That's an RTG, isn't it?"

"Yeah," Nora admitted. "I found it by accident the other day; we're not supposed to know about it. Trent said I'll actually have to be debriefed by army security people just for seeing the damn thing."

"I guess so. If terrorists knew this was here, they could use it to make a dirty bomb if they could get to the source material. Probably Cesium 137."

"Trent said the army's not worried about it. The source is buried in the middle of fifteen tons of steel-reinforced concrete."

Loren chuckled. "Oh yeah, that makes me feel a lot more secure. Shit, Nora, maybe it's leaking. Maybe the RTG is causing the mutations."

"That's impossible, and you know it. It's only a couple of rads heating up a thermocoupler. We've seen these things in our own field. They're safe, and their power is exaggerated."

"We better hope so. Greenpeace would *love* to hear about this. Let's call Nader."

"Just come on!"

Another black cable paralleled another scratch of a trail. Nora and Loren followed it through a small clearing. "No anoles or iguanas," Nora said. "Have you noticed that?"

"Unfortunately, yes." Loren pointed down, a look of disgust on his face. "And check that out."

Another possum lay dead at the base of a tree. Bloated and quivering. Nora peered a little too closely and noticed newly hatched pink worms—not a half inch long—exiting the animal's ear and anus.

"And look there," Loren added. "But don't get too close."

A rusted sign stood before them on metal posts. It read U.S. ARMY MISSILE COMMAND—RESTRICTED AREA.

At first Nora thought the quarter-sized pocks were just spots of corrosion, but then they began to move.

"Those are the biggest ova yet," Loren noted.

"I know. They must grow selectively, like the *Polychaetes myerus*. It's all in the genes. While some ova hatch early, others hatch late, to evade predators or hostile climate."

At least ten fat, yellow ova crawled along the sign's metal face. With them this large, Nora could see that the red spots on their outer skins were oval-shaped: The spots seemed to move, too, as the outer skin very slowly throbbed.

Nora felt cruxed. "These things are all over the place. They're in the water *and* on land. They're infecting everything . . . So why haven't they infected us?"

"That's a good question." Loren stepped closer to the sign, checking at his feet for ova that might be on the ground. "They probably sense carbon dioxide, sweat, and pheromones, like lots of worms and insects." Then he exhaled toward several of them. Just as the ova had done in their field lab, these immediately began to move in Loren's direction. "And we've been out here for most of a week, asleep in our tents, out in the woods sweating up a storm. That girl told me her entire party was killed by these things, and most of them were infected the first day they were here. How have we managed to not attract these things for all this time?"

"Maybe luck," Nora said. "Plus, we've been spraying ourselves constantly with insect repellent. We know that direct contact with the repellent kills them." She looked at her wrist. "Oh yeah, and we've got these things." She held up her wrist, showing the repellent-laced plastic bracelet. When she moved the bracelet closer to the ova, they began to back away.

"Well, that's good to know," Loren said. "At least it's a little protection."

"Sure, but let's be practical. Tiny worms and ova are one thing, but these little bracelets aren't going to stop a large, fully mature worm. The one that attacked me in the water wasn't the least bit affected by this bracelet."

"Yeah, and neither was the twenty-footer that got Annabelle. She had a bracelet too."

"We better put more spray on now that we're thinking of it," Nora said and withdrew the narrow can from her pocket. She aimed the can down at her legs and pressed the button. Nothing came out.

"It's all gone!"

"Terrific," Loren said. "We better hope that Trent has some more."

Nora tossed the empty can. "Come on, let's keep going anyway. Just be careful."

They burgeoned forward through heavier brush, and after just a few more yards . . .

"See it?" Nora asked.

"Yeah . . ."

The old blockhouse building looked jammed into the woods, overrun with brush, Spanish moss, and vines that crawled down from the trees above.

"The control center for the old missile site," Nora said. "Just like Trent told us."

"Shit, that place *looks* like it hasn't been used for twenty years," Loren observed of the squat, bunkerlike structure.

"Maybe it's just *supposed* to look that way. So no one bothers with it." Nora kept her eyes on the station, imagining what might be inside. What did she suspect? A secret barracks, a camouflaged field lab or research outpost? *I don't know WHAT I'm thinking . . .*

They both crept up slowly.

"No windows," Loren noticed.

"Of course not . . . but there's the door."

A black, metal-framed door stared back at them, with a similar warning: RESTRICTED. Loren noticed it at once: "Look. The doorknob."

Nora saw what he meant. There actually *wasn't* a doorknob anymore, just a rust-rimmed hole. Loren hooked his finger in the hole and pulled, but the door didn't budge. "Maybe it was welded shut when they closed down the site."

"Then why do I see light inside?" Nora questioned when she leaned over and peeked into the hole.

"You're kidding me . . ." Something caught Loren's eye. "But check this out," he said and pointed down to a heavily cased air-conditioning unit. It sat midbuilding, bolted to a cement grounding. It was rusted through, its grate corroded. They could see the fan deeper down, caked with more corrosion.

"That thing hasn't turned in years," Nora said.

"So that means there can't be anyone inside. With no windows open? It's 110 in there."

Fine. But why's there a light on? Nora went back to the door. Head-level against the frame was a black plate of some kind. "What's that? A military dead bolt?"

"Feels almost like plastic or polycarb," Loren said after he brushed his fingers against it. "The temperature's cooler than the door metal. It's a tack weld or something. If it was a dead bolt, there'd be a keyhole."

Nora touched it too. "There is—at least I think so. See that?"

Loren squinted.

There was no sign of a key cylinder, but there was indeed a tiny slit in the black plate, perhaps an eighth of an inch long.

"You can barely see it," Loren said. "Must be some high-tech security lock."

Nora was unconscious of the impulse; she was reaching down into her pocket and before she even knew what she was doing, she'd withdrawn that pendantlike object she'd found in the woods: the strip of metal on a neck cord.

"Interesting," Loren said.

Nora put the end of the pendant into the slit. Out of reflex, she tried to turn it, as one would a key, but it began to bend.

"Don't turn it," Loren directed. "There's no cylinder like a regular lock. Just push it in as far as it'll go."

Nora did so, and—

Tick.

The door popped open an inch.

Both of them stiffened.

"I guess this is what we wanted," Loren said with no enthusiasm at all.

Nora was suddenly scared herself. *This is a new lock on a very old door.* That key she'd found on the trail the other day could only mean that military people *were* using this island, in secret. Not even Trent knew about it . . .

"Cool air," she whispered to herself. Another question mark. With no sound of an air conditioner running?

"Yeah, feels like seventy degrees in there," Loren said. "You tell me."

"There must be fans on or something," Nora replied. "But I'd say we've got bigger questions to answer."

"How's this for a question: Who's going to be the first to go in?"

Nora peered ahead into the murk. "How about *you?*"

"Why? Because I'm the man?" Loren frowned into the doorway. He didn't hear anything but he did see some dim lights on. A clean-floored hallway led straight down the middle of the building, with doors on either side.

"This was my idea," Nora owned up.

"Yeah. Plus, you get paid more than me."

Nora almost laughed. She stepped inside, and Loren followed.

"Shhh," she reminded him.

She took long, slow steps. The coolness inside sucked around her, which felt good after being in such dank, humid heat. When they'd first stepped in, the building seemed dead silent, yet after a few steps Nora heard something humming. Odd white lightbulbs that were small and circular dotted the wall up near the ceiling. They both stopped at the first door. There was no dead bolt on it like the outside door. A sign read PROCESSING UNIT, but it was peeling at the corners, obviously very old.

"Are we really going to do this?" Loren whispered. "What if there's somebody on the other side?"

Nora didn't want to think about it. They'd come here for information, and chickening out now seemed worse than pointless. "We'll run," she said and turned the knob.

Old hinges creaked as she pushed open the door.

"Wow," Loren said.

No one stood waiting for them, but they immediately saw old desks and tables pushed together to form a platform for some very fancy-looking security monitors.

"These are the highest-tech LCD flat screens I've ever seen," Nora said of the dozen one-foot-square panels. Each panel framed a different area of the island.

"We were right," Nora said. "All those little cameras are operational."

"They're monitoring the entire island." Loren leaned toward the glowing screens. "Look, there's the shower, our campsite, and—shit!" He pointed to a frame. "I was just there! That's where the girl killed herself, on that boat."

Nora saw the canopied Boston Whaler anchored in a small lagoon. "We never even knew that lagoon was here."

"Here's *another* lagoon," Loren said and pointed. "And another boat . . ."

This panel showed another lagoon hemmed in by trees and mangrove roots. Tied off to one of the roots was a small, unoccupied skiff.

"Jesus, there really have been a lot of people on this island," Nora guessed.

"Yeah, and they're probably all dead now, infected. The girl who shot herself said they were being used for a scientific test, and that these military people in the gas masks were monitoring them."

"Which means they've been monitoring *us* too," Nora reminded him.

They both chewed on the thought for a while. The silence began to unnerve Nora.

"Why monitor the north beach and not the others?" she said next, looking at the one frame that showed the shore.

"Well, for one, that's where the bristleworm nest was."

"Yeah, and it's also where the trench is, where these guys parked their submersible." She'd almost forgotten about that. "They came here in it, in secret, to set up. But I'm sure there's a lot more than this," she said of the room itself. Security equipment was suspicious. But Nora needed more proof.

Proof of genetic experiments.

"Let's look in some more rooms."

"Or let's not," Loren posed. "This is crazy coming here in the first place. We're going to get caught. We already know the navy or army or some military agency is engaged in a secret project. So let's just go."

"You go, then. Go back to the campsite and wait for Lieutenant Trent. I'll only be another few minutes."

Loren scowled. "Shit. Come on, I'll go with you."

They left the room and went into the next. More screens on more tables, and old shelves filled with cases almost like tackle boxes.

"More of that code," Loren said when he looked at a screen.

"It must be their research data after being encrypted."

The screen was filled the same dots and dashes they'd seen on the cameras and the key.

The first line on the screen read:

-.-:-.::-.-.:::.-.::-.-.:.:.-.-.:.:.-.-.:.:.-.-.:.:.-.-.:.:.-.-.:.:.-.-.:.:.-.-.:.:.-.-.:.:.-.-.:.:.-

"I wish I could take a picture of this," Nora said. "Or print it out."

Loren looked around. "I don't see a printer hooked up to any of this gear."

She pointed. "Look and see what's on those shelves. I'll check this closet."

A rusted door narrower than the others stood in the corner. *I was wrong, it's not a closet,* she thought when she opened it. It was another room, illumined by more of the small round lightbulbs. Hanging along the wall were several black rubberized suits with hoods, and widely visored gas masks. From pegs on the opposite wall dangled narrow black belts, and connected to the belts were fabric pockets containing tools.

The tools, too, were black. Nora slipped one out. *What the hell is this? A ruler?* The tool extended via a slide mechanism, but for the life of her she didn't know what it might be used for.

These narrow doors must connect all the rooms, she gathered when she opened another door like the one she'd used to enter here. She was looking into the first room they'd searched, with all the surveillance monitors.

"Nora," Loren whispered. "I think I hit pay dirt."

She went back out. Loren had taken down one of the cases and opened it. It reminded her of the blood-sample cases that doctors' offices sent to labs. When the case had been opened, racks popped up on either side. The racks contained what she could only guess were—

"Specimen tubes," Loren said, holding one up. "They're square instead of round, but it's obvious that's what these are. Check it out."

Nora took the tube. Floating in a fluid that looked like light mouthwash was a spotted ovum identical to those they'd seen all over the island.

"Here's another one."

The next tube contained a half-inch-long worm.

"There's your proof," Loren said, "so let's go."

Nora looked at more tubes, which all contained either pristine examples of ova or worms. *Are they alive?* she wondered. *Preserved? Are they prototypes?* Ultimately, it didn't matter.

And Loren was correct: Here was proof of what she'd come here to find out. *A military test in the field. A worm that's obviously a cross-species, the product of either a mutation process or a genetic splice . . .*

And humans are what they're testing it on.

Loren put the case back, then squeezed her arm. "How can I put it more eloquently, Nora? We have to *get the fuck out* of here."

"All right, all right . . ."

He practically dragged her out of the room. The door remained opened at the end of the hall, light pouring in. Nora peeked in the first room as they brushed by; then she tugged back at him.

"Wait a second—"

"Damn it, Nora!" he whispered. "We're going to get caught in here!"

"I don't think anyone's here right now," she said.

"Then where are they?"

"Outside. Look at that . . ."

She was pointing to the security monitors in the first room. Loren edged in behind her, seeing what she meant. "That's one of them," he said.

On one of the higher screens, a man was kneeling— a man in a gas mask and decon suit. He was kneeling at a large slab of concrete.

"That's the RTG, isn't it?" Loren noticed.

"It sure is." A chill went up her back. "We were just there a few minutes ago."

"And look, there's two more of them—"

Yet another screen briefly showed two more masked and hooded men moving down a trail.

"Three of them total," Nora counted.

"Plus the one I shot . . ."

Both of them looked back at the RTG screen, and the mysterious figure kneeling before it. A gloved hand produced a small black box and rested it on the slab. Then he opened the box and withdrew a black disk that looked like a hockey puck.

"What the hell is he doing?" Loren asked.

"That disk," Nora said. "What's that rod he just pulled out of it?"

They both stared. The man extracted a short rod from the disk; from the end of the disk, he seemed to remove a cap.

Then he pushed the rod against the slab's cement face. A moment later, the disk had been mounted onto the concrete.

"The rod must be some kind of stand," Nora said. "And . . . shit. I've got a bad vibe about this."

Loren looked right at her. "Me too. Nora, why do I have a funny feeling that black thing is a bomb?"

"I . . . don't know . . ." She was thinking the exact same thing. "It's not big enough to be a bomb is it?"

"A piece of C-4 the size of a hockey puck? It could probably break that concrete slab in half."

"And then the pressure from the explosion might split the fuel-source casing."

"Instant dirty nuke. Shit, Nora. If that really is what he's doing . . ."

"It would look like a terrorist operation," she realized. "The radioactive dust from an explosion like that would contaminate the entire island."

"And anyone or anything on it would die from radiation sickness in a matter of days."

This is madness, she thought, still staring at the screen.

Then the man in the gas mask got up and walked away, leaving the disk propped up on the slab.

"We're out of here," Loren insisted, but just when they would turn to leave, a security monitor in the corner began to blink.

"What's happening *now!*" Nora exclaimed.

It was the screen showing the north beach. The panel's frame was suddenly bordered by a blinking red line.

The camera showed the water beyond the beach . . .

"That's where the trench is," Loren murmured.

"And where their sub is . . ."

They stared fixedly at the screen.

Nora supposed she could guess what was about to happen even before it did. In a few moments the water beyond the beach began to stir.

"Holy shit," Nora muttered.

"Uh, yeah," Loren agreed with her, because they both saw it very clearly.

The sub was surfacing.

CHAPTER TWENTY-TWO

(I)

There he is, Trent thought.

The clearing.

Then another thought: *What if he's not dead?*

The man whom Loren had shot lay utterly still, gloved hands outstretched, legs and booted feet sprawled. The visor of his gas mask was tinted; Trent couldn't see through it.

Probably the latest generation decon gear, he thought of the flat-black finish. He knelt and touched it—the material felt like sheer polyester. Trent tried to pull off a glove but then saw that it was fastened somehow, perhaps snaps on the inside.

He was about to pull off the mask but something dark caught his eye.

A dark gray patch over the left breast. In the U.S. Army, that's where a troop's name tag would be sewn.

But this tag bore no name, only this, in black marks against the gray:

..:-:

That shit again . . .
Trent fished around in the man's pockets, eventually pulled out a plasticized card.
The card read:

:.-:.-::.-:

He felt creeped out. *How could that stuff be a code?* he wondered.
Next, he tried to pull down the hood. He needed to get inside the suit, for the ID tags that would, by regulation, have to be around his neck.
Damn it!
The hood wouldn't detach from the mask. Was the entire suit integrated, a step-in?
Trent stood up, grabbed the lip under the mask's chin, then yanked upward.
The mask pulled off after several tugs.
Trent stared.
He doubted what his eyes were showing him at first. Was it a disease? Something from the worm?
The open-eyed face stared up at him.
Trent could see red arteries and blue veins webbed across the man's face. And he could see the skull beneath the flesh, because . . .
The flesh was transparent as glass.
Hands shaking—and his mentality breaking up— Trent yanked open the jumpsuit's front, popping unseen snaps down the middle.
More clear, jellylike flesh, embedded with blood vessels, nerves, and the rib cage.

A lower glance to the abdomen showed more transparent flesh encasing obvious digestive organs.

Trent simply stood there looking down, a reasonable response. He tried to conceive the inconceivable, and eventually he acknowledged what lay before his eyes:

This guy's not in the navy. He's a fucking alien—

A final squint showed him what he'd been looking for all along. A small, rectangular plate on a cord around the figure's neck.

Trent leaned over and looked.

..:-:, the plate read.

His mind churned as he continued to stare. Then the next thing he knew, an impulse caused him to dash out of the clearing and hide.

Why?

He'd heard footsteps thrashing through the woods.

Trent prayed it was Nora and Loren . . . but he knew that would not be the case.

Two more figures in the same black gear entered the clearing and stopped at the corpse.

Trent held his breath, gun in sweaty hand.

The figures seemed to be communicating, yet no words could be heard. Radio gear inside their hoods? It didn't matter. They looked back and forth at each other, glancing alternately at the body of their comrade.

Then one of them produced something that looked like a pen. When he aimed it at the corpse, something issued from the "pen's" tip. Trent absurdly thought of Silly String, but this stuff was black.

The man sprayed the pen back and forth, eventually covering the corpse in a bizarre black web.

Then the two figures walked away.

Trent kept his eyes on the webbed corpse. He heard a definite hissing sound, then saw bluish, sooty smoke rising.

By the time a full minute had ticked by, the web had completely disintegrated the corpse, and itself.

Trent walked back out to look more closely.

The area where the corpse had lain was clear. It was as though the corpse had never been there at all.

(II)

Nora's and Loren's mouths hung open as they kept their eyes nailed to the monitor.

The hundred-foot-long submarine had fully surfaced now, and sat there in the frame, floating on the calm water. It shone black in the sun. Modest fins could be seen forward and aft of the perfectly cylindrical hull, yet the ends weren't rounded or pointed like typical subs. There was no conning tower. There were no windows.

And there was no propeller.

"I've never seen a submersible like *that*," Loren said. "No prop? Must be impeller-driven but . . . I don't see any intakes for the impellers."

"Loren, I don't see any *anything* on that. It looks like a giant black Pringles can sitting in the water."

The monitor frame continued to flash.

Then the vessel began to rise.

More slack-jawed silence as Nora and Loren tried to comprehend what their eyes were seeing on the screen.

The vessel was levitating ten feet above the water now, and a moment later it began to move forward, toward the island. As it did so it began to change color, the stark black giving over to the green blue of the water. Eventually it moved out of the confines of the frames.

Nora finally broke the silence. "You're thinking what I'm thinking, right?"

Loren's Adam's apple bobbed when he gulped. "Yeah. It's not a submarine or submersible—it's a spaceship. And it ain't one of NASA's."

"I don't believe in that kind of stuff."

"Neither do I, so what are we seeing?"

"Hallucination," Nora suggested. "Side effects of sunstroke, maybe. Maybe we *have* been infected by these worms, and one component of the infection is psychosis. There are many roundworms as well as ova of roundworms that can corrupt a host's DNA with a mutagenic virus. Maybe that virus is now in our brains and we don't even know it."

Loren smirked at her. "Do you believe that? That we've been having shared hallucinations because of a roundworm infection?"

Nora shook her head. She knew that she had no confidence in a single word that had just issued from her mouth.

"Aliens, then," she said.

"What else could it be?" Loren stalked around the room. "We know that the box full of worms in the other room and the ones that have overrun this island can only be the result of a gene-splicing and DNA-manipulating process that is beyond the technological capabilities of the modern scientific community." He reached up and took down one of the strange round lights on the wall. "How do you like that? A light that doesn't give off heat, doesn't have batteries, and isn't connected to a power source."

"Just like the cameras in the woods, too," Nora said.

"Sure. No power source, no electrical connections of any kind, not even an antenna, but—" He pointed to the bank of monitors. "They work better than any surveillance cameras we've ever seen." Loren was starting to get a little giddy with his acknowledgments. "Not to mention these monitors, which aren't connected to a power source either." He fiddled with the corner of one of the monitors . . . and eventually *peeled* it away from the others.

Nora brought a hand to her mouth in shock.

The monitor was nothing but a clear sheet—like a plastic cover sheet for a term paper, and just as thin. Loren held it up, flapped it around, then rolled it into a tight tube. When he unrolled it again, it still held the perfect image of the sea where the vessel had just lifted off.

"How do you like that?" Loren said cockily. "Boy, that's a really cool monitor, isn't it? I'm sure you could go to Circuit City right now and buy one just like it."

Next, he pointed to the screen rolling the strange markings:

```
·::·-·:::·-··-·:-·::·-··-·:·-·-·:·:·:·-·::·-·:-·::·-·:-·:··-·::·-·:::·
·:··-·-·:-·:::·-·:::··-·:··-·:::··-·:··-·:-·::·-·:::·-·:::··-·:··-·-·:·
·:··-·:-·:::·-··-·:-·:·-·:··-·:-·:·-·:··-·:-·::·-·:::·-·:::··-·:··-·::
·-·:-·::·-·:::··-·:··-·:·-·:··-·:··-·:-·:·-·:·-·-·:-·:::·-·:::··-·-
··-·:-·::·-·:··-·:::··-··-·:-·:::·-··-·:-·::·-·:·-·:::-·::·-·:··-·:··-·:
:·-·:::··-·:··-·::·-·:··-·:·-·:·-·:··-·:-·:·-·:·-·:··-·:-·:::··-·::·-·:
·:··-·-·:-·::·-·:::·-·:··-·:·-·:··-·:::·-·::··-·:::··-·:··-·:··-·-·:·:
·-·:-·::·-·:··-·:··-·:··-·:·-·:··-·:-·:·-·:··-·:-·::·-·:::·-·:::··-·:··
:·-·::·-·:··-·:::··-·:··-·:··-·:·-·:··-·:·-·:::·-·::··-·:::··-·:-·:·:
·-·:-·:::·-·:::··-·:::··-·:··-·:::··-·:-·:··-·:·-·:-·::·-·:::·-·:::··-·:·
·:-·:::·-·:··-·:::·-·:::··-·:··-·:·-·:·-·:-·::·-·:::·-·:::··-·:··-·:::·-·:
:·-·:::··-·:··-·:::··-···—·:··-·:::·-·:··-·:··-·:·-·:-·:::·-·:::··-··:
·:··-·-·:-·:·:·:··-·:::··-··-·:-·::·-·:·-·:··
```

"That ain't no military *code*," Loren balked. "It's not an encryption. It's fucking Microsoft Word from another planet."

Nora felt tiny looking at the screen and all of its ramifications. *An alien language,* she thought.

"And to top it all off, we've got these guys in gas masks—who are obviously the *crew* to that thing we just saw levitate out of the fucking Gulf of Mexico, and they've been running around this island the whole time, instigating what can only be a field test of a genetically created parasite. And we just saw one of those guys put a fucking *bomb* on a live RTG. What's that tell you, Nora?"

"It tells me that their field test is over," she said with surprising calm, "and now they're getting ready to leave. They know enough about the modern human species to know that if they blow up an RTG, the radiological dispersion will contaminate the island so effectively that our own authorities won't be able to investigate the perimeter closely enough to ever realize that an advanced race from another planet was here doing tests on us in the first place."

"Exactly."

More silence. It was too much to contemplate, and too much to believe even after all they'd seen with their own eyes.

"There's got to be a way we can defuse that bomb," she finally said.

Loren laughed out loud, bug-eyed. "You're kidding me, right? We don't even know what it'll do. Just because it's only the size of a hockey puck doesn't mean much when you consider the technology base of the people who put it there. Nora, it could a million-megaton bomb."

"Yeah, but it probably isn't," she reasoned. "It's not logical. What's logical is what we just said. They don't want *our* authorities to know they were even here. So they're going to rupture the RTG core with a small nonnuclear device because they know the U.S. military will simply quarantine the island and believe it was some terrorist cell trying to make a point. I guarantee you, our side will believe that a lot more readily that they'll believe an alien entity came here to do a genetic field test, and then left without a trace."

"Whatever," Loren said in haste. "But there's nothing more we can do except leave *right now* before all this shit happens and we get turned into dust."

Nora's mind raced. Her eyes were all over the room, along with her thoughts. "Trent wanted to inspect the dead body, but we already know what he found, so I want you to go back to the campsite, and—"

Loren's look of incredulity couldn't have been more glaring. "No, Nora, *we* go back to the campsite, get Trent, then go to that girl's boat, and get off this powder-keg island."

"You go," she said. "It'll only take a few extra minutes. Get Trent and come back here. *Then* we'll all go to the boat together."

"Bullshit!" Loren yelled.

"I want to look around here a few more minutes," she insisted. "There might be some way to deactivate that bomb. There might be some tool here or something."

"Some *tool*! You're crazy! Come on!"

Nora shoved him for the door. "Just go!" she yelled back. "I'm still your boss, remember."

Loren honked laughter. "Big deal! What, you're going to drop my T.A. credits back at Worm School because I refused to help you defuse an *alien bomb*?"

"I don't care!" she yelled. She was determined. "Leave without me, if you want. I'll swim back."

"Yeah, Nora, the bull sharks will love that."

"Just get out! I've made up my mind!" She shoved him hard for the door.

"All right, already. Annabelle was right. You've got serious PMS."

"Blow me!"

"I'll go get Trent and come back," he agreed. "If I get

eaten by the alien worms or abducted by the spacemen, then it'll be on *your* conscience."

Loren jogged away, shaking his head.

Now Nora could think. She knew her decision was unsafe and stupid, but there was just too much here for a scientist to walk away from. She edged back out into the hall, then quickly walked down to a far room. More of the weird white light bathed her face when she entered.

She froze.

There was no smell, but there was also no mistake that what she now faced was a rotting human corpse, half eaten by a multitude of infant worms. The white male victim lay bloated, as if the slew of dead worms and ova around him had initially been inside his body and then burst out. There must've been thousands of worms and ova composing the morbid pile.

This guy was a test subject, she thought through a wave of revulsion. *They abducted him, infected him, and put him in this room to record the results . . .* He must've been dead for several days; she knew just by looking that the corpse had entered the stage of decomposition known as karyolysis, where the molecular lipids that form body fat begin to liquefy, and now the corpse and dead worms alike all lay suspended in that liquefaction: a congealed mass of organic rot. It was repulsive to look at but . . .

I should be gagging right now, she knew.

Why was there no death stench in the room?

Very slowly, Nora reached forward into the air, then—
What the hell is that?

Her finger came into contact with something, a barrier. She opened her hand against it, could feel it as surely as she'd ever felt anything in her life. It felt like her hand was pressing against a pane of glass.

But she couldn't see it. No streaks, no shine, no reflection of herself.

A quarantine barrier, she thought, mystified. When she tapped it with her fingernail, the sound ticked exactly like glass. *It's solid, and obviously nonpermeable—* Then she rapped it with her knuckles.

Clunk, clunk, clunk.

—and totally invisible.

She left the room, numb now from all of the impossibilities she'd witnessed. Of course, their technologies would vastly surpass that of her own race. *It's not so impossible when you think about it . . .* The realization summoned worse thoughts, though.

What other technologies might be waiting?

She was about to enter another room when she heard . . .

Rattling?

Loren had closed the door at the end of the hall when he'd left, but now—

Shit!

The door was opening.

Nora ducked back into the first room just as a wedge of sunlight widened on the floor. *It must be that guy we saw at the RTG!* Nora's heart revved; her gaze tore back and forth for a place to hide, but just when she realized there was nothing, the knob on the door began to turn.

She ducked back into the uniform room during the same second that the door opened.

She held her breath, watching through the crack . . .

The figure entered, a stark shadow in the black suit and hood. No facial features could be detected beneath the mask's tinted visor. He turned, his back now to Nora, and he seemed to be inspecting the items on the shelf.

Nora glanced to one of the belts hanging on the wall next to her; without thinking, she pulled out a strange flanged tool. She couldn't imagine what purpose it served but it did feel like metal . . .

If I could only hit that bastard in the head . . .

But her chance was gone before she'd finished thinking the thought. If she jumped out now with the tool, he'd scarcely even be surprised.

He'd taken something off the shelf, something Nora had already seen. The small square box—

Another bomb, she realized. *Just like the one he put on the RTG.*

He opened the lid and removed the hockey-puck-size disk. Again, he retracted some sort of rod from the disk's side, removed a small cap, and stood the disk upright on the desk. Either the rod had a base she couldn't see, or it had some sort of glue that enabled the disk to stand on end.

Next, the figure's gloved fingers produced a small black cube. He merely touched the disk with the cube, and—

Oh, shit, this is really bad . . .

A circular line of green light—thin as thread—instantly circumscribed the edge of the disk.

And the line began to blink.

Nora didn't need to see a clock to know that he'd just set the timer on the bomb.

At least it meant he and the rest of the crew intended to leave soon. *But HOW soon?* she wondered. With no clock hands or numbers, she had no way of knowing how long the timer had been set for.

I screwed up huge, she realized. *I should've left with Loren. Shit—I should never have come here! We could be on the boat by now, leaving this place. Instead, I'm stuck in an alien coat closet, and I just watched one of the aliens activate a bomb!*

She caught a breath in her chest when the door opened and two more men in black suits and masks walked in.

It was clear—by the way they moved and looked at

each other—they were communicating, yet Nora heard no words spoken, alien or otherwise. It seemed that the first figure was giving orders to the others, because a moment later they were taking things off the shelves and carrying them out.

They're taking their gear back to their ship.

But would they take it all? How potent was the bomb? Would it destroy anything they left behind?

Too many questions that had no answers.

Then the scariest question:

This room . . . The uniforms . . .

Nora watched through the crack as the first figure turned and made for the narrow door that led to the room she was hiding in.

She wanted to scream but her fear sealed her throat shut. *Oh, please, God, get me out of here!*

She could hear the doorknob being turned, could hear the hinge keening, when by another stroke of luck she found another narrow door in the corner. She was through it just as the figure had walked into the room.

She remembered now, how the rooms all seemed to be connected by the narrow inner doors, probably alternate fire routes for the old missile station.

Thank you, God, she thought.

But what room was this? One she'd been in previously?

Her next glance around told her no.

The image that glared back rooted Nora to the floor. It was too vivid . . . and impossible. It was . . .

A woman.

She was naked, and she hung from the back wall as if suspended in midair in a cruciform position. Strange black bands girded her upper arms and wrists, yet there were no cables attached to them.

What was holding her up?

It didn't matter. Nora's frozen stare ranged the woman's features, most notable of which was a swollen belly like that of a woman eight months pregnant. Her head was arched backward as though she were staring at the ceiling, a mane of long black hair hanging in line with her spine. When Nora stepped closer and to the side she discerned the next most shocking feature: The woman's left eye was opened and appeared normal, but the right eye was an empty socket. A black tube or wire looped into that socket, having been threaded through the optical canal to reach the brain. A second black wire had been fed into her mouth and down her throat.

A young college girl, Nora managed to guess through her horror. There were bikini lines, plus a generic vine tattoo around one ankle. Piercings that had been removed left telltale holes above the navel and through the nipples.

She simply hung there.

Nora detected respiration; then the left eye blinked. *Still alive . . .* Obviously another test subject they were monitoring directly. The bands around her wrists and upper arms were the only things she could be held aloft by . . .

Some sort of gravity-reversing technology . . .

How could Nora possibly get her down?

The answer lost all significance when Nora reached forward and encountered the same invisible pane she'd discovered in the other room. If felt identical to glass but lacked any frame, any point of foundation. *A containment barrier,* she realized. *A giant test tube.*

Her cognizance snapped back.

The doorknob again.

Shit!

She ducked into the leg well of a desk against the other wall.

They'll put ME in that thing if they catch me!

The black-garbed figure entered and looked up at the

naked girl. He extracted something from his belt, touched it, and—

Nora couldn't contemplate the next thing she saw. *Haven't I seen enough today!*

Via some arcane command from the tool on his belt, the entire transparent barrier she hung behind immediately changed tint. The room darkened while the screen itself began to glow . . .

Like a big MRI machine, Nora guessed. *But an ALIEN one . . .*

Now the image of the girl was being displayed like a living X-ray. The ventricles of the heart expanded and compressed, the aorta throbbed, internal organs expanded and contracted. But if that weren't enough, her next revelation surely would be.

Another command from the implement threw a square border of light right over the girl's belly. Then the image within the square increased in magnification times three.

The image alone nearly caused Nora to scream. But how could she, with this otherworldly technician in the same room?

The magnified image now displayed the girl's grievously expanded womb.

The womb contained a quivering, coiled-up worm. It looked like a roll of hose packed into her belly.

Just then Nora only knew one single thing in the world: *When that guy turns around, there's no way in hell he won't see me sitting under here . . .*

It was either sit there and die, or . . .

The figure remained examining the uterine image, his back to Nora. Nora stood behind him. When she raised the flanged tool high, the floating girl's head moved forward, her left eye watching . . .

The black figure had only turned halfway when Nora brought the tool down on the back of his skull.

He collapsed . . . and Nora reached for the door to the hall.

The split-second thought told her she had no choice but to take the chance. Had the other two figures returned to their vessel?

Or were they standing right outside in the hall, no doubt with weapons beyond her imagination?

She flung the door open.

The hall stood empty.

Nora jogged for the exit door. It was closed but she whipped out the object she now knew was a key. Her fingers felt around the face of the bizarre dead bolt, found the tiny slot, then she put the key in and instinctively turned it—

Snap!

The end of the key broke off in the keyhole.

Nora shuddered. She hadn't pushed it in far enough, and she'd forgotten to not turn the key itself.

I just broke the key off in the fucking lock!

She banged her hands against the door.

Of course, it didn't budge.

Oh my God, I just locked myself in an alien lab, and one of the aliens is still here!

Even if she'd killed the one in the room with the girl, the other two would certainly be back for him, if they weren't already.

Nora knew the door wasn't opening unless she found a way to push the broken tip all the way into the keyhole.

But with what?

She felt imbecilic trying to blow on it. Then she banged it with her fist. Nothing happened. The one she'd knocked out would probably have a key, but that would mean searching this body . . .

And with her luck, that's when he'd wake up.

She didn't know if it were a prayer or just a figure of

desperate speech when she pleaded: *Holy shit, God, please help me find a way!*

The idea snapped in her mind.

Her cross . . .

She broke the fragile chain off her neck, felt the body of the gold cross between her fingers. The post of the cross felt just about the same width as the key . . .

Nora stuck it in the slot, closed her eyes, and pushed.

The door clicked open.

Thank you, God, she thought and ran off into the woods.

(III)

Loren jogged the trail back toward the campsite. *Lieutenant Trent better be there,* he thought. *And Nora better not be too far behind . . .*

Nora.

Shit.

Suddenly, he was grimly aware of the pistol in his waistband. *I should've left the gun with her . . .*

The bulk of the desalinator and purification machines caught his eye, then slowed him to a stop. *The RTG,* he remembered. It was just a few yards away from all that. He turned and followed the power cable, where it ended at the concrete slab.

And there it is, he thought. At once came a sensation like ice water in his belly.

He was looking at the bomb . . .

The small black disk sat propped up on the rod, just as he'd seen on the surveillance screen back at the station. *Is that thing really a bomb?* he questioned. *How do we really know?*

Then his certainties returned the instant he recalled everything else they'd seen, particularly the hundred-foot-long vessel levitating out of the sea and moving toward the island, changing color to match the terrain. Perfect camouflage.

A fucking spaceship. Shit.

Then a glance back down to the puck-sized disk. A border of light was flashing on it, as if counting off seconds. *Like a timer,* he realized.

Loren dropped to one knee, took a breath, then grabbed the disk with both hands. He pulled with all his might but the disk didn't move.

Christ! What did he do? Drill the damn rod into solid concrete? Loren had watched the entire process on the screen, and there'd been no sign of a drill or any other kind of impacting tool that would be able to drive the rod through the cement.

What if I . . .

He put the barrel of the pistol against the rod . . .

On second thought that's a really BAD idea.

Loren couldn't figure a way to remove the disk. *It's not my problem,* he tried to rationalize. *It's beyond my control.*

The easy way out.

Maybe I can pry it off, he considered, then sprinted into the woods. If he could find a branch sturdy enough to wedge between the slab and the disk . . .

"Holy Mother!" he yelled when the worm—in the space of a blink—shot out from under the thicket and began to coil about his legs.

Loren tried to kick but the worm's hoselike body encircled his thighs tight as a metal clamp. Loren collapsed.

His heart squirmed as more glistening pink coils raveled up his body. The worm had hooked his ankles with its tail end and was working upward, now past the waist. Its efforts were turning him into a mummy of pink coils. The musculature of its coelum made Loren feel like he was being swallowed by a pulsing mouth . . .

His left arm flailed free, but the right had been caught under the coils. How much sooner till it got to his neck?

Loren couldn't think. His adrenaline pumped uselessly through his body; the harder he tried to move, the more he couldn't.

Then the worm's head loomed.

Loren nearly lost consciousness at the sight: the eyeless pink cone. A tiny, meaty hole at the end suddenly expanded, revealing a pulsating throat. Stylets like transparent fishhooks emerged. Loren knew that the hooks would seek his mouth so that the worm could secure a grasp before it would start pumping its acid-like digestive enzymes down his esophagus, whereupon his innards would be liquefied and then sucked back into the worm's body, for nourishment. After the hearty meal the creature would fill Loren's emptied body cavity with ova, to incubate.

His right hand had managed to slither to the pistol in his waistband, but the coils were too tight to drag it out. Even in this revolted paralysis, his subconscious knew that there was nothing to lose in firing anyway—

Bam!

Did the worm actually squeal? Loren felt the gun kick beneath the mummifying coils, felt a bullet blow through the side of his swim trunks.

It also blew a hole in the worm, midbody.

The gun barrel burned against Loren's thigh, but he didn't feel it. He'd managed to squeeze off the shot just as the worm's head was lowering to his face. Worm blood and stored seawater flooded Loren's legs; then the coils began to loosen, shuddering in their own pain.

Gotcha, you fucker! he thought when he grabbed the head with his left hand, pressed it to the dirt. Only now was he able to drag his gun hand out.

He pressed the barrel to the worm's skull-less head, and—

Bam!

Chunks of pink meat speckled Loren's face. In the other direction, more seawater, white blood, and a tea-colored ichor flew. The plume hit a tree and—

Shit!

Loren began to frantically wipe his face off, remembering that the worm's enzyme duct was in the head. He could see spatters on the tree smoking, sizzling, those same fluids burning through the bark. It was Loren's very good fortune that none had gotten on his face.

The worm limpened in death after a few reflexive spasms. Loren shrugged out of the coils.

He got up and looked closer at the tree. The enzymes became impotent after a minute, but not before eating a crater into the hard tropical wood.

As the sizzling from the acid died down, a thought began to sizzle in his head.

He grabbed the worm's neck, clamping hard with the ring of his thumb and forefinger, leaving eight inches of exploded head hanging off. Loren dragged the dead thing back toward the RTG.

Can't hurt to try . . .

It was like dragging a great length of hose. When he arrived at the slab, he carefully held the worm's ruptured head right against the black rod on which the disk had been mounted.

Loren squeezed a few feet of worm . . .

More fluids evacuated, mostly the tea-tinged slime.

The cement around the rod—

It's working . . .

—began to sizzle and smoke.

Loren jiggled the disk as the acids worked deeper. Moments later, he yanked it out of the cement slab, like dragging the stick out of a thawing Popsicle.

The enzymes liquefied the cement!

He'd gotten the bomb off the RTG but—

Holy shit . . .

Now Loren found himself in the most bizarre predicament of his life. *I'm standing here in the middle of the woods, holding a bomb from another planet . . .*

He looked at the blinking border of light around the disk.

With each blink—he noticed now—that border got infinitesimally smaller.

Loren shook his head.

Question of the day, he thought. *How the HELL do you get rid of an alien bomb?*

No answers were forthcoming. He at least knew that he had till the border ran out to think of something.

With nothing else to do, he put the bomb in his pocket and headed back to the campsite to find Trent . . .

(IV)

Robb was strong, all right. His mottled yellow hands turned Ruth upside down, and hauled her shorts off. The terror merged with the stifling heat, and of course, the "zombie's" stench of rot and metamorphosis. The fetor in the room could be likened to fresh-ground beef, sperm, and a restaurant Dumpster in the sun. Ruth landed on her head when Robb shucked her out of the shorts, which dangled off one ankle. She saw proverbial stars as Robb's hands began to wring her implants like dishwashing sponges.

When she was able to see through gaps in some of the stars, her scream ground down to a disgusted gag. Robb had shed his own shorts previously, to reveal a groin that looked more like an open wound. There was no penis, for instance, just a rot-gnarled nub with a hole in it, and a bloated yellow scrotum. Were small things moving in the scrotum?

Ruth was too racked with horror to ponder the question very deeply, but given the circumstances, a passer-by might beg another question: With no penis, what did Robb intend to rape her with?

Muscles flexed beneath yellow, red-spotted skin. In Robb's infection and sequent decomposition, aspects of his college-athlete physique remained: pillars for thighs, bulging biceps, pectorals, and lats. Ordinarily, Ruth might even have been turned on by the flexing washboard abdominals.

But not when they were covered by red-spotted yellow monster skin.

All 110 pounds of Ruth put up a formidable fight, hands slapping at the mindless, wedgelike face, fingers poking at the eyes, which looked so watery they might somehow have aspirated their inner humors. The big chunk she'd bitten out of his cheek was now covered by something that looked more like a wart than a scab.

One big wet hand pinned her chest to the floor, while the other, now, wriggled for her groin. Ruth's legs moved like fifty miles an hour on a stationary bike; she was going nowhere, but her body was trying anyway.

Her senses disconnected. None of her brain bothered to curse Slydes—that big hairy redneck coward—for leaving her here. None of her brain wasted any synaptic energy on the useless regret that if she'd stayed in school, never done drugs, and never gotten involved with creeps like Jonas and Slydes, then maybe she wouldn't be pinned to the floor in this infernal toolshed by a sex-crazed zombie with no penis. Maybe, just maybe, if she'd kept going to church instead of opting out for strip joints and coke at age eighteen, and penny-ante tricks in between sugar daddies . . .

It seemed likely that she would never have had occasion to meet her noxious death on an island full of giant pink worms.

Ruth didn't bother thinking about any of that.

Instead, she thought this: *The fuckin' barbecue fork!*

She'd brought it in from outside, hadn't she? More senses shut down as stout fingers began to play inside her womanly orifice. Her auditory faculties didn't register Robb White's ruined efforts to speak:

"Bluckin' blig-tit blitch! Gublunna pull bloor gluts out frew bloor plussy!"

Whatever.

Ruth's eye had already caught sight of the barbecue fork, lying not three feet beyond her reach. *If I can get this big zombie fucker's hand off me just for ONE SECOND,* she realized, *I could get that fork!*

Something unexpected happened then, almost in synchronicity with the thought. The yellow lids on Robb's glop-for-eyes shot open. His body stiffened as if seized by a sudden pain, and his gestures of molestation . . . stopped.

He pulled away. When he pulled his hand out from Ruth's spread legs, it didn't all come out.

The yellow, red-spotted skin peeled off like a rubber glove.

Robb held up the hand in mute, zombie astonishment. His hand was now a raving, shining *pink*.

He stood up in haste, shaking through a confusion. Then he began to take his skin off like someone taking off clothes.

The "shirt" of yellow skin crinkled wetly as it was removed from Robb's back. The sleeves turned inside out; then the entire mess was tossed away. What existed beneath was more of the same brand-new, clean, raving *pink*.

The same color as the worms.

The new pink arms, in fact, looked more like fat, sturdy worms themselves. No nipples or navel adorned the chest, just a remnant human musculature covered by fresh pink skin.

Even in this utter madness, Ruth was able to think: *What the fuckin' FUCK is happening?*

A transformation was happening, not that she could've been technically aware of that. After all, she still thought Robb was a zombie. He was actually now a late-cycle mutant. His robust health had allowed him to survive a full mutagenic conversion, his altered genes bidding this successful wedding of human DNA with genetically transfected *worm* DNA.

Next, Robb pulled off what was left of his scalp, revealing a glistening pink head with an aperture at the top. His head seemed to collapse, the skull cracking heartily, and then that aperture expanded and expelled the chunks of Robb's cranium. Without the support of bones now, the mass of pink flesh on Robb's shoulders distended and looked a lot like one of the eyeless conical heads of the worms.

Two species were merging into one before Ruth's eyes. But there was still the yellow skin from the waist down . . .

Robb stepped out of it, like stepping out of a pair of pants.

Gleaming pink legs stood V'd over Ruth. What covered Robb now, clearly, was worm skin. Even his toes looked more like the ends of worms than human toes.

But Ruth couldn't have cared less about the toes.

Her eyes shot to Robb's crotch.

What hung there was purely and simply a fat, ten-inch worm.

Oh, fuuuuuuuuuuuuuuuuuuck, Ruth thought.

Now Robb had something to rape her with, and worse still was the fact that the worm . . . was erecting.

That's when Ruth grabbed the barbecue fork and hooked it right into the pulsing column.

Blood that was white shot out on hot jets, painting Ruth's determined face. The sound that Robb made in objection bore no semblance to anything human now. More like stabbing a barbecue fork into a rhino's penis.

The shed shuddered around the concussive sound.

Ruth became a blond maniac dynamo. The fork blurred as she jammed it in and out of Robb's abdomen. Then more jabs in the neck, then a few more in the boneless sack that used to be his head.

Dust rose from the wood floor's seams when the fully mutated Robb White collapsed. Ruth jabbed the now-flaccid penis-thing one more time, then ran like a banshee out the door.

Her brain still registered very little. All she knew was that she was no longer in that Shed from Hell, and she was breathing fresh air, not monster-stink.

Her shorts still rung her foot. She pulled them on and sprinted off down the first trail she saw. She only knew that she was going to run straight to the beach and start swimming.

It was worth the chance, even with the sharks.

(V)

First Nora checked the camp. *They're not here,* she thought in the biggest disappointment. That meant she'd have to go looking, and there was precious little time for that. She found another can of repellent in Trent's tent, then sprayed herself down liberally. *For all the good it'll do against those things,* she told herself, remembering just how big the worms could get.

Frustration overwhelmed her now. She jogged down the trail. *That was stupid!* Her heart still hadn't let up. Maybe God really *had* saved her. *But for what?* she wondered.

Did she really deserve to be saved? How different

would her life be if she survived this mess? Even amid the chaos and all the impossibilities, some recess of her mind seemed to dwell on that.

Try to do some good, she told herself.

She veered off back toward the RTG.

I'll find a way to disarm it . . .

But when she got there . . .

"How the hell?" she muttered.

It was gone.

She squinted down at the cement slab. The area where the black disk had been seemed blemished, even corroded somehow. *Well, that's sure some shit . . .*

Then it occurred to her, *One of the guys in the masks must've moved it. They must know we're onto them . . .*

So what now?

When she turned she almost shrieked.

A dead worm lay like limp rope across the clearing. End to end, it must've been thirty feet long.

She felt caught in a cross fire of confusion. *Back to the campsite,* was the only recourse she could think of. She took back off running . . .

An unseen impact slammed her chest and plowed all the air from her lungs. It happened too fast for her to think. Had she run into a branch?

Her back slammed the ground.

Consciousness began to fizzle, her peripheral vision going from gray to black.

Nora had been clotheslined, but not by a branch.

By a girthy arm.

A bearded face hovered over her.

Echoic words floated from slow-motion lips. "Hey, baby. My name's Slydes. What's yours?"

Then a knuckly fist to the forehead knocked her out cold.

(VI)

Loren stood dumbfounded at the campsite. *Yeah, I need this headache!* Trent was not to be found.

He foolishly checked all the tents, if only because he could think of nothing else to do. *Right,* he thought. *Like the lieutenant's going to be taking a nap. . . .* He was about to start calling out, but thought better of it. *Trent's out there somewhere . . . but so are those guys.* Loren had no choice but to think of them as that: those *guys.* Those men in the masks and black hooded suits. He simply didn't have it in him to use the more specified label:

Alien research technicians.

But it was true and he knew that. And he knew they were still on the island. He'd seen a total of three of them on the surveillance screens.

What should I do? a voice unlike his own demanded. Perhaps the voice belonged to his more courageous alter ego. He walked anxious circles around the site, glancing incessantly at his watch.

Five minutes. Ten minutes. Fifteen . . .

Nora said she'd be right behind me, he thought. *She should be here by now, and so should Trent.*

He stood still and listened. Just then the island utterly lacked any sound at all. Not even a parrot squawked. Not even a lizard scurried up a tree . . .

Where is everybody?

Loren, of course, already knew what he should do: *Got to look for them!* he thought. *Find Nora, find Trent, and then we can get to the boat and leave! Unless . . .*

Unless those guys in the masks and black suits—*the ALIENS,* he forced himself—had already killed Nora and Trent.

Or maybe something worse . . .

Maybe the worms or their ova had gotten them by

now. He'd seen how fast Annabelle had been lost. *It could just as easily have happened to them on their way back here, and come to think of it . . . It could happen to me, too.*

Of course it could.

And he still had the bomb in his pocket. He removed the puck and saw with some unease that about twenty percent of the blinking border was gone. *How much more time before this thing goes off? And what the FUCK am I going to do with it?*

Loren didn't care for pressure or stress, and he wasn't much of a decision maker.

But providence was changing that today. He could either stay here, or he could bone up and go search for Nora and Trent.

Do it, the other voice demanded. *Don't be a coward . . .*

Loren took the gun out of his waistband. *Three bullets left,* he knew. Then he pocketed the disk and decided he'd cut through to the other side of the island and throw it as far out into the water as he could.

He jogged off down one of the trails. Trent said he was going to check the body, so it made sense to look there first, then ditch the bomb, then track back to the control station. He could think of no other tactic.

Immediately the trail seemed more dense, hemming him against the paranoia that pressed from either side, below, and above.

The worms could be anywhere, he knew.

He moved very slowly, examining his field of vision. Gun in lead, he felt foolish. He knew a bullet would kill a worm with a head shot, but he only had three bullets. *There are a hell of a lot more than three worms on this island.* Worse, he was squinting through each forward step, peeling his eyes for signs of ova that, by now, probably existed by the hundreds of thousands.

One further question haunted him: *If I don't find Nora or Trent, what am I going to do?*

He'd have to go to the boat and leave without them.

"Loren," a peep of a voice seemed to seep through trees.

"Nora!" he replied. He wasn't sure which direction.

"Oh God, I think I broke my leg . . ."

Not Nora's voice—

He stepped a few yards off the trail and saw her, lying sprawled in the thicket.

Annabelle.

Loren stared down, gun poised.

She lay naked, inclined on her elbows. When she tried to lean up farther, she groaned. But what Loren noticed first and foremost was this: *She looks . . . normal.*

She winced through obvious discomfort when she looked more closely at him. "What's wrong with you? Why are you pointing that gun at me?"

"I—" He didn't lower it. He saw no ova on her, and no yellowed skin like the girl in the boat.

No sign of infection.

But . . . that worm . . .

"Put that gun away and *help* me!"

"You—you must be infected," he finally choked out. "You *have* to be."

"Don't be an idiot, Loren!" she snapped. "Do I *look* infected?"

Loren eyed the robust breasts and healthy, tan belly. *Actually,* he considered, *you don't.* "But that worm— Trent and I saw it. It was dozens of feet long, Annabelle, and it lifted you up into the trees."

"Tell me about it!" she griped in her normal voice. "That goddamned thing was trying to go down my throat, but once it got a whiff of this"—she held up her wrist, showing her plastic repellent bracelet—"it gagged and dropped me. I must've fallen twenty feet!"

Loren's brain ticked. He had no choice but to doubt what she claimed; it didn't jibe with the science. Those bracelets, as well as the bug repellent they'd been using, were only strong enough to discourage small insects with microscopic sensory pores that would easily be overloaded by the small traces of chlordane and diethyl-based irritants. *But a twenty- or thirty-foot worm? It would be like killing a wild boar with a mousetrap.*

Then again . . . bug spray killed the ova and smaller worms, he remembered. *And as a matter of fact, I haven't been infected, and neither has Nora or Trent— and we all used bug repellent and the bracelets.*

"Loren! Just when I was really starting to like you, and now you're *really* pissing me off! Would you stop being a chicken and come over here and help me!"

He knew what Nora would do; she'd help her. Plus, if anything, Annabelle looked one hundred percent as healthy as she had earlier. The trickle of remnant attraction assailed him as well, even under these conditions. Any real man would feel the same thing. Her raw beauty lay before him, and she was in pain: the ultimate damsel in distress . . .

Loren put the gun away and went to her. "You said you broke your leg?"

She ground her teeth. "I think so, when I fell out of the tree—my right leg. It hurts so much."

Loren placed his hands on the warm leg, felt for signs of fracture. "I think you lucked out," he said, trying very hard not to steal a glance at her breasts. "There's no swelling, and I don't feel any bone fragments under the skin. You probably jolted the cartilage in the knee and hip, though, and that's going to hurt for a while. Let me help you up, see if you can walk."

She groaned again, head arched back, as he got her to her feet.

"Can you put any weight on your leg?"

She clung to him with one arm, and gingerly stepped forward. "Yes—damn! It hurts, but I think I can walk."

"Good. Let's take it slow."

At least Loren had some direction now, but . . . *Jesus, I've got to move fast. Got to get Annabelle to the boat, then find Nora and Trent and get THEM to the boat. And then get out of here . . . AFTER I get rid of this bomb in my pocket!*

They limped along down the trail. This was going to take a while. The bomb ticking away in his pocket only reminded him further of how little time he had to get everything done. And . . .

How powerful IS this bomb? the worst dread kept forcing him to think. Loren didn't need that question distracting him, and a distraction he needed even less was Annabelle's warm, curvaceous body pressing right against him. One big breast kept rubbing his side, and every time he cast a tiny glance down . . .

Oh, man . . .

During one such glance, he could swear her nipples were erecting, which hardly made sense given the situation. *Stop looking at her, you pervert!* he yelled at himself.

He didn't see the kudzu vine crooked out from the base of a palm tree. His foot hooked it, and—

Flump!

They both fell.

"Shit! I'm sorry," Loren bumbled. "Are you all right?"

Annabelle lay atop him, her luscious, hot weight pressing him down. He expected that the fall had hurt her leg, but she made no protest. Her face opposed his, strands of blond hair falling to either side of his neck. It looked like she was about to say something, but then her eyes bloomed . . . and her lips lowered to his.

The shock stiffened every muscle in Loren's body. He felt agog at what was happening. Her tongue traced his lips, delved into his mouth, then slipped down to his ear where she whispered, "I've been hot for you since the day we got here . . ."

More shock on Loren's part, and more stiffening, especially about the groin. *I can't believe it,* came the thought through so much hot fog. *I'm finally making out with her . . .*

At last he relaxed and slipped his arms around the small of her back. Her bare legs spread wider, her groin grinding down. Her breathing issued as a series of wanton pants and gasps. She raised herself on her hands then, and hitched herself up.

To a guy like Loren, the mother lode had arrived.

The two perfect orbs of her breasts were now level with his face. Then she positioned herself more precisely, and a swollen nipple began to brush across his lips.

"Suck it," she whispered. "Hard. Real hard . . ."

The instant Loren obliged, Annabelle moaned.

The way her bare hips were grinding down, Loren wouldn't last long. Her warm body encompassed him: She was a cocoon of his most erotic dreams. She traded her nipples back and forth, "Harder." And then one hand slid down, caged his crotch through the meager swim trunks, and squeezed.

"Take these off and fuck me," came the next desperate whisper. "I can't stand it anymore. I've *got* to have you in me . . ."

Just hearing her say that almost spent him. This would be tough. Even if he got that far, how long would he last?

Only a few of his closest friends knew his secret: that he was indeed a virgin. He'd told Nora some contrary jive because—well, it seemed the right thing to do, not to mention that he had the hots for her, and not to mention that she was his boss.

But . . . *this?*

No one would believe him, and he didn't care.

Cringing, he was about to pull the gun out of his waistband and push his trunks down when the situation's true gravity slapped him in the face:

Wait a minute! I've got an alien bomb I've got to get rid of, two people to find, and a boat to get on . . .

I don't have time to have sex!

"Annabelle . . . we can't do this now. There's some stuff you don't know . . ."

The wanton desperation on her face . . . changed.

Suddenly her face turned blank, like a sleepwalker's . . .

She sat upright, still straddling his groin. When he looked now, it seemed that her belly was swollen, and . . .

Ooooooooooh no . . .

Her skin seemed to be tinged with the faintest off-yellow streaks overlain by tiny red spots . . .

"Get off me!" he shouted, shoving up at her.

Very softly, she said, "I'm going to sit on your face and feed you my worms . . ."

Her fists were suddenly in his hair, holding him down. She kneed herself higher, trying to position her groin over his mouth . . .

Loren almost fainted when he glimpsed several narrow wormheads peeking out of the folds of her sex.

He tried to lever her off his body, couldn't, but found enough room to grab the pistol and swipe it upward.

When the gun's blue-steel top strap clacked the back of her head, she fell over.

Loren's heart was a squirming lump. He crawled away backward, stood up against a tree, and aimed—

Several pink worms—pencil-thin and a foot long—squirmed farther out of Annabelle's sex. Her strangely pushed-out stomach seemed to be churning.

She was getting up—

Bam!

He squeezed a shot off into her belly.

Loren managed to not pass out when he witnessed the results of the shot.

The bullet gave her a second navel. Upon impact, a half dozen foot-long worms darted from her vagina, along with a slew of crawling ova. More ova foamed out of the bullet hole.

Then a ten-foot worm snaked out of her mouth, and began to sidewind very quickly toward Loren.

Loren ran faster than he ever had, not at all sure that it would be faster than the worm.

(VII)

Slydes dragged the skinny dark-haired woman by the crotch of her one-piece swimsuit—a convenient handle. He wasn't quite sure why he didn't just kill her right there, but he supposed it was curiosity more than anything.

She might know something.

And Slydes definitely wanted to know what these worms were all about, and those little yellow things, and the shit that had happened to Jonas. The skinny woman might have a clue.

It didn't take him long to get to the farthest head shack, where Jonas grew the bulk of his pot. He dropped the woman, made for the door, but stopped short.

Shit, I gotta piss like a racehorse, it occurred to him.

What *didn't* occur to him, however, was this: Why the sudden need to urinate when he was so severely dehydrated?

Slydes immodestly opened his pants, then began to go . . . or tried to. *Jesus,* he thought. His bladder felt bloated, but only a trickle popped out. *I ain't got all day!* He pushed, pushed harder, then—

"Ahhh, there she goes."

Suddenly Slydes was voiding his bladder like a flood-gate just opened. A few seconds later, though, something struck him as . . .

Not right.

Slydes looked down—and blanched.

He expected to see a golden arc of urine. But urine wasn't what his bladder was voiding.

It was an arc of BB-sized ova.

Oh, my fuckin' shit!

He couldn't very well stop now; he had to get them all out. Slydes pushed and pushed, thrusting his pelvis ludicrously forward. The clotted stream just kept pouring, and another thing: The more he urinated, the more discomfort he felt.

It was supposed to be the other way around, wasn't it?

He saw now that the ova shooting out of his urethra had gradually gone from the size of BBs to the size of peas. He was literally peeing a *pile* of ova.

He felt even sicker when he looked at his penis.

It was yellow. With red spots.

"Oh, my fuckin' shit," he groaned.

"Looks like you're infected in a big way," the skinny woman said. She was up on one elbow, watching the grotesque spectacle.

"I ain't infected!" he bellowed. "And who the hell are you anyway? What do you know about this shit?"

"A lot," she said. "My name's Nora Craig, *Professor* Nora Craig. I'm a marine biologist with the college. You've been infected with what appears to be a genetically hybridized parasite that's part trichinosis worm, part ribbon worm, and part pinworm."

"I ain't infected!" he repeated. "It's—it's—it's . . . just a few of 'em. Once I piss all of 'em out, I'll be okay."

"You're dreaming, Paul Bunyon. Once you piss all of them out, you'll still have the worms. A lot of those little yellow things already hatched—in *you*."

Finally, Slydes was done. One last ovum—the size of a gumball—squirmed out.

His face looked understandably sick. He pulled up his shirt, looked with more nausea at his red-spotted beer belly.

What am I gonna do now? he wondered.

When the pile of ova began to move toward Nora, she withdrew a small can of something, and sprayed them.

"What's that?" Slydes demanded.

"Bug repellent. It kills the ova, and the younger worms."

"Give it to me!"

Nora laughed. "It's not going to do you any good, pal. You've got those things *all through* your body. By now they're insinuated throughout your major organ systems. And some of the ova have already released a virus that's going into your brain. It'll change your behavior too, it'll change your DNA, to make you a more adaptable host. You're a breeding ground for the worms, buddy."

Slydes saw that the pile of yellow things had stopped moving. *She ain't lying. It killed 'em.* "Gimme that can, bitch! I'll drink it, and it'll kill any of 'em left."

She laughed even more boisterously, holding up the can. "This is poison, asshole. It'll kill you in a few minutes. But you know? I'd rather die from poison than die from those things." She threw him the can. "So go ahead. Drink up."

Slydes looked at the can. He wasn't much of a reader, but he could indeed read the words WARNING: POISON! and the universal skull and crossbones under it. Slydes swore and threw the can away. Three long strides took him over to Nora. He grabbed her hair and dragged her toward the head shack.

Nora shrieked. Slydes liked that. *Sassy, smart-ass bitch. If you think THAT hurts* . . . He'd cut on her good, but first . . .

He needed some water.

That's the ticket. I'll be all right. I'll get me a good long drink of water, and that'll be that. This bitch is just tryin' to scare me. I'm sure I've done peed all them things out . . .

Wishful thinking for a desperate man . . . but a desperate man who was also a sociopath. "You're gonna be a of of fun, baby. I saw ya the other day—wanted to do a job on ya right then, lemme tell ya."

"You're a busted redneck no-account loser," Nora said, and yelped louder when he twisted her hair some more. "You're a fucking walking worm farm and you're gonna die."

"Keep talkin'. I'm a gator poacher. Did you know that?"

She responded through grit teeth, "Sounds like the perfect job for a big redneck moron like you."

Slydes whipped out his Buck knife. "But gator ain't the only thing I know how to skin." Then his big bearded face broadened in a grin. "I'll be nice'n slow, too. Might even pop ya a few times while I'm doin' it."

But first, the water. He dug the key from his pocket, and unlocked the dead bolt.

Even in her distress, Nora had to ask: "How do you have a key to that?"

"Damn it!" another voice barked out.

Slydes and Nora turned in startlement.

Trent stood behind them, his face stamped with anger. "Let her go, Slydes."

With a smirk, Slydes released Nora. "Lieutenant Trent!" she almost squealed in delight. "Thank God you're here!"

But Trent glared at Slydes. "I told you to *never* come here without my permission! I *told you* I was escorting a photo shoot! I specifically *instructed you* to stay away until it was over!"

"Jonas got more buyers," Slydes said, "and ran out. We needed to come out here to get more product. We'd planned to be in and out real quick but . . . things didn't work out."

"You're not kidding they didn't work out!" Trent yelled.

Nora looked mystified. "You *know* this guy?" she asked Trent.

"Yeah, I know him all right. The dumb son of a bitch is my brother, and so is Jonas. I gave them the key to these two head shacks."

"What for?"

Trent frowned. "For hydroponic marijuana. Jonas, my other brother, is a pot grower, and Slydes brings him back and forth in his boat. I've been letting them use these facilities for the past two years."

Nora looked deflated by the information. "I've read all about it," she said. "Hydroponic pot is twice as potent, and has double the street value. The only problem is the need for constant electric light and fresh water—but that's not a problem out here, is it?"

"No," Trent said. "It's all unmonitored and it's all free."

"And you get a cut of the profits . . ."

"Of course I do. It's just pot, for Christ's sake, it's not like it's heroin," he tried to justify. "I didn't see any real harm. The RTG'll be producing electricity for the next fifty years. And since I'm the only one who checks the island . . ."

"What the army doesn't know won't hurt them, huh?" Nora goaded.

"Something like that." Trent shook his head. "Shit."

"The army'll know now," Slydes spoke up, " 'cause this bitch'll tell 'em." He whipped out his Buck again. "Lemme just kill her right now."

Trent drew his gun. "You're not killing anyone, Slydes."

"Can't believe you're pointing a gun at your own brother!" Slydes growled.

"Speaking of brothers, where's Jonas?"

"He's dead," Slydes said.

Trent looked astonished. "Dead? Are you sure?"

"He was sure as shit dying when I left him. Them yellow things got him. They're, like, eggs. He was coughing them up, and turnin' yellow. He told me to split before his mind went and he tried to infect me."

"Same thing'll happen to you," Nora interrupted. "Soon."

"Bullshit! I'll cut your skinny throat!"

"Just shut up!" Trent yelled. "I've got to think!"

"There's nothing to think about," Nora said. "One brother's dead and this one's dying of the same thing."

"Don't listen to the bitch! She's lyin', tryin' to turn you against me!"

Nora's face lit up in a cynical grin. "Lieutenant, he just passed a *pound* of ova out his bladder." She quickly pointed to the mound of dead ova.

Trent stared at it, then at Slydes. "You fucked everything up, Slydes. You should never have come here. I don't know what I'm going to do now."

"First thing you can do is let me turn this bitch into cold cuts. Then we can get out of here."

"Where's that girl with the funny lips you always got with you?"

"Dead, too," Slydes told him.

"No big loss there."

"Some big guy got her. He was all yellow, looked like he was rotting. Even looked like he was changing underneath his skin."

"Mutagenesis," Nora cut in. "It's not an uncommon

trait among certain nematodes. Their ova will attack a potential host with a DNA-changing virus, to make the host's living body more habitable for the worms." She pointed to Slydes again. "That'll be happening to you real soon. It's *already* happening."

Slydes stepped toward her with the big knife. "I'm skinnin' her right now, so help me!"

"Back off, Slydes." Trent cocked his pistol. "I'm not thinking too clearly right now, so just . . . back . . . off."

Slydes stepped back, grinding his teeth.

"Did you examine the body of the man that Loren shot?" Nora asked.

Trent looked grim. "Yeah . . ."

"And it was no man from this planet, was it?"

"You know?"

"Loren and I got into the old control station. It was full of all kinds of alien shit," she said. "They turned the place into a field lab and were implanting worms into humans. And that thing in the trench we thought was a submersible . . . it's hovering over the island right now."

Just as Nora had said it, a dark spot drew over them, like a cloud moving in front of the sun.

They all looked up.

What they saw appeared inexplicable: a long rectangular dark spot whose covering had turned sky-blue. "It can camouflage itself," Nora said. But running underneath the object was a bright glowing white line. "And that line of light can only be its propulsion system."

Trent and Slydes just stared, dumbfounded.

"It means they're getting ready to leave," Nora added.

"Well, that's good, isn't it?" Trent said.

"No, Lieutenant, that's bad, *real* bad. They've planted some bombs on the island—"

"Bombs? You're shitting me."

"Wish I was. And God knows how powerful they are."

Trent was chewing his lip in confusion. "Where's Loren?"

"He's probably waiting for us at the campsite, to take us to the boat," she told him.

Slydes finally snapped out of his daze. He looked at them both and said very slowly, "What the fuck is going on here?"

"Some really fucked-up shit, Slydes."

The bearded brother looked upward again. "And that thing is . . ."

"It's an alien spacecraft," Nora put it bluntly. "And those guys in the black suits and masks are its pilots. We think they created a new species of parasite by genetic manipulation."

"What the fuck for?"

"Oh, I don't know. Maybe to decimate the human race. The worm grows hundreds of times faster than any other parasite, and it can live on land and sea, and anyone it infects becomes a concealed carrier. They're not doing it just for shits and giggles."

Sunlight moved back across their faces as the macabre object in the sky hovered past.

"Looks like it's going to the control center," Nora figured. "To pick up its crew and their research. Then they'll leave and you can bet your ass those bombs'll go off."

Trent rubbed his face. "Holy shit, I don't know what to do."

"Kill this clown so we can go!" Nora shouted.

"He's my brother!"

"He's *infected,* Lieutenant. And if you don't kill him, he'll infect *you.*"

Trent and Slydes stared at each other without blinking.

"You're one low-down slimy shit-house rat to even *think* about killin' your own brother," Slydes said, "I ain't infected, I peed 'em all out! And even if I didn't, once I get back to the mainland, I can go to a doctor and get an antidote or somethin'."

Nora laughed at the bombast. "It's an *alien parasite,* you asshole! Penicillin won't cut it."

"She's right, Slydes," Trent groaned.

"Our daddy'd be ashamed if he saw you right now, holdin' a gun on your own brother."

"Our daddy was a thieving cracker scumbag, Slydes," Trent intoned. "Just like you."

Slydes pointed a big finger. "Listen here, *little* brother. The only person you're gonna be killin' is this skinny smart-mouth bitch. Now quit pointing that gun at me 'fore I shove it up your ass."

Trent didn't lower the gun.

"Kill him," Nora implored. "He's infected. The longer you wait, the more he changes."

Trent's confusion made him cross-eyed. "Then how come *we're* not infected? We've been on the island longer than him."

"Mosquito repellent, suntan oil, these things on our wrists, who knows?" Nora said.

"And where are all these damn worms? You're making it sound like an epidemic. How come I've only seen a few of them?"

"These worms are obviously spawning," she answered. "And when worms spawn, particularly round-worms and similar species, they tend to nest."

"Where?" Trent demanded.

"Either out in shallower water where the temperature will be higher, or some place on the island's surface—any place that's moist and warm. There have got to be thousands of them on the island now, and the bulk of them are probably nesting. That's why we're not seeing a lot of them. But you've seen the ova—they're all over the place. At least half of those ova contain infantile worms."

"I don't know what to do!" Trent yelled, face reddening.

Nora looked right at him. "You better do something fast, because we probably only have a few more minutes to get out of here."

Trent just kept staring at Slydes, the gun still pointing.

"You always were the pussy of the family," Slydes challenged. "You ain't got the balls to drop that gun and go man to man with me."

"Shut up, Slydes."

"I kicked your pussy ass when you were a kid, and I'll kick it now. Daddy always knew you were the weakest of the boys."

Trent smirked. "I'm the only one who made anything for himself."

"Shit. You? The army? You ain't never had the balls for nothin', and you know somethin'? You ain't got the balls to pull that trigger."

Trent sighed. "I'm glad you said that, Slydes—"
Bam!
The round Trent squeezed off hit Slydes right in the nose and flipped him over backward. By the time he landed on his belly, he was dead. In only moments, ova could be seen exiting his mouth.

"Now let's get out of here," Nora said.

But Trent stood still through the veil of gun smoke. Now the pistol was trained on Nora.

"Oh, come on!" she yelled. "What? You're afraid I'm going to tell your superiors that you were letting your brothers grow pot out here? *I don't care* about it! I won't say anything! Let's just go!"

"I can't take the chance," he feebly replied. "It's my career."

"You're kidding me, right? Right now there's more crucial things going on than your little pothouse! Pardon me, but didn't you see the *fucking spaceship* that just flew over our heads?"

Trent was melting down from the pressure. He was standing right in front of the head shack on the end, which still had Slydes's key in the dead bolt. Just as he raised the gun's sights to Nora's face—

Something thunked on the head shack door.

Something inside.

Trent's eyes widened on her. "What . . . was that?"

"*Who cares?*" Nora shrieked, her face red as a cherry. "Let's *go!*"

"I'll bet it's Jonas," Trent murmured. "Slydes admitted he didn't actually see him die . . ."

Another thunk on the door. Trent reached out.

When he turned the knob, the bolt clicked, and—

"Holy fucking shit!"

—the door popped open as if hit by a battering ram. Nora saw at once what had been exerting such pressure against the door . . . and so did Trent:

Hundreds of pink, shining, twenty-foot worms.

The scorching air that gusted from the head shack smacked Nora in the face with a smell like fresh manure. The worms existed as a shivering mass, covering the head shack floor to a depth of several feet until Trent had opened the door. It was a dam break, and Trent found himself instantly standing in the mass that poured out.

Shock and revulsion turned Trent's face white. When he tried to scream, only the most meager gasp escaped his throat. He all but uselessly emptied his magazine into the creatures that quickly coiled up his legs.

Nora moved backward, half paralyzed by the sight herself. She noted that she'd been wrong in her estimation, as she saw now that some of the worms were stout as firehoses, and much longer than twenty feet. Several reared their eyeless heads above the mass as if to gloat over their catch, while Trent failed very quickly to escape. He was halfway to the knees in shivering worms.

Bugged eyes sought Nora: "Help me!" he begged.

Not a chance, Nora thought.

It was all Trent could do to stay on his feet. Worms coiled up his arms now, and his waist: Soon he was cloaked in them. He tried to wade out of the mass when one fatter worm spun round his neck and shot its head down his throat. The worm's body began to throb in waves as it began to empty its digestive enzymes into Trent's stomach. Two more thinner worms struggled down the back of Trent's shorts, seeking an alternate orifice. Trent's eyes looked on the verge of ejecting from their sockets.

More and more of the mass poured out, making a shivering pink carpet before the head shack. Nora kept stepping backward.

Eventually the largest worm of all emerged, raising above the mass cobralike. It was close to a foot in girth . . . and God knew how long.

Though its head had no eyes, it seemed to look right at Nora.

Nora ran.

(VIII)

If their vocalizing could be properly converted and heard by a human, it wouldn't sound like "words" at all, but something more like Morse code. They didn't communicate via sonics, in other words, but by fluctuations in ambient pressure transceived by the theta waves in an autonomic cerebral ventricle. When they were out of their own atmosphere, transponders in their masks trafficked their speech back and forth, through pulses of aneroid signals. They spoke in millibars and dynes, not sounds.

But they had words, just like humans or any highly evolved life form. They even had their own equivalent colloquialisms, profanities, and figures of speech.

"Where's the damn colonel?" the major asked.

The sergeant was wondering that himself as the manometer in his mask relayed his superior's query. "He said he'd meet us at the debark point, sir." He checked the grid readout on his task strip. It read: -:.:-:... "And this is the debark point."

The major looked up. "I don't see the LRV. Maybe the regauge system didn't fire."

He's really worrying, isn't he? the sergeant thought, amused. "It's right there, sir."

The shadow roved over their faces. It took some squinting but eventually the major saw it, and sighed in relief. "That's incredible. The obfuscation systems work so well in this atmosphere."

"It's the nitrogen, sir."

The line of the particle synchrotron element glowed faintly above them, extending from one end of the ship to the other. The ship was called a lenticular reentry vehicle, which counterrotated gravity by manipulating nucleons and forcing them to divide and permute their para-atomic particles within a controlled field. It was simple.

Not so simple was the dilemma of the colonel.

"Maybe he was killed," the major said.

"By the humans?"

"Why not? They killed the corporal."

"The corporal wasn't very smart. And our reflexivity is twice as fast as the humans'."

"Do you think one of the specimens in the field got him?"

"Not unless the methoxychlor dispersors in his utility dress malfunctioned. I wouldn't worry about it, sir. The colonel probably wanted to double-check the control station one last time before debarkation."

The major didn't respond. It was clear he was concerned. One troop was already dead.

They remained in the small clearing as the LRV hung silently above them. To the sergeant's side hovered a Class I antigravity pallet, loaded with the specimen samples and prototypes, plus all their data-storage pins. Everything else had been left at the control station and would be destroyed by the blast.

The major was rubbing his gloved hands together. Nervous. He checked his own task strip and shook his head.

He doesn't know what to do, the sergeant realized. *They should send field officers on these missions, not science administrators.*

The major tried to maintain his acumen of authority, but wasn't doing a good job. "Sergeant . . . what exactly are the emergency operating instructions for a . . . situation like this?"

"We must be fully debarked and out of this planet's stratosphere at least ten points before count-off, with or without all personnel."

"When is count-off?"

"Fifteen points from now, sir."

The major stared off.

"Sir, if the colonel doesn't get back here in time, we have to leave him. The data from the mission is far more important than one officer."

"Right," the major said. He sighed again. "Open the egression port, Sergeant. Let's man our stations and prepare to debark."

The sergeant smiled behind his protective mask. *It's about time.* "Yes, sir," he said and pressed the proper sequence on his task strip. *I've had just about enough of this planet.*

(IX)

"Push! Push!" Loren yelled.

"What's it look like I'm doing! Playing fucking polo?" Nora pushed for all her adrenaline was worth, her hands pressed up against the aft of the Boston Whaler. When she'd stumbled into Loren back on the trails, she'd followed him to the lagoon he'd promised was there . . . and the boat.

"It's only midtide!" he fretted. "I don't think we can get it over those rocks!"

"Don't think negative, damn it!" But Nora could easily see the large boulders pocking the shallow water. *It's this . . . or swim,* she knew.

The water rose up to Nora's chin as she pushed. The side of the hull scraped some rocks. Water churned around her body, the current at her knees almost strong enough to push her off her feet.

"I don't think it's going to go, Nora!" Loren shrieked.

Nora could see up ahead: two outcroppings of rock sticking out of the water. The grim fact whispered in her ear . . .

We're going to have to thread this boat between those rocks. Otherwise, we'll have to swim and— wouldn't you know it? It's hammerhead season . . .

"Push! Hard!" Loren wailed.

The hull grated against the rocks. Just as their forward motion would stop, a high swell came in, lifted the hull, and then the boat glided through.

"We did it!"

Loren was taller, but Nora had already submerged.

Bubbles erupted from her mouth as her feet were no longer touching bottom. *Shit!* she thought. *I'm too low to grab the rail . . .*

Water splashed; Nora was jerked by one hand out of the water. She flopped over on the deck, dripping.

"Can you believe that shit? We did it! We're clear!"

Nora leaned up and looked ahead. The current was sucking the boat out of the lagoon now, and sending it straight into the seemingly limitless Gulf of Mexico.

We made it, Nora thought, a tear in her eye.

"Looks like something's finally going our way," Loren said, flopping down on the deck. The current was taking them fast. "In ten minutes we'll be a mile or two out."

Safe from the bombs, she hoped.

The sun blazed overhead, welcome sea breezes drying their faces. Loren stood back up and grabbed the wheel at the console. They didn't have power, but he could rudder with the current to get them out faster. He held the wheel with one hand but was looking back.

"What are you looking for?" Nora asked. She helped herself to her feet by a gin-pole. "The ship?"

Loren squinted hard. "There it is. See it?"

Nora shielded her eyes to cut the glare. It looked like a slightly darker piece of the skyline but, yes, after a few moments she could make out its long cylindrical configuration. It was hovering about thirty feet up, near the beach at the far end of the island.

"Those guys," Loren said next, in a lower tone.

Nora could see them, too. Two of the men—or whatever they were—in the black suits and masks. They were both standing immediately below the almost invisible craft. Something bulky stood next to them—a cart full of boxes?

Then the cart levitated upward and disappeared into the ship.

"Jesus," Loren muttered. "Those guys really are aliens, aren't they?"

"What else could they be?" Then she thought, *Oh my God,* at what they saw next.

A hatch of some sort seemed to cant out of the bottom of the craft. One of the masked men had something in his gloved fist. When he raised his fist overhead . . . he, too, began to levitate up to the craft, as if he'd been hauled up on a winch.

But there was no winch.

Then the second crewman rose into the craft the same way.

"I've seen everything now," Loren said, eyes peeled.

As the boat coursed farther away, they stared another few minutes at the spectacle they were certain no one would believe: the otherworldly vehicle hovering in midair.

Then—

"This is it!" Loren said.

—the vehicle began to rise, very slowly at first, and then—

It seemed that in the course of two or three seconds, the craft launched straight into the air so quickly it didn't even blur in their eyes. It was gone in a blink.

There were no exhaust gasses, no shuttlelike roars of burning propellents, no expected blastoff.

The ship simply darted upward and was gone.

"At least we were right about one thing—they were getting ready to leave just about the same time we found out about them."

"Yeah, but you know what that means . . ."

Nora did indeed. "Now that they're gone, the bombs will go off. And we know there are at least two."

"Two?"

"Yeah, after you left the station, one of them came

back and activated one of the disks in the room with all
the monitors. But—shit!" She'd forgotten to tell him.
"I hit the guy in the head and knocked him out, and
when I went looking for you, I passed the RTG. And
guess what?"

"The bomb we saw the guy plant there was gone,"
Loren said smugly.

Nora's jaw dropped. "How did you know?"

"I'm the one who took it off the slab."

"How?"

Loren shrugged as though it were nothing. "I killed a
thirty-foot worm and melted the connector with its digestive enzymes. The stuff turned the cement to butter,
so all I had to do was pull the bomb out."

"Loren! That's fantastic! That bomb would've ruptured the RTG's core and blown radioactive fallout
halfway across Florida!"

"Sure it would've. But I took care of it, no problem."

Nora gave him a giant hug. "Loren, you're the
world's first polychaetologist *hero*!"

"It was nothing."

"So what did you do with the bomb?"

"I put it in my pocket, figured I'd try to find a safer
place to ditch it."

Nora's eyes widened. "Loren. Tell me that bomb's
not still in your pocket?"

Loren rolled his eyes. "Of course not. In fact—" He
paused and snapped his gaze back toward the beach.

"Look! There's the third guy! His buddies left without him!"

Nora could see the frantic black-clad figure standing
on the beach. He was looking to the sky.

"That must be the one I knocked out in the control
station. When he didn't get back to the ship in time,
the other two left."

Loren broke out into hysterical laughter. "Oh, shit! That guy's really screwed!"

"Loren, what are you talking about? There's a live alien on the island now! Who knows what kind of weapons and technology he has! Jesus Christ, if he gets to the mainland—"

Loren crossed his arms and shook his head. "Take my word for it. That asshole's not going anywhere."

"What do you mean!"

"After I got the bomb off the RTG slab, I stuck it in my pocket. Then I went to look for you. I went *back* to the control station, and that guy was lying on the floor, unconscious."

"So?" Nora shouted.

"Nora, I put the bomb in *his* pocket."

Nora stared. "You mean—"

"Then I ran back to the campsite."

Just as the words left Loren's lips, the detonation took place.

There was no sound, no cacophonic explosion as they might expect.

Instead, just the sensation of a sudden monumental shift in air pressure.

The entire island *jolted,* its trees swaying as if swept by a hurricane wind. The point on the beach where the figure had been standing was suddenly a throb of light that rose, then fell. A similar throb occurred deeper on the island, where the old control station had been.

That fast.

The light dispersed, forming a crude dome over the entire island, and a second after that—

Nora was fingering her cross. "God in heaven . . ."

The diffuse dome flattened all at once.

The concussion knocked Nora and Loren flat on their backs. No heat wave or scalding radioactive flash assailed them. No mushroom clouds emerged.

When they got back up, they looked back at the island . . .

It was on fire, from one end to the other.

They could feel the heat even this far out.

"Incineration," Loren observed. "How convenient."

"It'll kill everything on the island, every worm, every ovum."

"And the third guy? He doesn't even exist anymore. You can bet everything they left in the control station will be ashes too."

"No evidence," Nora whispered.

"Look at that shit. Unbelievable . . ."

The fire raged for only seconds. Then it went out as quickly as it had bloomed. Even the smoke dissipated in a matter of moments.

But the island was a blackened clot now. Every tree on it had been reduced to a charred stalk.

"No evidence is right," Loren said. "But it doesn't make sense."

"Maybe it does but we just don't get it."

Loren stroked his chin, contemplating. "Why did these people come here, from God knows where, to create a hybrid bienvironmental parasite that grows exponentially and infects humans faster than any known virus . . . only to destroy it all in one puff and leave?"

"Just a field research exercise, I guess," Nora muttered. "A scientific test on their equivalent of laboratory animals."

"Only in this case the rats were *us*."

"Has to be. We do the same thing sending probes to Mars, and mice in space, and setting up research stations on the North Pole."

Loren chuckled, wiping sweat off his brow. "No reason to even tell anyone what really happened."

"Not unless we want everyone to think we're crazy," Nora added. "Our authorities will think the RTG melted down, that's all. It'll get pushed to the last page of the newspaper."

Loren shrugged, eyes ahead to the sea. The boat bobbed as the current claimed it. They'd probably drift back to the mainland in an hour or so.

Loren looked at her in subtle shock. "But something just occurred to me."

"What?"

"We're alive."

Nora let the two words sink in. *Yeah. How do you like that?*

"Oh, and I have to be honest enough to admit something," Loren remembered. "I lost the bet."

"The bet?" Nora blinked, trying to remember. "Oh yeah. I bet you dinner that Annabelle would put the make on you. Did she?"

Loren gulped. "Oh yeah. So where do you want your free dinner?"

Nora gave the matter some serious consideration. *I almost got killed by aliens today. I didn't but . . . I'm still a virgin.*

"My place," she said.

"I was hoping you'd say that," Loren replied.

They slumped down next to each other, hips touching, and let the sea carry them away.

EPILOGUE

Bad luck had pursued Ruth for essentially every living minute of her life, so . . .

Why should it stop now?

The small skiff she'd found lashed in a secluded lagoon had indeed seemed like a turn of her typical luck. She'd managed to get it out to the gulf in spite of the lower tide, and next thing she knew the current was gliding her back toward the mainland. *I don't fuckin' believe it!* she thought. After all she'd been through, she managed to escape. She could never be aware of the irony, though: that the selfsame skiff that saved her life had once belonged to a young man named Robb White . . . before he'd turned into what Ruth continued to believe was a zombie.

Her luck only lasted another half hour, however. That's when the skiff began to sink.

What the fuck?

She peered down in terror, only now noticing the tiny holes in the skiff's aluminum hull. *Those fuckin' worms again! They ate holes in it, just like they ate holes in Slydes's engine!*

So much travail for poor Ruth. She'd survived giant worms, zombies, and two redneck psychopaths but fate still had not finished toying with her. The boat took water very slowly, which only worsened the truth: first to the tops of her feet, then to the tops of her ankles, inching coolly upward while Ruth just sat there jerking glances at the water which would eventually claim her. When the skiff was finally swallowed, Ruth bobbed like a buoy, gasping, "Fuck, fuck, fuck, fuck, fuck, fuck, *fuck!*" as her feet paddled manically.

She snorted salt water, her eyes stinging. She could see a stretch of beach on the mainland, less than a mile away. It seemed like a mirage, rising up and down with her vision, whispering to her: *Swim! Swim! It's not that far!*

Ruth swam, as best she could given her clinical exhaustion, dehydration, and extreme malnourishment. One too many adrenaline dumps left her limbs enfeebled, her consciousness winking in and out.

Would a shark get her first, or would she just drown?

Ruth expected both to happen at once, with her luck. Dizziness swept a grainy veil over her eyes. Her heart was missing beats. How much farther?

When she could move no more, she thought *Fuck* . . . one last time, and sank into the sea's green depths—

She tumbled beneath the surface, like clothes in a washer. Any energy left in her body seemed fit to burst along with her lungs.

The grainy veil turned black . . .

And there was only stillness.

Voices chattered above her: "Somebody go get help!"

"Is—is she dead?"

"Somebody get one of the seniors!"

The chattering sounded like little girls. When Ruth's eyes opened, she eventually focused on a ring of little chipmunk faces peering down.

"Who the fuck?" Ruth croaked through a parched throat.

"She said the F word! She said the F word! I'm telling the Den Mother!"

"Shut up," someone else said.

They're little girls, Ruth finally realized. *I washed up on the beach and these little girls found me . . .*

The girls all seemed between ten and twelve. They wore tan shorts and tuniclike blouses with stark, colorful patches.

"Look at her boobs," another one marveled. "Wow!"

A hush.

"I think she's a bum who sleeps on the beach. You know. One of those homeless people."

"Oh yeah, and we're supposed to help 'em."

Homeless? A bum? Ruth finally leaned up on sore elbows. "What the fuck are you little shits talking about? I ain't no bum."

The girls squealed. "Gosh! She said the F word *and* the S word!"

"I want boobs like her."

Ruth couldn't see well; the sun blared in her eyes. *I didn't drown,* she finally realized. *And I didn't get eaten by a shark!*

"Hey, lady, are you all right?" one of the little girls asked.

"Yeah, do you want us to get the Den Mother?"

Ruth saw that one of the girls had a round canteen. She grabbed it—

"Hey!"

—and emptied it down her throat. *Oh God, that's
good!*

"Did you fall off a boat?" one of the girls asked.

"Something like that," Ruth replied, refreshed by the
water. "Where am I?"

"You're at Fort De Soto Park."

Ruth had heard of it; it was near St. Petersburg, and
she knew that St. Petersburg had a Greyhound station.
She slipped a finger in the shorts she found at the shed.
The cash was still there, over a hundred bucks—more
than enough for a bus ticket back to Naples. "Who are
you girls anyway?"

"We're Girl Scouts—"

Ruth looked beyond them, to the park. *Holy fuck,
look at them all . . .* Past the beach stretched a vast
campground full of tents and barbecues.

Hundreds of Girl Scouts milled about.

"You're having a campout?" Ruth asked.

"It's the National Jamboree," a girl said. "There's
over a thousand of us here."

Fuck, Ruth thought. *A thousand annoying little girls
all in the same place.* She steadied herself, then stood
up. "There must be some adults here," she presumed.
"I need somebody to drive me to the bus station."

"We'll take you to our Den Mother . . ."

"Hey, lady," another girl asked. "Are those boobs
fake?"

Ruth smirked. "Of course not!"

"Wow!" several girls said in awe.

Jesus . . . Ruth took shaky steps off the beach, following the drove of girls. Only now was it truly sinking
in: She'd survived.

When they got closer to the woods, Ruth saw the
sheer density of Girl Scouts populating the vast campsite. If anything, it looked like *more* than a thousand.

Soon she was in the midst of them all, one little chipmunk face after another giving Ruth the eye.

"What's Yuck Foo mean?" a girl asked, pointing to Ruth's pink shirt. "Is that Chinese food?"

"Uh, yeah," Ruth said. "Come on, come on, take me to this Den Mother, will ya?"

She followed them deeper into the veritable *sea* of Girl Scouts. Then another one asked, "Hey, lady?" She pointed to Ruth's belly. "When are you having your baby?"

Ruth gave a hard scowl. *What the fuck is this little pain in the ass talking about?* "I ain't pregnant," she asserted.

"You're *not?* Jeez, you must eat a lot."

The little shit! Then Ruth looked down . . .

Her belly was bloated, indeed, like a woman close to term. Ruth's eyes widened, her hands feeling the distended stomach stretched pinprick tight.

Holy fuck. I wasn't like this a few hours ago . . .

Very slowly she raised her T-shirt up over her stomach—

"Eww! Look! She's got cooties!"

Several of the girls stared, while several others ran away.

The skin of Ruth's swollen stomach was yellow as custard, with bright red spots.

She looked around in the deepest dread, surrounded by a thousand Girl Scouts, and she had a funny feeling that her water would be breaking any minute now.

THE
BACKWOODS
EDWARD
LEE

More than memories await Patricia when she returns to the quiet backwoods town where she grew up. A woman strangled half to death and buried alive. Children who scampered off to play, never to return. Men and women strung up and butchered for sport. Corpses dug up and bodies found—with parts missing. All these greet Patricia. All these and more…

Something from the darkest heart of the night is stalking her, while the town itself seems cursed by a nameless evil. Lust-filled dreams fuel deadly obsessions, the bodies pile up, and the blood flows. Black secrets are revealed and nightmares live in… *The Backwoods*.

EDWARD LEE
FLESH GOTHIC

Hildreth House isn't like other mansions. One warm night in early spring, fourteen people entered Hildreth House's labyrinthine halls to partake in diabolical debauchery. When the orgy was over, the slaughter began. The next morning, thirteen of the revelers were found naked and butchered. Dismembered. Mutilated. But the fourteenth body was never found.

The screams have faded and the blood has dried, but the house remains…watching. Now five very special people have dared to enter the infamous house of horrors. Who— or what—awaits them? And who will live to tell Hildreth House's ghastly secrets?
